The

Storm

A Story of Reincarnation in the Golden Era of Film and Music.

By
Michael DuBasso

Cover design by Greg Kain / Creative Juicez
Interior design by Brian Schwartz / AuthorDock.com

ISBN: 978-1629671925 (Paperback)
ISBN: 978-1629671932 (Hardcover)
Library of Congress Control Number: 2020917242

rev 93

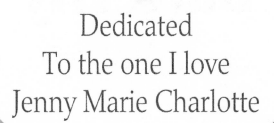

Dedicated
To the one I love
Jenny Marie Charlotte

Most Beautiful Butterfly

In Peru, there was a mountain range called La Malanese.
Very high up in that range was a rain forest
Where the walnut trees grew,
And in these trees lived Exandu, most beautiful butterfly
In the world,
And she had never been seen by man.

In the village below La Malanese lived Miguel, and his
Dream was to catch the elusive Exandu.
As Miguel grew to manhood, he knew it was his destiny to find
This love of nature and bring it down to his village.
Never had anyone seen this
Most splendid myth.

And one day with the sun's rays just rising,
Miguel arose as by call of God and ascended the mountain,
And in the middle of the rain forest there was a glow
Of ethereal light, and in the middle of the light
Was Exandu, and Miguel took her, for
She was life itself.

In his descent, the glow of her life consumed
Miguel, and he felt love for all mankind.
And as he neared his village, Exandu's glow faded and a
Great sadness was in Miguel's heart, as he realized
He could not possess the
Beautiful butterfly.

In the village under La Milanese lives an old man
Who sits in the sun each day and smiles.
The villagers love the old man, as he exalts the very
Richness and love of life they would all like
To feel. The old man is especially loved by the children, as
He tells them of the story of Exandu, of how he captured
The jewel of life—

The old man, having seen this most
Beautiful butterfly and felt its glow
Ebbing as he brought it down
The mountain, had freed her,
Knowing, had he kept her, she would have died.
Miguel wanted Exandu to live.

He could not possess her and thus freed her.
No one can be possessed, only loved and let go.

Table of Contents

Preface

The Storm is a novel about four intriguing people: Jean Delacroix, Marie Savoie, Vanessa Daniells, and Tristan Taylor. Born on two continents, my principals have fascinating lives, which will entwine in an exciting manner. My novel tells first the life of each person to a certain point before they become greatly involved with each other. However, to introduce you to each briefly, I have taken a day in their lives, interestingly enough the same day, so you can come to understand the adventure you are about to begin.

Reincarnation was made popular to some by the 1956 novel *The Search for Bridey Murphy*. Other books have been written since then about the subject. My novel is based on incidents that occurred in my own life, starting with a near-death experience at age seven, when I nearly drowned at Lake Elsinore in California. As I was underwater, memories of my short life passed in front of me. I went through a vortex, not of water but a passageway with unearthly lights. I was rescued at that point, and since that day have seen and experienced extraordinary visions. I wish to bring some of these experiences to my readers in my novel, *The Storm*.

INTRODUCTION: JUNE 26, 1955

Jean Delacroix — Saint Moritz, Switzerland

Chateau Delacroix

The structure lay on top of the mountainside like some great edifice created for a god. Quite large for a chateau and too small for a palace, it nevertheless was an imposing sight. A dark-gray granite citadel with turrets, towers, and enormous rooms, too many to consider counting. Corridor followed corridor on five levels, most filled with museum furniture and spectacular works of art by European masters: some landscapes, many portraits of the rich and famous or notorious characters of centuries past, long departed to resting places, mostly forgotten by current generations. In places, the corridors reeked of different odors, some strange and unpleasant, perhaps from the mildew of ancient tapestries, old and far too valuable to clean, or furniture paddings also giving forth their ancient odors. The interior could be quite frightening; the chateau was dimly lit, and tomblike silence prevailed. The relatively large staff of servants was devoured in the maze of corridors.

A modern elevator had been installed that led to all floors. The chateau's four imposing corner turrets were really large suites designed for different functions. The largest housed the master living area on the fifth floor. The elevator could reach that level only with a special key. There the elevator door opened into a foyer. The small entrance astonished the few allowed into that area. A green marble floor and walls — carved from the same quarry that had yielded the sarcophagus for Napoleon — gleamed under a sparkling chandelier. Mirrors in beautifully carved ebony frames hung on the walls, and a large alabaster stand held dozens of antique walking sticks, each a conversation piece in its own right. The entry doors were clear glass allowing visitors a glimpse into the apartment and its awesome living room, a room from a time past when money could truly produce works of art only found in museums any longer. Visitors of common means would never conceive, though earning great income for modern times, that it would take a lifetime of wages to furnish just a tiny part of that one room. Beyond the living area were other rooms, one of them occupied that glorious, sunny day in June.

15

Jean Delacroix stared at himself in the intensity of the makeup lights. Still in his thirties, he smiled at the image reflected back from the sharp light of the mirrors. Dark gray-blue, piercing eyes were set in his oval face. He had a wide nose and a large but well-formed mouth. A dark mole rested alongside his right brow, the brows full and as black as his hair, which he wore shortly cut. He was not handsome by any means, yet not unattractive. His body was in great physical shape— sinewy muscles from hours of workouts and a dark tan from what little sunlight he exposed himself to daily. He made up for that with his cosmetics company's artificial tanning oils, applied daily by his servants.

Jean knew deep in his soul his physical attributes did not make him attractive; the power radiating from his very being made others both admire him and, at the same time, feel intimidated in his presence. He looked again at his reflection with satisfaction before leaving the master bathroom.

Walking through the bedroom, where exquisite oil paintings by the French masters hung in proficiency on each wall, Jean considered momentarily the madness of one person owning such art. In reality, each masterpiece should belong in the greatest of the French museums, not in a private home. At one of the large open windows, he stood in silence, admiring the spectacular view as the sun set behind the mountains of Saint Moritz. The sky was a blaze of orange. The lights in the village below twinkled with the very life Jean felt as he reflected on another gratifying day.

Jean was the richest man on planet Earth, and that by far. He had taken the Delacroix Empire and expanded it as no predecessor had. Not since the day the great Napoleon had cut the original deal with his ancestors had the Delacroix fortune risen to such heights. That he was eccentric, that he wanted to share the planet with no living person, he admitted, and he thought about those he knew hated him, envied him, even wanted him dead. Well, to hell with all of them, the countless imbeciles who walked like ants around him. Jean beamed at those thoughts as he anticipated the excitement coming in the next few hours.

The girl would be waiting in one of his guestrooms. Jean had seen her momentarily before ascending the elevator to his special bedroom suite. She was magnificent, resembling a legendary Amazon; taller than he, very young and very blonde. Jean started an erection but paid no interest to that as he threw on a brilliant-red satin robe.

The room Jean used for his sexual fantasies was located in a basement area of the immense chateau. At one time, the long, narrow domain was used for storage, but Jean had converted it to a gymnasium complete with weights, workout equipment, and climbing ropes attached to a ceiling twenty feet from the floor. Against one wall of the gym was a gun collection consisting of rifles and handguns, the latter used for practice almost daily. The walls were entirely covered with primitive art, mostly the works of Henri Rousseau. Ultraviolet lighting was used to enhance the paintings and the mood of the action that took place there. A spacious dressing room with wall-to-wall makeup mirrors adjoined the gym. High-intensity lights, all on dimmers to adjust the concentration of light on the mirrors, were used while putting on makeup and the costumes Jean used on those *special occasions.*

Jean entered the gymnasium and locked the steel doors. Only he and two trusted servants had a key to that room. He pulled the robe closer around himself and turned on the heating system. Somewhere deep in the chateau, the near-silent generators would soon fill the large room with warmth. His slippers rustled softly against the hard linoleum floor as he entered the makeup room. Jean turned on the lights to their maximum capacity. He removed his robe and stared briefly at the image looking back. Moving quickly to a huge eighteenth-century armoire, he opened the carved doors and carefully examined the costumes neatly hung inside. After ten minutes, he stood back, not finding anything his mood called for.

Next to the armoire was an antique Queen Ann chest of drawers. Jean slowly opened each drawer, smiling occasionally at one item or another he had used on a previous occasion. Then he remembered the special package that had recently arrived from Georgetown, Guyana. It lay to the side of the chest, unopened, its burlap paper covering showing several South American stamps. He opened the package silently and marveled at the new costume inside. A tight-fitting bodysuit made entirely of anaconda skins—soft, with brilliant shades of green, orange, and black that glistened in the intensity of the lights. He donned the costume, covering his face with its wonderful skin hood. He could see only his eyes then as he admired his reflection. With a sharp awakening, he realized his dark blue eyes were not in sync with the colors of the snake skins.

Makeup tables spanned the length of the room and held every possible chemical and color used for making up the human face and body. He opened a small chest that held his contact lenses. Inside, he examined shade after shade of colors, many tinted to the eye colors of living animals. He tried on various hues and finally smiled at the dark green-and-yellow eyes in the mirror.

Jean paused a moment, glancing at an old wooden desktop cabinet. Christie's had auctioned the cabinet in London years ago. It was the talk of the sale, and much bidding was anticipated from the strange museums that catered to the bizarre. Madame Tussauds wax museum boasted they would pay any price for the cabinet and its special contents. In the end, an anonymous bidder hammered down the lot for the monstrous sum of £100,000. Jean, of course, was the bidder.

The cabinet had once been the personal property of the Marquis de Sade. Taking a small silver key from his pocket, Jean opened the cabinet. He picked up several of the instruments inside, caressing their handles. With a light, lingering touch on their sharp edges, he returned them to the cabinet. They were stainless steel surgeon's scalpels, all used by the marquis to torture and mutilate his victims—many of them boys and girls—before he killed them. Closing the cabinet, he exited the room.

Back in the gymnasium, Jean opened an ancient elm-wood armoire containing the control system of his music center. Selecting a favorite soundtrack, he turned the system on. Jungle music emanated night sounds with a cascade of waterfalls constantly in the background. With another control system, Jean dimmed the ultraviolet lights to a low glow, pitching the room into near blackness. The paintings came alive with Rousseau's magical animals, which seemed to follow him around the room. Jean looked about and smiled in ecstasy.

Jean turned on the intercom and called his trusted servant. "George, I'm ready for her . . . what is her name . . . oh yes, Melissa. Very good. Bring her to me now, and please, make sure you secure the door. You may go back to the village until I call you."

Two waist-high counter chairs stood in the center of the room. They were made of steel, with their metal struts loosened purposely so that when one stood on the chairs, they wobbled slightly. Jean smiled, an erection again starting, which pleased him immensely. Unconsciously, he rubbed his penis and testicles. The coming events would be magnificent.

There was a brief flash of light as the outer door opened. George closed it after the girl entered, the sharp snap of the locks echoing through the calm of the jungle music. The semidarkness and quiet resumed as Jean walked up to the girl. He spoke softly. "My dear Melissa, how very beautiful you are. Madame Alexandra has instructed you about my . . . habits?" The girl tilted her head slightly, and smiled broadly at Jean. "Excellent. Please step out of your robe and let me feel your body against mine."

The money Jean would pay her was ten times a normal fee. That figure did not count the gift he usually gave his willing accomplices. It was rumored he paid his girls in diamonds, just as the shah of Iran did. But Jean always got his money's worth.

The girl came into Jean's arms. He held her tightly as he contemplated the sexuality of her long body. Both smiled as he softly stroked her. A small scar on her shoulder interrupted an otherwise near-perfect figure. He recognized at once her rather clumsy attempt to appear sophisticated with the overuse of makeup. Jean always forgave that in the young and the naïve; if the girl was asked to return, he might teach her the arts of makeup and dress. He gently touched the scar, wondering what accident had befallen her, and in that moment, his erection came to life.

"Melissa, I'm going to blindfold you now, and we will have intercourse in an unusual position. I will tell you what I'm doing to you so you will not be frightened." He led her, blindfolded, to the two chairs. "I'm going to lift you up on a chair, Melissa. The chair will not be steady. Don't be concerned. I will hold you very tightly as I make love to you. I will first engage you in front of me. I will then enter you anally and consummate in that position before we take a brief rest. Don't worry about the chairs. I won't let you fall."

Jean lifted the girl onto one chair and climbed onto the other. He reached up and grabbed one of the climbing ropes suspended from a steel bar in the ceiling. Taking the end, which had been formed into a noose, he lowered it over her head. The rope was made of a soft silk, and Jean talked to her soothingly. "I'm placing a collar around you, Melissa. Don't move now."

Reaching up again, Jean took a second rope and placed it over his head, tightening the noose. Gently he reached over and tightened the girl's noose but not so tightly that she would become uncomfortable. He took a few moments to melt into his surroundings. His erection then was enormous. He had always felt endowed by the gods with good fortune and control of his glands, and he paused to absorb the enchanted surroundings.

The paintings even more alive, Jean felt his innermost being swept into the magical world he had created for his pleasure. The girl's body melted into his. She gave a small cry of pleasure as he entered her, and he held her very tightly as he began the sacrament. The ultimate pleasure on the planet was flirtation with the greatest ecstasy of life and the finality of death. Jean smiled broadly, knowing that with one false move, both would die. They would hang in ignominy with their bodily poisons running from them if he lost control.

Jean's mind raced with thoughts of his own existence, the purpose of life. Control. Was that not what living was about? Was that not what heightened the sexual act to its maximum excitement, the escalating pleasure of intercourse in combination with the threat of instant death? That extreme form of masochism was practiced long ago by another, the master of all S&M, the Marquis de Sade.

Jean ground himself into the girl, the sweat pouring from his body and hers. Ten minutes passed, and his body screamed for an ejaculation. Jean slowed himself and came out of the girl. He turned her around and entered her tight ass slowly, holding back the burning semen that wanted to erupt into her.

A quick thought of what Jean would give the girl for the performance briefly entered his mind. A wave of passion swept over him as never before. She was breathing hard and seemed to be enjoying the encounter as much as he. He wanted to do things to her he had never dared before. Wild thoughts entered his mind—dark imaginations.

Jean looked away briefly at the paintings, so alive then that he imagined he had been, in another life, the painter Henri Rousseau. His imagination took him to another place, and he abandoned rational thought. The tigers were looking back at him, communicating with him, pleading with him to become one of them. Wild thoughts went through Jean's mind. His male core was on fire, and he forced himself into the present. Jean pulled back, turned the girl toward him, and pressed himself into her young breasts.

Without warning, the girl reached up and removed her blindfold. That startled Jean; no other had ever dared to do that before. She ran her hand along his snakeskin costume and glanced about the room, stopping at Jean's neck. Her hands moved to the noose about her own neck, and her eyes widened. Her body stiffened. Pushing away from Jean, she screamed and struggled against him, at the same time pulling at the rope around her neck.

Jean's powerful arms held the girl in check for a few moments, but her youthful strength, along with her flailing, resulted in both chairs falling away. Jean and Melissa dropped sharply a few inches, and the nooses cinched tightly around their necks. They hung, struggling against the ropes. The harder Jean fought, the tighter his noose became.

The oxygen was going from his lungs, from the blood flowing into his heart.

They were moments from death when an urgency overcame the mind of Jean Delacroix. He had survived the German occupation of France and the Holocaust. His life could not end yet. By force of will, he reached for the rope with his powerful hands, lifted his strong feet above him and wrapped them in the rope, slowly pulling himself toward the ceiling. The pressure shutting off his air eased as he climbed. He gasped for breath and continued climbing until he reached the steel bar from which the rope hung. He jammed his feet between the bar and the ceiling and pulled up, causing greater slack in the rope. Instantly, Jean loosened the noose and tore it from his neck. Not waiting to slide down the rope, he dropped to the floor.

Jean landed twenty feet below, both legs collapsing under him. A sharp crack and the searing pain in his left leg let him know he had broken it. Using a great force of mind, he stood up. Placing one chair upright, he climbed on top, ignoring the pain from his broken leg. He lifted the girl and removed the noose from her neck. Jean lost control then, and the chair collapsed, bringing them down in a heap.

Jean held the girl tightly and stared into her lifeless eyes. A smile crossed his face. Even with the pain of a broken leg, he felt a wave of sexual pleasure as never before. Jean had not wanted the act to end that way. But fate had provided him a new sensual experience. His leg was throbbing, but so was his maleness amidst the insanity. He bent over the girl and lifted her against him gently, then tightly, then erotically. How long he held her and what he did to her, he would not remember. Those moments would consciously be erased from his memory. His body had gone into shock; shock from the broken leg, but mostly from the experience.

When he completed his perverse acts, Jean hobbled to the private phone directly connected to a chalet in Saint Moritz. It was time for his most trusted employee to take over. He dialed the four-digit code.

"George Saint-James here, how may I help you?"

"Wolf, come here at once. I'm in the gymnasium. We have a problem. I need you."

Marie Savoie — Paris

Marie Savoie, at thirteen, was so striking in appearance that it was difficult for her to walk the streets of Paris alone. Men would stop and stare at her, in most cases their looks betraying more than a passing interest. She was mature for her age, with a petite figure. Dark auburn hair, worn very long and slightly wavy, framed a diminutive face with large, sparkling brown eyes. Her long lashes, full mouth, and small nose were aligned in near-perfect symmetry. Standing just above five feet tall and always tastefully dressed, she was admired by men and women alike.

Marie lived with her mother, father, and grandmother in a beautiful apartment complex near the site of the famous old Bastille. Grandmother Catherine had snow-white hair that cascaded to her waist. With auburn hair in her youth just like Marie, she too had been favored for her looks. She still appeared regal with soft, sparkling black eyes, and lived solely for her Marie, whom she spoiled enormously.

On a warm June day in Paris, Marie was enjoying one of her favorite pastimes. She and her grandmother had spent the entire day wandering the Tuileries Garden and park before taking a long, enjoyable lunch nearby. Marie ended the meal by feeding the pigeons, which waited near all the outdoor bistros for any tidbit that might enable them to survive another day. She noticed the annoyance of the bistro owner as he eyed her with obvious distaste for attracting the birds. When he turned his back, she coyly stuck out her tongue, to the dissatisfaction of her grandmother.

Catherine scolded her quietly. "Marie, the birds need to eat, but you can't tempt them into the bistro. They poop everywhere, and the patrons might step into it or, God forbid, even sit in it."

Marie, who would go through life with much humor and her own coy rules, smiled irresistibly at her beautiful grandmother before responding. "Yes, Grandmother Catherine. I know you're right, as always. I'm going to the toilet, dearest, and then we can leave." Marie rose up and, carefully making sure she was not noticed, lifted a rather large piece of fresh pigeon poop from the ground with a napkin and smeared it on the owner's chair as she went to the rear of the little restaurant. As she walked toward the back, the owner, not having seen her maneuver, scowled again at her. Marie displayed her sweetest smile at him and sauntered past as if nothing had occurred.

That night, Catherine came to tuck Marie in bed. It was a favorite time for both. Making sure her father was in another part of the house,

Marie begged Grandmother Catherine to tell again the ancient story of their family history. She could not hear enough about it. Marie's family was descended from Louis XVI of France. Marie was in reality a princess, a descendent of Marie-Louise de Savoie, the Princess de Lamballe, first-lady-in-waiting to Marie Antoinette. They had all died in the French Revolution.

After Marie-Louise's death, her son and his children prospered in Austria. At the beginning of the twentieth century, a son returned to France, at the same time changing the family name to simply Savoie. "Late in his life, on a cold October day," Grandmother would tell Marie, "a daughter was born of that family. That was you, my darling. Marie Louise. Named after our famous ancestor. And just like her, you are quite beautiful." Uncannily, on Marie's right breast was a small birthmark resembling a rose.

In spite of her son's admonishments, Grandmother Catherine described what had happened to Princess Marie-Louise de Savoie, her imprisonment. She had studied a detailed history of the princess's family, and over the years had reiterated the fateful story so many times that Marie knew it by heart. Soon, Marie fell into a deep sleep and the dreams came. Often the dreams were the same and very frightening. In her dream, she heard Grandmother's voice reciting the familiar story; and as Marie sank into a deep sleep, she became Marie-Louise de Savoie, Princess de Lamballe. The vivid dream took her to a cold winter morning, August 4, 1792.

Paris — August 4, 1792

La Force Prison, Number 2, Rue du Roi de Sicile, was located on the left bank of the Seine River in the Paris district of Saint-Paul. Marie-Louise de Savoie, lady-in-waiting to Marie Antoinette, was half-dragged out of her filthy cell and led to the courtroom of the French Tribunal. It was there that the aristocracy were interrogated. At precisely 1:00 a.m., having been awakened from a deep sleep, Marie-Louise was brought before the president of the Revolutionary Tribunal, the famous journalist Jacques René Hébert.

Upon Marie-Louise's arrival, René scowled and asked, "Who are you?"

Marie-Louise felt the blood drain from her face. Had her imprisonment of six months killed the spirit in her? Her response at first was weak. "I am Marie-Louise, Princess of Savoie."

René sneered at her and continued. "What was your position in the palace?"

Marie-Louise thought hard. Surely the man knew of the fierce loyalty she had given the king and queen even after they were incarcerated. The Tribunal had ordered her to be separated from them upon their arrest. One could only assume they had hoped to alienate Marie-Louise against the monarchs, to use her rejection of the royal family as an example. "I was in charge of the queen's household."

René looked at the princess, approaching her closely. She was seated in an old wooden chair. She no longer cared about the deterioration of her appearance during her imprisonment. Once beautiful to look at, she must resemble a streetwalker. She would never become accustomed to the increasingly foul odor of her unwashed body, and she noticed with some degree of satisfaction that René brought his hand to his nose as he neared her. With a disgusted look, he walked away from the princess. Better a stench without than a stench within, Marie-Louise thought.

Walking over to his desk, René picked up a gold snuffbox, took a pinch of the white powder, and inhaled deeply. Turning again to Marie-Louise, René asked, "Were you aware of the conspiracies at court on the tenth of August?"

"If there were conspiracies, I had no knowledge of them."

René approached once more, maintaining a certain distance. He faced her directly and raised his voice to a shriek. "If you wish to live, swear to love liberty and equality, and to hate the king, the queen, and all that was royalty! Do so and you are free to go."

A strong wave of calm swept over Marie-Louise as if a great weight had been removed from her. She responded, "I would willingly swear the oath of loyalty to the New Republic, but I cannot swear the other. I shall always be loyal to my king and queen." She sat taller and raised her chin.

René's mouth fell open, and he leaned forward. "Do you not know what this means? It will be your death." He straightened and turned his back to her. "I will give you thirty days to consider taking the oath." Calling on one of the guards, he instructed the man to take Marie-Louise back to her cell.

As Marie's dream neared its conclusion, she stirred in her sleep. It was the ending of the dream that terrified her. Marie's father had admonished Grandmother Catherine many times not to upset her with the real story of the long-dead princess. Grandmother's voice told the story as it unfolded. "Thirty days passed . . ."

La Force Prison — Paris
September 3, 1792

The dungeon of La Force Prison was pitch black at night and dimly lit during the day by a few smoky torches in the stinking corridors. Starving prisoners, many beaten badly during the day, cried out in their misery. Rats the size of cats prowled the passageways at night, eating the flesh of those too helpless to fend them off. Those were the sounds and smells of a world gone mad.

Marie-Louise sat on the damp floor of her cell, contemplating the fate of France. The most creative men and women were locked up in the prison, and the lunatics were in charge of the asylum. History was repeating itself. Since time began, civilizations had prospered, then a period would occur when the masses rose up against the powerful and wealthy, and took control. It had happened in Rome, but unlike Rome, Louis had not provided the people with "bread and circuses." Marie-Louise sighed. Perhaps if he had, the French aristocracy might have survived.

Marie-Louise and her identical twin sister, Francoise, had been described once as two of the most beautiful women in France. Marie-Louise had come to dislike the word beautiful, when so addressed by an admirer. When not wearing a silver wig, her long dark-brown hair glowed with natural radiance. She possessed a classic face with sculpted features, small nose and mouth, tiny ears, and large brown eyes that could make any man fall in love on sight. On her right breast was a birthmark resembling a tiny rose.

When she was arrested, she was given no change of clothes, and the once-elegant gown she wore, originally sewn with enough salt-water pearls to ransom a nation, was all but destroyed. The pearls had been stripped from her on the first day of the Revolution, leaving the dress in tatters. Only her undergarments kept her from freezing to death at night, and they were filthy after six months. She loathed the stench of her unwashed body and others in nearby cells.

The High Court of the People had special plans for her. She had been Marie Antoinette's favorite and loved by Louis XVI, as well. It was rumored that Marie-Louise's only son was not by her husband but the king himself. Thankfully, their son had been whisked away by a Swiss guard of the court and was safe in Austria; thoughts of him kept her alive. She dreamed and prayed of being spared from the madness of France so she could reunite with him, and the king and queen. Certainly they dared not kill the reigning monarchs.

The guards came for her. They mocked her, addressing her as the favorite bitch of the king and queen. The guard in charge kicked her in the back. "Well, yur ladyship, the king and queen await yur pleasure, along with our favorite doctor, Dr. Guillotine. He has a special gift for ya today. Come, me love, yur to see the sunshine in the park. You even get a horse ride to the lovely square we knows you been waiting fer. But first Citizen Hébert will see you, before yur executed."

Marie-Louise looked up at her tormentor in silence. The burly man's leering face was scarred, probably from a terrible knife fight. He had hardly any teeth, and those that were left were black. He reminded Marie-Louise of the gargoyles that decorated the Notre Dame Cathedral.

The guards led Marie-Louise through the dark corridors of La Force. As they passed the main entrance, she heard a mob outside chanting, "More, more, more," but she had no comprehension of what that meant. Inside the courtroom, the shuttered windows made the room dark, even with the wall torches and candelabras burning. The smoke was almost unbearable, as there was no place for the fumes to escape. The windows could not be opened that special day because of the clamor outside.

Marie-Louise was seated again in the wooden chair and left alone with René Hébert. He walked around her, again maintaining some distance, and greeted her coldly. "Ah, the royal consort of our beloved king. I have been busy this day meeting one royalist after another. And now I have before me again Marie-Louise de Savioe. Your associates have had the sense to plead for mercy. Have you also come to give your pledge of loyalty to the new government? It would please me to provide you the depth of compassion I have extended to them."

Marie-Louise was certain those people must have been desperate. She could only imagine the severity of his "compassion." She looked up at René. "I pledge my allegiance to France but will not forsake my king."

René bellowed for one of the guards to return. The ugly man who had brought Marie-Louise to the courtroom appeared. "Bring out the other de Savoie bitch now."

Francoise was brought into the smoky room, disheveled in the same manner as Marie-Louise. She appeared frightened beyond imagination and was crying uncontrollably. Francoise rushed to Marie-Louise and embraced her. They had not seen each other since Marie-Louise's arrest.

René's mouth formed into a crooked smile, and he crossed his arms. "How touching." Marie-Louise ignored his sarcasm. He yelled at her then, getting her full attention. "Your sister has taken the oath of allegiance! Tell her, Francoise!"

Francoise whispered that she had and begged Marie to do the same.

"This is your last chance," René said forcefully. "Swear an allegiance to France and disavow the monarchs. Do it at once or face your death."

Marie-Louise held her sister in a tight embrace. "I love you as my own soul, but I can never betray my king."

René smiled broadly, exposing his yellowed teeth. "So be it, my dear." Calling two burly guards, he ordered them to escort her to the massive oak doors leading to the street. The doors were opened, and only then did Marie-Louise realize the manner in which her life would be lost. Strewn across the street were dozens of dead bodies, all mutilated grotesquely. She cried out in horror as she was forced to walk on top of the corpses. When she fainted, her remaining clothes were ripped from her body. She awoke naked amidst howls of laughter from the mob. Mercifully, one man in the crowd struck a savage blow to her head, killing her instantly.

Grandmother Catherine's voice completed the tale. Many in the mob pierced the princess's pale flesh with pikes and lances as a ritual to prove they were in favor of her death. At noon, her head was cut from her body and taken to a nearby tavern, where drinks were ordered in celebration of her desecration. The leaders took a vote of the mob, who decided to place Marie-Louise's head on a pike and take it before Marie Antoinette. However, several of the women present demanded that the head be cleaned and the hair given a coiffure first. After that was accomplished, the delirious mob escorted the gruesome remains under the windows of the king and queen of France, principally to remind the monarchs of what was in store for them.

Marie awoke with a start, focused on something from the stories Grandmother Catherine had told her. History had never recorded what happened to the twin. Sitting up in bed, Marie looked out her window at the dark night and wondered what fate had befallen Francoise de Savioe.

Francoise de Savoie
October 1, 1792

Four weeks to the day after Francoise had lost her sister, she was awakened by two guards. One of them handed her a blue dress of plain fabric and a wooden pail filled with clean water. He told her to clean herself and change clothes. As she did so, they laughed mockingly at her. When she was finished, they escorted her outside into the light, which was at first blinding. The day was frigid, and the wind made her shudder. The sky, though, was a clear blue. A solitary dove glided in the air above her.

Another abhorrent guard pulled Francoise into a horse-drawn cart and held her up for the crowd to see along the procession. The cart carried her to an area adjoining the Tuileries Garden. The crowd jeered Francoise. The guard rasped in her ear, "Ayre you flattered now, missy? No worry, these folks pay kind regards to all the noble guests we brings this way."

When they reached the courtyard, the guard guided Francoise up a wooden flight of stairs to the top and left her standing for all to see. Suddenly, the light faded, all sound ceased, and she looked directly into the deep blue of the sky, toward the heavens. The crowd roared, but she heard nothing; she had found the peace she needed so desperately, as she sincerely believed she was soon to be reunited with Marie-Louise. Some sense told her death was not the end, only a beginning.

The executioner pulled Francoise down onto the curved block of the guillotine. The blade was released, and Francoise saw a great flash of light, as if the very heavens had opened, revealing the sun in enormous intensity. She felt herself spinning in a dark vortex, but without becoming dizzy. Momentarily, she could not feel anything, as if she did not exist. Slowly, feeling returned; breathing, an awareness of her body.

The vortex ceased, light returned, and with no warning, she found herself sitting in a field of yellow wildflowers. She looked about and discovered she was in a veritable sea of brilliant yellow daisies. Green mountains appeared in the distance, and as she stood, thousands of brightly colored butterflies rose from the flowers and blocked her vision. The butterflies lifted her sprit to the heavens, and she entered another vortex. From a great distance, a voice called out, "Vanessa. Vanessa Daniells, it's time to come home. Your father's packing the car. Come now, we'll be late."

Vanessa walked toward her mother. That day had been special, her seventeenth birthday. The following day, she would start a career in film, having landed the starring role in *Where Is Achilles*. The fabled Bond Studios had selected her from thousands of young girls who auditioned. Vanessa unconsciously pushed up one of the straps that held her dress, briefly revealing on her right breast the tiny birthmark resembling a rose.

Tristan Taylor and Vanessa Daniells — Hollywood

Tristan Taylor drove south on Rodeo Drive, lost in thought about the audition he had just performed for a role in *West Side Story*, a new Broadway musical. Final casting would be in four weeks in New York.

The production was holding preliminary auditions in every major city in the United States. The producers had been advertising a search for fresh talent never seen on Broadway. Tristan was almost eighteen, looked twenty-one, and was a local prodigy who had spent two years in Rome studying opera. He was a marvelous tenor with natural but unexploited talent.

The young singer was handsome. Tristan stood over six feet tall with strong masculine features. The slight crook in his nose and his chiseled facial contours reminded one of a young Roman general. His lively deep-blue-green eyes were wide apart, with a twinkle that promised a zest for life. His mouth was full and sensitive with a dimple on his lower lip. There was a certain feeling in the way Tristan easily smiled, the way the corners of his mouth trembled ever so slightly when upset. In time, Tristan would attract the most beautiful women in the world.

Always soft and shiny, his wavy dark-brown hair had gold sun streaks that glistened in the warm California sun. He wore his hair long, a cascade of curls resting on his tanned shoulders, something not done in the fifties. It was a bit unruly around his forehead such that, in moments of passion while performing on stage, he would push the damp curls away from his temples. One day, women in the audience would wish they could do it for him in the privacy of their dreams.

Tristan's skin was a golden brown from spending time at the beach. He maintained a healthy physique by surfing, running, and lifting weights, as Maestro Paulo Nolanza, his voice teacher, had stressed diet and gymnastics to keep his young singers in good health and attractive appearance. The aspiring singer worked continually to maintain an attractive image. The amalgam was of pure innocence that would prove to be a fatal combination for the opposite sex. All parts perfectly formed, begging, by the gods, to be held and kissed.

Over the wheel of his red '49 Ford convertible, Tristan glanced to see what California beauties might be in front of Jax's, a fashion clothing store for women. Some of the most beautiful and sophisticated women in the world came to that store to be fitted in tight slacks that would show off all their curves. Returning his attention to the road, he just had time to slam on his brakes before hitting a pink Cadillac convertible. Tristan thought he would avoid contact, but it was not to be. His front bumper collided with the rear of the Caddy, breaking its parking lights. Noting a young woman was behind the wheel, he jumped out to apologize.

Tristan recognized her instantly — Bond Studios' brightest star, Vanessa Daniells, his favorite actress. What he would give to just tell her how much he adored her. He had just read about the twenty-two-year-old actress entering into her third marriage, to an older but wealthy European aristocrat. Her screen image was breathtaking, but in person, she appeared even more so. She had blue eyes — no, violet — in a heart-shaped face; deep, full lips colored ever so slightly in a pretty shade of pink; and intense black, slightly wavy hair. She wore pale-yellow Jax's slacks, white bobby socks, and sneakers. A pale-tan linen shirt with buttons open at the top revealed a superb cleavage. The total image was breathtaking; she was the most beautiful woman he had ever seen.

When Vanessa's eyes met with the young driver who had hit her car, she instantly took over. She recognized Tristan Taylor as having performed at the Horn the previous weekend. Vanessa had gone with a girlfriend to see the aspiring opera singers perform at the Santa Monica landmark. Taylor had stood out among them with his rich tenor's voice mixing classic opera with modern pop and Broadway tunes. His boyish charm and charisma had turned her on almost at once.

Vanessa studied him then, noticing the instant childlike infatuation reflected in his eyes. Then something awoke deep inside her. There was something else in the young man. His spirit. She slowly became aware that the life he radiated was familiar, as if she had met him before. Vanessa was into an occasional affair if the person was very special. The young man seemed that and more. So young, so naïve and undeveloped. Even so ... perhaps he could carry on a conversation. *How delightful. I'll pretend I never saw him coming.*

"Please, Miss Daniells," Taylor stammered, "I'm so sorry about hitting you. I'll pay any damages."

Vanessa looked with amusement at the handsome young man. He appeared near her age, yet the electricity that took over her was dangerous on occasion. Well, why not? All she had to look forward to over the coming weekend after a grueling week on the set of her new film were Baron Holstein's frantic calls about the details of their pending marriage. Everyone in Hollywood, including Louella, was yelling, "Marry the man. You'll be set for life." Yes, she did want the financial security the marriage would bring, yet . . .

Having just celebrated her birthday, Vanessa was on top of the world. A new studio contract, a fabulous home given to her by her studio for completion of her last film, *My Father's World*, and soon a marriage into one of Europe's wealthiest families. Her attorney had just worked out the financial arrangements for the marriage. A ten-million-dollar trust had been set up for her, free of any encumbrance, in exchange for any claim she might make if the marriage failed.

Giving Tristan one of her winning smiles, Vanessa said, "Forget it. My studio will pick up the cost. Come join me for a bite. I'm famished." Which, of course, she was not. Tristan was turning her on with his boyish look. Vanessa was feeling very horny over the past months and had found no outlet for her frustrations. During the current filming of *Lions*, she had thought her leading man, Carlos Montoya, was interesting, and had hoped he would pursue her. As it turned out, he was more interested in Tab Brown, the director. "You haven't told me your name, young man, and how old are you?"

"My name is Tristan Taylor, and I'm twenty-one," he said, not convincingly, "and I know who you are from your films, Miss Daniells."

Well, he was at least eighteen, and that meant no statutory rape. She smiled again and responded, "I like to be called Vanessa." Sensing Tristan's shyness, she reached out and took his hand.

§Ɔ

Tristan's sexual experiences were not what one would consider enlightening. They had consisted of either inexperienced young ladies or one of the over-the-hill gang that followed his limited singing career. None had taught him much in the art of love — the younger ones from lack of experience, the older from just wanting a young lover to perform the basic act so they could rush back home to husband and family. He had one wondrous affair in Rome, but it had ended painfully.

Tristan gazed into Vanessa's eyes, lost in that amazing shade of violet. *She's in love with me.*

"What are you doing this afternoon, Tristan, and if you aren't busy, come see my new house. If you're hungry, I'll fix you something there."

They took the Cadillac, Vanessa driving and really turning on the charm. She made small talk, but with an incredible smile and flirtatious glance. Vanessa talked mostly about her work as they drove north from Bundy Drive to Sunset Boulevard and east to Benedict Canyon. On a small knoll north of Sunset, her home lay just behind the Beverly Hills Hotel. The comfortable house rested on one-half acre of ground, not terribly large but very comfortable, especially for a single person. It had been designed for the studio star.

Entering through a marble hallway, they stepped down into a large living room. Taking Tristan's hand, Vanessa led him through the house to an enormous master bedroom. Thick white carpets covered all the floors. The bedroom had a heart-shaped bed covered entirely in pink. The immense bathroom contained a large step-down marble bathtub the size of a miniature pool.

Tristan was not paying much attention to the tour; he had fallen in love and was like a little puppy wanting to please its wondrous master. Vanessa ran a fingertip down Tristan's arm. "Come," she said, taking his slightly trembling hand. "Let's have a glass of wine to celebrate our meeting today." She took him back into the living room and poured two glasses of California Chardonnay. Tristan did not normally drink, but took the pretty crystal glass and raised it as she did.

Vanessa led Tristan to the sofa and gazed at him. He melted into her glance. Tristan knew nothing of eye contact, nothing of the control one can have over another. Silently, they sipped their wine. As Vanessa refilled his glass, Tristan reached out instinctively and pulled her to him. Her eyes never left his, and she smiled, but there was something powerful behind that smile. He hesitated. Then he pulled harder, but she leaned away, still smiling.

"Come, Tristan. We need to bathe first." He followed Vanessa through the bedroom to that fabulous, inviting pool. As Tristan drained his second glass of wine, she turned on the faucet then filled the bath, adding her favorite fragrances. Vanessa reached up and unbuttoned his shirt. Her hand moved over his chest and back. Tristan grabbed her. Again the smile and the push. He reached out wanting to undress her, but that was not to be.

Tristan felt completely dominated by Vanessa, not daring to offend her in any way. Her dominance was also a pleasure, one he had never experienced in that manner — her authority, the enormous waves of sexual desire. He let them encompass him. She could do whatever she wanted.

Vanessa removed her blouse and slacks and kicked off her shoes. Turning her back to him, she removed her bra and panties then stepped into the bath. The warm, clear water hid nothing. Again she smiled, that time inviting. Tristan removed his clothing and stepped in. She moved next to him, and again he reached out to hold her. She slapped his face so hard he could feel a welt rise up.

"No, Tristan. Don't touch me now. You're unshaven and you'll scratch my face with your chin. Let me shave you first." On the edge of the tub was a fresh razor and soap. She slid next to him and shaved him, twice. He never moved. She took a small vial of clear liquid and applied it to his face. Using the fine oil, Vanessa shaved him a third time, all the while moving her pointed breasts against his body as his maleness expanded.

℘

Vanessa was enjoying herself immensely. All her special lovers got shaved, and only if she really cared for them. She never felt cheap or promiscuous, as she was only attracted to extraordinary men, a premonition of sorts leading her into each new affair. She cared deeply for her lovers, enjoying the game of domination and control. It made sex much better, and never in her life had she lost a man.

Massaging Tristan gently, Vanessa continued to contemplate her personal philosophy. She would have in her life whomever she chose, and continue the relationship for whatever length of time suited her. She occasionally thought she was in love and had consummated that feeling in marriage. No marriage had worked out so far, and she wondered if one ever would. Vanessa once confided to a close friend, "I feel like a free spirit not bound to this earth with any human relationship in any permanent manner. I'll live my life dedicated to all my friends and lovers. I will always be loyal to those loyal to me, and any man who on occasion might fall from grace and need me, I'll always be there for him."

As they stepped out of the bath, Vanessa studied Tristan. He was quite handsome and obviously worked out. His upper body was tight and his long, well-formed legs strong. She ushered him to the pink bed. "Tristan, I'm going to tell you what I want. If you're a good little boy, you can make love to me. If not, we will just be friends. I want you to kiss me gently, nothing else."

ॐ

Tristan dreamily gazed at Vanessa, seeing that incredible body he had fantasized about when watching her films. Her iconic face showed no signs of makeup. Her body appeared well toned and . . . her beautiful eyes controlled every move he made. As he reached for her, he noticed on her right breast a small birthmark. *How strange. It resembles a rose.*

When Tristan kissed Vanessa, his body turned to fire. That was his first kiss of consummate passion. All before were as nothing; there had never been the kind of warmth that was coursing through his body, his mind. His temperature even elevated, an experience he would have only one other time in his life, far away in another country, another time, with another woman destined to pass through his life.

Vanessa was the teacher, Tristan the willing pupil. And she did teach well. The caress of her lips, lightly, oh so lightly at first, a gentle exploration of the mouth, the taste of each other. Her fingertips gently caressed his hands, neck, face. A soft touch of nails, gently, then stronger, but never too hard. As Tristan started to lose control, to accelerate his feelings toward the final ecstasy, Vanessa whispered to him, broke the spell a bit, and taught him the blissful art of prolonged love.

For the first time in his life, Tristan just allowed the control, commanding his body to flow with Vanessa's. Everything was in slow motion, but the excitement was building; their bodies were in complete sync, intensifying for the next step in the lovemaking. Gently she pushed him down. Taking his hand, she showed him all the wondrous and secret ways a woman likes to be loved and caressed. Tristan followed every instruction leading to the final intimacy.

Vanessa pulled Tristan slowly to her, into her, never allowing his eyes to leave hers. He understood not to build to a climax without her eyes telling him, without her body telling him the rhythm she wanted. At long last and in perfect harmony, the lovers relinquished themselves to the ultimate ecstasy, only to begin again.

ॐ

Vanessa woke at 5 a.m. Their lovemaking had gone on through the night, and Tristan was asleep. He had been eager to please, as she knew he would be. She allowed herself a gratified smile. Tristan had virtually no experience but made a fine lover. The gods had certainly smiled down on them with that little test of finding each other. She considered a continued affair, but her pending marriage and financial security were too important to jeopardize. Vanessa would just make sure she could stay in touch.

Going to the dresser, Vanessa opened Tristan's wallet to look for his address. His driver's license was there, and she stifled a sob. He was almost eighteen, *almost*! In California, intercourse under eighteen was considered statutory rape. Vanessa's film career, as well as her pending marriage, could be finished. She resisted the urge to shake Tristan awake and confront him.

As surely as all Vanessa's previous lovers had, this young man had simply fallen for her, hopelessly and without thought of any consequence. Her panic subsided, and she went into the living room. The sun was just pushing the darkness aside, and Vanessa looked out the large plate glass window. Without warning, a vision appeared.

Vanessa saw Tristan. Where had she known the handsome young man? As the moments passed, she realized she had known him in another life; he was a kindred spirit from a faraway past, another time and place on the planet.

Vanessa had received visions since she was ten. They normally were harmless, perhaps she would see someone surprise her with a gift before it happened. She occasionally would see her mother or father, even when they were out of town. The premonitions were always preceded by the dimming of any light, natural or artificial. All sounds would cease. She had told her mother once about the visions and was reprimanded as being mentally deficient, a daydreamer. Her mother talked of special doctors and hospitals if her fantasies continued. Vanessa never mentioned them again, and so far most of them were not disturbing.

The vision of Tristan was terrifying. Vanessa rushed into the bedroom, packed a small garment bag, and quickly left a short note for him. She drove to the studio and entered her private cottage, used as a residence while shooting during the day. Her thoughts drifted back to Tristan Taylor. "I won't think about this anymore," she told herself. "He'll be all right. I know it."

PART I: VANESSA DANIELLS

Culver City, California, 1949: Bond Studios

John Schafer was tired and depressed and had hardly slept the previous night. He had been absorbed in Orwell's new book — and *1984* hit too close to home. Constantly monitored, scrutinized. Control the "Great Studio"? Fat chance with Big Brother riding his ass.

Where am I going with my life? he thought. He was already forty-five. As head of Bond Studios the past decade, he held long-shattered dreams of producing epics. Each time he proposed to the board a truly significant film dealing with an issue that might influence a few good ideas or promote a better standard of life, he was put off by the executives who controlled the studio's productions.

Named head of Bond Studios by its founder ten years before, he had been told he could create a new generation of films that would educate the public and raise their awareness on issues of integration, politics, and other issues close to the heart of middle America. John had tried to produce, among others, a radical film utilizing an all-black cast. That was not to be; the executive board complimented him on his strong moral views and voted down the offbeat script dealing with segregation and bigotry in 1940s America. To appease John, they had allowed him to film a black-and-white documentary on the subject, a film that was quietly hidden away and never released.

John was seated at an ancient desk in his executive office. The day was overcast, and he had not turned on the ceiling lights. The office appeared somber and foreboding even on a well-lit day. Many of the studio's staff thought it was a dismal room reminding them of a hostile lawyer's office. Occasionally, one got the feeling bad news might be coming, and more often than not, such was the case. If it wasn't bad news directed to John from the executive board, it might be in the form of John having to fire a long-term-contract actor who had served his time in the studio system and was no longer box office draw. John was always the one who had to sit down with a former star and give the bad news.

Two years before, John had called in Robin Jackson, who had just developed Parkinson's disease. When John told Robin that Bond Studios was not exercising its option on him, the man fell out of his chair and died of a massive heart attack. John was so upset he had to leave the studio for several weeks, secretly going away to the Serra Retreat hidden in the Malibu mountains.

In the shadows of the office, John walked to the Victorian mirror on the west wall. A tall man with a receding hairline looked back. He had dark-gray eyes set closely together, a small mouth with narrow lips, and an oversized nose. Many of the executives snickered behind his back. He had actually overheard one of them say, "his work is excellent, but he looks like a clown who should hurry into his makeup and hide from the world."

John thought about his appearance as he dressed each day, realizing he was not born with the gift of great semblance. He vigorously tried to make up for that in his dress. An expensive wardrobe of colorful suits, shirts, and elegant shoes was his passion. His long arms resulted in his buying suits requiring extensive tailoring. Medville Brownstone, his personal tailor, tried to no avail to steer John toward more conventional selections. John's naïveté in good taste in clothing prevented him from seeing the light.

Ambling back to his desk, John reflected on the previous week's news. A directive from the board had informed him Bond Studios was going to produce *Where Is Achilles*, a new version of one of its classic epics. John had read the directive with disdain. *Hooray, another piece of shit to add fodder to the great Bond image.*

The executive board wanted the film to introduce a new young face to enhance their stature. One thousand aspiring fifteen- and sixteen-year-old girls were interviewed for the part. Ten of the thousand were handpicked by the board. They ranged from the daughter of one of the executives to a favor owed by the studio to one person or another. He had seen all but one, Vanessa Daniells, whose tie to the studio was Lois Derson, one of America's most famous movie commentators. Lois was Vanessa's aunt, and John wondered what kind of sixteen-year-old spoiled brat was going to walk into his office. He had been at the interview game off and on all week.

John was also tired of fabricating excuses to his wife why he would be late for dinner, again. He would arrive home with a splitting headache then have to go through one of Angela's tired Italian meals loaded with garlic, oregano, basil, and thyme. After dinner, he would listen to her complaints about poor household help, the shortcomings of their children, and the big fight she had with her bull-dyke hairdresser. John would follow that with a visit to the toilet for his nightly Alka Seltzer. To finish off the evening, he would collapse in bed to await his grossly overweight lover pounding his tired body into

unconsciousness as she moaned and screamed ecstasies of which he
had no comprehension.

Those were the thoughts going through John's mind when the
office door opened, and he sat paralyzed with the vision in front of him.
Casting must have grossly screwed up. The nymphet before him had
to be no younger than nineteen or twenty — long, intense-black wavy
hair; eyes a color he had never seen before: blue, no, lavender, no
something in between. She was dressed in tight slacks and open pink
blouse revealing perfectly shaped breasts. A miniature Helen of Troy,
or an American teenaged Venus. And the way she looked into his eyes,
John was momentarily hypnotized.

"Hello, Mr. Schafer, I'm Vanessa Daniells and hope you might be
interested in my playing Laura in your dog movie."

John's eyes grew wide as he listened to her. Her voice was
mesmerizing, rich and soft. No little girl there; sensuous undertones
implied something sexual, but on the surface nothing. He wanted to
embrace the young lady; she was vulnerable, needing someone to
shield her from the demons of the existing universe.

As he came back to reality, John found himself stammering for
words. "How old are you . . . sixteen . . . how in heavens can you be
sixteen?" But sixteen she was. Well along into sixteen, but no question
at all, a sixteen-year-old nymphet, sitting in his office, giving John an
erection, whereby he could not rise from his chair.

Cast the part? What part? The role of Laura belonged to Vanessa
Daniells. She would have landed that role if it had been designed for a
twenty-year-old. How in the world could he *not* cast her? John's gut
yelled that such an unbelievable sex kitten would sell *Achilles* to
audiences who hated dogs. So, if he could just get up with a straight
face and un-engorged cock to greet Bond Studios' newest ingenue, he
could get on with adding that beauty to his life. Then he remembered
his wife and twelve-year-old daughter. No. He had seen Vanessa's
application containing her birth certificate. She really was sixteen.

John awkwardly stood to greet the vision in front of him. "Vanny,
tell me a little about yourself. You're so mature for your age."

With a tilt of her head, Vanessa smiled. "Please, John, don't call me
Vanny. Call me Vanessa."

&

It was not the first time a mature man had fallen for her. Vanessa had
looked deeply into John Schafer's eyes and known at once he was hers,
known the power she would have over him. Some of her father's

friends, when visiting the family, were obvious in their infatuations. John was no different.

A studio car drove Vanessa home to Venice Beach, a sleepy oceanfront community known for solitude, white-sand beaches, and Charles Atlas, Mr. Universe. In the 1920s, those beach bungalows had been used by the wealthy as weekend retreats. As the affluent became aware of larger summer crowds sometimes making too much noise in Venice and adjoining Santa Monica, they moved out to a rural area called Malibu. The Malibu beachfront community was developed in such a manner that access was difficult to the public, and the Venice cottages became available to the middle class as year-round residences.

The Daniells resided within sight of the blue Pacific, sitting back from the expansive white sandy beach. Above the clean, gleaming sand, sea gulls and pelicans glided along the water's edge in their hunt for a late-afternoon meal of sand crabs, and the setting sun was a brilliant orange globe sinking over the horizon. Winter was approaching, and the beaches were no longer crowded.

The neat white cottage with its blue-edged shutters stood out and would always bring great warmth to Vanessa's heart when she reflected on those times later in life. She would think back, realizing how fortunate it was to have been born and raised in such a carefree lifestyle. She walked along the beaches then with no thoughts of being harmed by animal or mankind. No stranger, high on some chemical, lurked in a doorway. It was a kind and warm time for mankind. It was in that setting that Vanessa Daniells grew up.

Vanessa exited the car, looking radiant after her meeting with the famous studio executive. Aside from an immediate sex appeal, young Miss Daniells was truly a wonder to look at. Quite mature at nearly seventeen, she had a lovely heart-shaped face, full mouth, deep lavender eyes, sometimes with flecks of blue but in a different light, shades of green. Her skin was unreal—like cream, and no blemishes except a tiny dark mole above her lip. Vanessa had a voluptuous figure for her age, with long, shapely legs and a narrow waist. Her lips were a naturally deep pink shade, her hair an intense shade of black and slightly wavy.

Vanessa's father allowed her no boyfriends. Michael Daniells was no prude, only a loving parent wanting to hold off the inevitable romances that would come and go in a beautiful young woman's life. He cared deeply for his only daughter, and that love had enabled Vanessa to grow up with such security that she never thought of receiving a rejection of love on any scale. Her father would say, "Please understand. Your mother and I want you to date, but your life is in front of you. There will be a world for you to explore someday, but not now."

Vanessa would listen obediently and nod to her father; but deep in her soul, she had the overwhelming desire to be independent, and the sooner the better. Her wild, rebellious side urged her to seek her freedom; but the other side, her strong loyalty and mostly a realization that she had time on her side, kept her beside her admiring and loving parents.

Having listened to and observed the adults around her, Vanessa often thought about her future. Her mother's female companions complained of the strange meandering of men, their thoughtlessness and careless infidelity. Early on in life, Vanessa decided her own relationships with men, and women, would be loyal to an obsession. Her mother had once taken her to John Astor, a famous astrologer, who, after completing her chart, stated the Vanessa was different. Her zodiac signs forecast nothing that, in time, would show her strengths, her weaknesses, her loves, her joys, her very sojourn into life. Her chart did predict that Vanessa would live a unique life and enjoy some of the greatest moments of ecstasy. She also would suffer the lowest and deepest sorrows one can encounter on life's astral plane. Astor had ended his session with her by saying, "One man is destined to come into your life whom you will love deeply but never recognize that he should have been your touchstone."

Later Vanessa said to her mother, "What complete nonsense. I don't believe a word."

℘

Susan Daniells loved her daughter so much that there were times she hardly knew any other person existed. She gave birth to Vanessa when she was only seventeen. The love affair between Michael and Susan was one for the ages. Susan was darkly beautiful with long black hair, full lips, blazing blue eyes, and high cheekbones. Some asked if she were of an Indian heritage, but in reality, her ancestors were Sicilian. Michael was tall and elegant, reminding her of the Ashley character from *Gone With the Wind*.

Both from broken homes, Vanessa's parents met in high school and fell into instant infatuation. Their parents, neither of which had remarried, tried to tell them it was only teenage love, that they were only attracted to each other for the moment, it would never last. But Michael and Susan's infatuation grew into a strong, loving bond. At sixteen, she was carrying Vanessa, and the love between her and Michael was so strong that their parents finally agreed to the marriage.

Both families had money, and Michael was able to graduate from UCLA with a master's degree in engineering. Howard Hughes personally interviewed him and placed him into his plastics program at Hughes Aircraft, producing lightweight parts for the aircraft manufactured there.

Susan and Michael eventually moved to Venice Beach, where wistful, beautiful Vanessa grew up loving beautiful, albeit war-torn, 1940s Los Angeles, especially the beach communities. Only the Great War in Europe caused alarm in America, and many just prayed for its end. In America, citizens owned the streets of their communities. No guns, no knives, no threats, just happy times. The sea breezes, the community, the natural beauty. Anyone growing up in Venice Beach had an exceptional lifestyle. For Vanessa, it was truly the good life.

Susan's mother had a younger sister, Lois Derson. Every evening after the news, KFI Radio broadcast *The Lois Derson Show*, a popular entertainment news program broadcast to her Southern California audience. Eventually, that show went nationwide, and whatever Lois said was taken as word-of-God. Lois made and broke motion picture stars. If Lois called them for an interview—be they Lana, Eva, or Greta—they met and talked. Either that or the studio had a "little talk" with them.

That was the age of the *Studios*. They asked actors to jump, and actors asked how high and what should they wear. For a select few, the studio man added, yes, they might have to fuck him. The famous actress Bette Davis tested them on that point, thinking she could work in London and void her studio contract. To her astonishment, she was blackballed, and only after a big kiss to Jack Warner could she work again, and only for the Big W.

Susan never asked anyone for a favor, but in 1949 it occurred to her that Vanessa was attracting attention wherever they went. The attention was far from just admiration. On occasion, mature men, not comprehending her daughter's age, would come up to them for an introduction, hoping for a date. When Vanessa would blurt out her age, admirers would sometimes jump from shock.

Lois suggested to Susan that she expose Vanessa to the studios in Hollywood. One day, Lois called Susan and told her Bond Studios was casting actors for *Where Is Achilles* and Vanessa might be perfect for the lead role, Laura. It would mean taking her out of school and having her work with the studio's teachers, something the Daniells were not sure about. They finally decided to see what might happen by having her try out.

Vanessa had gone straight to her room when she arrived home. Later her mother and father had dinner laid out, and as the family ate, Susan questioned Vanessa about what took place that day. "How many girls came in for the auditions? Were they beautiful? What did Mr. Schafer look like? Did he like you?"

An awkward smile spread over Vanessa's face. "I think he liked me. I believe he has some speech problem, Mom. He kept stammering for words. You know, like some of Daddy's friends. He told me not to worry about not having experience. Whoever is cast will have six months of training before the filming starts."

Michael said, "I still can't believe you might end up in a major motion picture. Did he tell you if you might get the role? Did they explain what the role would be?"

"Kind of. It's about a girl and her love for a German Shepherd. The dog becomes lost, and the whole picture is about trying to find him."

Michael blinked. "How can you make a whole picture about a lost dog? I won't pay fifty cents to see a movie about a lost dog."

The conversation went on, Vanessa's parents coming to the conclusion that the entire episode would end with Vanessa not getting the part anyway, and who cared about lost dogs.

Vanessa's seventeenth birthday was just a few weeks away, a very busy period as the new school semester was starting in two weeks. The day after Vanessa's visit to the studio, Susan was going over her daughter's school clothing when the phone interrupted her, probably Michael calling to say he would be late for dinner.

"Hello, is this Mrs. Daniells? My name is Wanda Canter. I'm in charge of casting for the new Bond Studios picture and wanted to tell you your daughter, Vanessa, has been selected to play Laura Diamond. She will attend the Bond Studios school. Please tell me if you can schedule her in for acting class starting this Monday. Mr. Schafer is anxious to meet you and Mr. Daniells to sign a contract. We don't know what agent you're using, but if you have none, we can make a suggestion."

Susan was dumbstruck; she never really thought Vanessa would get the part. With the professionals available to them, how in the world could they give the leading role to an untried youngster? What would Michael say? Their lives could change forever. All the self-doubts and consternation any parent would have entered Susan's mind. It was one thing fantasizing a show business career for Vanessa, but the animal had arrived and was about to cart her daughter off to who knew where.

෩

Life would be changing considerably. After some time on the beach, Vanessa entered the Daniells' single-story cottage. She passed through the living room furnished simply and tastefully in an early-American style with large, soft chairs in brightly colored pictorial fabrics set in dark wood. Comfortable, but not her style. Avoiding her mother in the small adjoining breakfast and kitchen area, she headed toward the back where there were two small bedrooms. She wanted time alone.

In the 1920s, these California Beach bungalows were used by the wealthy as weekend retreats. As the affluent became aware of larger summer crowds sometimes making too much noise in Venice and adjoining Santa Monica, they moved out to a rural area called Malibu. The Malibu beachfront community was developed in such a manner that access was difficult to the public, and the little Venice cottages became available to the middle class as year-round residences.

Vanessa's charming room faced north, and she could easily view the beautiful Santa Monica Mountains every day the sun was out. She loved the peaceful setting. The room was a tiny jewel. No early-American furnishings for that little princess because she and her mother had made up the room in a fairy tale setting. It could have been right out of "Aladdin." The petite circular bed was enclosed partly by a canopy of bright silk fabrics and a fine netting to keep out the few mosquitoes that found their way in.

The room was painted a soft shade of pink. Pictures of circus animals lined the walls, and on one wall hung a movie poster of Shirley Temple alongside W.C. Fields, given to her by her aunt. The carpet was an imitation tiger skin, perfectly reproduced, including a glaring head. A bookshelf was adorned with *Grimm's Fairy Tales*, *Aesop's Fables*, and many stories of youth and innocence.

Vanessa had sat in her room for hours reading under the shadow of the distant mountains, hearing the crashing waves of the Pacific and the wails of the terns and gulls. She imagined herself on the carpets of heaven, visiting places, falling in love with her Prince Charming, becoming a great actress like Jean Harlow, meeting the new young heroes of film — Errol Flynn, Tyrone Power, and Cary Grant.

As she approached seventeen, Vanessa often daydreamed, leaving behind her childhood and developing into a lovely young woman. It became a time of aspirations and loss of innocence as she noticed others around her experiencing the bitterness of the realities of life.

One daydream would never fade. Even before landing the role of Laura, Vanessa believed she was preordained to become an actress. Had she been born in Siberia, Vanessa would have ended up in Hollywood and become the star she was meant to be. It was simply her destiny.

ℰ◌

The studio school Vanessa attended was unique to the youngsters enrolled. Only a handful attended full-time, and the various teachers assigned to the studio loved their jobs. They cultivated the minds of budding stars, with ideas and aspirations for a future world of acting. They taught the students to act in every way the studio system wanted them developed. Youngsters who could not dance learned everything from ballet to modern jazz. Those with left feet became only passable dancers. Some would go on to dance professionally after failing to create a star image acting on the silver screen. Others would be passable actors and go on to gain a modest threshold in motion pictures or onstage. Very, very few would become legendary stars.

Vanessa's 1949 class was exceptional. It would produce a handful of stars ranging from comedic to serious actors. There were no drugs available, or any interest in drugs. The youngsters were serious about their acting and took pride in the accomplishments that would earn some of them the great fame and fortune that would make them film legends.

Santa Monica Mountains, California: Where Is Achilles?

Costarring with Vanessa in *Where Is Achilles?* was a veteran child actor who had already gained the fame of his time with energetic roles — eighteen-year-old Jimmy O'Connor. He had been a child star at eight, and all his films were popular to the audiences seeking diversion from the still-affected economy of post-Depression America and World War II. His roles were lightweight soap operas dealing with high school romance. Americans wanted the innocence they had lost during the Roaring Twenties. It was America's turn to pay back, to reclaim what they had lost to a decadent society.

In one television series, Jimmy was cast as a macho male trying to win the heart of a local school cheerleader. His role as Beaver Jones brought back part of America's innocence. Moviegoers commiserated with Beaver; they lived his simple joys and disappointments, laughing through his films, knowing that in the end, he would win out over the campus bully or end up with the school cheerleader.

℘

First on the Bond Studios set, Jimmy seated himself onstage, directly in front of the red velvet rope that blocked off the living room setting to be used in the filming later. In his hand was the day's shooting script, and he momentarily set it aside as he stared into space. Leaning back against the large thirty-five-millimeter cameras that had been set in place the day before, he looked around the sound stage.

Jimmy glanced at his short legs. After eighteen years, when was he going to grow past the five feet four he stood in elevated shoes? When would he become the six feet two inches his father was? Or would he never grow another inch, never become the Errol Flynn or Tyrone Power he so yearned to be? Other thoughts came to him as he rested onstage. He had always had serious problems with his lines, having a slow memory. He long ago realized he was a poor actor at best, who came through his roles based on the sheer vitality and charm he pushed out for each film. He let no one know he felt insecure in his roles. He wanted to succeed more than anyone in the Bond Studios family, the studio system.

Those thoughts were taking Jimmy into a bad space, and he wanted to be in good humor when he met that new actress, Vanessa somebody. Rising into a sitting position, he smiled mischievously as other thoughts crossed his mind. Had he not screwed every costar he had ever worked with—young, middle aged, and to Jimmy's mind, even older? Jimmy was aware he possessed something many male actors did not. He was in the truest meaning of the word, a serious *Cox man*. Nature had bestowed on him the equipment to perform, and the natural ability to find every woman's sexual buttons.

Jimmy would meet a girl for the first time, take her to a dinner party, sit with her for a meal, and by the time everyone got up to join in after-dinner conversation, he would have the surprised young lady in an upstairs bedroom. A trail of clothes, a locked door, and it was no unusual occasion that a piercing scream would descend from upstairs. It was never an amazement to the host or most of the guests. Not only unknown aspiring stars wanted Le Jimme. Major stars, not finding in a taller man the attributes they wanted for gratification, would date, nay, even want to marry, the short man. But lo, the Cox man, like most of his kind, sooner or later met with fate. His current lady would catch him nipping the buds of a newcomer, and the relationship would terminate. He happily stayed friends with all his ladies, and seldom was heard the proverbial discouraging word of bad feelings.

Jimmy laughed loudly on the empty sound stage as he came back to the present. *To hell with my personal appearance. I'll grow taller later this year.* It was approaching six in the morning, and he picked up the script again, gritting his teeth and viewing the opening lines for what he described to friends as *Achilles Stay Lost*.

Rumors had reached Jimmy that the ingenue for Laura was smashing but very young. Well, how young was his youngest? Thirteen. There was some miserable quote about a girl of thirteen, but he suppressed the thought. Maybe he would not be interested; yes, he would develop a new friend instead. He had never just made friends with his costar before, but some sense told him that during *Achilles*, it would be extremely wise. He would be wise.

The stage door opened, then, accompanied by a woman who must be the mother, the vision appeared. Miss Universe. Italy's Venus de Milo had just landed. She was not buried in Italy; she was not standing armless in the Louvre in Paris; she was in front of him. No, it was Botticelli's Venus emerging from the sea. It was one of Raphael's paintings come alive. She was a walking volcano, and he was expected to work with her, keep his hands off her—easier to climb Mount Everest in a day, no, in an hour or two. *I better control myself; she'll think I'm crazy.*

"Well, hello, little Miss Vanny. My name is Jimmy. I'll be working with you today on some walk-throughs. What do you think of our big studio, and have you learned any of the lines?"

"I'm so happy to meet you, Mr. O'Connor. Yes, I've learned all my lines for the entire picture, and do call me Vanessa, please. I don't like nicknames."

And so, into Jimmy's world came the virgin Vanessa Daniells. She had not so much as kissed a boy, let alone an experienced man who had a reputation for seducing every young lady he took a fancy to. Well, who cared about that? Vanessa's life was ready for an awakening. She was a seventeen-year-old girl with a woman's body, and he would take her to unimaginable sexual heights.

With no warning whatsoever, Jimmy started an erection. Vanessa's voice was like velvet. He grabbed a chair and sat down to hide his embarrassment. Meanwhile, the stage and light crews were coming in. Had they seen Jimmy's reaction? He could hear Jay Lester, the main grip, snickering as he said beneath his breath, "Jimmy's going to have his hands full with this one."

Jimmy stared at his costar in amazement. Her eyes were like none he had ever seen, or in reality ever would again. Like a ton of marble, he fell hopelessly in love.

$$\infty$$

The day was scorching hot; the two actors had been reshooting a scene where a farmer spotted what he described as a lost German Shepherd. Laura and her caring neighbor, Peter, played by Jimmy, were searching the hills for the lost Achilles.

The film was progressing into its sixth week and right on schedule. Vanessa was a natural. The daily reviews of her film indicated that, as breathtaking as she was in person, the camera loved her even more. A new star was in the ascendant. It was lunchtime, and she was too hot and tired to sit with the cast and crew to eat. Jimmy suggested a short walk along one of the trails he knew leading to a tall, lush growth of eucalyptus trees.

The six weeks of filming had been exciting and stimulating for Vanessa. And Jimmy never seemed to take his eyes off her. He spoke to her often, but the two had never been alone together. The mountain path wound through lush vegetation, and after five minutes, an enormous grove of eucalyptus trees came into view. The two sat down, and Jimmy took Vanessa's hand. He looked intently into her eyes. "I'm in love with you," he said.

Vanessa's reaction was startling. A warm feeling, starting from her toes and running directly to her essence, lifted her to an instant recognition of intense sexuality. Previous rare flirtations with boys her age had induced little but an embarrassment for the little boys that might have grabbed her for an immature kiss or embrace. But there in the shade of the trees, with a sexually intense young man whom she certainly was attracted to by his animal magnetism, Vanessa had a strong desire to allow him to do whatever he wanted.

Jimmy pulled Vanessa close, and she smiled invitingly. He leaned over and kissed her gently on the lips, then tenderly on her neck. They embraced, and Vanessa felt an enormous rush—her heart raced; she felt a flame over her entire body. Signals inside her, telling her to pull back, were ignored. She would flow with the feelings, knowing someone or something would protect her from the ultimate act. Vanessa had never seen her parents make love, but instinctively she knew what it might be like. Both parents always cautioned her about sex should she be in a situation like she was then.

&

Jimmy was on fire. He had never had that kind of high before. He recognized something he had never felt before. It had to be love, intense love. This ripe young virgin was in his arms, and he could feel her passion. His hand wandered to the back of her dress, and he undid the top buttons. She moaned gently as he slid his hand inside then under her tight bra to feel her breasts. She had the body of a fully developed young woman. Everything was tight all over. His hand reached under her lace panties and with no warning at all, for the first time in his life, Jimmy ejaculated all over himself.

&

Vanessa returned to the set hysterical with laughter. The cast and crew had some idea of what Jimmy's intentions were. They smiled at her, wondering what in the world she could be laughing about. They all knew how young she was, and some thought Mr. Wise Guy probably got rejected.

Vanessa approached the key grip, Jay Lester, just as she had been told to do. Leaning over she whispered into his ear the information Jimmy had given her. "Mr. Lester, Jimmy needs a fresh change of clothes." Then with a mischievous grin, she added, "He can't come back to the set the way he is now."

❧

Where Is Achilles was a box office smash. But it was not the script and not Jimmy O'Connor that brought nationwide audiences to the theater. All of America had fallen in love with Vanessa Daniells. Bond Studios had a blockbuster star, and one man had decided to control her destiny.

West Hollywood, California, 1! ~~54~~
Valentine's Day

> On Valentine's Day in 1954, Chasen's would be closed to
> the public for a private party hosted by John Schafer for the
> entire staff and contract actors of Bond Studios. The young,
> the old; actors, dancers, choreographers; stage crew and
> grips would all be seated at Chasen's as per their rank in the
> Great Studio.

The restaurant had various rooms segregated by rows of booths.
Running to the famous Back Bar, a T-shaped area at the front of the
restaurant represented the *place to be seen*. Only the best actors sat with
the executives in that area. Legendary actors would call ahead, and if
they could not be seated there, they simply would not come. The rest
of Chasen's seating areas were divided up in such a manner that tables
near the best tables would go to less notable patrons. Seating near the
toilets and kitchen was, of course, for the nobodies.

As Valentine's Day approached, John Schafer, famous studio head
and visionary, reached a major crisis. He had turned forty-nine the
previous June, and deep inside his mind and body, a voice cried out for
changes in his life. Compulsions he had never felt before descended on
him like a plague of locusts. Going home to his wife and children was
agonizing. He prolonged leaving the studio, sometimes until late into
the night.

Sitting in his depressing office, John tried to concentrate on what he
was feeling. But no relative or rational thoughts came to him. Just an
overwhelming desire to change his life, to run from everything and
everybody he had ever known. There was one exception to his
madness. No matter how strong those thoughts of change were, he
wanted only one thing for certain. He wanted to take Vanessa Daniells
with him into a new life.

As he focused on his passion for Vanessa, John decided, against his
better judgment, to seek help. He turned to his family physician,
Ludwig Obermeyer. Dr. Obermeyer was a charming man, not yet
seventy years of age, with a happy cherubic face and matching
disposition. He had been John's personal doctor for as long as he could
remember. John explained what was going on inside him and patiently
awaited the doctor's response.

"Yes, John, I do understand what you're going through. I'm going to give you a book by Carl Jung that basically describes a kind of male menopause. I want you to read it carefully. You're apparently going through a powerful change in your biological makeup. Dr. Jung explains this in the book. But let me tell you, Jung suggests many things to contemplate, which might answer your current dilemma. However, in the end, only you can decide what to do."

John took the book home, and on the eve of the Valentine's party at Chasen's, he finished reading it, sadly acknowledging the reality of his situation. Like so many admirers around Vanessa Daniells, he had fallen hopelessly in love with her. Over the last few years, he had pretended to be a father image and thought he had everyone fooled. Everyone but himself. He had not once professed anything to Vanessa except advice on the roles she was offered. He listened to her complaints, her inspirations, her dreams. He had been the perfect mentor to her, or so he thought.

John prepared for the party. Valentine's Day would be the happiest in his life. Hadn't he started Vanessa's career, molded her acting style, and selected the parts that had made her a star? She must certainly be aware of that and welcome him as her soul mate with open arms. John finished dressing and viewed himself in the bedroom mirror. How smart he looked in his purple blazer, black pinstriped slacks, and red crocodile shoes. He hesitated ever briefly, wondering about the shoes, and as second thoughts went through his mind, he shrugged. *To hell with it. After all, it's Valentine's Day.*

ℂ

George Borshe, president of the board of directors at Bond Studios, spotted the maître d' greeting John Schafer as he entered. He cringed as John came toward him, smiling broadly. George was no fan of John, realizing over the past years that something unseemly was going on in his life. A plain man with strong business sense, George realized John was infatuated with Vanessa Daniells. He was also fully aware that John knew nothing of George's own feelings about her. He turned to his wife, Muriel. "God almighty, look at who's coming our way. You would think the man would learn to dress appropriately."

Muriel smiled. "Oui, mon cher, but if it wasn't for my influence, you'd look like John, too, wouldn't you?"

John greeted the two warmly, complimenting them on their attire.

"Why, John," George said, "how impressive you look in those alligator shoes, I didn't know alligators came with red hides."

John's eyes enlarged. "Of course they don't. Alligators aren't red. And this is crocodile, not alligator. I bought them at Sy Devore last week, and Sy told me these crocs are bred for their hides. They give them a diet of special pink carnations resulting in a pink hide. Then they die them red. By the way, I'm looking for Vanessa. Have you seen her?"

As John moved off into the crowded bar area, George and Muriel locked in an embrace to hide their laughter. "John's in sooome kind of trouble," George said.

"Perhaps the board should consider a replacement?" Muriel whispered.

℘

A few miles away in her Venice Beach house, Vanessa finished dressing for the gala event. She, too, was thinking about John Schafer. She had known from the day she met him that he was hers to control any way she saw fit. During her life, she had come to believe she was born with strong intuition and possessed the gift of clairvoyance. She instantly could feel the aura surrounding others near her. She had long ago decided to use the gift throughout her life, as long as it hurt no one.

Vanessa immediately knew if a man was infatuated with her. His eyes and physical demeanor said everything, and she read body language very well. John Schafer could not look at Vanessa directly because he had fallen in love with her. Not only his eyes told her that but everything else—his stilted speech in her presence, his slightly hunched back when he stood in front of her, and occasionally the erection he could not hide. When he talked to others and was not conscious of her presence, none of those mannerisms occurred. She had observed he could look forcefully into a director's eye without having a speech impediment, and he stood straight as a Coulter pine as long as he was not with her.

The party that night would be crowded. Vanessa would mingle well, and avoid John as much as possible.

℘

Had John realized Vanessa could read almost every thought in his head, he might have hesitated in his pursuit. John's hands trembled slightly whenever he might come into physical contact with her. He was vaguely aware of occasionally stuttering when he spoke to her. John thought he was just a little nervous in her presence. His eyes could not meet hers, but John had always had a problem meeting the eyes of a woman he was attracted to.

John could no longer hold back the enormous feelings he had for Vanessa. The changes he felt in his mind and body had become unbearable. Having read in the Jung book what he might be experiencing, he chose to ignore most of the suggested remedies. It was time to do something about the way he felt … start a new life. He certainly was aware of the social suicide he was committing, but fighting against everything that said no, he just let go.

An hour had passed since John arrived at Chasen's, but there was no sign of Vanessa and his patience was wearing thin. When he finally saw her enter, he walked over and, without a greeting, took her hand. Pulling her sharply, he said, "I must speak with you." He led her to a private office in the restaurant and locked the door.

John immediately put his arms around Vanessa, holding her tightly. As he had never before dared to, he whispered, "I love you, I want you. I'll do anything you want to be more than a friend now." John told Vanessa of his long-harbored feelings for her, how he adored her and thought of nothing else, day or night, but winning her to him permanently. He would give up all — his wife, family, whatever it took. He looked forlornly at her. "I'll make you the biggest star this studio ever produced."

℁

Her mind racing, Vanessa tried to think her way out of the mess. *I must be clever, control my reaction until I decide how to resolve this without jeopardizing my career.* She allowed John to kiss her, stalling for more time. An outright rejection, as she was not attracted to him in any physical way, could end her career at Bond Studios. Vanessa thought momentarily of her virginity. That silly idea was not so important to her, but she certainly did not want John Schafer to be the first of her loves. She must come up with the right answer and be more clever than ever before.

Vanessa held John close, even as his hand started to caress her where she cared not to be touched. She resisted the urge to throw up. Controlling her voice, she said, "John, you silly, marvelous man, you know how I feel about you. I'm so attracted to you, but you must give thought to your wife and children. I'm only twenty-one, and Mom and Daddy will do something very silly if we get involved now."

ℛ

John had the taste of Vanessa's lips on his mouth and, losing all control, started to grope Vanessa everywhere. His hands were caressing her breasts, were inside her dress, and without thinking rationally, he started to pull her clothes off.

Vanessa stared straight into John's eyes and said forcefully, "No, John. I want you, too, but not now. You must wait. And stop trying to take my clothes off. I'm having my period."

John had never heard that authoritative edge in Vanessa's voice before. She sounded almost like his drill instructor in boot camp. He had served in the Marine Corps, and that kind of military training never quite left a person. John came back instantly to the present and, losing all control, burst out crying. He knelt in front of her, realizing what a fool he had made of himself. In his mind, what Vanessa had really said was that he must bide his time until she was free of her family, then she would come bounding into his life.

"Of course, my love, I'll wait. I'm so sorry I behaved this way. You will forgive me? It won't happen again. Just promise me you'll be mine when the time is right. Don't let any other man near you till then." His voice, which had started in a normal tone, ended in almost a whisper.

ℛ

Pulling her clothes off had been the last straw, but Vanessa smiled sweetly at John anyway. *So this moron thinks I'll wait for him exclusively. Fat chance of that, now that I know where you stand, buster. I've made myself invaluable to this studio, and should you try to fuck around with me, there will be another studio waiting. You told Mom and Dad not to use an agent and waste the commission, that you would act as our friend and agent. My contract comes up for renewal in two weeks. Guess who's coming to your office for lunch when you ask us to come re-sign the dotted lines; it won't be Bugs Bunny. It will be the best agent in Hollywood.* And all the while, she held John's hand, smiling her sweet smile.

Yes, Vanessa Daniells could be the best of friends with people throughout their entire lives, but woe to those who crossed her or tried to take unfair advantage. General Patton could do no better in battle than that little wildflower.

John led Vanessa back to the fabulous Valentine's party all had come to enjoy. His shoulders were slightly hunched, his hand trembled, but the moment he turned away from her to engage one of the studio executives, he stood tall, his hands stopped shaking, and his voice was strong and commanding.

Vanessa smiled to herself. Were all men that silly? How in the world did they get to run the country?

℘

The executive offices at Bond Studios, in particular the main studio office, were designed for intimidation. John Schafer's office consisted of two rooms. His executive secretary, Jean Collins, occupied the first room, which was furnished in a contemporary design—traditional desk, sofa, chairs, light-colored walls covered with George Hurrell photographs of the studio's greatest names, and a huge oil painting of flowers, not unlike a Van Gogh copy, hung on one wall. In all, a pleasant atmosphere.

A petite woman in her forties, Miss Collins sat behind her desk, wearing a warm smile. The setting was designed to relax first-time visitors in the reception area. The studio head wanted them to be at ease in that room, a bit like being at home prior to entering the snake pit. Fresh flowers were always present, and Jean was trained in matter-of-fact politeness. All of the secretarial staff were sent to a specialized school that educated them in the cordial manners the studio wished to extend to those coming to see their chief, Mr. Schafer.

As charming and relaxing as the reception area was, John's mahogany-paneled executive office represented another matter. Shelves of law books occupied an entire wall. A large painting of Louis B. Mayer occupied the wall directly behind John's courtly office desk. Another wall displayed an old master painting entitled *The Rape of The Sabine Women*, a classic reprint of a famous museum painting. Next to that was an allegory illustrating the castration of Muslim slaves. Many an actor never understood their feeling of total insecurity in that room when complaining about one part or another. Many had a compelling urge to leave the executive's office, the sooner, the better.

John's massive desk was a copy of a nineteenth-century French Regency piece, displaying beautiful bronze inlays depicting lion heads on each corner. A prodigious, throne-like chair sat behind the desk, and in front were small discomforting cane-like chairs, brought forward depending upon the total number of visitors present at a given time. The overall appearance of the office was purposely designed to intimidate any and all who dared ask to see the executive of the studio. After all, if actors came to complain about the roles assigned to them, or agents came to negotiate contracts, the studio wanted them to feel like nobodies coming before the reigning monarch.

Louis B. Mayer, who formed the Great Studio, set that practice into being years before. It normally worked splendidly. On more than one occasion, an angry star threatening one thing or another ended up leaving the office, tail between legs, grateful to still be working.

In that setting, John sat relaxing, happily drinking a strong coffee while anticipating the arrival of Vanessa Daniells and her sweet mother. His day was in the ascendant; visions of young Vanessa and the glorious future coming for them were on his mind when Miss Collins buzzed him to announce their arrival. In walked Vanessa and Mrs. Daniells, but what John did not anticipate was the appearance of the thorn in his side, Tony Zefferino, the strongest Hollywood agent of the time.

Mr. Zefferino was responsible for more studio switches than the rest of the Hollywood agents put together. He retained the top actors. His specialty was big bucks. If there was one fear for any of the major studios, it was developing a top star only to find that Iron Balls was to handle the new contract negotiation. John sat back in total disbelief. His sweet little Vanessa, how in the world did she contact that motherfucker? What enemy of the studio had plotted that little surprise?

As Zefferino came forward, extending his hand, John stared icily. "Hello, my dear old friend, John. I'm so happy to see you today so we can discuss the career of the greatest newcomer to motion pictures since Gloria Swanson. You devil, John, keeping dear Vanessa employed for less than you pay Miss Collins, your secretary."

John sat back seething but put forth a phony smile. He felt like he had bit into a sour lemon but pretended to enjoy it anyway. "Well, Mr. Zefferino, so nice to have my Vanessa represented by the best agent in town. Has she told you how well we treat her and that I may feature her in a picture that could turn her into a real star? We have just optioned Mary Todd's best seller, *The Stallion*. Should we feel it appropriate, we might use Vanessa in the lead role."

෨

Tony had not come to the Great Studio unprepared for battle. He had been through the wars and paid his dues; arriving to negotiate a contract unprepared was not his specialty. During the two weeks since Mrs. Daniells contacted him, Tony had spent time in serious confidential negotiations with Warner, Paramount, and Twentieth Century Fox, pleading his case that the best contract ever offered in Hollywood should be awarded to Vanessa Daniells. He conferred with and educated the Daniells family on what were the salaries of the time for every major actor, male or female. To their amazement, he listed the side issues such as limited approval of roles, as well as the perks offered the best actors of the day. Such issues as credit, accommodations while shooting, perks to family members, transportation, and special gifts for getting the film done on time were all laid out. Tony had by then elevated the Daniells family from their ignorance of the Hollywood motion picture business to the light of what really went on behind the public's awareness.

To the meeting, Tony carried letters of intent from two of the studios and one very strong verbal offer for Vanessa. The verbal offer would hold, as he knew the studio head well and they wanted Miss Daniells very badly. Having those cards to play against Bond Studios, Tony handed John a prepared letter asking Bond for the largest sum of money paid to any actor in history. The amount was frankly staggering. He knew that even if John agreed, it would take the executive board's approval to consummate the contract.

∞

John took the letter of proposal and, in stony silence, read it carefully through to the end. Maintaining a poker face, he stared intently at Zefferino a few moments. "Is this a joke, Mr. Zefferino? Miss Daniells is a twenty-one-year-old aspiring actress with no major picture behind her, and you want me to sign a deal calling for the equivalent of the Taj Mahal? I understand you're making demands in excess of what you anticipate, but how can I go before the board with *this*? We have no place to negotiate from. We're going to have to tear this proposal up and just talk candidly" — his hands gestured toward Vanessa and Mrs. Daniells — "as one big family."

However, John had a sixth sense there was more going on than he knew about. He was caught totally off guard by everything that was happening. Never in his wildest thoughts did he anticipate Vanessa showing up with not only an agent, but the biggest agent in town. The studio had tried to hide the box office receipts and even the fan mail, all indicating they had a major star they could ill afford to lose. Zefferino had gotten the information anyway.

Why is this — A sharp image from a few weeks ago came into John's head. Chasen's? No, it couldn't be; his sweet little lover-to-be would never do that to him. It must be the mother. Vanessa did not possess the kind of mind that would enable her to realize what she needed in that cutthroat business. It had to be her mother. John consciously made a mental note to be wary of Mrs. Daniells from that day forward. She would be an enemy in the camp and not to be trusted. *Vanessa? My word, never.*

Breaking John out of his sudden stupor, Zefferino announced, "John, I'm not going to play the little theater game with you. You've known me for the past decade. I didn't come here unprepared. You know me better than that. I'm not going to disclose which studio has the most interest in Vanessa, but I do possess letters of intent from all the studios.

"You used the words *talk as family.* I've informed the Daniells family of exactly what this business is about. Do you want to tell them what you do when you're finished with a contract actor? How they're thrown out in the streets after a lifetime of devotion to your family, the Great Studio family? Vanessa has become number one in box office popularity. You want her, pay for her or she's gone, John.

"And as to the film you're talking about, it's a children's picture. Vanessa will not star in that film. I personally know you're going to make a new version of *The Winds of Ireland,* and I want Vanessa starring in the lead role. That's part of the deal. You're casting James Montgomery as the male lead. Vanessa will star opposite him."

John's beloved Vanessa *had* betrayed him. He thought immediately of Judas betraying Christ. A sick feeling in the pit of his stomach did not help the situation. He had just yesterday happily informed the board that he would announce to the public that Vanessa Daniells would have star billing in *The Stallion,* a much-anticipated film and certain to earn the studio a small fortune.

Zefferino was not bluffing. That tiny man from Italy, with beady eyes, receding hairline, and slight limp from a case of childhood polio, represented to John the biggest obstacle of his life. All his frustrated sexual fantasies, along with the potentially biggest star of the studio, were coming to a crashing end.

John was pinned against a wall. The only thing available to him then was to salvage as much as he could with the figures Zefferino had given him. And how in the world could he convince the executive board to dump Gene Tierney in *The Winds of Ireland* for Vanessa? The money Zefferino was asking for was staggering and probably exaggerated. John's clever spies, located in competing studios, would reveal to him within a few days what were the real proposals for Vanessa.

John stood up then, not noticing the hunch of his back or the slight stuttering in his speech. Under the watchful eyes of the Louis B. Mayer painting behind him, he spoke almost in a whisper. "Tony, Vanessa, Mrs. Daniells, we want Vanessa with us. We know you want to be part of our family no matter how badly Mr. Zefferino has painted it. We all love you here. Allow me to go before the board with your proposal. I'll do whatever I can to keep you with Bond Studios."

&

The office was empty later, much like the way John felt. Had it been Mrs. Daniells after all, or could that ingenue, Vanessa, be not so innocent? If that was the case, where would their relationship go? It wouldn't go anywhere, and what repercussions the executive board would pound him with for the casual, short, original contract he had offered Miss Daniells became fixed in his mind.

John opened the desk drawer in front of him and pulled out the beautiful copy of a Colt Buntline .44-caliber handgun made originally for Wyatt Earp. The studio presented it to John after *The Life and Times of Wyatt Earp*, a great film of Bond Studios. He had sponsored that epic when he came to the Great Studio so many years ago. A much younger man, just starting a family, greatly in love with his pretty wife. What had happened to him? Why had he become so obsessed with young Vanessa? John lay his head on the great desk and closed his eyes.

Biarritz, France: The Winds of Ireland

Susan was packing when Vanessa entered her parents' small bedroom to have a private talk. "Mom, I love you, but you can't come with me to France. I must be alone to concentrate on my role. James Montgomery told me all about Lee Strasburg's classes and how important it is to try and become the real character you're portraying. This film will cost a great deal of money, and Mr. Schafer said it was my best opportunity to go to another level with my acting."

"I see. Well, what does a mother know about such things?"

"This is just what I was afraid of. I—"

"No ... no. We have to let go sometime. This may as well be it." With a sigh, Susan reached out and took Vanessa's hand. "My little princess has grown up. What will be, will be. You just be sure to watch out for yourself. And call us every day."

Vanessa heard her mother crying that night. She would get over it. Vanessa needed to find her own identity. The coming acting opportunity would test her strength of character, and she was ready to plunge into whatever lay ahead.

සා

On the Bay of Biscay in France near the Spanish border, Biarritz was a resort to the wealthy for centuries. Located near the Pyrenees Mountains, it was a small but pleasantly active town. The production company had set up residence in a little chateau converted a century before into a hotel in the nearby village of Espelette. *The Winds of Ireland* was to be filmed just outside the village, where some of the most beautiful landscape in the world could be seen as summer began. The low hills surrounding the hotel were located at the foot of the snow-capped Spanish mountains, allowing spectacular settings for the film.

La Petit Chateau contained twenty rooms and had been set aside exclusively for Bond Studios. The chateau was constructed in 1612, and most of the original interior had been preserved carefully the past three hundred years. Nearly all the rooms were small yet adequate for the actors, crew, and lead department heads. The two costars were given the chateau's two large suites. Tom Lynch, the director, and his assistants would stay a short distance away in a beautiful eighteenth-century manor home.

At the rear of the inn, Vanessa's room was a special delight. Large picture windows framed the lush hills leading to a view of the Pyrenees. Having never been in a foreign country, Vanessa was ecstatic as she walked around her room. No other building was in view, and she could pretend none existed. The room placed her in a world of her own.

The suite was lushly furnished. The soft sofas and chairs were in Vanessa's favorite pastel colors. A large canopy bed in one room was beautifully covered in floral silks. Across from the bed was a stunning fireplace. Pictures depicting hunting scenes, horses, game birds, and flowers adorned the walls. Modern comforts were provided, including a refrigerator hidden in an old cabinet. Seating herself in one of the chairs looking out at the countryside, Vanessa was grateful to rest after the long trip from America.

The production company allocated the first few days for cast and crew to adjust to the time zone change. Everyone was up before dawn the first week. Tom Lynch, the director, took full advantage of that by allowing an early day's finish to get the most out of everyone until they became adjusted to the time. Breakfast was at five in the morning, and cast and crew, excited to start that grand film, arrived at the breakfast table, making jokes and drinking strong coffee.

Timothy McClarin, the inn's host, was on hand to orchestrate every meal. Timothy and his nephew Jamie had been hired by the hotel owners to run the French landmark, as well as the famous stables nearby. The family was from Scotland and had been hostlers for centuries. They brewed American coffee, and tea for the more civilized. English-style breakfast was the fare and enjoyed by all. After breakfast, the assistant director took over, and rehearsals were organized for the first scenes.

Over the next few months, everyone would become emotionally attached. Most films attracted the cast to each other like a family. They couldn't even picture a time they would be apart, until the film was complete. Then, like gypsies, everyone moved on to another film, another family, in time forgetting the previous one. That was the motion picture business. A few who developed close relationships stayed in touch by phone or mail, but for most, the friendships ended until they worked again with the same cast and crew on another production.

Vanessa's costar arrived a week after the others, traveling by train from Paris. James Montgomery was a young and talented actor, and many film critics considered him to be America's best. He was the first to emerge from Lee Strasberg's Actors Workshop in New York and find tremendous success almost at once. Jim, as most people called him, had been finishing a film in Mexico. Tom Lynch had taken one of the production company cars to pick him up in Biarritz and was just returning as the cast and crew finished the evening meal in the hotel.

Vanessa had heard many rumors about James Montgomery and that he was exceptionally shy. No one seemed able to identify him with an affair of the heart. That evening, she was sitting with Arthur Beal, the assistant director, when Tom and Jim entered the dining room. They approached Vanessa's table, and as Tom made introductions, her eyes met Jim's. His dark-brown eyes sparkled with life. A warm smile covered his kind face, which appeared to redden slightly as he returned her warm gaze. Jim's long, thick brown hair was combed back and cut sharply in the rear, exposing rich layers. Vanessa realized he must have been letting it grow long for the film.

Jim reached out and took Vanessa's hand, gently pulling it toward him and softly kissing her fingers as he bent toward her. He spoke quietly, but she barely heard his words. She felt her cheeks redden, and the warmth between her legs spread toward her heart and turned to fire. Vanessa's eyes widened as she realized she had fallen into instant lust.

ℴ)

The weather was sympathetic to the film crew, and the days went by quickly. They finished a famous love scene where Heathrow expressed his love for Catherine and the two became lovers for the first time. In their version, the love affair consummated, unlike the original Samuel Goldwyn classic of 1939, in which it was only implied. The sequence was filmed in a remote mountain section at the foot of the Pyrenees. Below the craggy rocks where they had been filming lay the lush green valley floor. Everyone but Vanessa and Jim had long since gone.

Vanessa was in a magnificent period dress of multiple layers of silk in soft shades of pink. Her lavender eyes and soft pink lips smiled at Jim invitingly. He was in gentlemen's attire for the period, and the tight suit enhanced his youthful physical attributes tremendously. Jim took Vanessa's hand, and they walked from the rugged mountaintop toward the valley. Partly down the mountain lay a cluster of willow trees surrounded by a deep green blanket of grass. He led his young star to the shade of the trees, and putting his arms around her, whispered in her ear the words she wanted so very much to hear.

They melted into each other's arms. As Vanessa smiled at Jim, he sensed the incredible power she possessed. He felt like he was being hypnotized. *Those eyes of hers. What color are they? Not really lavender, there's no such thing. And why does she look so innocent, so breathtakingly beautiful?*

He had heard she was young. How could that be? She had the figure of a mature woman. He watched a bead of sweat run down her neck and disappear into the bodice of her dress. Her complexion was blemish free; a tiny dark mole broke up a perfect heart-shaped face. He focused on her lips, imagined the bright crimson color was natural. He had never seen such a beautiful mouth.

Vanessa pulled him closer, and he reached up to caress her face. Her eyes never left his. She softened into his body ever so gently, and before he had any idea what was happening, he was holding her very tightly, kissing those wondrous lips, still gazing into her eyes.

Jim felt like he was falling from a very high place. The hillside seemed to move slightly. His chest constricted, and with no warning, he felt Vanessa's warm, moist tongue in his mouth, exploring the inside of him as if she had been doing that for a very long time. Jim's hands caressed her all over through her thin dress, and Vanessa moaned softly. He began to lose all control of what he was entering into. She was so young; what they did could lead to deep and serious consequences. But a tremendous passion welled up, chemistry took over, and he entered into the ecstasy of pure sexual pleasure.

Jim started to pull off Vanessa's clothes, throwing them on the ground with his own. Without thinking, he dropped to his knees and began to kiss her feet, her thighs; pulling down her scant panties, he put his head into the very core of her.

℘

Vanessa had never come close to that type of intimacy. Her inner self was on fire. She did not want any of that to stop but realized where it was heading. She had started something that only she could control. It was her first experience of that kind, and much was going to be learned from it in retrospect. She had dreamed of the conquest and envisioned a pursuit of James Montgomery that might take her weeks, months, or even longer to win him. But the reality of what was happening already came to the fore and she tensed.

℘

Jim felt her hesitation and pulled away, realizing intercourse was not what *he* wanted that day either. Vanessa reached for him, but he merely put his arms around her. Holding her tightly, he said softly, "Vanessa, I'm so sorry. I love you. I want to make love to you, but not today."

And there was an explosion inside him. His mind raced with thoughts he afterward erased from his consciousness. It was as if his entire life had flashed inside his mind — thoughts repugnant, memories of things that had occurred in his past, all detestable. Memories of his mother, their last meeting, his confessions to her, her ruminations of him — bad boy, sick boy. He began to tremble. The trembling turned to almost uncontrollable shaking, then came tears, a flood of tears.

Vanessa held him tightly against her, stroking him. "Jim, is it me? I want you to love me now. What's wrong?"

He saw the genuine affection in her eyes, those enchanting eyes. He stood and clung to her. Thoughts went through Jim's mind, thoughts he could not share with any living soul.

Night was falling, and the heavens blazed with stars. A breeze, refreshing and cold, chilled him, as well as the act that regrettably had not taken place. Night sounds — an owl, seemingly close by, calling for a mate or warning others to stay away, a sea of crickets from the nearby woods — all created what should have been an enchanting setting but for two sad people on an island of desolation. They dressed slowly and headed back to the comfort of the hotel and their adopted family.

Back at the chateau, Jim made an excuse and went to his room. He opened the large windows, revealing the distant snow-capped mountains beautifully illuminated in the moonlight. He allowed himself to reflect. James Montgomery had reached an exigency in his life. He desperately wanted Vanessa's physical love. He wanted to fulfill the ache he had, and knew, sooner or later, she would be there for him. A virgin, he knew from their intimate conversations. And what man would not envy the fact that if he were to love a virgin, let it be Vanessa.

Until that point, he had not faced a situation in which the imbalance of his soul and the difference in his chemistry surfaced. And surface it did. He never understood the sexual pull *away* from women just as he was consummating the act. Although he was initially attracted to a woman, he drew away when the relationship became close. And what represented close? Jim could not and would not consummate a relationship with a woman sexually. He was not physically attracted to women, only mentally, and would not consciously face that fact.

As he thought of those things, he suddenly focused on a thought that had always bothered him. His mental attraction toward women caused him, on occasion, physical attraction, but when he thought to culminate that with sexual intercourse, he found himself repulsed. At the moment, he was with a woman he wanted to fully love more than any that had come into his life. What Vanessa did not know, and what was then crashing down on Jim like an avalanche, was that he had lost his virility just as Vanessa was still in a heat of passion. That she had stopped him from continuing was in reality a miracle, as he could not have performed the act anyway.

ⅎ

A little after six in the morning, the second week in Espelette, Vanessa walked down the dirt road that led from the small village to the countryside. The sun was coming up, melting the Pyrenees mist. It would be a spectacular day. A feeling of euphoria overwhelmed her. Everything was deep green, with scattered patches of sunflowers accenting the hillsides.

A large building appeared just off the roadway, and neighing filled the air. Vanessa was instantly drawn to the sprawling barn where the sounds were coming from. An old wooden gate was open, and not being able to resist, she walked into the cavernous building. Long horse stalls lined both sides of the barn. She wandered aimlessly back and forth, greeting and touching the splendid animals. At the end of the barn, she came across the Clydesdales, a breed she had heard about but never seen. They were magnificent standing so tall and large. She marveled at their massive feet. Vanessa was lost in admiring them when someone touched her shoulder. Vanessa let out a scream.

A handsome young man responded, "I'm sorry. I didn't mean to startle you, lass. I'm Jamie McClarin. You're one of the cast doing the film here, I believe. I'm just feeding our little group of animals, aren't they beautiful?"

"Well, hello, I'm Vanessa Daniells, and you nearly frightened the life out of me. Can I stay while you're feeding them? Tell me about these great . . . Clydesdales they're called?"

Jamie appeared about twenty and was very muscular in his jeans and T-shirt. He had a kind, sun-tanned face with light-brown eyes, long, thick reddish-brown hair, and was at least six feet two. He looked a bit like a Greek legend she had read about, and oh, that amazing Scottish brogue.

Jamie described the horses to Vanessa, and she was happy he did not visually undress her as most men did when they spoke to her. She could see his love for the animals and the great knowledge he had of the different breeds he was in charge of. Jamie explained some history about the animals. "All the horses in the nearby providence are stabled here when one of the farmers leaves the village and no one else is available to take care of his horses. Ya see, dear, the residents love their horses like one would a family member. And here we treat their animals like our own."

Jamie and Vanessa traversed the stalls as he talked. Suddenly Vanessa realized a great deal of time had passed and she would be late for rehearsal. "Jamie, I loved meeting you. Do you think I can ride with you one day when I'm not working? You could show me the countryside. Bye for now." And she hurried out.

℘

Jamie McClarin was the most sought-after man throughout that area of France. His popularity extended beyond taking care of horses. Many women, single or married, craved his special companionship. He seemed to know what women liked most, and his charm and exceptional looks left him with no conquest unaccomplished. What Jamie saw, Jamie got, and it mattered not if she were young or old, single or married. To many a lass, he was simply irresistible, and deep inside a bit of a scoundrel.

As he fed the animals, Jamie thought about that great beauty, Vanessa Daniells. She was naïve, and he bet a virgin, by all the saints. How delightful, how delicious, and he hummed a favorite tune as he finished his chores with the beautiful animals.

℘

Filming progressed quickly as the summer deepened. *The Winds of Ireland* was a classic story about the daughter of a middle-class Irish family, who falls passionately in love with a young gypsy who was brought up with her. The parents disapprove of the love affair and pressure the boy to run away. He returns years later, enormously wealthy, finding his sweetheart married to another, leaving a dramatic and ghostly finale. The original film would be nominated for five Oscars, surprisingly winning only for cinematography.

Filming went well over the next month. The mornings were early, and the days mostly long. Cast and crew got along well and became a big family, as always. Vanessa and Jim continued their relationship, which to others seemed very close indeed. Forgotten for the moment was the unfulfilled sexual encounter. They touched and caressed as if, in reality, they were lovers. No one on the set would have guessed otherwise.

Nearly every morning at dawn, Vanessa wandered down the dirt road to Jamie McClarin's stables to see the horses, especially the Clydesdales. Jamie was there, of course, and after a week or two with no sexual overtures, Vanessa began to wonder why. He was polite to an extreme, and that drove her mad as time went by. Jamie was one of the first men in her life not to fall all over her.

In the beginning, Jamie's apparent disinterest was a curiosity to her, but as time went by, her curiosity became an obsession. He wore his simple working clothes unusually tight in the waist, exposing a rather large bulge at the front. His back and thighs resembled one of those marble gods she had seen in the Metropolitan Museum of Art in New York. His blue-denim shirt, unbuttoned to the middle of his chest, exposed a dark thatch of hair. Though not perfect, his white teeth gave him a natural look, unlike so many celebrities she encountered who had corrective dentistry to enhance their appearances. Vanessa herself had been ordered early on for a visit to the Great Studio's dentist to have a few of her teeth "improved." She was given special powders and solutions to maintain those pretty teeth.

What really turned Vanessa on was the neat, clean appearance Jamie had at all times. He worked hard in the stable and was always helping his father at the inn. She saw him lugging in boxes that were obviously heavy. She observed on many occasions the perspiration on his brow while he worked, but never detected the sour odor one usually encountered with men when they were doing menial work. That puzzled Vanessa, and attracted her.

The film wound down, and soon there was only a week left for local shooting. The cast would then fly back to Los Angeles to finish filming at Bond Studios. Many of the interior shots would be completed there.

At the end of a cold and windy day, Vanessa and Jim finished a scene outside the village and, having borrowed two horses for the ride to the site, lingered awhile watching the sun as it prepared to settle for the day. Most of the flowers had vanished as summer ended, and the lush, green of the grass had turned brown. The leaves of the trees were beginning to turn color and fall as the season changed. Deeply covered in snow, the Pyrenees Mountains were almost blinding on occasion. Vanessa and Jim wore long heavy coats — western style, lined in lambs' wool — comfortable in the crisp air of France.

As they sat on the dry grass, he took her hand. Neither said anything. More and more sensitive to feeling others' unspoken thoughts, Vanessa understood from Jim's eyes what was in his heart — conflicting emotions, regret? He assisted her onto the chestnut mare Jamie had given her and got on his horse.

As they headed back to the stable, she wished to feel ecstasy again. Perhaps Jim would try to consummate the relationship that day. Her mind drifted. *It must be his shyness. I'll get him to overcome this silly modesty. I'm in love with Jim, but I must have a physical relationship soon.* Vanessa's sexual frustration had reached a pinnacle. She had never had an affair. She had been attracted to men occasionally the past few years, but she wanted the right man, a man who represented Camelot — Sir Lancelot, the perfect companion. And she, Guinevere. That day would be memorable. If there were gods above, they certainly were in attendance, looking down with bated breath. Vanessa offered up a silent prayer. *Let it finish one way or another.*

Coming back to reality as they neared the barn, she heard the horses neighing. Whatever had kept her and Jim apart sexually must finally end. She would culminate the relationship at almost any cost. She willed that to happen, and it would happen immediately. Her body tingled at the thought as they entered the stable. Vanessa knew Jamie would not be there at that hour. He had informed them in the morning that he had to drive to Biarritz for the day. He asked them to hose down and feed their horses; he would be back in the evening to secure the stable.

§

The huge barn was eerily silent. Jim locked the stable doors and led Vanessa to an area away from the stalls. Finding some clean blankets, he made a comfortable area to sit on. He took Vanessa in his arms, caressing her. He kissed her fervently. Moments later, he pulled away. An erection that had started before they entered the stable suddenly evaporated, as the dew disappears from the morning air when the sun rises.

Again baffled why he could not sustain his inner desire with a woman, Jim realized with finality that if he could not love Vanessa, he could not love any woman on the planet. Tears coursed down his face, and he buried his head in her lap.

She held him tightly, not quite knowing what was happening to them. Totally exasperated, she looked at Jim through her own tears. "Tell me what's happening. I don't understand. Is it me?"

"Vanessa, I . . . I . . ." Jim stared at her blankly. Time passed, and still he did not get the words out.

Having loved Jim in all the ways a woman could besides one, Vanessa tried desperately to understand. But no matter how hard she tried, in that case, her inexperience could not be offset by her clairvoyant mind. She just didn't have the years yet to perceive the many ways of men and women — their strengths, their weaknesses.

His voice breaking, Jim looked into her eyes and said, "I love you, Vanessa. I just don't know what's happening to me. I never wanted anyone as much as I want you. But when we get close, my body just . . . I can't . . . There's something inside me that's not right." He sighed raggedly. "You're perfection. If I can't love even *you* like that, what woman will I ever satisfy? I know you love me. Can you forgive me? Please forgive me, and give me a chance to find out what's wrong with me. I must go." And as she gazed after him, he was gone.

The stable was quiet then except the rustle of the horses, an occasional neigh. The lights cast strange shadows along the dark walls. Vanessa felt terribly alone and empty inside. The bitter disappointment was overwhelming. She also felt rejection. Could it be she, was there some problem that she could not identify that had turned Jim off?

A central heating system was used to warm the old barn. Growing too warm, Vanessa shed her clothes and lay on the soft, worn horse blankets, letting her thoughts drift. Still very much aroused, she began to caress herself slowly and gently, the large tips of her nipples hardening at her touch. Sexually frustrated, she reached her fingers between her legs and touched the inside of her sexuality.

Hay bales were stored at the front of the loft above Vanessa. She and Jamie had climbed up there once to view the snow-capped mountains through the open loft doors. A soft rustling noise emanated from the loft, frightening Vanessa for a moment. Jamie was peering down at her with a sheepish smile on his face, like a child caught with a stolen candy bar.

Climbing down the long ladder, Jamie sat close to Vanessa. He gazed into her eyes. "I'm sorry, love. Didn't mean to be here or listen to you both. I got back from my work early and just wanted to take a wee bit of a snooze before dinner chores at the inn. I didn't hear much of your conversation, really." Taking her hand in his, Jamie looked at Vanessa with intense sexual meaning.

Shirtless, Jamie had on a pair of faded, tight jeans torn in places. Again Vanessa noted the physical attributes that made him so desirable. His large dark-brown eyes riveted hers.

Vanessa looked into his eyes, still caressing herself without realizing it. She was breathing rapidly but was not aware of that either.

℘

Jamie was aware of everything. He watched every move Vanessa and Jim made when he could. He noted nothing of a romantic nature between them, even though they acted the part. It was Jamie's turn, and his worldly experience left nothing to chance. He realized exactly where Miss Daniells was in her mind. She was gazing into his eyes when he pulled her to him, not roughly, and at the same time not gently. A moment's hesitation would lose him the opportunity. He brushed his lips against hers, holding her tightly. Vanessa responded by taking the back of his neck, and he pulled her to him even more tightly.

As Jamie's mouth melted into hers, he reached down and caressed Vanessa's entire body starting with her thighs and reaching to her voluptuous breasts. Her nipples hardened, and she sighed heavily. He kissed Vanessa's neck, her breasts. Removing his clothing without hesitation, Jamie continued the foreplay, moving his face lower and caressing her with his tongue along her thighs and into her soft center. Vanessa was convulsing rhythmically. He had not entered her and certainly did not want to prematurely end their lovemaking with an oral climax. Completely aware that she was a virgin, Jamie pulled away and kissed Vanessa deeply inside her beautiful lips. He tasted her mouth, slowing her somewhat from the intensity of the previous moments. When her breathing slowed slightly, he entered the tip of his finger into her gently, ever so gently. He could feel her virginity, and behind that, her very essence.

Vanessa was virtually on fire. What she imagined she might have from Jim intensified with each moment with Jamie. She did not want that feeling to end, and neither could she control herself at all. She knew Jamie was slowing her, and tried to stay with him, but inside she felt like the center of a volcano. Vanessa never noticed he had removed his clothes, never felt him carefully exchange positions, gradually placing the tip of his manhood into her. When he finally entered her, she felt nothing but a great explosion of happiness and release of emotions. Vanessa climaxed, never experiencing the discomforts of first love.

Jamie engorged Vanessa with himself, expanding his manhood into her and rocking her to an abandonment of any inhibitions she might have. Staring into each other's eyes, they emitted exclamations that neither intended. He made love to Vanessa for nearly an hour, until he felt she had drained herself of all emotion. Finally, Jamie let himself explode inside her. Then he lay next to her, completely exhausted.

Delicious indeed. Thoughts of Vanessa overwhelmed Jamie. What a shame neither could go on with a serious relationship. Their worlds were too different. He held her tightly and kissed her gently.

As Vanessa looked up at Jamie, she too realized that would be a passing moment, a precious passing moment in life, but just that. The two would see each other almost every day until shooting ended. Her introduction to the roller coaster of sexual love had begun with that beautiful man Jamie McClarin. Like the few women who were fortunate to have a warm and experienced lover for their first affair, she would never forget that first day or the first week. Jamie would always be in her thoughts as the years went by. Vanessa would keep in touch with him as a friend. She loved people and would always remain connected with those who touched her life.

$\wp$

At the end of their time in France, Tom Lynch set the last evening aside for a *wrap* party to celebrate. Taking Vanessa aside, he said, "I want tomorrow night to be a very special occasion for you. An admirer will be giving the party to celebrate the end of the film. He's one of the most respected men in France. I'm sure Jim will appreciate that fact, though he might have a personal interest in you. It wouldn't be a bad idea to see the host of the party and pay a little attention to him. In the past, he's financed several French films of rather remarkable distinction."

Vanessa picked up the innuendo from Tom and smiled anyway replying, "Yes, Uncle Tom, and if it's not too much to ask, just who is Mr. Rich and Holy?"

Tom smiled back sheepishly, laughing. Gasping between chuckles, he said, "You clever little nymph. Of course he wants your ass, who doesn't? His name is Jean Delacroix."

$\wp$

It was not only raining in Paris; a cold sleet descended from the skies, causing the few pedestrians in the streets to run for shelter. Jean Delacroix watched from his rooftop gardens as the skies darkened. He was dressed in light slacks and a white linen shirt. His soft slippers made little noise as he moved among the flower gardens occupying the entire roof. Encased in clear glass, the area was temperature controlled to allow the flowers to grow year round, no matter the weather. Artificial sun lamps with ultraviolet globes were set to run when the sun failed to shine. With the added help of the most skillful gardening staff in Paris, the flower gardens were the finest imaginable.

One of Jean's Japanese gardeners was carefully cutting his Egyptian lilies for the party he was hosting at the Palace Hotel in Biarritz the following evening. He spoke softly to the gardener. "Mr. Chang, when you're done with the lilies, make sure you pick the best of my roses. Use only the Queen roses, mostly pinks, reds, and the new violet ones we've been experimenting with. Put them in the refrigeration unit overnight. I want them on my private plane no later than six tomorrow morning. You will personally accompany me to the hotel and arrange the flowers as you know I like them."

Jean left the gardens and took the elevator to his private suite. The rooms were furnished in French period furniture, the quality higher than any museum in the world. From the walls hung the greatest master paintings, one finer than the other but all complementing each other. In some rooms hung nineteenth-century impressionist paintings by Renoir, Van Gogh, Matisse, and Pissarro. The south wall of the main salon was mostly glass, framing not only a fabulous view of the Seine, but also the great cathedral, Notre Dame. That was Jean's private office, and his massive King Louis XVI desk was situated in such a manner that he could view the river and church as he worked.

Seating himself at the desk, Jean examined the files laid neatly on top. They contained a history of actress Vanessa Daniells, as well as the archive photographs he had requested from Bond Studios. Presenting the prospect of using Vanessa in an advertising campaign for his cosmetics company, he had convinced the studio to persuade Miss Daniells to meet him. Jean's mind raced with possibilities. He had toyed for years with the idea of promoting an international celebrity for his clothing and cosmetics lines. Though Vanessa Daniells had not achieved international recognition yet, reports in the film community predicted she would achieve that status as no other before her. And he would be first to cash in on the fortune to be made with her. Other thoughts occupied his mind about her, but first things first.

෴

Built by Napoleon III for his wife with no expenses spared, the Palace Hotel was located on the seafront in Biarritz. The splendor of the place was much to Jean Delacroix's taste, but not even his fortune could accomplish such magnificence anymore; craftsmen of that skill were too few. As Jean had instructed, everything was in order.

Tables were set with every delectable food he thought the cast and crew would enjoy. And he went much further still. In the center of the room, a three-foot tall dolphin, sculpted in ice, sat on a wide circular table covered by a flowing white tablecloth laced with silver thread. Beside the sculpture sat an enormous hand-cut crystal bowl of Beluga caviar flown in from Russia. Surrounding that delicacy were finger breads and crackers arranged on silver trays ringing the entire table. Another table held wonderfully aromatic cheeses from Switzerland, Scandinavia, and France. From France and Germany came countless pâtés and other treats.

Jean had provisioned his wine cellar with the best money could buy, mostly from France and its famous Bordeaux vineyards. Château Lafite Rothschild, vintage 1945, was one of Jean's standard house wines, and he had ten cases on hand for the party. Additionally, Haut-Brion Bordeaux, and from the estates of Roederer, their finest champagne.

Beautiful bouquets of flowers filled the room. To top it all off, a stunning red-headed lass from the citadel-town of Carcassonne entertained everyone with her harp and golden voice. Every detail of Jean Delacroix's instructions was complete.

The party was well under way when Jean arrived. Tom Lynch came to him immediately. "Ah, Mr. Delacroix, a great pleasure to meet you, especially in this setting. I can't begin to thank you for the occasion. Our film family is feeling no pain. I'll introduce you to the most important actors and staff, but frankly, I see a few of them are already too tipsy. I hope you'll be kind enough to forgive anyone who responds inappropriately."

Jean chuckled. "No, Tom, I fully understand the circumstances, and after all, isn't this what a great party is for—celebration and inebriation?"

Tom took Jean around the vast banquet room and introduced him to many people. Polite conversation between the two resulted in a fast bond of friendship. Jean stood near the huge windows facing the bay. On the veranda outside, he saw two figures silhouetted in the semidarkness. He touched Tom's shoulder. "Is that Miss Daniells? I've been looking forward to meeting her."

Tom stared into the misty night and after a moment said, "Yes, of course. She's with her costar, James Montgomery. I'll introduce you at once." He led Jean outside and walked slowly toward the couple, who were obviously deep in conversation. Tom introduced Jean to his stars and excused himself. Jim politely excused himself also, saying something about nature calling, and left the two alone.

Jean studied Vanessa behind a veil of smiles. A rush overcame him, as it always did when he encountered his prey. The ultimate game for

Jean was to capture or win his quarry, whether it was a competitor in business, the deal itself, or in the case at hand, a woman. He knew Vanessa was only twenty-one, but immediately sensed she was no young innocent he was dealing with. He continued his charm, utilizing his smile and keen wit. "Do you know the history of this hotel? What do you know of France — is this your first trip abroad?"

෨

An alarm went off in Vanessa's soul as she studied Jean Delacroix. She had discovered he was one of the wealthiest individuals in the world, with a fortune not measured in monetary value alone. Timothy McClarin had said, "Mr. Delacroix has a reputation of being ruthless in business as well as in the pursuit of young and beautiful women. Beware, Miss Daniells. Me nephew and I have come to love you, you know." Vanessa had blushed at his statement but also realized he was sincere, and the thought that Jamie had said anything to his uncle about their affair was quickly dismissed.

Looking at Delacroix, Vanessa's clairvoyance rose up strongly. She needed no one to warn her; she knew. Deciding to make a friend if possible, she put forth her best front. "I don't know much about France or its history, Mr. Delacroix, but enlighten me."

Delacroix maintained his smile and charming conversation. Taking Vanessa by the hand, he gave her a private tour of the hotel, including the suites of Napoleon and his wife, not open to the public. He seated her in the Grand Salon, where Napoleon III greeted his own guests. With great charm, he described his personal interest in her. "I have a proposal for you that has your studio's approval, if you're interested. A portfolio from Delacroix Couturier Clothing and Cosmetics is awaiting you at the desk. You will receive it this evening when you leave. I'm interested in your representing my firm exclusively in my advertising. The contract I'm offering you won't interfere with your film career for the first three years. It's a five-year contract and includes an option for renewal. I'm prepared to offer you one million dollars per year for the five years."

Vanessa's mouth opened, and she barely controlled herself from accepting at once. The offer was staggering. No star — and she was not yet a real star — had ever earned that kind of money in film. Her response was straight forward, immediate, and honest. "And pray, sir, what catch is there? What does it mean that the first three years do not limit my acting, what happens after three years?" Her mind was racing.

How did he know there were only three years of her contract left with Bond Studios? What did he want?

Still smiling warmly, Delacroix laughed aloud. "In the portfolio, you'll find a draft of my proposal. I know you're stopping in Paris for a few days before departing to America. You must be my guest on Ile Saint-Louis. The small island is charming and in the center of Paris. Let me be your host for a few days. I'll answer all your questions then." He stood and escorted Vanessa back to the party.

When Vanessa caught up with Jim and they ordered a round of champagne, Jean Delacroix was gone. Jim looked at her with a pained expression. "I missed you. You were gone forever. What did that man want from you?"

Vanessa looked at him as if he were a stranger. The world around her had changed, and she knew there would be no serious relationship with her costar from that day forward. She had become a woman in the village of Espelette, and no thanks to James Montgomery. Part of the little girl would be gone forever. Jim started to speak again, but she put a hand on his side and said quite strongly, "I want us always to be friends, Jim. Please stay in touch. And if you should ever need me for anything at all, I'll be there for you." Seeing the bewildered look on his face, she continued in a softer voice. "I have my own life to live now, and certain things that are private I don't care to share with you."

Jim lowered his head, and tears formed in his eyes. Grasping the moment for what it was, Vanessa took his arm and led him back to the other actors. As she turned from him and walked away, she laughed merrily and said to him, "As to Mr. Delacroix, he just gave me a little history lesson."

The cast and crew were not accustomed to the delicious tastes of either the food or the champagne. Considerable drinking went on into the morning hours, with many of those present finding themselves in an advanced state of inebriation. Declarations of everlasting friendships were made among many with deep sincerity. The acting profession and its related occupations often attracted loners who were breaking away from home, seeking something that would give them an identity they could not find elsewhere. Many were like gypsies wandering here and there searching for those identities. Most rarely found them. On the set of *The Winds of Ireland*, cast and crew worked so well together that, for a moment in time, they became one. Of course, excellent food and wine boosted that, and nothing better than a wrap party.

Jamie McClarin was noticeably absent that night, to Vanessa's great disappointment. He had said he would try to be there but might have to work late and away in the next village. She knew deep inside that the affair was over, that in reality they might not meet again because it would never be the same. She realized his absence was really telling her, *I loved you. I cared for you. I was the first person in your life.* He really did not fit in with her life and wanted to end their relationship without that last night. In time, Vanessa would realize exactly what he had done and why. She left the party early, not wanting a scene with Jim.

Vanessa had packed her suitcases for Paris the day before. Knowing the cast and crew would sleep late, she instructed Timothy McClarin to wake her at six. He had made arrangements for an early train to Paris, leaving her just enough time for a light breakfast and last view of the mountains. The party was a delightful experience for her. She was ecstatic and would read Jean Delacroix's proposal on the train to Paris.

Vanessa entered her beautiful room, removed her makeup, and pulled the warm blankets around her, falling into a deep sleep.

She was in a dark room with a man and another young woman. The girl was her sister, and she must convince her to say something to the short, ugly man in order to save her life. She cried and pleaded with her sister to say some innocent words that would reunite them. They would be free of the little man. But her sister only stood there and said no.

Vanessa awoke with a start. Her nightgown was soaked with perspiration. She arose and went into the bathroom to shower and change. As she looked into the mirror, she almost cried aloud. In the dream, everyone spoke French, including herself. Vanessa was mesmerized; she knew not one word of French.

∞

In Paris, young Marie Savoie awoke from the same dream.

Paris: Ile Saint-Louis

A Mercedes limousine picked Vanessa up from Orly Airport. The drive into Paris was exciting, especially after coming within view of the Eiffel Tower. The ancient buildings and bridges were incredible to see, but an underlying feeling Vanessa could not identify bothered her. She called upon her special gift of understanding, but there was no answer to the odd feeling. At first, she thought it was her apprehension of seeing Delacroix, but, no, she decided it was something else. As she neared the city, the feeling grew stronger. Something amazing was in Paris.

When the limousine crossed over the stone bridge to Ile Saint-Louis, the feeling turned to déjà vu. The tall spires of Notre Dame came into view with their grotesque water spouts, and Vanessa realized suddenly that everything was familiar; she had been there before, another time and probably centuries before. Having come to that realization, she relaxed. Her decision to meet with Delacroix was predestined.

The building adjoining the Seine was not remarkable from the outside. Surely the man could live in a more prestigious building. But when Vanessa arrived at Delacroix's spacious apartment and saw the entry, she was speechless. He greeted her with the same smile as in Biarritz, his voice soft as he spoke. "Welcome to my home and to Paris, Vanessa. You will have a magnificent stay, as I have made arrangements to lavish you in kindness. I would like to be able to say I made Paris your second home."

Smooth. Vanessa put on a heart-winning smile. *He plays a brilliant game. I wonder if I stand any chance.* "You already have, Mr. Delacroix. Your party at The Palace was great. The entire cast will be buzzing about it for days."

The smile disappeared momentarily as Delacroix said, "Please, call me Jean. Only my family calls me mister." He smiled again and laughed at the joke he had made. "Vanessa, I have made arrangements for you to stay at a small hotel nearby called du Jeu de Paume. It's just around the corner. I would prefer you be here with me in my little home, but alas, though you will see I have spacious apartments, neither you nor I would have privacy. One of my personal guards will escort you while you are here in Paris." Without turning, he called out. "George, please come meet my guest."

A hulking man came from somewhere behind Jean and stood towering over her. George bore no smile and had a pale complexion. Steel-blue-gray eyes stared at her as he extended his hand. Vanessa's smile faded. A cold shudder swept over her as she took his hand. He bowed politely and left as if on cue.

"Yes, my dear. George Saint-James is intimidating, but he has been a trustworthy employee for nearly a decade. You must understand, no harm will come to you when you are with him. He is very good at what he does. But come now, I have a light meal ready for us."

Jean escorted Vanessa through the main salon to an adjoining dining room. Though her knowledge of fine art was limited, her senses were not. She had never seen decor the likes of which she saw there. She had only seen furniture like that in books and magazines. Such art existed in a private residence? Some of the art she recognized. In school, she had done a report on the Van Gogh oil painting that adorned one of the dining room walls. Like an avalanche, she recalled the owner named in the report; of course, it was Jean Delacroix. Her paper had said he was the richest man in the world. Vanessa formed a new respect for him, dissipating the strange but slight repulsion she had felt about him before.

Courteous through dinner, Jean suggested different wines for each course, of which Vanessa was careful to imbibe only moderately. They finished the meal, and he led her to his private offices. He pushed a device on his desk, and the velvet curtains opened, revealing the Seine and Notre Dame, both brightly illuminated at that time of night. Vanessa stood momentarily, taking it all in. Recognizing her lack of worldly knowledge, she could not think of anything to say.

℅

Jean realized what young Vanessa was experiencing. Everything was working as he had planned. He had brought her to that place mentally; it was time to go for the kill. "Vanessa, would you like an after-dinner drink or another glass of champagne, some sherry perhaps before we discuss my proposal?" He seated her in a small, almost-uncomfortable chair with her back to the windows, himself at the desk, and smiled comfortably. "I see you're admiring the desk. It was King Louis the Sixteenth's personal desk, removed from Versailles at the time of the French Revolution and secreted away in a farmhouse in the country. I had it restored to seventeenth-century condition."

ॐ

The more Vanessa's mind opened to that New World, the more insecure she felt. For a twenty-one-year-old, no matter how mature she felt, she could not put herself on a level with Jean Delacroix. As she listened to the words of the French aristocrat, she marveled at his worldliness, remembering her lack of the same. Then she realized Jean had asked her a question. She reddened slightly. "I'm sorry, what did you say? I was lost in thought for a moment."

Jean smiled. "Are you tired, Vanessa? We can discuss business tomorrow if you would like."

She was not really tired, just overwhelmed, but at the moment, her curiosity over Jean's proposal was paramount. "No, I'm interested in your offer. I read the proposal several times on the train and am frankly puzzled why you want me to represent you. I've done only one film. Maybe my next will not be well received. And no one knows me in Europe."

Jean studied Vanessa for an instant. "Your first movie has set box office records everywhere in America. The film's limited showing in Europe has done very well. I have many reasons for employing you commercially. I'm expanding both my cosmetics and clothing lines in America. I expect rather substantial sales with you as my figurehead.

"I'm also no novice to the motion picture business, having financed a number of worthy European films. I know a good movie when I see it and can tell by a script and casting whether it will be a success. With your studio's permission, I've seen some of the rushes of *The Winds of Ireland*. You will not only become a star with this film. You will become an international star, as well."

Vanessa listened attentively to Jean's logic and, after a moment of silence, addressed the issue foremost in her mind. "I'm concerned about part of your proposal. After my contract with Bond Studios expires, you have the option to take over my film career for the next two years . . . why?"

He looked her directly in the eye. "I can make you the biggest star the world has ever seen."

"How can that be proven?"

"You will just have to trust me."

Vanessa hesitated. Dare she raise the question in her mind then? She decided she had no choice. "Your reputation precedes you, Jean Delacroix. Others have said you only give serious attention to those who become your mistress. Is that what you're seeking with me?"

Jean laughed heartily, but he was surprised the young woman had any information on him at all. His ploy of veiled honesty was getting him only so far, and he decided to delay further discussion. "I've made dinner reservations at Maxim's for tomorrow night. George will escort you home. Let's have a nice evening tomorrow, and we will continue our conversation." Not giving her a moment to respond, he called for his bodyguard and walked with them to his front entry. Taking Vanessa's hand, he kissed it and walked away. Leaving Vanessa puzzled would heighten her curiosity.

ဢ

As George escorted Vanessa to her hotel, her only thoughts were, *goodness, what an interesting man, but beware, beware.* And her favorite nursery story came to mind: "The Big Bad Wolf."

ဢ

Jean walked to one of his favorite Renoirs, a small canvass depicting a dark-haired French girl looking wistfully at whomever would view the canvas. Reaching next to the painting, he pushed gently on a switch known only to him, hidden behind the brocaded velvet wallpaper. The painting swung open, revealing a circular wall safe. From the safe, he removed a small velvet box. Opening the box, he smiled. A brilliant glow radiated from the box momentarily, and he reflected on the gem's history. Jean snapped the box shut and took it to his bedroom suite. After placing the box carefully in the jacket of his favorite tuxedo, he retired.

ဢ

Early the next day, a wardrobe arrived at Vanessa's hotel, along with dozens of fresh red roses. A note stated:

> *Hoping you are having a splendid time. Please accept whatever you want from my couturier line for this evening. And don't even think of insulting me by returning any of the clothes you might like. Think of it as an advance on our having you represent me.*

Vanessa picked a magnificent dark-blue full-length gown with a fleur-de-lis pattern in glittering sequins. In the lining of the dress was an embroidered label with the name Propriété de Coco Chanel. Even Vanessa recognized the word meaning *property* in French. Hesitating, she also selected at the last minute a full-length Russian sable coat. Wrapping it around her, she experienced a delicious feeling of outrageous wealth.

Maxim's was amazing. Jean met Vanessa at the entrance, wearing a striking tuxedo. Vanessa was unknown in Europe, but as she entered on the arm of Delacroix, the restaurant became alarmingly quiet. It seemed that every eye in the room was watching them as the maître d' escorted them to the restaurant's premier table. Vanessa lost count of the number of courses served during dinner. Each was more delectable than the last, and more elegant than even the restaurant itself.

Jean kept the conversation light and seemed to avoid any discussion regarding his offer. As the evening wore on, Vanessa thought perhaps he had changed his mind. She enjoyed herself immensely, and all too soon, the dinner was over and they were back on the small island in the middle of the Seine.

As they entered the elevator, Jean turned to Vanessa. "Let me show you my gardens. There are flowers I'm growing not to be found anywhere else in the world."

The overcast skies cleared as Jean and Vanessa emerged from the elevator, and she found herself in a fairyland of sorts. The full moon illuminated a sea of blazing colors. Jean led her enthusiastically from flowerbed to flowerbed. "This Queen rose in deep lavender has taken us a decade to grow. Look closely. The color matches your eyes. And look here at my Nile Lilies, have you ever seen a combination of colors like this?"

Vanessa was astonished, as the colors of the lilies were deep orange, yellow, and red, all on a single stem.

Jean took Vanessa's hand and led her to a corner of the garden overlooking the great cathedral and the river. A small table set for two and a single glass of Napoleon brandy appeared as if by magic. He seated her facing the river and said, "I'm ready to answer your question about the contract now. I'll be honest with you, as I feel you're older than your years and would see through any deception. Let me start by telling you about the history of my family. I am a direct descendent of the Delacroix family that has served France for the past one hundred and fifty years. Our fortune has multiplied beyond any imaginable means, and my lifestyle is one not to be compared to any living soul.

My staff enjoys enumeration far beyond their skills, and I'm generous to those loyal to me. This leads me to our possible relationship. When your studio contract is over, I can create for you, if I choose, roles and film scripts surpassing any studio here or in America. You need only choose what movie you want and what part you wish to play."

Vanessa sipped the brandy slowly, listening to discover what Jean really wanted. She did not have to possess the years of experience another might to know he was not about to lavish that proposal on just anyone. As those thoughts went through her mind, he interlocked his fingers with hers. The intimacy was no different than his having embraced her. She did not pull away but briefly reflected — the financial arrangement was huge; the chance to live that lifestyle, and much more, would certainly never come again.

Jean withdrew his hand and removed a velvet box from his tuxedo jacket. "I have made arrangements for us to fly by my private plane to Zurich tomorrow. I wish to show you my estate in Saint Moritz. Please don't open the little gift I have given you now. Do so when you have time to reflect on it. George will escort you home and pick you up tomorrow afternoon at two."

℘

Vanessa entered the hotel and went to her room. The rooms in the hotel were mostly small, and only hers was sumptuous — a sitting room decorated with French period furniture and a bedroom befitting a princess, with gilt mirrors and an eighteenth-century canopy bed draped completely in red satin. Large windows looked out over the hotel's courtyard.

Seating herself near the open windows, Vanessa opened the velvet box. The bedroom lamp on the table was not bright, but the flash of pink light from the box nearly blinded her. She stared in disbelief at the diamond resting inside. Vanessa had never seen a gem so large. Next to the jewel was a small card from Jean. It merely stated, *Marie Antoinette wore this for a single evening.* Vanessa picked up the gold chain holding the huge diamond and walked over to the dressing room mirror. Circling the chain around her neck, she stared at the flashes of light emanating from the stone.

The night sounds from the street outside ceased, all light faded, and Vanessa was thrown into a deep vision. Something was happening to her that she had never experienced. In her momentary trance, she felt motion.

Vanessa was spinning, and she descended through a wide tunnel. She sensed that time was standing still, then she plunged into a deep green sea. She was in another place, another time. From the depths of the sea, she ascended into the heavens. Suspended above the earth, she looked down from the stars. She came closer to the planet, and as she did, it seemed to be changing. At first, she saw only water, then great upheaval as massive continents were born. Suddenly, she was falling. Air rushed past, and storm clouds with unimaginable torrents of rain. Vanessa was terrified. Her past visions had been brief moments, never so three dimensional, so realistic, and she cried out in terror.

As if someone knew her thoughts and fears, a voice carried to her though she saw nothing. "Do not be afraid, Vanessa. You are witnessing the birth of your planet. The experience shall be exhilarating for you. You are special to the gods and will be allowed to witness this miracle of ours. Enjoy what you are seeing, it may never happen again for you."

The Voice faded, and Vanessa cried aloud, "How can this be? Will I return to my time again? Please, I don't understand. How can I witness in this short time the creation of earth?" She heard distant laughter, but it was like thunder as the Voice spoke to her again.

"Yes, I wish I could answer your questions, Vanessa. If I tried to tell you all, your mind could not absorb my words and you might perish from the knowledge. Your mind and the minds of twentieth-century mankind are not prepared for those answers. God, as you mortals think of the creator, placed you on the earth for his purposes only a short while ago. I can answer one of your questions, though your mind will not fully understand.

"You are witnessing the birth of your planet, and in a moment, the evolution of a life form that is tied to your present life on earth. The gods are watching this happen, as we did millions of years ago. To us, this is actually taking place in what you mortals call a moment in time. Time for you, measured in millions of years, is to us an instant.

"Concentrate on what you can envision as all the grains of sand on all the beaches on your planet. Picture your earth as but a grain of sand lying on one of those beaches. Now imagine that grain lying on a beach on another planet far away in the solar system and that the entire solar system is, in turn, only a grain of sand lying on a beach on another distant planet. Each grain of sand is a tiny particle on a large beach, and so on into infinity."

Vanessa tried to think about what the Voice said, but she became dizzy as she concentrated on the theory. The earth beneath her came closer, then she was standing on the ground. But the ground was moving beneath her feet. At first, the land had no vegetation. Then the landscape changed and was covered with brush and small trees. The trees and plants grew into a dense jungle, and with that change, everything became still.

Vanessa had transcended to a part of Mother Earth that would someday be the nation called India. Through the jungle foliage, the deep-red sun turned orange as night fell. Vanessa was jolted by a massive tremor under her feet. She knew it was an earthquake but was no longer frightened. The Voice had calmed her spirit, and she knew no harm would befall her. Another tremor, larger, almost made her fall. Quickly, dawn came, then dusk. That repeated rapidly, and Vanessa instinctively realized time was passing — weeks, months, years, all in the moment of her vision. Suddenly, everything ceased and once more it was nightfall.

For the first time in her life, Vanessa's gift of visions took on a deeper meaning. She was able to experience and comprehend what was occurring, as the gods enabled her to understand the remarkable vision. A marvelous sight appeared before Vanessa. Uncannily, she knew it had something to do with the pink diamond.

Vanessa stood next to a small, elegant leopard and four tiny cats, that ignored Vanessa completely. The leopards were beautiful and had an unusual color. It was crimson red because their main diet was the deep-red salmon the mother leopard hunted in the many lakes of that area. Somehow Vanessa knew that even the animals' bones were crimson red. She was mesmerized by the sight in front of her and tried to approach the animals. But the gods pulled her back into the heavens and toward the earth of her time before she could reach them. The gods continued to reveal the leopard scenario to her as they brought her back.

The little family of red leopards had lost their male leader, and only the mother was there to protect her cubs — four hungry cubs to guard and feed, an endless day-and-night task. The magnificent female leopard was fiercely loyal to her cubs and would die for them, even if facing the largest of her predators. But that night there were no enemies, and the winds were unusually calm.

The family had feasted on fish all day, and it was time for slumber. The mother was sleeping when she felt the first vibrations. Under her feet, the ground shook as if some force were coming to the surface. Indeed, a force was coming. Gas from the center of the earth was looking for a release and chose that lush part of earth in which to burst forth and form a volcano. As it traveled the last miles from the center of the earth, the gas built up an enormous amount of pressure and molten heat. The area under the surface had been an ocean bottom eons before, and the gas mixture brought forth the sand from that ocean, melting it into a liquid.

The cat family never felt anything. The heat asphyxiated them in an instant, and as the molten lava rushed out of the bowels of the earth, it encompassed the little animals, melting them into a mass of light, sandy liquid. Then a wondrous thing occurred. The little leopards' bright-red bones combined with the unusual substance that forms diamonds.

When the temperature cooled, a large, lightly colored pink diamond lay on the surface of the planet, many miles from the new volcano. The sun's rays lit upon it, and the brilliant shade of pink radiated from the twelve-inch crystal. As eons passed and rivers formed over the area, the diamond was hidden in the earth, awaiting the time for man to find it, just as the gods had always intended. Some who learned the history of that splendid diamond – including Marie Antoinette, who wore it for a single day – claimed it was the talisman that started the French Revolution.

Vanessa came slowly back to the present, eventually aware she was still in front of the mirror and covered entirely in sweat. In fact, she was soaked. As she showered, she was radiant from her vision. She would never forget what had just happened. Not wanting to remove the diamond, she wore it to bed that night. As she drifted off to sleep, her last thoughts were, *I wish never to be parted from this stone, but can I pay the price of my soul?*

Vanessa awoke at dawn, feeling disoriented. She dressed in simple dark slacks and a warm sweater that hid the precious diamond. A compulsion to find something, or someone, drove her from her room. The hotel's restaurant was not open, so she walked out in the mist of the early morning light. Crossing the stone bridge, Pont Saint-Louis, she strolled to the small garden adjoining Notre Dame, which marked the spot of departure for thousands of French Jews ferried away during World War II. From there they were taken to trains and deported to the death camps. A chill passed over Vanessa as she hurried past the famous cathedral. She crossed the Seine again, over Pont au Double, and followed the bank west toward the Eiffel Tower, which she could see in the distance.

A strong force within her drove her along the river. There were few people about, and most appeared to be vagrants lying wherever they could find shelter from the cold. Drizzle began to fall, but Vanessa was oblivious as she followed the riverbank. She felt the diamond against her breast as she walked, the immense stone rubbing ever so slightly with each step. Pont Royal appeared on her right. When she hesitated, a sudden force pushed her toward the large stone bridge. She crossed and immediately saw the Tuileries Gardens. The trees were bare, the flowers long gone, but Vanessa recognized the little park as if she had been there a day ago. She briefly looked to her right as she entered the gardens, recognizing the immense palace called the Louvre, which had never been a special place to her. She walked through the grounds toward Place de la Concorde at the end of the park. Sweat ran from her body as her pace quickened. Leaving the gardens, she recognized in the distance the Arc de Triomphe. She was on the wide sidewalk adjacent to the Concorde, and though it was still early, the traffic was immense. Cars were honking, and even the pedestrian traffic was busy.

Vanessa sensed something monumental was progressing around her. She reached up to her breast and touched the magnificent diamond hanging from her neck. The skies darkened, and gradually all sound ceased.

When Vanessa looked up, there were no cars. The sky was a clear blue and filled with pigeons. The walls that surrounded the park behind her were gone. In front of her, the landscape was a dirt field, filled with the smells of another world and the deafening noise of tens of thousands of people. They were dressed in plain clothes, as if they were peasants from a thousand years before, though it was in reality the end of the eighteenth century. Vanessa was dressed quite well in a yellow velvet dress. Though it was not ornamented, she certainly stood out from the others.

She felt a sudden sharp pain in her arm. A shabbily dressed old woman grabbed her, saying in a coarse peasant's accent, "Well, deary, what's brought the likes of you to watch the special events today? Yur dressed like a lady. Yur not one of the elegants are yus?" She cackled. "No, of course not, or you'd be all locked up in La Force Prison. Come quick wit me. I'm gonna get a better gander at what's gonna be today."

The old crone took Vanessa forcefully by the hand and yanked her into the crowd, cursing at anyone who would not move as she forced herself toward the middle of the field. "Move yur bloody ass. It's me who helped start this revolution. Get the hell out of my way, or yul join those who have their appointments with the Doctor." She pushed and screamed her way through until they were standing in front of a tall scaffold. An area in front was blocked from the crowd, forming a thoroughfare in which a horse-drawn cart was approaching.

Vanessa stared at the toothless crone. Saliva was running from the old lady's mouth, and a look of pure passion rested in her wrinkled face. She turned to Vanessa and with a maniacal glare said, "I waited me entire life for this moment, deary, and I knows it's special for you, too."

The cart pulled up in front of the scaffold, and Vanessa saw it contained two persons, a man and a woman. Two guards who had been inside the cart with them led their apparent prisoners out and toward the platform. Vanessa studied the scaffold. Her twentieth-century mind recognized it then for what it was: a guillotine.

The prisoners were led toward the stairs that ascended to the top. They would pass directly in front of Vanessa. As the two came near, the old crone grabbed Vanessa's arm tightly and shrieked. "Well, behold, it's the king and queen of France coming for a visit to Dr. Guillotine. Where's yur fine robes and jewelry now? And looky here who's I got with me."

The old woman pulled Vanessa closer, and as she did, Vanessa's eyes met those of Marie Antoinette. A spirit within, a memory of another time, passed over Vanessa, and she began to cry. The queen seemed to recognize Vanessa, but in reality, the creature that had survived so many months in prison was almost beyond understanding. She was emaciated from lack of food; her hair was so thin her scalp was visible. But her eyes were alive, and a glint of recognition swept over her as she stared at Vanessa. A feeble smile came to her lips as she passed by and climbed the stairs to the executioner.

Fierce, angry hands pulled Vanessa and held her head tightly against the old woman's face. The smell of stale beer and onions, mixed with something worse, descended on Vanessa as the woman spoke into her ear. "I knows you. You thought you'd fool an old lady, but I recognize you. Yur the Princess Savoie, and we tore you apart long ago. You must be a devil, reborn to be kilt again. Don' try and run away, Weel just watch yur friends beheaded, and I'll drag yuself up after for the same." The old lady tightened her hold on Vanessa, all the while snickering and howling with insane laughter.

Realizing she was having a vision and that what she was going through would end soon, Vanessa watched the king and queen and braced herself for the execution. The sky darkened, and distant thunder announced the coming of rain. Taking flight in great numbers, birds fled for safety from the approaching storm. The enormous crowd of people quieted as the executioner placed the queen's head against the wooden block.

Vanessa stood mesmerized at the sight, and unexpectedly within the vision, she experienced something new. The murmuring of the crowd ceased, and a glow of light surrounded the scaffold. The blade was released, and descended in slow motion. As the blade came close to the neck of Marie Antoinette, the world exploded in a flash of white light. The crowd disappeared, the scaffold vanished, and Vanessa was suddenly covered in yellow butterflies, millions of butterflies. The pretty insects seemed to be carrying her, as she felt weightless.

The vision disappeared and Vanessa found herself standing in the middle of the Concorde. Cars rushed past her on both sides, and two gendarmes appeared to lead her back toward the Tuileries Gardens. Back in the park, she glanced at her watch. Jean Delacroix would be picking her up in one hour.

Without a moment's hesitation, Vanessa knew what she must do. She had just enough time. A Paris taxi was parked at one corner of the square, the driver eating a croissant and sipping a cup of coffee. She walked over and, putting on a winning smile, begged him to take her to her hotel.

℘

Jean looked at the bronze-and-marble inlaid clock across from his desk and noted it was almost two o'clock. The Mercedes limousine was parked in front of his apartments, and his luggage was already inside the car. Behind the Mercedes was a smaller car that would accommodate all of Vanessa's luggage. He exited the building and waved off his driver, walking to Vanessa's hotel just around the corner.

As Jean entered the hotel, he greeted the manager politely, noticing that the man was new. Looking around, Jean hesitated, noticing no sign of Vanessa or the beautiful Louis Vuitton luggage he had sent over. Turning pointedly to the young man across the desk, he said, "My name is Jean Delacroix. Is Miss Daniells in her room?"

Alarmed, the young manager stuttered slightly. "N-no, sir. Miss Daniells left the hotel a short time ago. She gave me her room keys and this letter to give to you."

Déjà vu swept over Jean as he turned his back on the young man and walked up the single flight of stairs to Vanessa's room. He opened the door and stood mesmerized for a moment. The wardrobe he had sent over was neatly laid out on the beautiful bed. On top of the clothes was the necklace he had given her. The new Louis Vuitton luggage was piled at the foot of the bed. Jean walked to the open patio window, the fresh Paris air flowing through the pretty room he had so carefully chosen for Vanessa. He sat down in the chair next to the window and abstractly studied the small patio below. A couple occupied two chairs and embraced tightly, the man softly stroking his companion's face, both oblivious to anything else.

Voices drifted up from the hotel lobby as Jean opened the letter. He read it with tightness in his chest, the words comforting, confusing, unloving, certainly nothing he had expected. Jean's gaze wandered back to the young couple, laughter drifting up, covering the tightness in his breast. A single unnoticed tear slid down his cheek. For a moment, Jean Delacroix allowed an image to enter his mind — something of youth, his mother and father; a young gestapo officer, and a scene from hell played out long ago and shut away from his consciousness. The images faded, and the rage came. He had lost, and Jean Delacroix could never lose at anything.

Jean slowly rose and left the hotel. Choosing to walk the short distance to his apartments, he waved away his valet and driver again. The anger he felt could not be directed at Vanessa; her letter did not allow that. He dropped it on the street without thinking. There would be another day and another challenge. A sudden burst of cold rain covered him, and he quickened his steps to his little palace on the Seine. The icy water took away the sting of defeat. He smiled, his last thoughts of Vanessa: what a classy little bitch, and so young to defeat him.

PART II: TRISTAN TAYLOR

New York City, 1955: The Roxy Theatre

Leslie Cole was New York's equivalent of Lizzy Borden and the Marquis de Sade but possessed the theatrical genius of Orson Wells. She was in charge of casting *West Side Story* on Broadway. At forty-five, she had been through all the wars, starting as an aspiring young actress who was told, "You got the part, honey. Now undress."

What did it matter what she played that game for? She liked sex any way she got it — upside down, backward, forward, mornings, evenings, from man or woman. Years later, she would laugh when she coined the phrase *I'd fuck a snake to get the part, and like it.* Leslie was striking and looked very young for her age, with a great figure and a spectacular face. To some, she appeared like a life-size Barbie doll with large blue eyes, a pink complexion, almost no makeup, and a sensuous mouth with full lips. She stood five feet ten in stockings, and had a thirty-six-inch bust that went perfectly with the rest of her.

The casting-couch years were behind her. Tired of acting and the payment often extracted for each job, she had met Chad Warner, a major producer of Broadway shows, mostly musicals. He introduced her to that aspect of the stage, and she took to it like a Nile crocodile to an overturned boatload of tourists. Leslie made a place for herself, gaining the respect she never had when she was an actress. It was her time to do the auditioning, and what a trip that was. The straight producers got laid any which way they wanted it. The fruitcake producers got whomever they wanted through her "auditions." As for Leslie, she got the pick of the litter, all through the casting process.

Leslie was reflecting on the new show. *West Side* was turning out great. The nationwide ads calling for open casting had worked wonders, especially for the pre-opening publicity. Leslie's mind raced with thoughts of the macho Puerto Rican studs with erections that never ended, and so willing to please. Then there were the pretty Latinas with great piercing eyes. One of her male casting assistants had told her recently after one especially beautiful Puerto Rican girl finished her audition, "If I get her in bed tonight, you not only might not see me tomorrow, but you just might have to bury me."

Leslie watched the aspiring Caucasian performers with incredible talent. Young starlet types appeared from all over the US and Europe, including one major Hollywood actress who could even carry a tune. The lads were outstanding, with muscular bodies ready for all kinds of

interesting action. Tall, short, most good looking, and a few who also
carried a tune. But, of course, none of them stood a chance of being
casted. Leslie kept a special list with the names she had already chosen
for roles in the musical, all from Broadway. The national program to
use newcomers was just so much rubbish, to promote interest in the
musical.

The weather that day was humid, and Leslie was happy to enter
Chad Warner's air-conditioned offices. Alone at the time, he stood up
to greet his casting director. She noticed Chad's gaze wandering over
her sleek black suit and white tux shirt, a hint of a smile as it halted a
moment at the cleavage he had fondled so contentedly when they first
met. But he was much younger then, and she eager to please. He gave
Leslie a brief hug, audibly inhaling the fragrance of her hair.

"Hello, gorgeous. How's it going?" he asked. "Have we set the cast,
and when do we start rehearsals?"

"Yes, but a small hitch. I haven't cast the lead role: Tony."

Chad looked at Leslie, his brow creasing in deep folds. "How can
you say that? Two weeks ago, you and I sat down with Gordon
MacRae, right here in this office, with his attorney, no less. We all
agreed to his playing the part for the first twelve months. That was a
done deal. You never told me anything happened to change things."

Leslie sighed. "I know, Chad, I know. But you seem to forget one
slight issue to that deal. Twentieth Century Fox had the right to sign
him in *Carousel*, and they did. He's out for us."

Chad paled slightly and sat down in his deep office chair. For a
moment, he was silent. Pouring himself a glass of ice water from a
thermos on his desk, he asked, "Who's out there that can fill the role?"

"No one. All the key people I wanted are committed to other shows,
either playing now or beginning shortly." Leslie took a breath. "I'm
considering a newcomer."

Chad glared at her. "I'm spending this kind of money, and you're
going to use someone untested. We won't get through the first week."

Leslie walked to Chad's desk and, without hesitating, said,
"There's no major singer out there! If you're not happy with my
suggestion, then cancel the fucking show until I get you a regular,
Chad. What do you want from my tired body. I can't get anyone."

Chad stared at her, finally realizing they had a mutual problem.
"Who do you have in mind?"

"A young singer from LA who has a great voice, an athletic body,
and I can work with—Tristan Taylor. Come in tomorrow, and I'll have
him audition just for you."

New York City: The Plaza Hotel

The small hotel room was situated next to the elevators. Seated on a tufted wingback chair, Tristan Taylor could feel the vibration whenever the elevator passed or stopped on the other side of the wall. A faint *ting*, when the doors opened, *ting* again when they closed. Well, at least he was in one of the best hotels in New York. His family had taken care of that, as they had everything throughout his brief career.

Tristan was at the threshold, a chance to go where few his age dared or could. He went to the window overlooking Central Park — a vast expanse of green as far as the eye could see, ringed by the Manhattan skyline. A beautiful summer's day had begun, an easterly wind blowing the trees gently. Once, only the wealthy had lived there on the fringe of the park: the Vanderbilts, Gettys, and Roosevelts. But Tristan viewed it only as an immense concrete jungle with a bit of green added for good measure. Tristan thought about his future, how much it held in store for him. In New York, he would penetrate the music business and someday change part of it forever. But that was in the future. A single woman stood between him and the beginning of his career.

Tristan went to his audition at the Roxy Theatre that morning. From her seat in the auditorium, Leslie Cole scrutinized him. When Tristan's turn came to sing, he gave one of the best performances he was capable of. As he sang, he sensed Leslie's eyes on him. *Remarkable. I know she's listening to me, but at the same time she's undressing me.* He finished his brief solo, performed the required *West Side Story* dance number, and sat down in the far left corner of the theater to observe the other actors.

One young man from Ohio had a marvelous voice. Leslie instructed him to perform the dance routine. He had practiced the *West Side* dance number and performed brilliantly, far superior to Tristan's somewhat clumsy attempt. Tristan noted that Miss Cole recognized that when she applauded after the dance routine, but she kept turning and staring at Tristan, even as Mr. Ohio went through his routine. So that was show biz; what else was new. Thank God she wasn't queer.

It had not been just Tristan's voice or his rigid dance steps. He knew that look as lust. A small victory over the other performers. Tristan felt confident, but he also realized that if Leslie Cole was interested in him sexually, she might just want to fuck him and nothing more.

Miss Cole listened to all the aspiring male leads that morning. There were three young men trying out for the part of Tony, and that day the field would be narrowed. She stood up and asked the three singers to return to the stage. She shouted to them to turn one way and another, to look serious, thoughtful, amused, depressed, then just to stand relaxed for a while. Several minutes passed, but for Tristan it was an eternity. The other two had extensive experience. Tristan stood still, feeling like a total outcast.

Leslie Cole pulled a dark pair of sunglasses from her jacket, placing them on. Tristan could no longer see her eyes. Then she addressed them gently, "Okay, young men, be back at six this evening."

Sensing that Miss Cole was still looking his way, Tristan gazed at her. *She still wants me. But what's with the frown?*

With a slight smirk, she said, "Mr. Taylor, on second thought, and as you're a newcomer to Broadway, I'm really not sure I want to have you back. I'll call you at your hotel and let you know later."

Tristan stared at her before leaving, again noting her head turned in his direction. *She's a fucking bitch.* He smiled flirtatiously at her anyway. When he returned to the hotel, a short message was waiting when he picked up his room key: *Auditorium at six. –Leslie*

Tristan showered and dressed for the six o'clock meeting, not sure any longer if he was in or out. He chose a new Italian-cut suit by Brioni, a custom tailor in Rome. Adding a pastel blue shirt, dark tie, and Oxford dress shoes, Tristan had finished dressing. Drawing away from the window, he checked his watch. Half an hour to spare. Tristan wandered into the Plaza Hotel's beautiful foyer, which also served as a dining area. They were still serving a late tea-and-sandwich buffet.

He sat under a tall palm tree that gave him privacy of sorts, and ordered tea. As he sipped from his cup, his thoughts drifted to Leslie Cole, the gorgeous, nasty Amazon who could undoubtedly start his career in earnest. He instinctively knew Leslie was playing some sort of game and had already decided who was to have the lead role in the play. He just wasn't sure whom. He was also aware of the backstage gossip that no one outside New York had landed a single minor role and that all the main leads who might have been a shoo-in for the role of Tony were busy on other shows. A newcomer was definitely going to get the lead for *West Side Story*.

Tristan ordered a second cup of tea. As he waited, he noticed a book on the floor, probably left by the previous patron. *Nobility of the French Revolution.* Tristan glanced at the illustrations and suddenly froze, unable to move past the face of a young woman on one of the pages. She was featured in a portrait called *Marie-Louise Lamballe de Savoie, Lady-in-Waiting to Marie Antoinette, Queen of France.* Tristan stared at her face, a strange sensation coming over him, but he had no inkling what déjà vu represented. Forgetting his tea, Tristan left money on the table and got up from his seat. He meant to return the book at the front desk but absentmindedly left with it in his hand.

Exiting the hotel, Tristan walked the five blocks to the Roxy Theatre. The streets were crowded, and many people stared at him. The cut of his slacks and tight shirt showed off his muscular figure. Was it too much? he wondered. The stares were not hostile—most were admiring, some envious, and from many of the women, plainly flirtatious.

ऒ

Leslie watched Tristan enter the old theater. He sauntered down the center aisle with ease and self-confidence, and she wanted to take him right there on the lush red carpet. Her mind raced, and her body turned to fire as a wave of lust coursed through her. It had been six months since her last affair and the resulting bitter disappointment. No man had come into her life since, and she had toyed with the idea of allowing no man near her again.

One evening Leslie had been invited by a close woman companion to attend a sadomasochistic party. Her friend said, "Come. You don't have to participate, just watch. You might even learn something new." Leslie hesitated, but her curiosity got the better of her and she attended. A young man greeted her as she entered and escorted her to a private room where he explained the rules of his club—what could be done, and what could not be done. She was amazed, having thought all S&M activities were perverted sexual orgies. That night opened her eyes, and she enjoyed what she saw. Though she did not participate, she took home a copy of a book on sadomasochism written by one of the members. Those thoughts filled Leslie's mind as Tristan Taylor took a place on the stage. She wanted to initiate him into her sadomasochistic fantasies. That night.

There would be no further auditions. Leslie had planned at least two more to eliminate, one by one, the talented aspiring performers who were giving everything they had to be at the top of Broadway's phony show-business world. How lucky most were in not making it. The years of payments would take a toll on their very bodies, minds, and souls. Leslie often thought they were selling their spiritual beings to the devil in return for paltry financial rewards and the superficial adoration of the audience, all for the possibility of being one of the few stars who rose from those ashes. Well, Tristan Taylor would be given the chance to rise from those ashes. That beautiful body of his would be hers for the run of the show.

Leslie waited until the candidates were standing at center stage. For a fleeting moment, she considered the possible folly of hiring Tristan. Deep inside, she was aware that a good part of her decision was purely personal and selfish. She had become more than infatuated with the young man. As coy as she had been with her obvious attraction to him, he in return was behaving badly, almost cock sure of himself. She wanted to punish him, and Leslie's punishment would be her newly discovered sadomasochistic fantasy.

With no further thought of guilt over her choice, and without taking her eyes off him, Leslie stated, "Tristan Taylor will be the lead of *West Side Story*. The rest of you, thank you and goodbye. Tristan, my secretary, Mr. Grady, will give you directions to my private office. Be there in one hour."

Hollywood, California, 1947: Radio Recorders Studio

Tristan Taylor was nine years old when his father, Ralph, a record producer, first brought him to the recording studio. Friday, June 27, 1947, 9:45 p.m., would be forever etched into his memory. Radio Recorders was the only studio in Los Angeles set up to record music for commercially produced singles and long-playing albums. The recording rooms were tiny, hardly allowing room for more than a handful of the talented musicians who brought to the world some of the greatest jazz, blues, and rhythm-and-blues songs of all time. B.B. King, James Brown, Lionel Hampton, The Platters, and endless other talents. Much of the music recorded there was "black," and due to segregation, most of it was not aired on the major radio stations.

Black music was taboo on white stations and, with very few exceptions, only played on small radio stations that catered to the black community. It was during that period that Ralph Taylor entered the entertainment business. A tall man of Italian descent, Ralph was a concert-violinist-turned-record-producer, who worked for Black and White Records, a little-known company whose specialty was black music, mostly blues. He was the label's Artist and Reputa Manager, organizing groups of musicians and the songs they recorded for the company, building their reputations.

That week had been difficult at best, and Ralph was not in a great mood. One of the company's music writers had been arrested by the United States Attorneys' office and charged with being a member of the Communist party. He called Ralph in the middle of the night for assistance. Fortunately, Ralph had the thousand dollars in bail and was able to get his friend released.

Ralph expressed his anger while having dinner with his family. "What in the world is happening in America when a person's arrested for joining a political group not popular to the majority?" His wife, Alice, listened without comment. He had made it clear from the day they met that he was politically to the left and a strong supporter of minority causes. Well, his life had been dedicated to exactly that, a white honky representing talented black singers in a country full of bigots.

On top of everything else, Ralph was pressed for time the next morning. He had booked a full-day music session. Radio Records rented studios by the hour, as it was costly to use the equipment and

they were the only studio in town. Ralph was using an unknown group
he had put together to record an early long-playing record of twelve
rhythm-and-blues songs. They worked from early morning until late in
the evening, finishing eleven songs. They needed one more song to
complete the LP, and there were only fifteen minutes of recording time
left.

Tiny Topsy, the lead singer, looked into his song notebook and
exclaimed, "Shit, man. We don' have a twelfth song, we only came wiff
eleven."

Ralph stared stonily at him. "Well, gents, who's got something
new?"

Musicians are not only talented artists; they're innovative and can
create a new song or lyrics, or improvise an old song to a new beat,
often on a moment's notice. Wanda Hastings, the group's female singer
replied, "I got a li'l ditty called 'Open the Door, Richard.' "

Realizing they had less than fifteen minutes to rehearse and record,
Ralph said, "Spit it out fast, girl." And Wanda did just that as Ralph,
closing his eyes, listened intently to see if it would work.

Wanda handed a copy of the lyrics to Topsy, and they began the
song, begging Richard to open the door. The musicians picked up the
melody. Jessie Parker, the band's drummer knew the song and joined
in with Richard's responses. The bantering went back and forth,
completing the song.

Ralph looked at the band, looked at the recording clock and the
irate studio technician glaring at everyone from the doorway. "I'm
shutting this place down in five minutes!"

"Group," Ralph said, "we got one take. Do it now. Do it right."
Without the band or singers rehearsing further, they did a perfect cut
on the first take. Ralph's nine-year-old son, Tristan, attending his first
recording session, took everything in with a wide smile, humming in
the background to Ralph's annoyance.

Years later, familiar with the recording, and the phenomenal sales
it had to its mostly black audience, many would declare that it was the
first big R&B single, a turning point that influenced music over the next
decade. From rhythm and blues, music would evolve to rock and roll.
And it all started with "Open the Door, Richard" that summer day in
1947.

℘

Inside all people lies a memory bank, and if they are very lucky,
that bank sends them a signal that influences what they might like to

do with their lives. In many, this little memory gene never goes off. If it does, it might awaken them at such a late point in their lives that they don't have the time or economic means to make a change. For Tristan, it went off that sublime summer evening, surrounded by a warm group of entertainers who had given their hearts and souls, creating music for the world.

In school, Tristan was unpopular with both boys and girls due to his anemic appearance. Having a great deal of time to himself, he spent it studying and earning good grades. In his spare time, Tristan studied the history of music, not just contemporary music but all music. He learned about early instruments going back thousands of years. He studied the accomplished singers of the twentieth century, especially those involved with the opera.

Tristan's greatest solace remained attending every recording session his father was involved in. As the musicians who surrounded him were black, Tristan experienced firsthand the extreme prejudices that existed in post-war America. And he would always love the black musicians who came into his life. In the privacy of his home, Tristan mimicked the singers while playing his guitar. Ralph sometimes laughed at the young soprano's voice, which was certainly not in sync with the black music of the time.

Rustic Canyon, California, 1953

Tristan's home was in Rustic Canyon, a small hillside community in Pacific Palisades. Many homes in the area had a view of the Pacific. The canyon had some of the most beautiful natural foliage in California. Tall green eucalyptus and pine trees and the natural brush of the area gave no indication of being near a large metropolis. The Santa Monica Mountains were to the north, gentle foothills on the east and west, the Pacific Ocean to the south. The neighborhood was upper middle class to wealthy, with some homes of modest size and some quite spectacular.

At fifteen, Tristan spoke fluent Italian like the rest of his family and was still not particularly notable in stature or appearance. Five feet ten inches already, he was a gangly 150 pounds. With all the blemishes of adolescence, his gaunt face presented a large Roman nose, which in time would blend nicely with his adult appearance but at the moment stood out dominantly. Tristan possessed one redeeming attribute, his deep blue-green eyes, which could attract others to him if he possessed any self-security. But he had none and would not for years. He was not popular in general, and years later he would be amazed when a friend told him others had viewed his shyness as arrogance.

Tristan had no father image to relate to, as Ralph spent all his time either in Chicago chasing down new talent or in Los Angeles doing recording sessions. Attending University High School in nearby West Los Angeles, Tristan was an above-average student in all areas except music. There he stood above everyone.

Like all young men, Tristan was hopelessly in love with one of the school's most beautiful girls. There were five in particular whom he gawked at incessantly: Julie, Jan, Happy, Tony, and Kathy. The one he admired above all was Kathy LaRoque, the lead cheerleader, but he knew that to girls like her he did not exist. He was just another dull boy—not athletic, not good looking, and heaven forbid, they were never seen with the likes of him. However, there were girls without beauty who did respond to Tristan. Whenever that occurred, he took them as good pals, much as he would a new male friend, and never saw them in a romantic light.

On one occasion, Tristan confided to his mother, "I'm in love with this girl, but she won't even look at me. She's beautiful, and I just don't know what to do. I also like her girlfriend, who's just as pretty, but neither will give me so much as a glance."

His mother quietly listened to all his laments. "Tristan, dearest, you mustn't fall for what you see on the surface of a person. Other girls are interested in you, but you pay no attention to them. Stop thinking about physical appearances. Try and find out what's inside."

Rather than telling him how to win attractive girls, she was steering him toward the plain ones? Tristan looked down at his feet. A moment later, Tristan realized his mother had stopped speaking. He met her gaze again.

"You have much to learn in life. And, Tristan dearest, when you moon over girls, remember one thing." Alice paused. "They sit on the toilet every day and perform nature's call, just like you."

Tristan heard his mother's words, but her wisdom did not take hold in his mind. And though he had dated a couple of lesser girls, he continued to seek after those whom he could not obtain. In the solitude of his imagination, when no one else was present, a Voice within would say, "The gods look down upon you, as you are here for their purpose. And someday in a faraway place, a very special person will come to you and all your fantasies will be fulfilled."

Tristan was hopelessly ruined by the attraction of beauty and did not realize that the appearance of the body was only that; the inside was what really mattered.

&

Peter Burton, Tristan's music teacher was a stocky man with wide, twinkling blue eyes set in an oval face. Peter knew quite well the insecurities of the young boy, as well as what his father was doing in creative music. Peter respected and enjoyed black singers and recognized the special singing ability Tristan possessed. Tristan was a general member of the choir, and Peter had not utilized him in a solo spot. That was about to change.

It was five o'clock and most of the students were tired and wanted to leave. Peter dismissed the choir and said, "Have a nice weekend, all of you. See you Tuesday for rehearsal, and, Tristan Taylor, please stay behind. You will sing solo this year."

A few students whistled, others groaned, and Kathy LaRoque said loudly, "When do the pigs lead the singing?" The students roared with laughter and left the schoolroom.

Tristan stood with his head down, his eyes watering. Peter placed his hands on Tristan's shoulders. "They don't know you have the only real talent among them. Let's show 'em a thing or two."

~~

The end of the school year was traditionally recognized with a celebration in the huge school auditorium. The school's fifteen hundred students plus their families would attend. The student body performed short skits, and the faculty handed out awards to outstanding scholars. That was followed by senior graduation. Peter Burton's responsibility was the music program. His fifty-student choir would sing mostly traditional ballads of that era with a token modern pop song thrown in.

Peter had been working with Tristan privately the last few months to culminate the singing program with the classic "Ave Maria." He had been unable to help the young singer overcome his insecurity. In the large auditorium one evening, Tristan broke down completely on stage, crying silently. Peter approached and sat next to him. "You have a splendid voice, Tristan. What is it that makes you so upset?" Tristan did not respond, but Peter was a man of infinite patience and waited for him to gather himself.

The silent sobbing stopped after a few minutes, and Tristan, looking forlorn, said, "I've really never spoken to anyone before about my feelings. I don't believe anyone understands me. My mother's busy with her life, taking care of me but mostly my father. Dad's not around much. He spends most of his time looking for new singers, then recording them and promoting their songs. I don't see him either. He laughs at me when I tell him I want to be a singer. He doesn't even know I'll be singing solo next week at graduation.

"As a matter of fact, no one in school even knows me. I don't participate in sports. I'm unpopular with most of the students here. So how can I go on stage and sing solo?" Tristan stood and walked to the front of the vast, empty stage.

Peter watched the young man and, when he returned, looked at him quizzically, saying, "And what is it that's really bothering you?"

The young singer looked at him sheepishly. "I'm terrified."

~~

At precisely noon, the school bell rang three times, alerting the campus it was time to go to the auditorium for the closing ceremonies. Tristan broke out in a sweat. No one in the school had ever heard him sing solo, and no one was aware he would conclude the singing program that day.

The audience was tolerant through the choir's concert, as that was the final presentation before graduation ceremonies. Families and students were used to that part, and to most, it was yawn time. Much yammering in the audience preceded Peter's Burton's final announcement. "I know everyone is waiting for the end of this program so you can all leave for the summer. Here at University High we have a very special young man I want all of you to hear. He is very talented, so please give Tristan Taylor your attention for our closing song."

As Peter withdrew, Tristan walked from the choir to the front of the stage and awkwardly adjusted the solitary microphone. A few students snickered loudly; others laughed, pointing at him and whispering to one another.

Tristan froze and, for the first time in his life, remembered nothing of the verse or lyrics. His mind was a complete blank. Anger rose up where none had ever been, and he realized he had the chance to make his mark. Tristan's thoughts flashed to the recording studio where his mentors had performed—Sam Cook, Jackie Wilson, The Platters, and that marvelous singer of soul, James Brown. His parents were sitting in the front row with their questioning eyes, especially his father. Was he looking at him with disdain? So, his father did not believe in him.

Tristan Taylor had arrived at his first pinnacle. His future would be measured by the next three minutes of his life. He caught the music teacher's eye and nodded, even though not a single word of "Ave Maria" would come to him. Peter waved to the student orchestra to start.

As with so many who perform for the first time, the words and music came into focus. Tristan had spent five years attending myriad recording sessions with his father, watching the finest musicians of his time record their extraordinary music, absorbing everything about them. Each entertainer had a special way of singing; two musicians could play the same instrument but make it sound unique. It was Tristan's turn.

He started softly. The audience paid no attention, only waiting for that part of the program to end. Half a minute into his presentation, Tristan hit a note that got the attention of every person in the audience. Half the girls he had mooned over would later say to each other, "Who is he? Where did he come from?" Kathy LaRoque would look in vain for that "new student."

As Tristan escalated his voice to impossible tenor highs, the audience grew still, and at the conclusion of his song, silence reigned for several seconds. Well-deserved applause followed; that time the whistles and catcalls were enthusiastic. But they all reached a deaf ear.

Tristan bowed to the audience and left the stage. The continuing applause did not mark his return. He simply exited and left the campus behind, walking into nearby Westwood Village.

Tristan didn't know why he had exited without an encore, but some sixth sense led him to it. He had watched many of his father's singers perform at the nearby Cocoanut Grove and the Shrine Auditorium and take as many curtain calls as possible. Maybe something he had seen from one of the more popular entertainers of the day had influenced him, or more likely what he had *not seen*. Tristan decided he never wanted to imitate any performer, at age fifteen or at the height of his career. He would be different in every way possible, including his exit at the end of his performances on stage.

℘

The next day, Peter Burton sat back comfortably in his aged black-leather reclining chair in his office near the school auditorium, silently congratulating himself for the success of the choir program, especially Tristan Taylor's solo. Peter was a soft-spoken individual. His forty-two years did not reflect in his face at all. Many who observed his boyish looks thought him to be in his early thirties at most. Peter was devoted to teaching music and in particular to his youthful singers.

Ralph and Alice Taylor sat in front of Peter and listened attentively as he spoke about Tristan's talent. "Yes, a natural control of the pitch of his voice and a powerful projection. I've never in my fifteen years here at University seen the likes of him at his age. During my summers in Rome these past years, I've had the opportunity to visit Maestro Paulo Nolanza's studio and watch the famous teacher conduct his summer classes. He offers a renowned two-year study group, as well, for only the most talented. I believe Tristan is capable of becoming a great American classical singer if given the opportunity."

Peter hoped Ralph would respond positively. Tristan had told him about his father's background in music. At age twelve, he had been awarded a musical scholarship and a trip to Russia to study violin with a renowned Russian violinist. Ralph might have become a famous violinist, but fate intervened and an auto accident severed all the nerves in his playing hand. He could not recover from the accident and funneled his talents into his profession in the recording business.

Ralph listened intently to Peter and, after a moment of silence, said, "What do you suggest, Peter? I have the means to send Tristan to Italy if that's what you recommend. As a matter of fact, he really doesn't like school here, and we would consider having Mr. Nolanza take him into the two-year study program. Do you think he would be accepted?"

Peter leaned forward. "I have no doubt he would be accepted."

Again Ralph hesitated. "My son is not really interested in classical music. He has a strong desire to sing commercial rhythm and blues. He copies the styles of my artists after he's heard them in concert or at the recording studio. Tristan doesn't realize how silly he sounds with his tenor voice. And I don't want him to develop as a popular singer. My father was an aspiring opera singer, and I'll back Tristan as long as he devotes his ability to classical music."

"I see," Peter said, the blood draining from his face. He hoped Tristan would pursue the opportunity. It seemed the only way Ralph was willing to support him.

Before Peter could say anything else, Ralph ended the meeting with, "I'll talk to Tristan about your suggestion. We'll let you know." The Taylors left the small room, leaving Peter to reflect in the quiet space.

Earlier in life, Peter Burton had aspired to be an opera singer, but his teachers considered his voice only "good." As the years passed, nothing came of his efforts to break into New York's prestigious operatic theater. In time, he had to take work teaching. As a middle-aged wannabe impresario, he was in California teaching mostly uninspired students the art of singing.

Peter glanced at the small mirror on the wall beside him. Why was he not born with the kind of talent Tristan possessed? The ticking of the old school clock on the opposite wall was the only sound in the room. He walked to the narrow window overlooking the schoolyard. The students were gone then except a loving couple embracing under an old oak tree. A breeze stirred the leaves of the tree, and Peter tried to imagine what the two lovers were whispering as they so tenderly embraced.

Closing his eyes, Peter drifted off into another world, somewhere far away, where he saw himself standing on a concert stage in Rome or Paris, singing in one of the great operas — Arabella or Pagliacci — to the thunderous applause of an audience visible only in his mind.

Rome, 1953: Maestro Nolanza's School

Tristan arrived at the infamous Leonardo da Vinci-Fiumicino Airport in Rome the first week of July. He was unaccustomed to the humidity the ancient city was known for at that time of year. The long TWA flight had been torturous. The roar of four large turboprop engines had kept Tristan up for the duration of the flight that left Los Angeles some sixteen hours before.

A customs worker looked at the awkward youth and reviewed his declaration. "Do you have fruits or any animals hidden in your luggage?"

"No, sir."

"What are you here for?" Tristan blurted out his upcoming education with Rome's finest music teacher. The customs man looked him over and let out a bellowing laugh. "You Americans come up with such big lies all the time. Who told you to say that, and why are you really here?"

By the time Tristan got through customs, retrieved his baggage, and found a porter to help him get a cab, he was beginning to wonder if Italy would be what he had envisioned it to be after all. Was Rome the city he had read about—where the very cradle of civilization had blossomed, where gladiators had fought, and the first leaders of the ancient world had ruled?

The taxi driver stared at Tristan in the rearview mirror. In Italian, he muttered to himself. "The poor young man. No family with him and giving me the address of the maestro! Perhaps the teacher needs some kitchen help or a house servant and has decided to give a break to a young American. Ahh, I will be kind to the poor boy and not overcharge him too much." Tristan had spoken English at the airport. The driver obviously did not know he understood every word of Italian.

That was Tristan's first stay away from home, and the long, sleepless flight took its toll. As the cab traversed the lengthy road to the maestro's palace, Tristan fell into a deep sleep.

No longer a gawky fifteen-year-old youth, Tristan was a famous opera singer making his debut in Teatro dell'Opera, Rome's most famous opera house. Attired in a spectacular costume, he stepped toward the audience to start an aria . . . and promptly forgot all his lines.

Tristan awoke in a magnificent bedroom, for the moment having no recollection of where he was, much less how he got there. Not having grown up in a European setting, let alone one of such splendor, he looked around in disbelief. The room was draped in gold and silver fabrics. The bed frame was a Roman chariot with a backboard made entirely of three-dimensional marble depicting, in motion, classic chariot horses with large, protruding eyes. The chairs and couches in the room were of ancient Roman style; the ambiance took Tristan back to a time when Rome was at its height of glory.

Tristan had slept around the clock, and the sun was setting over the ancient city. The view from his large patio balcony was spectacular. The palace was situated on a hill behind the Roman Forum. Tristan looked out at the remnants of the forum with its old marble columns and capitals. To one side, stood the legendary Colosseum where the gladiators had fought to the death. And beyond that, the great city itself, came alive with sparkling lights as the sun set in the distance.

℘

Wanting all of his young pupils spoiled rotten as to the ascetic values of life, Paulo Nolanza pampered them in a lifestyle of beauty. The maestro loved great beauty, whether it was the furnishings of his home or the women that came into his life. His home was a palace built in the sixteenth century for a Roman family of nobility. The villa was made entirely of marble, most of which came from the mountains of Carrara, made famous by the lifelike sculptures of Michelangelo. The rooms were immense by any standards, and within each room, a modern bath had been installed in the 1920s.

The maestro had intentionally planned that setting. How else could he take the immature egos of his little men and build them to the grand, competitive personalities of the greatest virtuosos? Using the arts of classical opera, he would work with all the pupils diligently, with love and compassion, to build their self-esteems. Paulo would scold them, cajole them, praise or dismiss them. He was a master of young men; he would come to know each of his students' weaknesses and each of their strengths.

Every student had his own room at the palace. When not working with the maestro, they practiced singing alone in the luxury of their own suites. The thick marble walls prevented sound from leaving their rooms, and no matter how badly they might sing off key, only they would hear it. There were eight young men, each selected by either the maestro himself or recommended by one of the worldwide music teachers, such as Peter Burton. Of those eight, Paulo envisioned producing a Caruso.

ဆဝ

Tristan was the last to arrive for the beginning of the two-year seminar and hardly spoke to the others during breakfast, his shyness getting the better of him. Afterward, one of the instructors escorted the students to the main studio, where Maestro Nolanza conducted his classes. Like the rest of the place, that room was spectacular. It had once been the main dining room of the old palace, according to the instructor. Master craftsmen had covered a domed ceiling in beautiful paintings some four hundred years before. The colorful baroque paintings depicted religious allegories of the Bible. A large stage with an aged wooden floor sat to one side.

Maestro Nolanza directed his students to the front of the stage and had them sit on the floor as he described what they would be accomplishing the next two years. "Welcome to each one of you aspiring young scoundrels," he began, speaking Italian. "So, one of you will be a Cesare Siepi, a Mario Lanza, or Enrico Caruso. I am here today to lay out for you the simple schedule we will follow."

Looking sharply at one of his students, Nolanza asked, "And you, young man, I see you are chewing on something. Pray, be it a piece of gum, or have you discovered some obstacle in your mouth that must be munched on?" The lanky boy immediately turned crimson. The maestro put on a formidable expression and addressed the young culprit. "What is your name, son, and where are you from?"

The boy hesitated before responding. "Guseppi Tonato, sir, from Bari." His heavy accent was difficult for Tristan to follow, as his own family spoke a soft form of Italian, a dialect of Florence, where Tristan's grandfather was born.

"Young man, there is one rule here: in this room, when I am talking, nothing moves in your mouth. If I catch you moving your mouth and it is not because you are responding to me personally, you will instantly swallow whatever it is you are munching. If you tell me there is nothing in your mouth, I shall provide you with something." Maestro pointed at a rather large cockroach on a nearby wall. "And if you lie to me, I shall provide you with a small tidbit like that bug, and you can devour that in front of your classmates."

A beaming smile came across the maestro's face. Some of the students laughed heartily. The maestro had a wonderful sense of humor, if not a bit bizarre. Tristan grimaced, picturing himself having to eat a live cockroach.

With their full attention, the maestro continued. "The program here at the palace is intense. Aside from learning to sing, you will be given instruction in every other educational area—math, science, reading, writing—all in Italian, English, and French. A limited amount of German will be taught for those operas written in the language. I stress physical education." His sharp eyes stared. "You two over there." Maestro Paulo pointed toward two of the largest boys in the class. "What are your names, where are you from, and what is your weight?"

Stammering, the two boys responded to the maestro's questions. One of them was from Germany, the other from Russia.

"Good. Until you lose weight, I shall call you Fat and you Fatter."

More snickers came from the small class, and the maestro smiled. "You will rise at five a.m. each day. Breakfast is followed by a workout in the rear garden adjacent to the tennis courts. In wintertime, you will exercise in the basement gymnasium. This workout will be one hour in duration. After that, I will work with you individually while the others attend our regular school classes. Lunch is served at eleven, followed by one hour of rest. At one o'clock, we continue our program until six, when dinner is served. Following dinner, you will exercise with weights for forty-five minutes.

"I do one thing here that is not done in other schools: teaching operatic singing. I expect that from this class of eight, one or more of you will not make it past the first month. Additionally, from the seven left, one will eventually have an opportunity to sing professionally. I will not waste the splendid talent you have by not providing you with an alternate direction to go should you fail as an opera singer. When I was a young man, I loved to dance. It mattered not to me what dance. I just enjoyed the movement. With your splendid voices and an ability to move your feet, you could end up as professional dancers.

"For those whose voices are good but not good enough to perform in the opera, you might become popular singers, like Mr. Sinatra or Mr. Tony Bennett of America. Having a good knowledge of the dance will enhance your career under any circumstances. Aside from that, it is great exercise anyway. You will learn all forms of modern dance except ballet.

"My schoolwork schedule is six days a week for the entire year with one thirty-day break during the Christmas season to visit your families. Should you wish to remain here with me at Christmas, that is also fine. Sundays are your own, but for the first month, you will be escorted around Rome so you may become familiar with this glorious city of the gods. Anyone caught leaving the palace at another time without my permission will be expelled from school at once.

"Do you have any questions, no, good. Then each one of you stand up for a few minutes, give your name, and tell us a little about yourself. I want a close and loving family here."

∞

Paulo waited until his last pupil went to bed. Retiring to his immense suite, he sat on an old black-velvet sofa. His thoughts turned to the day's events and the new class of aspiring singers. Would one emerge above the others? Would he have a new Caruso to give the world?

He walked to a long wall filled with photographs of many of the young men he had worked with over the decades. Paulo beamed at the great stars he had developed. Stopping here and there as he meandered through his photo gallery, he fondly remembered the familiar faces. Great singers like Maurice Renaud and Nicolai Gedda. He stood in front of one large photograph taken at the Metropolitan Opera in New York, where four of his protégés had performed together in Giuseppe Verdi's *Simon Boccanegra*. The maestro whispered their names softly, remembering those young men as they were when they first came to him — Lawrence Tibbett, Giovanni Martinelli, Paulo Ananian, and the prodigious Ezio Pinza. Paulo went to sleep that night and dreamed the sweet dreams of a remarkable teacher, going back in time, working again with the marvelous young men he had such good memories of.

∞

A young group of aspiring singers worked eagerly to make the grade in Paulo Nolanza's school. The music teacher had struck the fear of God into them the first day, and no one wanted to fail. And no one did as the summer danced away with surprising rapidity.

Surrounded by the remarkable atmosphere of Rome, Tristan attended class with enthusiasm. The daily routine was exhilarating, as the two teachers who tutored the general classes were inspiring. Ule Edel taught math, history, and foreign languages. Mario Gilbrati filled in with all other areas of learning, including physical education.

It was Mario's weight program that interested Tristan in the beginning. Mario called it bodybuilding. Although it was not popular in America and few men in the general public utilized the activity, the name alone attracted underdeveloped Tristan. When Mario first introduced his students to the weight room, he looked at them in mock surprise, saying, "You never lifted weights? What is wrong with you?" And to the two Americans, he said, "Charles Atlas. You don't know of Charles Atlas? Shame on you. Now let me demonstrate how we will all become supermen." The program consisted of lifting barbells of different weights while utilizing a carefully regimented posture. They "pumped iron" three times a week, allowing one day in between for their muscles to recover.

The maestro assigned diets to the students, designed for each's weight. Those overweight, especially Fat and Fatter, were put on weight-reducing programs. Fruits and vegetables were the mainstay of their diet, with a small amount of protein. Tristan and the others, who were mostly on the thin side, were put on protein diets, with an emphasis on meat during the midday meal.

For Tristan, the day started with a large breakfast consisting of eggs, potatoes, bacon, ham, cereals, fruits, and milk. The midday meal included steak, pasta, vegetables, and watered wine. The evening meal was fruit and water only. Within four weeks, Tristan had put on ten pounds. The gaunt look in his face disappeared, and his body began to develop.

Johnny Williams became Tristan's friend and confidant in Rome. His room adjoined Tristan's, and the two had much in common. Both started at the school feeling like Don Quixote in quest of an identity. A small, friendly rivalry began between the two that, in effect, caused both to advance beyond the rest of the class. Johnny was confident and had a special magic that attracted the opposite sex no matter what his appearance might be. Looking much older than his years, he had blond hair, piercing jade-green eyes, fine aristocratic features, and a pleasing, natural physique.

Tristan would have to work twice as hard to gain the confidence his friend already had. By observing others, he developed his own magnetism over time. But Tristan's naïveté would follow him through the mountains and valleys of life, never quite abandoning the mystique he acquired.

Having settled into a routine of waking early and retiring early, the students were full of energy on weekend mornings, especially Sunday. It was a brief break from the rigors of school. Many of them looked forward to the pursuit of young girls, and where could it be any better than in Rome, or so they initially thought.

For the maestro's young men, there were no responsibilities concerning life's distant but inevitable burdens. It was a time of youth, when their summers offered glorious opportunities and their winters only learning. There were no thoughts of aging with dreams unfulfilled, or that a day might come when their summers became shorter and the winters of their lives longer and harder.

ℰℭ

One of the most famous strips of land in Italy, the Via Veneto, started in front of the Hotel Diplomatic and extended three blocks. Two famous hotels served lunch and drinks at tables on the walkways in front, giving patrons a view of the foot traffic. Those tables were filled to capacity during the lunch and early-dinner hours.

Paulo Nolanza warned his students not to be taken in by the charm of their settings, particularly the Via Veneto. He began with a painstaking explanation why it was nearly impossible to find single girls in the sprawling city. On the eve of their first liberated Sunday, he said, "To understand the social climate in Rome relative to young girls, one must understand the basic concept of the family mindset regarding dating. In Rome, no girl from a respectable family dates without family permission and the presence of a *duenna,* a chaperone. A boy cannot stroll around the vast city during the day and meet single girls. Should you encounter a girl you admire and want to take her to a movie or have a meal with her, you must meet the mother and father and receive permission to escort the daughter to some activity. And then only guarded carefully by the duenna." Paulo looked at his young students and smiled noticing the skepticism from a few.

"Now let me tell you about the *other* group of young women who *do* walk the streets free of parental supervision. They are mostly streetwalkers, what Americans refer to as prostitutes." Noting again from some of his young men a look of bewilderment, he continued. "What makes the streetwalkers of the Via Veneto stand out so very specially is the tremendous beauty most possess. Some are absolutely stunning. And now my warning, and I will give it to you one time only. There are two reasons I ask you to resist the temptations of starting up with these women. Firstly, some have venereal disease, and though you might like the delicious taste of their wine, you will not like the hangover that follows."

He looked at the ceiling, lost in thought. When after a few moments he did not continue, Tristan blurted out, "Maestro, you said 'two reasons.' What's the other?"

Paulo was a startled for a moment but regained his composure. Lowering his voice, he said, "I once had a gifted student who did not heed my advice. He met a girl who had run away from home. They took to each other, and soon the two had fallen in love. The boy disappeared from school. His parents were enraged but could not find him. He had no money, and in time, the girl left him. I heard much later that he had become an alcoholic, and for many years wasted his young life."

Again the maestro became disoriented, and again Tristan addressed him. "But, Maestro, what happened to the boy? Did he stay an alcoholic? Did you ever see him again?"

Maestro looked at his aspiring singer and smiled. "Yes. I met him when he regained sobriety. He turned out to be a productive human being though he never married or fell in love again. Anyway, enough said about the subject. Stay away from the girls."

Tristan was impressed by what his teacher told them, and that night, as he was drifting off to sleep, he puzzled over one thing. He would remember to ask Maestro the next morning how he knew that the unfortunate man had never fallen in love again. Of course, when he awoke the next day, he forgot to ask.

℘

One Sunday late in August, Tristan and Johnny set out for a day's venture into the life of the great city they had been learning about. The weather was absolute perfection — the sky an intense blue with high billowing clouds, the air clear, the city a bit quiet at just past six. They walked past the Colosseum with its population of abandoned cats mewing their morning serenade and hoping soon one of the citizens would bring them stale bread or leftovers, as they had for centuries. The boys made their way to the foot of the Spanish Steps, where each could order a café au lait or espresso. The vendors were just settling themselves up and down the famous landmark. At the top of the long flight of stairs was the Hotel Excelsior on Via Veneto. It had stood there for a century and was the most expensive hotel in Rome.

The young men ordered espressos and rolls and watched the vendors set up their stands among the thousands of pigeons that flew and pranced amidst the activity. Johnny looked at Tristan sheepishly. "What should we do today? I really want to check out the Via Veneto for you know what."

Tristan studied him for a moment, hoping his friend was not going to try to find a prostitute. "No. I don't know what. Certainly not this nonsense about the girls. Maestro said to stay away from Via Veneto and not to gawk at the girls. I know what you have in mind, and it's going to get us into trouble."

Johnny let out a guffaw, staring at Tristan, who then felt as if he were some small insect. "Don't be naïve," Johnny said. "You're nearly sixteen, and you're still a virgin. When're you gonna wake up? You can't go through life without tasting the fruit. God put girls down here to taste, and I'm going to get a taste. Today."

Tristan wanted everything Johnny did but was frightened at the prospect of it happening in such an unromantic setting. A prostitute was not compatible with his concept of sexuality. His brief moments of romance had involved a lot of tenderness and caring. Two girls had entered his life, leading to touching, caressing, and the innocence most encounter when they are young. One of the girls asked Tristan if they could go all the way. A strange sense of guilt prevented him, and nothing came of the relationship after that.

He and Johnny finished their early breakfast and spent the rest of the morning in Vatican City, admiring the Sistine Chapel and the splendid treasures in St. Peter's Basilica, including Michelangelo's *Pietà*. They marveled at the Sunday crowds.

As lunchtime approached, they strolled to the Via Veneto. Tables were still mostly empty of customers. Umbrellas covered each table and were designed with the motifs of different wines or aperitifs. Tristan thought that set the hotels apart from each other in a funny way. He could tell a friend to meet him at Cinzano for lunch, or Parazolla. They chose the Hotel Diplomatic and sat down at one of the farthest tables. Johnny told Tristan he wanted to be able to leave his chair and check out the action without the other patrons gawking at him.

Adorned with a small bouquet of fragrant pink and white carnations, the table was covered in white linen and set for lunch with the hotel's fine dinner plates and large crystal wineglasses. The atmosphere was conducive to having a splendid lunch, or just drinks. From the expensive menu, the boys carefully ordered a salad and Punticelio a Marinaro, commonly called "whore's pasta," a delicious blend of olives, capers, anchovies, and small, whole tomatoes mixed in with the pasta. Their lunch passed delightfully as the tables filled with the luncheon crowd — mostly workers from the nearby embassies, and tourists sitting in the warm Italian sun and delighting in the atmosphere.

While Tristan was enjoying everything, he noticed the dark beauties who paraded by. Most of the street's infamous girls were very tall, and all wore high heels and revealing, short skirts. And the legs, Tristan would never forget those stunning legs, the way the lovely ladies walked by. Their figures were nearly perfect or better.

The young women ranged from late teens to middle or, in a few cases, late twenties. None of them stopped, or started a conversation with the male patrons. That was taboo and understood by both the girls and the men. If a man was attracted to a girl, he merely made eye contact, rose slowly from his table, and followed her for a short distance. A conversation would ensue, and the two would go off together to perform the oldest routine in man's brief history on the planet.

The man, generally a well-to-do businessman, was usually married. His wife would never acknowledge that he had that little indulgence, and at the same time, would be shocked if she discovered he did not. That was the Italian theme song. Man may, woman may not, and God forbid if the woman did and the man found out.

It did not take long for Johnny to find girls to his liking. As he commiserated with Tristan about the attributes of each girl, Tristan became annoyed. He respected his friend immensely but could not fathom his interest in those prostitutes. As Johnny continued to talk, Tristan interrupted him. Lowering his voice so no one could hear, he addressed his best friend. "Maybe I'm wrong, but back home in Los Angeles, many of the boys, and even a few of the girls, were interested in just one thing about sex. They enjoyed the act but couldn't care less about who they were with. Sometimes I wondered if a few of the same sex screwed each other. That's how indifferent they appeared about feelings. I wasn't popular at all in high school. I only had two girlfriends, but even though we never went all the way, at least we cared about each other."

Johnny listened quietly for a few moments, but as Tristan continued talking, his smile grew until it was a huge grin. Realizing he did not have a captive audience, Tristan also smiled, reaching out to poke Johnny in his side. "That's okay, Johnny, I understand you. We're just different, you and I. Go ahead and do your thing, but I'm not joining in."

Johnny seemed lost for words, but just as he started to open his mouth, a beautiful girl walked by and he got up, following her down the street and out of sight. He soon returned, sitting down heavily in his chair. "Mama mia, one hundred thousand lire. I'll be broke for a month." Yet he continued to go after various girls down the Via Veneto.

Soon Johnny did not reappear, and Tristan was alone. He sipped his soft drink and looked at the life unfolding around him, lost in the sea of faces and sounds of the great city. The bright sun began to fade as more clouds filled the afternoon skies. Unaware how long he had been there, Tristan suddenly felt a presence, looked around, and discovered a beautiful face watching him from several tables away. He recognized at once that she was older than he, but her smile was welcoming, though he detected amusement in her face. She was alone, and Tristan, with his shy disposition, hesitated before rising to say hello. With hardly any assurance of himself, he nevertheless found himself at her table and smiled back into one of the most radiant faces he had ever seen. He noticed her light-olive skin, and her long light-brown hair seemed to glow with a life of its own. Her dark eyes had flecks of green and were almost too large for her oval face. He could see that she was amicably endowed behind her white open blouse.

"Hello, young man. You are American?" she asked with an amused look on her face. She had an Italian accent but spoke English perfectly.

Tristan paused, warmth rising in his face, and responded in Italian. "Yes, of course. How did you know that?"

"Sit down, my fine young American. It's the way you're dressed, of course. Only Americans wear baggy blue jeans, unlaundered shirts, and shoes that should be worn only by factory workers. Your belt is brown, your shoes are black, and though you look freshly scrubbed, I'll bet your clothes haven't seen a cleaning in weeks. But don't look so dismayed. You are very attractive. How old are you, and where in the world did you learn that dreadful Italian you're speaking?"

The warmth in Tristan's face had heightened with each syllable, and stammering for words, he spoke in English, exaggerating his age by several years.

The girl smiled at Tristan, making him blush even more. "And what are you doing here in Rome? Who is your friend who disappeared with Annette a few minutes ago?"

Tristan was astonished. "Annette. You know who Johnny disappeared with. Is she a friend of yours?"

The girl burst out laughing, causing those at nearby tables to stare at them, and Tristan's face grew even hotter. "No, not a friend. But if you are a regular customer here, you get to know all the pretty girls who work the street. By the way, my name is Sofia. What is yours?"

"I'm Tristan, Tristan Taylor, and I'm here in Rome alone, attending Maestro Paulo Nolanza's school to learn how to sing."

The smile on Sofia's face turned from amusement to interest, and Tristan began to relax. Talking about the school put him at ease. Sofia told Tristan she, too, had once aspired to sing and was aware of the renowned operatic school he was attending.

They talked through the afternoon, and before Tristan knew what was happening, Sofia got up to leave. "Tristan, I really enjoyed our little talk, and hope I see you again." And the ray of sunshine who had come was gone. Tristan tried to see where she went, but the traffic was at its peak and she was nowhere to be seen.

Johnny suddenly appeared and sat down. His face was glowing. "I did it. I really did it. I'm not a virgin anymore. She was astonishing. You can't believe what she did to me." And Johnny went on endlessly, describing the act performed for so many millennia and expressing himself as if no person on earth had ever been laid before. Tristan tried to listen attentively, but all the while, his mind drifted to that splendid apparition who had gotten up and left. Perhaps she would be back the next Sunday.

The next week went by slowly for the first time since Tristan's arrival in Rome, his thoughts drifting to Sofia. How much older was she; what did she do; where was her family or duenna to look after her? He fantasized as all young men do, and the more he did, the slower the week passed.

Since arriving at the beginning of the summer, Tristan had grown another two inches and added twenty pounds of muscle to his frame. The warm Italian sun had bronzed him as he ran through early-morning calisthenics; and his skin, once embellished with the plague of youth, was clear of blemishes. The diet had somehow added color to his eyes, intensifying them to a deep blue at certain times of the day. He noted almost nothing of those changes, but others around him did, including a curious Italian girl who momentarily felt it in her best interest to stay away.

෨

Paulo coached Tristan in every phase of operatic singing the young man was capable of learning at his age. Mario Galbrati, the maestro's capable assistant, questioned Paulo on why none of the boys were pushed to perform to even higher expectations. The two were dining alone in the kitchen late that particular evening, and the maestro responded, "You can only go so far with a boy of fifteen or sixteen. This is a time of their youth that brings about many changes. Their bodies are forming. Their minds are developing.

"One of the physical changes is the voice. A boy of this age will see his voice change from soprano to alto, or even to tenor or base. I am always mindful of these potential changes and never stylize a student's voice, knowing it is sure to change. Instead I teach these young men to use their lungs, in order to bring forth the sound of their voice. It is more important for them to build up strength in their lungs and learn to control the pitch of their voices.

"Perhaps now you might understand why I have you train them with weights. My little men will all be powerful physically so as to be able to develop their lungs. That is one of my best secrets."

After they had finished their meal, Mario asked Paulo, "Do we have any special talent this year? It's been a long time since we gave the world a new virtuoso."

Paulo reflected on the question for a while and pensively responded. "We shall see. There might be one, but he is very insecure. One of the Americans: Tristan Taylor."

℘

The weeks flew by, and each Sunday Tristan and Johnny set off to explore little streets and alleys in Rome, settling around noon on the Via Veneto, in search of their identities. As the summer lengthened into fall, they came to know the pretty girls who flaunted themselves on those afternoons. Johnny tasted as much of that life as he could afford. His family had given him a generous allowance, and he made the most of it, sampling those God-given fruits as no other his age could.

Tristan was not interested; he had fallen in love with the pretty Sofia. The summer was ending and still no sight of the beautiful young woman. After the day she talked to him, he became aware of how important it was to dress smartly, even while wearing denim jeans. He asked his teachers about dress styles and began matching his clothes correctly. Never again would he venture into the world without checking if he was attired properly.

Johnny disappeared as usual, and Tristan was lost in thought that Sunday afternoon, when someone sat down next to him. "Well, hello, young American. I see you are dressing better these days, and tell me about your singing career. How is it going?"

Tristan looked up into two large dark eyes and was spellbound.

"Has the cat caught your tongue? You are turning red. What is the matter?"

"No, I . . . no, Sofia. What happened to you? I've come every Sunday, and you never came back."

She laughed, and Tristan wondered at her perfect white teeth and sparkling eyes. "I have been acting in a film. My second. And I think this one will make me a star. Of course, it's an Italian feature film and will probably never be shown in America. You Americans only watch your own films, which is a pity."

And all the while, Tristan gazed into her eyes, thinking that if life were something very special then Sofia would be a part of his.

"I'm ravished," she said finally. "Let's order something to eat, and I'll tell you about my film. And you can tell me about your famous school and the maestro everyone in Italy talks about. Does Paulo Nolanza really work you boys until dawn, and does he feed you only bread and water if you misbehave?"

The afternoon sped by like a freight train. Then Sofia abruptly got up to leave, and Tristan stood, taking her hands in his. "Please don't go. Let me walk with you. I must see you again."

She smiled at Tristan, allowing him to hold her hand as they walked along the Via Veneto and through the embassy area and surrounding villas. Leaves were falling from the trees, and almost no flowers embellished the expensive homes then. The air was chilly, and Tristan put his arm around Sofia's waist in a friendly manner, not implicating sexual need, just one desiring the warmth of another human being.

℘

Sofia sensed Tristan's sincerity, his innocence, and wondered why she was attracted to the lonely young man. Something about him reminded her of her own loneliness, her own spirit, and she felt a deep affinity to him. For the moment, Sofia had no guilt about her companionship with Tristan, just a pleasant feeling, and even she had no idea where it might go. They approached a shabby apartment building, and Sofia gave Tristan a hug and started up the stairs. At the top of the landing, she smiled and said, "I'll see you again next Sunday, same time, same place."

"No, Sofia. Please come to see me sing this Saturday at the maestro's villa. He's allowing each student to perform a short aria, and we can invite one guest. Please come and hear me." He looked into her eyes like an adopted puppy.

Sofia responded with a nod and disappeared into the ancient building. As she climbed the stairs to her apartment, she again reflected on her feelings for the young American. How in the world could she refuse him, even knowing she would have hell to pay if she were to tell her mentor, film producer Sergio Vaskeli. In Europe, he was considered one of the best Italian film directors. It was he who had first discovered Sofia and told her he was going to make her a star. He was her mentor, protector, and lover, and also twice her age. That forceful man would never understand her wanting to see a youthful singer under any circumstances. She would beg an evening to see her family instead. Tristan would be her secret.

℘

Tristan strolled back to the Hotel Diplomatic to find Johnny and listen to another hour-long description of what he considered to be true love. It was nearly five o'clock, and the streets were filling with people leaving work. Dark clouds hung in the sky, and even the pigeons were absent. The streetwalkers were again plying their trade but, at that hour, were on the side streets adjacent to Via Veneto.

How beautiful most were and, at the same time, how sad it seemed to Tristan. Why was it that some, who possessed the incredible beauty God gave them, ended up there on the street, while others, born with much-less-natural comeliness, lived a happy, meaningful life. How strange it seemed to him. In his youth and innocence, he thought he saw the realities of life.

Tristan couldn't know that the views he had then would change so dramatically with the passing of time that he would one day view those pretty streetwalkers as the ones possessing a real life, while those in high society often appeared to him as wasting theirs.

℘

Maestro Nolanza encouraged his students to perform in front of small groups. That way, the singers had the opportunity while others listened and watched. Most of the young men had performed in their local schools or church groups and were anything but shy. Paulo strove to have an audience attend the monthly recitals, no matter how small they might be. He usually invited close friends and other singers, who would critique the style and quality of each vocalist. Competition between students was strongly encouraged, as it brought out the best in almost everyone.

That Saturday the performance would be special. Two of Italy's finest baritones and impresarios were attending, including world-famous Leonard Wood, who was in Rome performing *Macbeth*. The renowned singers would judge and speak about each student. It was for that special evening that the students were allowed to invite a friend. Tristan, of course, had invited Sofia, who called to say she was not sure if she could come but would try.

ℰℛ

Monday morning, Tristan's voice was gone. Because of a changing pitch, he had been practicing in earnest for the upcoming concert. Had it been too much? By midweek, the maestro approached him. "Ah, my young Mario Lanza. Come have a glass of wine with me after class tonight. I want to help you through this difficult period. Did I ever tell you about how Enrico Caruso went through a similar change? He remained without voice for six weeks. Come back to class. We all miss you."

Tristan smiled at the maestro, and placing his arms around the esteemed teacher, he whispered gently, "I'm really fine, my teacher. Just give me space this week. I will sing on Saturday, and everything will be good."

Tristan went to his room and locked the door. He did not have six weeks; he had six days. He turned on the background music for "Ave Maria." Donning an outfit Sofia had insisted on having fashioned for him by Gessepi Brioni, he examined himself in the mirror. A fine wool suit in a dark shade of gray with just a hint of pin striping, a silk dress shirt and tie—he was self-conscious in such expensive clothing. But Sofia would be coming for the performance, and he wanted to please her.

ℰℛ

Over a glass of Italian brandy, Paulo met privately with his two assistants. The three talked somberly about each of the students, lamenting the lack of a rising star among them. Distressed, Paulo said, "And to cap off everything, one of my young American boys, Tristan, has lost his voice. It has been changing. Last week, we tried together to see whether he would remain a soprano or if his vocal chords would change him to tenor, and only gibberish came out. I calmed him with a glass of wine and told him to rest his vocal chords, but no, he refused, running to his room to rehearse for this week's little concert. It seems there is a girl involved he wishes to impress. What else is new in life? Why is it a woman has to come along in all men's lives and ruin everything? If it is not the mother then it is a girlfriend."

Mario laughed heartily. "Paulo, we all love the women in our lives. It is their nature to try and disrupt things for us. What in the world would you have them do with their lives?"

Having finished his third glass of brandy, Paulo looked at Mario with a serious expression. "Cook pasta, of course."

ℰↄ

The week passed, and Tristan did not rehearse in front of Paulo at all. On the evening of the intimate concert, Paulo confided to the two impresarios his fear that one of his singers might have a problem with his vocal chords. The opera stars agreed to be sensitive with their critiques, which would be in front of all the performers. They were "fully aware that the students' voices have not developed to their full potential and will not discourage them in any way."

ℰↄ

Early on Saturday, Paulo took Tristan aside. "Tristan, you have been noticeably absent this week. Is your voice all right? I do not want you to sing unless you are up to it."

Tristan smiled warmly at Paulo, noting the concern in his teacher's voice. He also noticed the physical change in the maestro. Paulo had lost weight over the past year. A tiny part of his immense energy was gone, and lines finely etched before around the teacher's eyes were deep creases. The two stood awhile in silence. "I'm fine, Paulo. I'm looking forward to this evening."

Tristan looked different to Paulo as he responded, almost as if he had gone into another plane, another place in his mind. The young man's words were softer, deeper. With a hand on Tristan's shoulder, Paulo listened carefully as he spoke. He instantly recognized the change in his voice. He would certainly never be a soprano again. But aside from the new sound, there was something Paulo could not put his finger on. As the maestro went about his daily routine, it dawned on him that Tristan had never before addressed him by his first name, though most of the other students had.

ℰↄ

At four o'clock, Tristan went to his room and removed his clothes. He showered a long time, letting the steaming water cascade over him, almost seeking to bury himself in the warmth. He realized a turning point in his young life had just occurred. He would never sing in the high pitch he was accustomed to; all of that was ancient history. Tristan had gone from the agony of failure to an awakening of new life, starting with the temporary loss of his voice five days before.

When he had alerted Paulo with the problem, almost nothing had come from his throat. His teacher tried to calm him, but Tristan panicked, locking himself in his room and trying to just speak, to no avail. All day and all night his vocal chords would not emanate any sound. He finally went into a deep sleep, and when he awoke eighteen hours later, he decided not to even try speaking. He gave a note to one of the servants, requesting a light breakfast. His body called out for liquids, and he consumed endless bottles of lightly gassed water, occasionally mixed with a small amount of red wine.

Day turned to evening, and he stood in front of one of the large gilt mirrors and smiled at his reflection. Wearing only a pair of briefs, he realized for the first time that his parents and few friends in California would never recognize the young man he saw in the mirror. His smile became a laugh, the laugh grew louder, and Tristan's voice miraculously returned. But the voice was no longer that of a boy. It was rich and surprisingly deep. To Tristan's amazement, the new sound had an unprecedented range of volume he had never achieved as a soprano. The remainder of the week was spent privately rehearsing in his room. He would give his finest performance ever.

Ↄ

Tristan was to sing last. As he stood to the side of the stage watching his friends perform, he noted in the small audience that his adored Sofia was not present. Sadness overcame him, as he had hoped with all his heart that she would be there for him.

Johnny finished his performance with Don Giovanni's "Dalla sua pace" and was enthusiastically applauded. Maestro Nolanza casually beckoned to Tristan to ascend the stairs to the small stage. As he did, the door opened and Sofia appeared. She looked ravishing in a red-and-black sequined dress, the likes of which Tristan had never seen. At her throat was a pure-white pearl necklace, and in her hair a small pearl tiara. Tristan's chest constricted intensely. For a moment, he did not realize the feelings that overwhelmed him. He simply had fallen into a deeper infatuation with that vision.

Sofia smiled as the maestro started playing the piano, and Tristan broke into "Granada." He had sung that popular song on many occasions, including previous in-house concerts. Audiences had applauded his beautiful alto-soprano voice, especially when he hit the higher notes. He started slowly, as was his way, controlling his new voice until he hit the midway point. Adding volume, he finished on a powerful note and broke into a heavy sweat.

Everyone applauded loudly, especially Paulo. Tristan took out a handkerchief and wiped the perspiration from his face. It had taken every ounce of his resolution to control the range and pitch of his voice.

No one in the audience seemed to notice, and the applause was enthusiastic, as he had anticipated.

℘

Paulo knew instantly he had a star on the horizon in Tristan Taylor. Tenors are the keystone to classical opera; and the maestro, having known Tristan had the potential of greatness, realized that with his new voice, he could go to the very pinnacle of the profession.

Tristan would conclude the evening with Paulo's favorite song, the beloved "Ave Maria," in Italian. Paulo began the introduction on the piano, but Tristan hesitated. Paulo glanced at him and started again. Tristan did not move, and he did not sing. Absolute silence hung in the room. Paulo whispered, "Tristan, are you all right?"

℘

"I'm fine, Maestro. Begin again." Intuition gave Tristan the answer to his quandary. He realized how tense he had been when singing the opening song. Subconsciously, he had tried to present "Granada" with the soprano voice he no longer had. He had sounded stiff, something between soprano and tenor but in reality neither. As he started "Ave Maria," he made up his mind to relax and use the new voice God had given him.

What came out was a stronger sound—a solid, deep voice, as if the instrument of his body had tuned itself and changed the lining of his throat. Aside from changing to tenor, his voice allowed him to lower it deeply to a baritone, something not traditionally done in opera. And again, if he wanted, he could approach nearly a soprano. He performed "Ave Maria" in a tenor's voice as if he had done it a thousand times before. He simply let the new sound emanate naturally from his throat—a husky, rich mahogany sound.

Sitting spellbound in the small room, Sofia closed her eyes momentarily. Tristan sounded at times like a black soul singer. Having never heard him sing, she was awestruck. Her silly infatuation for the strange young American turned instantly to something else.

Maestro Paulo, ever aware of everything around him, watched her expression closely and recognized exactly where Sofia was. To his observation, she was simply in lust. Tristan's new voice was phenomenal, but more than that, it was sexual. He would have a talk with the young singer about that.

When Tristan finished "Ave Maria," not a person in the audience made a sound. No one had to say anything. He walked off the stage, took Sofia's hand, and led her out of the house. Neither said anything as pure chemistry took over between them.

Tristan sensed in some way the power his singing could have, mesmerizing another person. That evening was the beginning of the domination he would have over the opposite sex, no matter their age or position in life. Men, too, would enjoy his performances, often closing their eyes and becoming the singer for just a moment in their own fantasies.

Sofia looked up and smiled at the newly discovered Adonis. Her apartment was free for the weekend, as her parents were visiting friends in Venice. Her lover, Sergio, was also away. She would have Tristan all to herself for forty-eight hours. The apartment off the Via Veneto was small—three rooms plus a kitchen and bath. A living room with nondescript furnishings led to two tiny bedrooms. Sofia's room was so small that the little bed provided room for just one. It mattered not at all.

Sofia undressed as Tristan sat watching. His gaze seemed to be not only adoration but naïveté, and she realized he had never made love before. She was no novice to sex. Her mentor had carefully instructed her in the art of love, and she would use that experience with Tristan to bring both to blissful fulfillment. She stood before him naked.

Sofia's figure was ravishing, and Tristan felt a strong wave of lust run through him. He admired her lovely light-olive skin. Her hair hung almost to her waist and was luxurious to the touch. She sat on Tristan's lap, and he felt her everywhere. Holding his face between her slim fingers, Sofia kissed him. She pushed her tongue into his mouth, and they tasted each other.

The feelings of those soon-to-be lovers were of youth and intense passion. The fruits were sweet. The aging process had not begun for either. There had been no real disappointments in life. Everything lay undiscovered, and only the excitements of the early joys of life were to be felt then.

They stood, and Tristan slowly undressed. He was oblivious to his manhood but did feel the rush of first love that happily overcame him. Sofia pulled him down onto the narrow bed and slowly, gently caressed his body, bringing him into a rhythm of sexual awareness.

Tristan rolled back, pulling her on top of him as with a small sharp gasp, she encompassed his maleness deeply. He felt his orgasm coming and made himself hold it back. Once that force was released, he would not be able to give pleasure to Sofia. With sheer strength of will, he focused his mind to hold that wild burning within. They made love that way for an extended period of time until Sofia let out a cry of passion, and he too released his own passion into her. She collapsed into Tristan's arms, and they lay there completely spent, holding each other until both drifted into a deep sleep.

When they awoke hours later, he explored her exquisite body, telling her how much he loved her all the while. They made intense love again, and the pattern went on for the entire forty-eight hours, neither leaving the small apartment for even something to eat.

℘

Paulo was amused with Tristan's performance at the concert. At his private critique the next week, he said, "I see you have studied the biographies of the most famous of my students. I am frankly amazed at your ability for a fifteen-year-old. Of course, you certainly don't look fifteen, perhaps thanks in some part to how we have trained you here. It is obvious to me you are emerging as my best student. However, be careful, Tristan. You are exhibiting a sexuality in your performance that you are not prepared for.

"How does one determine what is sexual? It is not determined. It is just there. I noticed how you were watching the audience adulate what you were doing. You saw them picking up the intensity of the moment. You took control of the lyrics and the melody and projected the power and volume to such a crescendo you blew the audience away completely. Your new voice is fabulous, my young man, but be careful and don't let it go to your head."

Tristan listened to his teacher with his head down. He had gone too far showboating with his performance and was expecting a severe criticism. "Thank you, Maestro. I won't."

"Now, before you go, tell me about Sofia. She is very beautiful, but isn't she a bit old for you?"

"Yes, she's seventeen," Tristan admitted. "But since coming to your country, living here with you and the teachers, something important has come into my life that makes me feel much older than I am. Among many things, I've bonded with you. You're not just my mentor — you've taken the image of a father. I want to be like you." Tristan stood to leave, and he and Paulo embraced. Tristan pulled back and looked at his teacher. "And I do regret leaving abruptly Saturday night. It won't happen again."

ℵ

Christmas approached, and with that, the four-week break when students and staff usually visited with family. Maestro Paulo, of course, kept his home open to the few students who had no family. Occasionally, a student did not want to leave Rome, and that was the case for Tristan. The school had become his life; Paulo had become the father image he lacked from his own father. He also had found his first romance and tasted those fruits that have no equal.

In a lengthy conversation with his mother, Tristan convinced her to allow him to stay in Rome. "Yes, Mother, I miss you terribly, but I don't want to come home now. The trip is too long, and by the time I adjust to California's time, it will be time to return to school." Only Johnny and Tristan stayed through the holidays.

With Tristan's allowance, he rented a room on the occasional times Sofia could break away to join him for a romantic rendezvous. Those times were far too few, but both made up for that with the wild intensity of their feelings for each other.

ℵ

New Year came, and classes started again. Paulo took stock of Tristan. His voice strengthened with each passing day. Not only his voice improved, but his entire body. He stood then nearly six feet tall and was evenly toned from head to foot. A dark tan accomplished over the summer made his deep-blue eyes more noticeable. Strangers who came into contact with him took him for eighteen. The maestro's female companions who visited the school whispered among themselves, deciding quietly that he was marvelous in both his strong voice and manly looks. Knowing he had something extraordinary with that student, Paulo worked ever harder to get his protégé prepared for a spectacular career in opera.

But Tristan had other thoughts about his singing career. He was not abandoning opera, but a feeling had overcome him that there might be something else in his future.

SERGIO VASKELI

The owner of Lion Studios in Rome was not pretentious under any standards. Sergio Vaskeli was in reality a plain man born of farm peasants. He was brawny, and his complexion was scarred from acne. Pale-brown eyes with a slight greenish cast did not lend to his appearance. His hair was intensely black and very curly.

Sergio had worked every job he could as a youth to stay alive in Rome—the City of Jackals. Sergio had delivered newspapers before dawn; worked for a grocery store in the day; and at sixteen, tended bar in one of the city's prestigious eateries. The freshly cleaned suit he wore at Costas gave no indication that he lived in a tiny room off one of the city's alleys.

Late at night, Costas was the place to be seen. Singers, politicians, actors, and the Italian aristocracy hung out there after midnight. In that setting, Sergio had met film producer Rocky Canicelli. One fateful evening, as the bistro was about to close, Rocky was seated at the bar, engaging in a boisterous conversation with Sergio when a young man rapidly approached. "Filth! Luring my little sister into your porno film! Only fifteen!" Flashing a long switch blade, he tried to stab Rocky. Without flinching a muscle, Sergio grabbed a silver serving tray and swung it down in time to block the blade. He jumped over the bar and sat on top of the attacker, who had fallen.

Rocky had credited his survival to Sergio's interference. He had hired him on the spot as a bodyguard and aide, and Sergio was brought into the pornographic motion picture business. In time, he was given a partnership, and when Rocky died, Sergio ended up with the company. Having tired of making kinky films, and the poor reputation that followed, Sergio created art films, including documentaries. As time went by, he developed a fine reputation and produced some epic Italian films starring new beautiful female stars. His latest star had turned out to be fateful for him, as he had fallen completely in love with her.

Winter had turned to a glorious spring; however, that particular spring day was not a good one for Sergio as he sat in his office. He had suspicions that his newest star, Sofia, was cheating on him, and had hired a detective to follow his Italian beauty everywhere. The lengthy report lay on his desk, and he dreaded reading it cover to cover.

When he had gone through less than half the report, Sergio threw the file across the room. Grabbing a favorite silver-tipped walking cane, which he used more for identification than anything else, he broke it against the wall. He picked up one end and smashed everything in sight, finally collapsing into an office chair, his hand bloodied by the violence. Taking his head between his hands, he rocked himself until the violent feelings ebbed. He composed himself with great will power and thought carefully about how he would handle the situation. After a while, he knew exactly what he would do to Sofia and her silly young lover. He would talk to her and give her the options.

The small offices were empty when Sofia came in. Sergio closed the door, locking it behind her. Their conversation lasted less than an hour. When it was over, he got up and left her alone to make the call.

∞

Tristan was lifting weights in the gymnasium when a call was announced for him. He was covered in sweat and really not in the mood to take any calls. When he heard it was Sofia, he rushed to the outside hall and grabbed the phone.

"Sofia, are you free tonight?"

"I can't see you for a while. I want to tell you why, but I can't."

"But I love you. I don't un—"

"Tristan, don't say anything. I really can't tell you. I promise someday we will be together. You just have to trust me. I can't see you now at all."

"You just can't—" But the phone went dead, and Tristan was left to his anguish. He dressed without showering and took the first cab he could to her apartment. A middle-aged man answered the door. Tristan had never met Sofia's parents, and the man who stood there then was hostile. It was as if a conspiracy had been made to blow up part of Tristan's budding life.

"You must be Mr. Taylor, here to see my daughter. Sofia is gone. She will not return, and I expect you never to come here again. I will call the polizia should you return." And with that, the door was slammed in Tristan's face.

He walked the streets in a daze. Sofia had become a part of his body and mind. The difference in their ages mattered not at all. His first romance had left him in anguish. Night fell, and the sky was unusually ablaze in stars. Tristan absentmindedly stopped to sit on the ancient Colosseum steps and let his mind drift. When he eventually walked back toward the maestro's residence for the evening meal, a plate had been left for him. He ate in silence in the empty dining room.

No one asked him why he had been gone, and only Johnny noticed Tristan's pained expression the next day. Johnny did not ask what the problem was, and Tristan did not venture a reason for his behavior. The days went by, the weeks went by, and the school year went by. Sofia never returned, and Tristan's weekly venture to the little table they had shared for so many Sundays on the Via Veneto remained solitary except for the memories that haunted the void in his soul.

As the next school year started, the memory dimmed. Sofia became a part of Tristan's past. He stopped trying to find her and no longer asked himself why she left. But the experience would remain an important part of his past, as years later, he would discover that it was one's past, present, and future that determined life's path. In time, he would find that those experiences were the building blocks of his life. Without them, he would not have grown and gone to where the Fates were leading him.

Eventually he joined his friend to experience the temporary bliss furnished by the girls of Via Veneto, or had an occasional affair with one of the maestro's female friends who attended the school's small, private concerts. But never did he find the sweet embrace he had so lovingly looked forward to with his darling Sofia. After a while, he ceased seeing any women for that purpose. A sexual encounter for him was meaningless without the intensity of romantic love. Instead, he devoted all of his energy to singing, occasionally experimenting, in the privacy of his rooms, with the black soul music he had come to love as a boy.

One night Tristan was belting out the Jackie Wilson song "Higher and Higher" when he noticed Paulo had entered his room. "I knocked loudly, but . . ." It was the only time Tristan noticed an indifferent look from Paulo, who never mentioned the episode again. Neither did the maestro ever open Tristan's door unless the singer answered personally.

As his second school year went by, Tristan stayed in touch with his family only by mail, avoiding their calls when he could. He was almost seventeen and unrecognizable as the gawky boy who had come to Italy two summers before. His body and mind had greatly matured. He had sprouted to six feet two inches and weighed a slim but muscular 180 pounds. Dressed in a T-shirt and blue jeans, he would have given any popular singer a run for his money. He had become, in all sense of the word, an extraordinary young man.

As Tristan's last summer in Rome approached, he attended the Apolito Theatre near the Spanish Steps, where his beloved Sofia was shown in her first seriously acclaimed picture, *La Dolce Vita*. She was superb in the role of mistress to an Italian nobleman in eighteenth-century Italy.

One love scene that bared all would create such a sensation in Europe that Sofia's career was assured. She would remain with Vaskeli all her life and never be unfaithful. And she would follow Tristan's sensational career, but neither would see each other again in that life.

Rustic Canyon, California, 1955: Home Again

The first week of June, Tristan returned home on a warm and splendid summer day. He expected his parents to be shocked by the changes in him, but at the airport, his mother almost walked past him. "Tristan? Oh . . . of course it's you." She laughed. "I hardly recognize you." As they left the customs area, she cast occasional glances at him and babbled about small things, fixing on the fairytale amusement park Walt Disney was building in Anaheim, California.

Tristan tried to steer the conversation toward his family. "Where's Dad? Is he all right?"

His mother—still casting glances—answered dutifully, "Your father's in Chicago, recording a new singer for King Records, Sam Cook. You may have heard his last hit, 'Kansas City.' "

Tristan laughed loudly. "Yes, Mother. I sang it at my last performance in front of Maestro Paulo, and had it not been my farewell, he would've kicked me out of the school."

℘

Having nothing better to do, Tristan wandered the streets of Westwood and the Malibu beaches with their white, white sand, noting the women eyeing him as if he were some Greek god. He stopped here and there, striking up a conversation in English, speaking in a heavy Italian accent, which they said was charming. Many of the girls invited him to parties, but Tristan smiled and politely said no.

In town the ladies stared when he walked by. As he had learned in Rome, he wore impeccable clothing of good taste. Not following the typical American dress standards, he chose a style of his own.

℘

Tristan's parents remained stunned. He had sent occasional photos, but in person his appearance was a complete surprise. He walked with the stature of a man, not a young boy, and it seemed no one realized he was not quite eighteen. Regardless of how old he might seem, they wanted him to have a high school diploma and registered him for the last two weeks of high school.

℘

When Tristan returned to University High in West Los Angeles, no one from his childhood recognized him. Those involved in the social scene at school whispered to each other, trying to guess who he was, why he talked with an Italian accent, but most of all, which of the girls could land him for the big senior prom and graduation party. No one could, but they all tried. Tristan was polite and just said he would attend alone, if at all.

Tristan remembered many of the students, especially those he had admired so much when he was a nobody in what seemed a decade past. One day, he noticed by chance four of the girls he had been so enamored of. They ceased their chatter and stared at him. Stopping in front of them, Tristan smiled. The pretty girls were wearing their club uniforms. Their deep-green jackets had the word Diamontes embroidered on the sleeves. Tristan broke into a huge grin. Refraining from laughing, he looked at each one. "Hi, Happy, Kathy, Julie, Jan. It's a lovely day, no?" He broke into a light Italian, informing them in a few well-chosen words how they paid no attention to him two years ago. He smiled all the while, knowing they did not understand a word of Italian.

Julie smiled back coyly. "That sounds lovely. What are you telling us?"

Tristan beamed as he walked away. "Just how pretty the four of you are. Arrivederci, ladies." The girls giggled behind him and lowered their voices in lively prattle.

A light breeze stirred Tristan's long hair as he crossed the campus. The summer flowers that encompassed the campus blazed colorfully against the thickening green of the trees and bushes. A thousand pigeons filled the deep-blue sky above as the day ended. The campus was deserted then except the old caretaker raking a few leaves and the debris from a careless student's lunch box. The sunset illuminating a brilliant red glow as nightfall descended.

ℰℴ

On June 18, 1955, Tristan graduated with a class that included child actress Margaret O'Brien and Alan Ladd Jr., who many years later would run Twentieth Century Fox Studios. One week later, Tristan auditioned for the lead role in *West Side Story* and met Vanessa Daniells. Leslie Cole cast Tristan in *West Side Story* on Broadway, where he became box office gold, attracting thousands of followers. That entourage would remain loyal and follow the singer's career, in all its ups and downs, throughout his life.

New York City, 1962: West Side Story

Tristan walked offstage to thunderous applause and ten curtain calls. It was the final performance of *West Side Story* on Broadway. The last two years were at the Mark Hellinger Theatre, as the Roxy had closed its doors in 1960. Tristan was elated and fatigued, and an overpowering sense of relief flooded through him as that part of his life was over. Walking quickly to his private dressing room, he showered, allowing the icy water to wash away the sweat and tiredness. Toweling himself, he sat in the chair opposite his makeup mirrors and stared at his reflection in the bright lights. He smiled at the face looking back—a dark tan from the Delacroix cosmetics company's new artificial tanning formula, and not a wrinkle thanks to Leslie's instructions on what creams to use morning, afternoon, and especially night.

His thoughts drifting away momentarily, Tristan worked his long, dark hair into a braid. He had achieved security from the success of the show over the past years on Broadway. Daily, mountains of mail arrived seeking everything from a simple signed autograph to the delicious but wicked requests for sex of all kinds. He laughed out loud at that thought, realizing that besides Leslie there was no energy or time to indulge in any serious affair, hardly an occasional one-night stand, and those were mostly reserved for the woman he adored most, Vanessa Daniells.

Tristan relaxed bit by bit, sipping a small glass of white wine as he studied the little dressing room in which he had spent the past two years. He wondered about the other performers who had been there before him, all Broadway stars, as that had always been the leading performer's dressing room at the famous Hellinger. If only the walls could talk, what interesting stories they might yield.

Feeling very good by then, Tristan wanted to remember that night and that moment in time. He had asked not to be disturbed while he was changing; and John Tibbs, the portly black security guard, was standing down the hall, politely telling well-wishers Tristan would see them at Sardi's restaurant later.

Finally, Tristan noticed the bright-red envelope Leslie always used for important communications. Opening it, he read the short sentence with annoyance—*my place, nine tomorrow morning*—knowing she was going to pressure him again to continue his role on the road. He had put her off for months, not giving her a final response, realizing that a no meant the company had to replace him. Though he had used a clause in his contract to respond that he was not extending, he had not yet officially stated so. Many performers did not exercise their options but utilized them to negotiate for more money. Time was running out; a two-week break before going on the road would hardly be time to recast the lead role, and the pressure on Tristan was building. He knew he had to tell Leslie tomorrow of his plans.

After he dressed, Tristan finished the last of the wine and opened the door, ready to join the cast at the famous old restaurant, Sardi's, for the closing night party. He had invited Vanessa to join him, not expecting to see her backstage, but suddenly she was there. His heart raced, and a huge smile spread over his face before she brought the incredible high he was feeling to a dismal end.

Tristan dreamed that night, and it was not like any dream before. *In a faraway place, an old city with beautiful buildings and parks, he walked hand in hand with a young girl. Surely Vanessa . . . but her face was veiled, and she seemed younger than Vanessa. They walked along a river. He tried to push away the veil from her face, but the girl just laughed and avoided him.* He awoke with a start, and it was morning. *Strange. What could the dream mean, and was it Vanessa?*

He took a cab to the Hellinger. Leslie's West Side apartment was normally a ten-minute walk from the theater, and that day Tristan was even a bit early. He looked up trying to see her penthouse from the street, but his angle was not great enough to see anything except blue sky. Using his passkey, he entered the private elevator and rode to the fiftieth floor.

Walking directly into Leslie's spacious apartment, Tristan found her in the kitchen area, having strong-smelling coffee. She was dressed only in a sheer pink nightgown. Tristan started an erection and would have made love to her on the spot if he could have.

Leslie smiled. "You want to fuck me, don't you, Tristan dear?" Leslie leaned back against the kitchen bar counter, exposing the dark mound under her sheer negligee. "Do you wonder what it would be like, my young angel? Perhaps if we continue to work together, I'll allow you to do whatever you want with me. What do you think of that?"

But unbeknownst to anyone on the planet except Vanessa and Tristan's new manager, he had already made irrevocable plans to change his life. There would be no more *West Side Story*; that part of his life was over. Tristan walked to Leslie, put his arms around her rigid body, and kissed her passionately, deeply, tasting her possibly for the last time. She melted into his embrace, her thin nightgown allowing him to feel all the soft, sexual contours of the beautiful woman he held so tightly. Pulling back slightly, he looked into her blue eyes and said, "I want my freedom, Leslie. I love you, but *West Side* has given me the ticket I need to go on with my life. I don't want to go on the road in *West Side*, or to play Broadway anymore."

Leslie's face blanched and suddenly appeared the leopard she really was. "What the hell do you mean you won't work for us, you inconsiderate bastard. After all I've done for you. I already told the producers you didn't want to continue in *West Side*, and now you're turning down the best musical lead since *Oklahoma*?"

With hidden amusement, Tristan watched Leslie go through her tirade. He had delivered himself to her as a young, naïve innocent and with her teaching and savvy, had become a man. But he had made up his mind to leave Broadway; as a matter of fact, he would leave America for a while. His new manager had already made arrangements for him to do small concerts in Europe to test the waters for larger things. *West Side Story* had made him a star in America, but many in Europe had either seen the show in New York or heard him sing the songs recorded by the producers when the show became so popular. Several small theater owners in France and Italy had sent him letters begging him to appear. The money was not much, but it was not the money that mattered.

Leslie was turning red, and without thinking, Tristan put his arms around her. "I love you, Leslie. I love you as my friend and as my mentor. You've taught me everything. I thought I had confidence when I came to you. And I did have a naïve faith in myself, but you showed me everything that took me to the heights we've reached with *West Side*. I couldn't dance, and your relentless coaching and endless hours of work made me a passable dancer. You taught me to flirt with the audience, to win them over using a charm I certainly knew nothing about."

Tristan had seldom defied Leslie, usually backing down in the end. For the first time, he noted a respect in her look. "I don't want to end my days on Broadway like so many before me. I read the script for *Grease* that you left for me *anonymously* last week. It's certainly going to make some new protégé famous. I like everything about it, and if things were different inside me, I'd jump to do it."

Tristan held Leslie tighter as he whispered in her ear, "I'll always love you, Leslie. I have to go and find myself. Broadway isn't me, and, no, I really don't know what I want."

Both were crying then, parting on a gentler note. Leslie pulled back slightly and smiled naughtily. With her most seductive voice, she whispered back, "Who's going to make me happy on Monday nights?"

Tristan turned to leave and, standing one last time in her penthouse apartment, said, "When I'm in town, anytime you need me I'll be here for you."

Paris, 1962: L'Hotel

Tristan had read about L'Hotel, a tiny landmark located on the Left Bank in Paris, far from the sophisticated Right Bank, known for the Champs Élysées with all of its famous stores and shops. Many of the large, famous hotels were there, such as the George V Hotel. Tristan did not seek that atmosphere, wanting a more relaxed, younger setting, hearing that many residents as well as tourists preferred the Left Bank.

In New York, a French journalist interviewing him for *West Side* had mentioned the hotel, known for its gracious host, intimate rooms, and especially the famous bar set in a jungle-like atmosphere with large parrots and a colony of wild ducks. L'Hotel had housed many famous, and infamous, persons. Oscar Wilde resided in the hotel, then called the Hotel d'Alsace, at the time of his death in 1900. The famous cabaret star Mistinguett once occupied the penthouse suite. Tristan admired her and wanted to stay in her rooms.

Guy Louis Duboucheron was in front of L'Hotel to personally greet Tristan as he emerged from the cab. "Welcome, Monsieur Taylor. I want your stay to be memorable. We have the suite you asked for. It has the hotel's most luxurious rooms."

Tristan smiled back weakly, wanting nothing but to lie down and sleep for twenty-four hours. Having had too much cognac and no sleep, he was jet-lagged and hung over. And that depressing scene in New York with his beloved Vanessa.

Mrs. von Snipes had come backstage to torment him after the closing act, informing him that no, she could not stay, everyone would talk, and no, she could not see him, even discreetly. "I just wanted to congratulate you for such a good performance. Must see the baron, you know, dear. I think he suspects we're more than friends."

Tristan had stared at Vanessa in disbelief. Good performance? He had killed himself knowing she was in the audience on closing night. Ten curtain calls, no less. What was she doing to him? He loved her passionately. If he had the money Baron Rolf had, her last name would be Taylor.

"Come to Vanessa and give me a big hug. You know I really love you, but what you want can't be. I just wanted to let you know how fabulous you were, and wanted to see you before you leave for Paris. I'm on my way to Rome to see Baron Rolf, love. I will always follow your career, and I'll try to see you in Paris. Come, give Vanessa a big kiss."

I won't come. To hell with you, he thought, but his body just walked over and melted into her as always. *What's wrong with me?* She held him closely, moving those unbelievable hands down his body. With a deep kiss, she was gone. And later he had been alone, waiting for his TWA flight to Paris and wondering what the hell life was all about.

Well, at least he was in Paris. Maybe the ancient city and a new career would take his mind off his melancholy. Waiting for his room key, Tristan stood in the small foyer of the hotel, contemplating unkind thoughts about Baroness Vanessa when Guy Louis approached him. "Ah, Monsieur Taylor, such a pleasure to have you with us. I hope you will not mind, but will you please sign the cover of *West Side Story* for me? And please, let me buy you a drink at the little bar we are so famous for."

Tristan, having no sleep the past twenty-four hours, didn't hear what Guy Louis said and responded with what was on his mind instead. "Baroness bitch."

Guy Louis's eyes widened. "Excuse me, what baroness? There's no baroness here. Come, young man, and let's have a drink. I'm sure whatever is ailing you can be alleviated with a glass of champagne."

Tristan finally realized what he had said. Feeling quite embarrassed, and though the last thing on earth he wanted was to sit down and have a drink, he was too ashamed not to. After he signed the album cover and accepted his key, he followed Guy Louis the short distance to his intimate bar area.

The owner seated him in "the room's best booth," calling to one of his waiters for a bottle of Dom Perigon. Turning to Tristan, he poured him a glass of champagne, and the two talked of his show in New York, life in Paris, and why women gave men such a bad time. Guy Louis reiterated his love for the music from *West Side Story* and admiration for the tenor who provided the world with some of that excellent music. Thirty minutes later, Guy Louis got up to conduct business, leaving Tristan alone with a fresh bottle of champagne. And that's when Tristan discovered the ducks.

ℰℴ

Guy Louis attended to business, greeting new guests as they arrived. Curious about Tristan Taylor, he walked back into the bar area only to discover he was gone. Calling over his maître d', Phillipe, he asked, "Where has our American guest gone?"

Phillipe hesitated, averting his eyes from Guy Louis's stare. "I'm sorry, sir, the American started feeding the ducks. Perhaps he drank too much champagne, sir. He started a conversation with two of the ducks. He ordered foie gras, thinking the ducks might be hungry. Of course, the ducks did not eat the liver pâté but did finish all of the bread."

Guy Louis fully realized his guest probably had too much to drink. "Come now, Phillipe, are you sure he was talking to the ducks, or just babbling from too much bubbly? Where did he go?"

Phillipe looked at the hotel owner sheepishly. "I'm sorry, sir. Monsieur Taylor took two of your favorite ducks and went to his room. He was talking to them when he got into the elevator."

Guy Louis could not believe what he had just heard and asked Phillipe very quietly so no one nearby could hear, "What was he saying to my ducks?"

Turning a bit pale, Phillipe responded. "Something about whether they were having a good relationship with each other."

Guy Louis went to the mahogany bar near the rear of the dining area, where he ordered a Fernet-Branca straight up. He normally took the aperitif when he had an upset stomach. The bartender asked if something was bothering him. Guy Louis looked at him despairingly. Surely he too had watched the crazy American disappear with his prize ducks. "You don't think he'll eat my ducks, do you?"

PART III: MARIE SAVOIE

Paris, 1962: Saint Germain des Pres

A young French actress drove her silver Citroen toward Paris. The sun was rising, and Marie Savoie had just completed the last scenes from *The Girl with the Golden Eye*, filmed at the Palace of Versailles. She was anxious to go home, to see her husband, Peter, but mostly to rest. The film, a story of lost love and betrayal, had been a letdown for her. She never liked the script; but everyone around her, including her agent and personal publicist, had encouraged her to do the film. Her last movie, *Romeo and Juliet*, had played to packed houses in America and Europe and had already made her a legend.

Golden Eye had been difficult, and Johnny Hanna, her costar, had given her no peace at all. From the first day of shooting, he was after her to start an affair. The harder she resisted, the harder he tried. Leaving that behind, she could relax with Peter and forget show business for a while. As she parked the car in front of their apartment, her mind wandered back to their first meeting earlier in the year and she smiled wistfully.

The streets were deathly quiet at that early hour. A black cat ran out in front of her, causing her to curse under her breath. She opened the trunk of the car and removed a large carry-on bag and her makeup case, laboriously walking the short distance to the entrance of the apartment building. How tired she felt, and mentally exhausted from the picture she had just completed. The producers had promised a longer break between *Romeo and Juliet* and *Golden Eye*; but lo, the shooting schedule had been moved up and there she was months later, tired beyond comprehension.

Marie's thoughts went back to her husband. His fashion photography took him all over the planet. When they met that spring, Peter Byrd had swept her off her feet. She was ready for that, anything to forget the pain of her last relationship. She had married him far too quickly. The attraction between them, so strong in the beginning, had waned after a couple of months, and things went sour.

The warm and charming man she had first met had a mysterious kink in his being that remained hidden from her no matter how much she tried to get him to talk about it. For no reason, he would suddenly become cold and distant. The coldness would leave in a day or two, so Marie believed the relationship would improve with time. A fresh smile spread over her tired face. She had finished the film three days early and would surprise Peter.

Looking at her watch, she silently opened the apartment door. It was not yet six in the morning. The spacious luxury apartment put together for her by her mentor and close friend Jean Delacroix was almost as she had left it. Whenever she was in residence, the rooms had large arrangements of white and orange lilies, at the moment painfully absent.

The bedroom door was ajar, and she tiptoed in carefully so as not to wake Peter. He looked so peaceful on their bed. Marie had covered the king-size oriental bed with many soft Scandinavian pillows and comforters to cuddle in on cold nights. As both liked lots of fresh air, a window was always partly open. Peter's clothes lay scattered on the floor with some others. Marie was fastidious from her upbringing, he just the opposite. She came closer, noticing his unshaven face and the strong smell of his body, among other odors. Peter was deeply asleep, a smile radiating from his face. Marie glanced about the room once more before making a hasty exit.

She walked quietly from the apartment and got into her Citroen, hardly noticing what she was doing. Her eyes met the piercing yellow eyes of the black cat, sitting atop the old Mercedes in front of her. The cat meowed loudly at her, and Marie sat hypnotized momentarily. Her overwhelming tiredness was then accompanied by despondency and a strange dizziness overcame her. Where was her most loyal friend? She needed Alexia desperately.

Intensely lonely, Marie felt a throbbing pain in her heart. Her mind roamed from one thought to the next: To love someone with all your emotions, even knowing it might someday end — the passions, the caring and loving, the tenderness and anger. All the emotions two lovers feel, and then to never feel those emotions with Peter again. The pain of love and, most of all, the rush of initial love, the embrace of the storm with its ebb of desire. It had been a hurricane, a great wind of passions ending with emotional destruction.

℘

Back in the apartment, Peter stirred, awoke, and sat up, smiling at the pretty girls he had brought home the night before. They were both still asleep.

Paris: Tristan Taylor

Marie's had separated from Peter, and a brief affair with Johnny Hanna was over. She decided to take a break from everyone except family and close friends, Alexia and a few other young women. They asked no embarrassing questions; they were just there, accepting her for what she was and asking nothing in return.

Seated in her elegant Paris apartment in Saint Germain des Pres, Marie complained to Alexia about her relationships with men. "One short, serious affair in my life, an even shorter marriage, and an unsatisfying fling. Do all attractive men have a Tarzan complex? Why is it they have to prove 'me Tarzan, you Jane'? I've just finished a very good film, the people I work with admire my acting, I've gotten three proposals of marriage from the stage crew alone, and the assistant director thinks I should be mayor of Paris. The real problem is I'm attracted to the kind of man who would like me to do the housework, cook all the meals, have his children, and go solicit another young woman for ménage à trois."

Alexia burst out laughing. A stunning blonde and thin as a reed, she was Marie's best friend. They had attended the Le Lycee school together in Paris and would be close friends always. Smiling, Alexia looked closely at Marie and said, "I have the perfect person for you. He will understand you completely, love your ideals, make you laugh, and be a constant pleasure in bed. He will love you passionately and exclusively. And to cap it all, he's the best-looking man in France."

Marie's eyes widened, and she smiled. "Introduce me to him at once."

"He doesn't exist. However, he just might be at La Poste tonight. Tristan Taylor is in town, and I have two tickets."

"Who's Tristan Taylor?"

"You're kidding me. You must've heard about him. Tristan was the lead singer in *West Side Story*. You know—New York, Broadway. The magazines I read said when *West Side Story* ended in New York, Taylor didn't want to go on the road. And he's here in Paris for one week only. Phillipe Anjou, the owner of La Poste, owed me a favor and gave me two tickets. They cost five thousand francs. Will you join me?"

Something came back to Marie: her funny experience one night in New York when she had seen a poor performance of *West Side Story*, the strange American restaurant, and her not meeting the principal of *West Side* because of some accident. "Sure. It'll take my mind off today's fiasco with Bryan Gilbere. That fat producer offered me a lead role in his film in exchange for you-know-what."

℘

La Poste was a quaint piece of French architecture. Located in Montparnasse, it was originally a post office in the mid-nineteenth century. When it became too small for its original use, the building went unused until the turn of the century, when two sisters converted it into Paris's most talked-about brothel. The interior was Napoleonic in all its original splendor. When the sisters were arrested and the brothel put out of business, the lovely building was converted to a small theater.

The building's main room was almost circular, supported by a dozen Corinthian columns beautifully carved in white marble. They rose twenty feet to a domed ceiling covered with a wondrous series of baroque paintings depicting mythical themes of love and romance. The room seated no more than one hundred patrons, giving it a warm, informal atmosphere. People in the audience felt that whoever performed did so for them alone.

Beautifully preserved, the theater was intimate, and exceptional for special, small gatherings. A fine gourmet restaurant during the week, it was an exclusive nightclub on Friday and Saturday nights, when popular singers performed. The entry price included dinner and, depending on who was performing, cost as little as one thousand francs to over five thousand. That night's event was a five-thousand-franc affair, and there were no empty seats.

Marie and Alexia arrived early, and the maître d' escorted them to a table. He brought over a glass of champagne for each. "Enjoy the show, ladies. Mr. Anjou will see you later."

Alexia turned to Marie. "Tristan Taylor is not only a talented singer, he also has a strong reputation of being one of America's most sought-after bachelors. Rumor has it he's been seeing Vanessa Daniells for seven years. Can you imagine? Vanessa could be his mother. His so-called secret affair with her is not only *not* secret, there's speculation that her marriage to Baron Rolf von Snipes of Holstein is in jeopardy over it. The best part, the trade papers say Tristan has numerous affairs, but no one remains with him for any length of time. He apparently is in love with Vanessa, and no one else can break him away. *Time* magazine interviewed him, and they concluded it just makes him more desirable."

Marie gave a pronounced yawn. "Who cares? La, if he's that gorgeous, I'll certainly have no interest in him at all. I don't even know why I agreed to come with you tonight. Perhaps it's just my curiosity after hearing what it cost to get in. I just hope the meal is good. If it isn't, I'm leaving early. And by the way, Vanessa Daniells is only thirty. Where in the world do you get your so called facts?"

From their table between two columns, they could view the performer but he could not see them easily. That suited Marie fine, and, speaking sarcastically, she said, "Dear Alexia, I will study this sensation the whole world is talking about. You know I learned singing in school. Later I will tell you all of his faults."

"You're just bitter about all men," Alexia said with a pained expression. "Isn't that what's ailing you? There is no perfect man. What would you have your next lover be like?"

Hiccuping from her drink, Marie leaned forward a bit, placing her cheek against her palm. "My next lover will stay at home and make dinner, take out the trash, and be there to take care of everything I need." Seeing the surprise on Alexia's face, she continued. "And one thing is absolutely for sure. If I want to bring home another man for ménage à trois, he'd better agree."

Dinner was delightful. The waiter suggested a combination of mousse of eel and mousse of crab, which was a splendid idea and quite tasty. Marie ordered another champagne, that time with Kir. Her evening was looking up. Coffee and dessert followed, and from the owner's cellar, the waiter delivered a rare decanter of nineteenth-century Napoleon brandy.

The stage lights came up, musicians tuned their instruments, and out stepped Tristan Taylor. Marie studied the singer closely. He was dressed in white from head to foot and had a dark tan—a difficult accomplishment for someone working in New York, she thought. His tie was loosely knotted. The clothes set off an attractive male body, over six feet, if she judged correctly. The designer cut of his clothes was better than most, probably Italian. His eyes appeared to be dark blue; in that light, she wasn't sure. His face was strong yet could become soft, changing with the mood of the music. His dark-brown hair was thick and long, pulled back in a tail, which was unusual.

After a few songs, Tristan untied his hair. Marie thought he resembled the legendary Sir Lancelot. Off came the tie; the shirt was loosened, his body exposed just enough to arouse those who fantasized living another life for a brief moment in time—Marie scoffed, looking around the room—the men, who likely toiled daily at work they hated, and the women, who yearned for some amazing man to enter their life.

Having imbibed a large glass of brandy, Marie turned to her companion and whispered loudly, "Tristan Taylor is full of himself. I hate him."

"Marie, hush up," Alexia whispered harshly. "He can hear you."

෯

Tristan heard no one. He had long ago trained himself not to be distracted by anything or anyone. The past seven years, he had learned many entertainment skills, and no part of his performance was made without hours of rehearsal. What appeared to be natural was well rehearsed. Tristan's experience with *West Side Story* had taught him that no commendable performer just walked onto a stage and gave a performance sure to win a Tony without hard work and preparation. No one.

He had worked to win the role in *West Side Story*. He hadn't gotten it because of his charm and voice. Leslie Cole had invited Tristan home for dinner after his final audition and enlightened him. "You want the part, you will service me in everything I ask of you, privately and for the show. You were certainly not the best of the ten who auditioned for this part. You know that and I know that. I'm going to work your ass off until the show starts, and when the show does begin, your precious Monday nights will be mine personally. Additionally, you will work with the cast not only during the week but every weekend. Your voice is fine, but your dancing sucks." Those thoughts were on Tristan's mind before every performance. It would always be that way. He was not a natural; there was no such thing.

෯

A short break in Tristan's performance allowed the audience to stretch and refill their drinks. Alexia and Marie went to the small but elegant bathroom to freshen up. Alone briefly, Alexia turned sharply on Marie. "You're a bit drunk, how can you go backstage afterward? What's the matter with you? Didn't you love the music? I did."

But Marie hardly heard Alexia. It was not the alcohol. There was a buzzing inside of her; something else was going on. When Tristan first appeared, she had felt annoyance, then an overwhelming feeling that she had met him before. But that was impossible. As his performance continued, other feelings overwhelmed her and she became annoyed with herself.

They returned to the table for the second half. The waiter poured Alexia another brandy and turned toward Marie.

Without meeting his gaze, Marie said quietly, "No. A strong coffee please."

To enthusiastic applause, Tristan returned to the small stage and motioned his conductor to continue. Starting with a few pop songs, he added some of the best Italian operatic solos in his repertoire. During the first half of his show, he had performed songs that were very good but not terribly powerful. Tristan wanted to build his performance to a climax, and in the second half, he utilized his best and strongest songs. He mesmerized his small audience and forty-five minutes later ended with "Maria" from *West Side Story*. It was pleasantly devastating, partly because the audience was not accustomed to hearing a powerful voice up close. Tristan's experience in Rome had left him with a strong tenor's voice. In such a tiny room, he could be overpowering, with or without a speaker system.

As a strong tenor, he knew how to utilize his voice when singing in a small theater. In a large auditorium or opera house, music was performed without a powerful sound system. In that setting, it was the singer's voice that dictated the listeners' hearing. Tristan had realized early in his career that if he could project his voice to an enormous audience with amplified sound, he might change the music business for all time.

The inner ear can actually radiate a highly sensual feeling while resonating with the sounds of a fine performer or instrument in close proximity. A small brandy in conjunction with a fine performance tends to push the experience to a higher level. One can feel quite rushed with the combination.

Alexia LaBrocque was numbed by the combination of a talented singer and the animal magnetism he radiated. And suddenly he was gone. She had never seen a performer give everything and walk out. No matter how much the small audience applauded, there was no Tristan. His arranger and composer, John Stiles, came out, took the microphone, and simply said, "Mr. Taylor thanks you very much and welcomes you to come another time."

Alexia took Marie's hand and almost wept. The owner, Phillipe Anjou, had promised her an introduction to Tristan after the performance, but it sounded like he had gone. She found Phillipe sitting in a corner, with a broad smile on his face.

Phillipe contemplated his new singer. What a coup he had pulled off! He was making a fortune from the engagement, whereas Tristan Taylor was not there for the money. He just wanted to try out some new material in Paris and never argued over the figure Phillipe originally offered. The only things Mr. Taylor seemed to want were the same room at L'Hotel where Mistinguett had lived and someone to accompany him in Paris and show him all of the historic sights.

Looking up at Alexia's pretty face, Phillipe suddenly remembered he was going to introduce her to Tristan. He recognized the girl with her at once, the beautiful Juliet he had recently seen at the cinema.

Alexia frowned. "Phillipe, you promised me!"

He laughed and said quietly, "John makes that announcement at all of Tristan's concerts. He's in the dressing room. I've already told him I have a special friend I want him to meet. But take care, he's not interested in anyone romantically. I'm beginning to think he might be odd. He's staying at L'Hotel, you know, and the owner also thinks Tristan's a bit daffy. Come with me, we're going to take him to la Coupole for something to eat. He dislikes large meals at night, but I'm sure we can convince him to at least have a drink."

Marie had been steadily absorbing the evening's excitement, but she had a strong urge to flee. There was absolutely no reason for that; always levelheaded, she handled every curve life threw her. There were no surprises she couldn't handle, especially after her last two disastrous relationships. She had no fear of anyone, and the word *shy* was not in her vocabulary. But some instinct urged her to get up and leave. She resisted it, hoping no one sensed anything unusual from her posture.

After the performance under the hot, bright lights in the humidity of Paris, Tristan enjoyed a cold shower and sat in front of his dresser, drying his hair. He was delighted with the performance that night—not a single mistake, and the audience had loved him. There was no Leslie Cole coming backstage to say his performance was fine, but . . .

Tristan had promised Phillipe to have a drink with a young friend of his. *I'll just get through it.* The door opened, and Phillipe came in with a blonde he introduced as Alexia LaBrocque and her friend, the actress Marie Savoie. Tristan greeted Alexia and took her hand; he always took a lady's hand. Maestro Paulo had instilled that in him. He turned to Marie and did the same.

As Tristan turned to Marie and reached for her hand, their eyes locked and his mind was transported someplace else. *How funny life can be, as if there are gods in the heavens, playing funny little games with the people on earth.* Someone had once told him that some believed people's souls were in their eyes. And perhaps once in a millennium, two people who had lived on earth's plane before could recognize each other's souls from another time and another place.

He did not let go of Marie's hand. The room was moving, but was not; each was saying something to the other, but he heard nothing. They were on the street, in a cab, sitting at an ancient table at la Coupole. The waiter was asking him something that Tristan did not really hear, but he ordered anyway. Alexia was asking a question; Tristan answered but had no idea what was asked. He could only look at Marie. *Her eyes are enormous. Dark brown.*

The restaurant buzzed with activity, yet Marie heard nothing. She returned Tristan's gaze. *His eyes are not blue; they're first blue, then green.*

Their dinner arrived; the conversation continued. Tristan talked and Marie talked. Alexia watched the scene. Something tremendous was going on, and with a falling heart, she realized it wasn't she he was looking at. And Marie. She seemed so strange, so lost. If her relationship with Peter was such a disaster and she was going to swear off all men, then what in hell was going on? Phillipe took Alexia by the hand, and they said their farewells.

Marie heard nothing, as if no one had ever been there. No conversation was going on then, had any before? Neither stopped looking at the other. Marie moved to the chair next to Tristan. As she took his hand, no words were exchanged. He caressed her face softly.

The air over Paris had been muggy, and black clouds were building. A storm was coming. In silence, they took a cab to Ile Saint-Louis, where they walked, holding hands. Marie's heart raced. Slowly, the world around her returned. The night sounds, a distant rumble of thunder. The wind picking up. Within ten minutes, they had covered the small isle and reached the Seine, which encompassed Saint-Louis. After crossing the bridge to Notre Dame, they sat at a small bistro table facing the cathedral. *His face, I want to caress it. I must put my arms around him. I think I'm going mad.*

Every feature in her face is perfect; her chestnut hair, I want to touch it. We have to get out of here. *Tristan held Marie's hand, and they touched each other gently — her neck, her hair, his face. Their brandy sat untouched on the table. Tristan wanted to speak but couldn't. He walked Marie to the curb and hailed a cab.*

Five minutes later Marie followed Tristan into L'Hotel, to the suite Mistinguett made famous, the same couch where she had taken her lovers.

The Storm was approaching, lightning radiating across the sky. The apartment was on the top floor, and outside the windows, each flash lit all of Paris. Dark clouds hung low; rain was coming.

Holding Tristan, Marie was unaware of the storm. He pulled her to him and gently kissed her. Marie's ears rang. His body was so warm. Her heart beat faster; she wanted to rush to her feelings. He kissed her throat, her ears. She ran her hands along his back.

The sensation of her touch was like a wave of electricity. Tristan knew he must be in control. The passion was immense for him, but it was not going to be any fast affair. They had an eternity. He controlled the pace as they undressed one another, caressing each other everywhere, kissing each other gently. He took a lock of her hair and caressed his face, then hers.

A bright flash of lightning struck, its blinding light bursting into their room, reaching for them as Tristan led Marie to the bedroom. Thunder battered against the windows, but neither paid heed as they became lost in the storm.

Paris, 1941: Marie Louise Savoie

On a stormy, windswept day in October, 1941, the rain was incessant. Lightning flashed in the Paris skies, illuminating the amazing edifices that had withstood centuries of rains, centuries of people coming and going through history. Once bright in their limestone casings, the buildings were dark with the soot of centuries past. The war that ravaged Europe would miraculously spare the splendid buildings of Paris, but the occupation would cause turmoil felt by its citizens for decades.

On that rainy day, a daughter was born to Martine Savoie, who was from a famous family of actors and playwrights. Her mother insisted the baby be named Marie Louise after a family member who had lived centuries before. Although it was never proven and never could be, it was said that the Savoie family had descended from Marie-Louise de Savoie, the Princess de Lamballe; first-lady-in-waiting to Marie Antoinette; massacred by a mob in Paris on September 3, 1792.

Family members had passed down that story for nearly two hundred years. Many in Paris laughed at the thought, while others believed the story and revered the family. When Marie turned ten, some thought she resembled the Princess de Lamballe. Some who came to know her and the history of the princess said she was the reincarnation of that great lady.

In the summer of 1979, an article would appear in the Los Angeles Times. Peter Hurkos, a famous psychic who had resided in France and moved to America, would tell an acquaintance that, indeed, Marie-Louise de Savoie had been reincarnated in 1941 in Paris. Hurkos would examine an extraordinary bracelet worn by the Princess de Lamballe and stripped from her hand the day of her death. Through the bracelet, he would make his psychic announcement of her reincarnation.

Mrs. Savoie named her daughter Marie Louise, as she believed the stories passed down from one generation to another. Her husband, Maurice, scoffed at the idea of his family being of nobility, and poor Marie would suffer her father's indignation throughout her life. Maurice, after all, was a heralded stage actor, much respected in and around Paris. When people asked him about the family history and whether his daughter might be a reincarnation of the fabled eighteenth-century Princess Marie-Louise, he would say, "Don't talk to me about that mumbo jumbo."

Unusually pretty at birth, little Marie grew so adorable in infancy that it was difficult to go out without people making a commotion about her. Though thin in her youth, one could see the marvelous bone structure in her face. Cascading dark-auburn hair framed her beautiful, classic face. Her dark-brown eyes were large. Full lips, a slightly upturned nose, and long, dark lashes caused many to turn around and stare as she grew.

As Marie matured from child to young teen, she developed a strong attraction for the opposite sex and, of course, they to her. There was always commotion in the Savoie household when it came to the boys. Some of those young men would show up at all hours of the day or night to call on her.

When she approached her sixteenth birthday, the boys her age suddenly disappeared from her life. The younger men had begun to bore her; men in their twenties and thirties became frequent admirers. They dressed maturely, spoke well, and knew how to make Marie feel good with their witty humor.

∞

Maurice and Martine allowed the company of those older men because they trusted Marie, but they made sure they knew who her admirer was before allowing their daughter to go out. Everything was all right until the evening Marie announced she was going out with a Monsieur Vincent Peret, owner of a large chateau in the Loire Valley. Nothing much was thought about that until the monsieur showed up. He greeted them politely, informing them he had known Maurice's father when he was a young man attending the Paris Theatre.

Vincent was a shade under sixty, and Marie was alarmingly and obviously attracted. That was the last straw. The Savoies grounded her, and at sixteen, she was chaperoned to and from school.

Paris, 1957: Le Lycee School

Marie attended Le Lycee in Paris and received top grades. And, of course, as the school was coeducational, every boy on campus fell into instant infatuation with the auburn-haired beauty. Most girls, on the other hand, were jealous. Brains and beauty did not go together at all.

She had only one close friend on campus. Alexia LaBrocque had a pretty face slightly distorted by ears that were much too large, especially at sixteen. Alexia's short fingers were her only other drawback. She hid her fingers by wearing gloves. Quite thin, Alexia agonized over any weight gain. "Look at me. Look at my tummy. It's sticking out terribly. What can I do about it? I have a date this weekend with Paul Brizot. He's going to want to not only kiss me but feel my body, and I really want him to touch me. What can I do?"

Marie looked expressively at her best friend so obsessed with being thin. *This could be fun.* "Hmm . . . if you're going to let him pet you and you're afraid of his touching your tummy, which *is* very big, obviously you have to tell him why it's too big."

"Are you crazy? What do I say?"

"Simple. Tell him you're pregnant."

The girls laughed heartily, Alexia stating the best thing after all was for her to go on a diet. She would not eat chocolate until she shed the weight. The girls were in the middle of the conversation when Marie's mother invited them to have some cake for dessert. Marie convinced Alexia her tummy was not really protruding. Instantly, all thoughts of dieting ended, and the two girls ate nearly the entire cake.

৪১

Alexia's dark-brown hair was so thick and luxurious that the stylists who trimmed it usually marveled over the texture and length. Even so, she fell into the shadow of beautiful Marie. Occasionally, young men desperately tried to get near Marie without success. The boys of Le Lycee soon figured out a tryst with la Alexia was better than nothing at all.

Unbeknownst to most of the girls at Le Lycee, Alexia did like to tryst. In truth, she had long lost her virtue and enjoyed sex with quite a passion. Miraculously, she was able to hide her affairs from family and friends alike. If a young man took her fancy, and she his, her one important condition was that the boy keep his mouth shut and not talk of her disparagingly. As most young men liked to talk or boast about their conquests, Alexia chose those who could either be fully trusted or attended another school far away from her own.

She took pains to hide her numerous affairs from Marie—not only for fear of losing the young men to her friend, but also a natural desire to keep Marie uninformed. In that environment, she became closer and closer to Marie as the years passed. There were occasions when her best friend questioned her because she *disappeared* for the moment. But when Marie asked directly if anything was going on, Alexia would look her straight in the face and say, "Who me? With that boy? You must be kidding. I'm waiting for Mr. Right. I can't even comprehend having some boy put that *thing* into me, can you? Isn't it marvelous that we're virgins?"

Marie would patiently listen, widening her large brown eyes yet completely believing her friend.

℅

Alexia was Marie's ticket to freedom. The girls often stayed overnight at each other's homes. Marie's home, a sprawling apartment in Montmartre, was on the top floor and gave no means of a nighttime escape if one wanted to leave unnoticed. But the LaBrocque's small, first-floor apartment in Saint Germain des Pres provided an easy, undetected escape for the two girls. Alexia's bedroom was at the rear of the building, leading to an alley. Her parents were gullible, and having to work from five in the morning to early evening in a local bakery, both passed into an early oblivion shortly after the evening meal.

℅

Fall turned to winter. It was quite cold that Saturday evening, and both girls dressed warmly for their sojourn to Castel, the hottest nightclub in Paris. The girls meandered the narrow, bustling streets nearby and stopped for a Kir at Café de Flore. Upon entering the club, they were politely escorted to a lush booth and seated next to one of the large brass bamboo sculptures that rested in front of most of the private booths.

Alexia nudged Marie and nodded toward the bar. Seated there was a man with an amused expression on his face as he studied the two girls, making no effort to hide his admiration. Alexia noticed he appeared mostly interested in her companion. He was not only examining Marie, he was undressing her with his eyes. A pang of envy ran through Alexia's heart. *Oh well, here we go again. Maybe he has a friend.*

෨

Marie never so much as blinked in the man's direction, but the instinctive little creature knew exactly what was going on. She had experienced to that point in her life one very disappointing affair. The man was Vincent Peret. He had wooed her secretly for months. A diamond bracelet, carefully hidden from her parents, was one of many gifts he had lavished on her. He promised marriage, stating he would divorce his wife and marry Marie. She laughed at his overtures but continued to see him out of curiosity. He looked exceptional for his age, had a great sense of humor, and was very worldly. His dress was impeccable, much better than her illustrious father, and what he gave her most was the love and attention she did not get from Maurice. Of course, she did not realize that, and when Vincent's attentions became more aggressive, she weakened one night. As a result, she terminated the short affair.

Two months after their last meeting, Vincent's family reported his untimely death in a boating accident. In reality, the poor man, cut off from the one great love of his life, had taken his own by stepping off his yacht in the South of France while the rest of his family slept. That fact had never been revealed to the public, and Marie never knew what really happened.

෨

The waiter approached their table with a silver bucket and lifted a bottle of 1952 premium Cristal champagne to show the two girls. Neither had enjoyed that little delight before. The bubbling liquid was exquisite, and Marie asked the waiter who had sent it over. Alexia already knew. They looked at the gentleman at the bar and smiled.

The man was tall and lean. He had a beautifully tailored suit that fit his body like a glove. It certainly was not from Galeries Lafayette, the local department store. His complexion was dark, his eyes blue, and his face rather kind with a strength that showed through his eyes. He came to their table. "Well, hello, young ladies. May I join in for a few minutes before I have to leave? I'm making a film just outside Paris and don't want to stay out too late. I am Pierre Remet. Please tell me your names."

෫ာ

His smile seemed genuine, his attitude relaxed—a man of distinction. Marie looked at him and responded with their names, turning on the charm with a sparkle in her eyes. She widened her eyes playfully. "You're making a film. Are you the director, producer?" She watched the man melt in front of her as she spoke. "What is the film about, and how about using Alexia and me. You know, we're very talented actresses at our school." A lie, of course.

Remet smiled and described the film he was producing in detail. "Yes, there might be a walk-on for you if you can get away from school and have your parents' permission. If not, come down next Saturday and you can watch some scenes filmed. Here's my card. Call my secretary during the week, and she'll tell you where and when."

With no further word except good night, he was gone.

෫ာ

The girls, of course, could not get out of school but were allowed on Saturday to visit the set of *The Door Closes*, filmed in a farmhouse near Orly Airport. Pierre Remet was having lunch under a large tent set up outside the old farmhouse. A corner table was reserved for the producer and director, away from the actors, and Alexia and Marie were escorted to him. Pierre stood to greet the girls, his sparkling eyes taking in the tight black jeans Marie wore. Her body was beginning to show the maturity she would in time become famous for—a stunning figure with long, well-formed legs. Framing her face, her hair cascaded full length to nearly the top of her derriere. Her large eyes flirted outrageously with him.

Nearing fifty, Pierre was youthful in his appearance and generally avoided any mention of his age. When asked, he would say, "Never mind my age. It's not the vintage that matters, only the taste." He seated his guests and motioned to one of the serving staff to bring more plates over. Barbecued chicken in a creamy Dijon-mustard sauce, served with fresh vegetables and Swedish lingonberries, was appetizing and set off the afternoon on a positive note.

෫ာ

The filming commenced after lunch, with a scene inside the eighteenth-century farmhouse. Alexia, caught up with the excitement, noticed the awed expression on Marie's face. Again she felt envy. She knew Remet was infatuated with Marie; additionally, she noticed something was going on in her best friend's mind as she watched the filming.

ℰℭ

A lightbulb had been turned on in Marie's mind. She was spellbound by everything taking place—the filming itself, the actors on the set, the stage crew, the camera crew. She looked everywhere, enraptured with what unfolded before her. She had witnessed her father onstage before, but it never really captivated her. In the setting of camera and cast, she was in an element that gave her enormous excitement and pleasure.

ℰℭ

Pierre watched the charming young lady with pleasure. The lust he had initially felt actually evaporated somewhat as he saw her genuine love for the filming. When the day's shoot ended, he escorted the girls back to Mrs. Savoie's car and introduced himself. "Your daughter is charming, Mrs. Savoie, and has an interest in what we're doing. Have you thought of sending her to the Conservatory? Call me next week, and we can discuss it. I lecture there several times a year and would be happy to sponsor Marie for the school."

Paris, 1958: Conservatory for Drama

Alexia was devastated. Marie had been transferred to the Conservatory for Drama within a single week of meeting Pierre Remet. Though nothing else would change in their relationship, Marie's absence from school was physically distressing. Alexia, who had maintained a high grade level, lost interest in her studies. Whereas before, her good grades made her feel somewhat superior to Marie, there was no longer any reason to improve herself with her studies.

Weekend visits to Marie were unhappy experiences over the following months. Marie babbled endlessly about the excitement of the new school. "You must hear about all the people here. They're so interesting and talented. I love my teachers, especially my ballet instructor, Monsieur Detarga. He's so handsome. He's taken a special interest in me, and, oh, Alexia, when he touches me—"

"He touches you. Where does he touch you?"

Marie, who had been serious in her description of school, noticed the look of shock on Alexia's face and decided to have tease her. "Oh la la, my dear Alexia. He touches me everywhere—inside my panties, inside my bra. He invites me to his room at night, and, oh, what he does to me. I can't even describe it to you." As she embellished her fictional romance, Marie saw Alexia's shocked expression turn to excitement, so she continued. "You know, I told Anthony you were coming this weekend to visit me at school, and you'll never guess what my teacher said. He asked me if we could indulge in ménage à trois together. And guess what I told him."

Alexia leaned forward. "Yes, yes," she said. "Let's do have sex together. This sounds fabulous. I've never done that before."

Though Marie had been playacting, she could not tell if her best friend was serious. She decided she had gone too far. "Are you crazy? I've been making the whole thing up. My ballet teacher is queer, though I adore him. You want to have sex with both of us?"

Receding into her chair, Alexia said, "Have sex with both of you, never. I knew you were joking, so I just played along with you. So there."

Marie looked momentarily into her friend's eyes and read only the truth. She smiled, laughed, and continued to tell her about the school, that time only with enthusiasm.

ℰↄ

Alexia listened to Marie, but deep inside, an alarm went off. In the future, she must be more careful to never expose to her beloved friend the way she really felt about her own sexuality.

Marie droned on about her love for the acting school. "I've discovered at seventeen exactly what I want from life. I'm going to hurl myself into it with abandon. At the Conservatory, the classes are my life."

ℰↄ

Alexia departed for home rather early after dinner Sunday evening. She did not take the metro, deciding to walk the quiet streets of Paris. It was a frigid night, and Alexia pulled her long, dark coat tightly against her body. A wet drizzle started, but Alexia ignored the moisture. What if Pierre Remet had asked her to become part of the Conservatory? Why hadn't he fallen in love with her instead of Marie? And mostly, why was she so fascinated with her friend? After all, they were in many ways opposites. Marie was such a prude.

Alexia realized she was soggy from the lightly falling rain. She looked into the dark skies, smelling the cold night air. Paris was her beloved city with all its ancient buildings and remarkable history. The drizzle stopped, and the winds cleared the night sky. As she ascended the steps to her home, she gazed up at the black heavens filled with so many stars that they looked like endless candles. Her mind raced in thought. *I love this ancient city. I shall always live here. I'll be more successful than my best friend and grow old gracefully, and then I shall die here.*

ℰↄ

Marie thrived at the Conservatory. In her first year, she was selected to play the main role in *Gigi*, which received standing ovations. The school also changed her romantic views. She was exposed to young men and women who had the same interests as herself. Many of the teachers were also young, most in their mid-twenties to early thirties. The Conservatory wanted a youthful direction with their teachers, and as a result, Marie's obsession for a father image diminished. She felt comfortable with the young men and boys around her.

Pierre Remet, who had felt that Marie had an initial physical interest in him, noticed it evaporate and sadly marked it off to his karma. As he sat with one of his assistant directors on his current film, Marie's name came up. "Ah, Marie. Of course I would have loved to possess her, but she thinks of me only as a father now."

The assistant director smiled. "Surely, it's not too late to try and bed her, don't you think?"

Pierre laughed heartily. "Too late, yes, far too late. The wine was a good vintage, but Marie won't even take a taste now."

Marie's ongoing performances in school attracted many notable film producers and directors. It was there that Jacques Demy discovered her, casting her that summer in his film *Les Demoiselles de Rochefort*. With a little cajoling, Marie was able to convince Demy to give a small part to her friend.

Excited at the prospect of acting in a film with Marie, Alexia discovered once filming began that she did not have an acting part. She was used in the background with dozens of other extras. She was nothing but added atmosphere; and though she tried not to, she felt resentful, as if it would have been better not to work with Marie at all.

℀

With the completion of *Les Demoiselles*, and as she approached her eighteenth birthday, Marie decided she wanted to make a change in her lifestyle. She was, after all, earning her own money and knew deep inside she would one day be a star. She invited her mother for a quiet lunch. Sitting at a small bistro in Saint Germain, she said, "Mother, I want my own apartment. I need to be alone so I can try and find out who I really am. I love you and father dearly, but I just won't find my identity until I'm by myself. Do you understand?"

Of course, her mother did not understand, and her father went into a rage over her request. The household remained in chaos for several days, but her mother realized that by holding their daughter from the freedom she wanted, in the end they would lose the open relationship they had with her. They agreed that Marie could have her own apartment; however, it must be situated close by.

The apartment Marie found was quite small — a narrow hall leading to a living area and single bedroom. To compensate for the tiny living space, she transformed the apartment into a small but beautiful jewel. Period fabrics picked up at flea markets were draped over the windows as well as the modest furniture. The fabrics were exquisite, some dating back a hundred years. In Marie's imagination, she was transported back to the time of Ali Baba.

Paris, 1960: Alexia LaBrocque

Spring came and with it the first real evidence that the sun still shone over the skies of Paris. The leafless trees grew the various shades of green that made the city come alive. Birds voiced the coming of spring, and the incessant rains of winter became sporadic. More people ventured out on the sidewalks, enjoying the petite cafés and bistros that were so numerous one wondered how they all managed to capture their share of business.

Late one afternoon, the phone rang in Alexia's room. A concession from her parents, the private line was somewhat new, and very important to her. Marie's chattered instantly. "See if your parents will allow you to film with me the next two weeks. Adriene Truffaut told me he needed a girl my age to play my sister. We're alike in so many ways, I convinced him you would be perfect. The lines are short, so he won't expect too much from you."

Although Truffaut was one of France's finest directors, the film was not one of his masterpieces and would almost not be released. It would do nothing for either of the young women except give Alexia a real taste of the motion picture business. Though not as infected as Marie, she enjoyed herself immensely, especially the attention she received from the cast and crew.

Alexia fell into a deep infatuation with the cinematographer, Olivier, and the affair was not exactly a secret. One morning when she tried to appear for a scene, her face was so "bruised" that no makeup could help, and the scene had to be canceled. In the picture, she played a blonde, and Olivier was so taken with Blonde Alexia that he never knew her wig was not real until he accidentally pulled it off while making love to her.

Realizing it would give her a completely different look and place her apart from la Marie, Alexia decided to bleach her hair to a magnificent shade of blonde. The outcome was beyond her wildest hopes. Her thick, slightly curly locks and professional styling gave her a spectacular look. She told Marie she would remain blonde for life.

The filming ended far too soon, as Alexia and Marie were having a good time working together. Marie went back to the Conservatory and Alexia to Le Lycee. The spring semester crawled by for Alexia, while her best friend often said she loved her work and wished school would never end.

As Alexia's graduation from Le Lycee approached, she formulated plans for the summer—sun, fun, and the Castel nightclub. Late in the schoolyear, she attended Marie's final performance at the Conservatory, the role of Henriette in *The Two Orphans*. Under the stage lights, Marie's character struggled her way through the French Revolution, finally reuniting with her lost sister, Louise. As Marie's realistic performance took the audience from tears of sadness to tears of joy, Alexia shed tears of envy. Would her dearest friend always outshine her? She feigned joy for Marie's success, but her heart remained jealous.

శ

The weather grew warmer as summer approached. The parks and grand mansions were ablaze in flowers of all kinds. Set in a background of lush plants and trees, Paris was indeed spectacular. Having dyed her hair, Alexia set it carefully in large curlers each evening so that when she combed it in the morning, it cascaded around her shoulders. The boys noticed; the girls noticed; everyone noticed. As Alexia's face began to fill in slightly and her cheekbones became prominent, a truly beautiful woman emerged. She could not keep the men away.

With all the attention she was receiving, Alexia became more selective. Young men bored her; she wanted those with sophistication to be near her. Looks were not important; money and worldliness were, and of course the sex had to be great. She realized what Marie had seen in older men. They were more interesting and experienced, and most importantly, had something the younger men did not—money to spend on all the yummies she wanted in her life.

Alexia made up her mind that above everything else, she would attain financial freedom. In her heart, she wanted to accomplish that in a straightforward way. Had she the choice, she would attain riches as an aspiring actress desired for her acting ability. Alexia made up her mind to become such an actress. She would show Marie who would be best. Screw the Conservatory, Alexia would make it to the top with no professional acting experience, no schooling. She would do it with her great looks and contacts.

Excited at the prospect of besting Marie, Alexia decided to have her horoscope read. Her history teacher had said that Napoleon never went into battle without his astrologer reading to him what fate lay in store on a particular day. If the great Napoleon had his chart read, so would she. Then she would show it to Marie.

Madame Tatiana, the "Gypsy Queen of Paris," was known for her predictions of catastrophic events as well as her astrology readings. Alexia gathered all of her hard-earned savings and called to make an appointment, giving Madame Tatiana not only her birth date but the precise time she was born. Based on that information, the fortune-teller would draw up an astrological chart of Alexia's life. Anxious to discover the wonderful things that would be forecast in her chart, she hardly slept that night.

Madame Tatiana was an older woman with pure-white hair. She was beautiful regardless of the wrinkles of old age. She smiled at Alexia and led her from the apartment entry into a darkened studio. The studio smelled of musk and ancient things; Alexia had not the slightest inkling what those odors might be. On one wall was an ancient mummy cloth, apparently the outer wrapping, as the shadow of a gilded face could be seen on the ancient cloth. A small table and two old leather chairs rested in the center of the studio. On the table, a single lamp illuminated the entire room, casting shadows throughout.

∽

Tatiana motioned Alexia to one of the chairs and seated herself across from her wide-eyed customer. Studying the girl in the darkened room, she opened a large white envelope, removing Alexia's chart. Tatiana thought momentarily of how many young customers had come over the decades to seek their futures, to be assured their lives would be filled with happiness, love, and prosperity. How sad that for most, life did not work that way. That day she would reluctantly talk to Alexia LaBrocque about her future. Based on the date and time furnished her, she had easily prepared the chart the day before. Tatiana reached over and took the girl's hand, which she noticed was trembling.

"Alexia, please don't be nervous. Your chart is quite interesting. Let me tell you a little about what the signs of the zodiac say about you. Your sun sign is Libra, and you love peace, beauty, and harmony. You are modest, artistically inclined, and neat. And at heart, you are a perfectionist. Your moon sign shows you are proud and ambitious and have no hesitation about assuming heavy responsibility or appearing in the public eye."

A thrill went through Alexia, as everything sounded just like herself. *Wait till Marie hears this.*

"Your ascendant sign is Virgo. Your shyness is a screen to keep others from discovering your intense need to be better than those around you, and especially from discovering how much you enjoy sex. In the sign of Uranus, you are unpredictable, erratic, and rebellious. Your life will be filled with separations from family and friends, and you will experience more than one divorce. Your sun is in the second house, which represents monetary status. It indicates you are interested much more in the prestige of wealth than in using your money wisely. Your moon sign indicates your need to be at center stage, so much so that you will push others offstage to gain prestige."

Alexia fell from the height of ecstasy as Madame Tatiana continued to read her chart. The desire to rush her excellent chart to Marie vanished, and she slid into a state of depression.

The look was not lost on Madame Tatiana. She tightened her hold on Alexia's hand as she continued the reading. "You approach affairs of the heart with cool, analytical curiosity. You are not spontaneous in your relationships, and as a result, you will continue to lose those men who come into your life. You will always have difficulty sustaining family ties or maintaining a happy household. Jealousy and arguments will hurt your relations with family.

"You prefer to work alone and cannot stay with one thing too long. You are a visionary with impractical goals. Your impersonal attitudes, aloofness, and eccentric habits will close doors and turn people off. You never stay with one project long enough to finish it, as your excitement to go on to the next project leads you to exhaustion.

"Lastly, you will go through life using sex to gain whatever it is you need at that time."

By then, Alexia had slipped into a deep depression. Madame Tatiana's words seemed to blur, and Alexia had an intense desire to escape. She felt desperate.

Again the wise old lady fully understood and tried to calm her. "Alexia dear, I knew before you came that this would be a hard day in your life, but I hope someday you will understand that by having knowledge beforehand of what fate may have in store for you, it will be easier to deal with life." But Alexia was inconsolable, and all Tatiana could do was lead her to the door, handing her the manila envelope that contained the devastating forecast.

Clutching the envelope in her hand, Alexia walked to the Tuileries Gardens, finding a place to sit amid a cluster of trees, well clear of the numerous Parisians meandering throughout the park. She opened the envelope and removed the contents, finding the wad of francs she had paid Tatiana. The old lady had not charged her for her chart, but she did not feel consoled. Instead, an even greater depression gripped her being. As the chart and the money fell from her hands onto the grass, Alexia let out a wail of despair. She was not even worth the price of the reading!

Madame Tatiana prepared an herbal tea and seated herself in one of the leather chairs in her old studio, reflecting on the sad girl who had just departed. She had decided the day before to reveal only certain information to Alexia. The chart and the reading were among the worst she had delivered in fifty years. The gods had sent the unhappy young woman to live out a virtual hell on earth. So young, so pretty, and full of expectations. Tatiana had not the heart to include some of the obstacles Alexia would encounter on her journey of life. She stirred her tea as she picked up one of the papers she had not given Alexia. It was a summation of her future. *You will lead a life filled with excitement, sorrow, success, and pleasure. You will reach financial security only to lose it. You will fall in love only once, and that love will take you to the stars. But the love will not be returned, and you will be cast into darkness. The last years of your life will be spent in despair and loneliness, as all those dear to you will be abandoned.*

Alexia walked across the wooden footbridge over the Seine and back to her family's apartment on the Left Bank. Marie had invited her for lunch on the set of her new film just outside Paris the next day. As she thought about the visit to Madame Tatiana, she made a mental note to never mention her meeting with the fortune-teller around Marie.

ॐ

Phillipe Vachon met Alexia on the set while she and Marie were having lunch, and fell instantly for her. He was one of the most sought-after men in France. A successful film director and producer, he specialized in casting gorgeous unknown girls in films where their natural attributes could be exploited.

Phillipe was separated from his wife, the fabled Dolores Pisier, a beautiful French actress. She had become ill on the set of *Moon Shadows* in Rome and flown to Nice without calling Phillipe to give him any notice. What she did notice very quickly were six beautiful girls engaged in an orgy with Phillipe, on *her* yacht, which was moored in Saint Tropez. When confronted by the enraged Dolores, Phillipe merely grinned and said, "What's it going to cost me?"

It had cost him a lot. She whisked their two boys away and served him with a monstrous lawsuit. The judge in Paris, a family friend of the Pisiers, smiled broadly at Phillipe in court and announced he could still keep his underwear, an ancient Citroen, and his typewriter.

Philippe set his sights on Alexia. While visiting Marie on the set, he noticed that an affair seemed to be going on between Alexia and Walter

Spier, the cameraman. Phillipe waited until the two-week film shoot ended and the two lovers were separated.

∞

Having developed an uncanny ability to feel the heat of a man, Alexia picked up on Philippe's interest and discovered, to her amusement, who and what he was. Giving no thought to the recent meeting with Madame Tatiana and her revelations, Alexia came to the realization that he might be her ticket to stardom.

Phillipe called on Alexia and, with her parents' consent, courted the young woman on a regular basis. He was very good looking, and popular with the celebrity element in Paris. He took her places she never dreamed of and introduced her to the most famous men and women of the day. They became lovers the first night they went out, and, to her extreme pleasure, she discovered in Phillipe a man of considerable sexual prowess. They made love incessantly, sometimes through the entire night with no rest. He took her from every position imaginable, and no part of her body was inviolate from his manhood. She enjoyed every moment, and after two weeks, found herself hopelessly in love.

Paris, 1961: Jean Delacroix

Marie was continually offered better parts, even though her first films were not notable. Producers and directors noticed her appearance and certainly her professional acting ability. Her first important role came in early 1961 in a film called *La Peau Douce*, the story of a man having his first extramarital affair after twelve years of marriage. The director was again Adriene Truffaut, and the film instantly catapulted Marie into international recognition. It was during the filming of *La Peau* that she met Jean Delacroix.

The Delacroixs were one of the most important and wealthiest families in all of France. Aristocrats dating to the twelfth century, the family produced weapons of war including cannon made for Napoleon Bonaparte. They added the manufacture of carriages then textiles in the eighteenth and nineteenth centuries. As Jean was very interested in the arts, at thirty-one, he had expanded the family's clothing line and added cosmetics, developing the finest, most famous products sold throughout the world.

A film aficionado informed Jean of the striking resemblance that Marie Savoie had to his favorite actress, Greta Garbo. Years ago, he had tried unsuccessfully to have an affair with Miss Garbo—the first rejection by a woman in his life.

Garbo had met Jean in New York after her publicist, Stockard Sheldon, insisted it would be of interest to her to meet the European notable. Her publicist had discussed Miss Garbo representing one of Delacroix's famous perfumes.

Jean had reserved a prime table at the exclusive 21 Club in Manhattan and arranged a special table setting, including a spectacular bouquet of red roses. After introductions by Stockard, who quickly disappeared, Jean exhibited his culinary expertise with his menu selections and appropriate wines. He was impeccably dressed that evening in a black vintage Delacroix suit designed by René Beaumont.

Noting an affectionate smile from Miss Garbo, Jean proceeded to impress her with a brief history of the Delacroixs. After appetizers and champagne, Miss Garbo seemed to be looking at him romantically. Calling over the waiter, he ordered a bottle of rare French Pomerol Petrus, vintage 1945.

When Greta opened a conversation about possibly representing Jean's most famous perfume, he invited her to see some advertising literature in his suite at his hotel. Once in his room, Jean promptly grabbed her and pushed himself upon her. He had spoken to Greta of a splendid contract, but the price was something that la Garbo was not willing to pay. If Jean delivered her the Hope Diamond—had it been obtainable—happily handing the precious gem to her for the privilege of conquering her exquisite body, she would have denied even that.

Jean was strong, and sensing a serious problem, Greta looked into his gray-blue eyes with a captivating smile. "Yes, Jean, but a moment, please. I need to use the restroom." She turned away, took two steps to the desk nearby, and grabbed a large crystal vase, smashing it, roses and all, on top of Jean's head. He got his star that night; he got lots of stars.

Two hours later, Jean awoke with a splitting headache, a scalp laceration, and a note from Miss Garbo:

> Dear Mr. Delacroix,
> So nice to meet you. Stick your advertising program up your ass! And by the way, you need to lose a few pounds. For someone so young, you're getting too fat.

Jean had smarted from the humiliation all the years since. When he heard rumors that a new French actress looked and talked like Greta Garbo, he was intrigued. Not wanting to lose an opportunity, he made arrangements to meet her.

ℛ

The set was dark after the day's shoot, and Mr. Truffaut had left Marie to read some changes in her script for the next day. Seated in her own director's chair in a large soundstage building, she was reviewing the changes when a man approached. He was lean and well-dressed, and had a certain air about him that instinctively told her he was someone important.

With an impressive smile, he said, "Hello, I'm Jean Delacroix. Adriene told me you were here reading lines for tomorrow's filming. I'm a fan of yours even though I've just seen one film you've done, and those beautiful photos of you in *Paris Match*. I wanted to meet you in the worst way. I think I'm in love with you."

Marie was amused. She knew of Delacroix, who didn't, and a little interesting company would be fun. Turning in her chair, she looked up and replied, "How in the world can you be in love with someone you know nothing about?"

Marie focused on his gray eyes . . .

§

. . . and proceeded to look into his soul. At least that was how Jean felt. Marie's voice sounded husky but at the same time like silk. Jean was mesmerized, vaporized; he had a sinking feeling in the pit of his stomach. Never before had he met a woman and experienced the sensations that were going through him then. Taking control of his emotions, Jean looked into her beautiful large brown eyes. "You can fall in love with someone having never seen them before. Let me tell you how I became so infatuated with you. There was a classic film made some years back in America, starring Jennifer Jones and Joseph Cotten: *Portrait of Jennie*. In the film, Joseph Cotten falls in love with a portrait of Jennifer Jones. He actually becomes obsessed with her picture. The lady had died in a boating accident, and later in the film, he meets someone who looks exactly like her. When I saw your pictures a few weeks ago in *Paris Match*, I fell in love with you. Come, now that I've told you this, have dinner with me tonight. We'll make it early so you can be on the set tomorrow, and I do promise to behave myself completely if you have heard the wrong things about me."

After the Garbo fiasco, Jean had made a decision to never take a woman for granted. It was a devastating experience discovering that financial wealth did not necessarily mean an easy conquest when it came to the opposite sex. He did not like losing at anything, and as sex was just another game, he made up his mind to never lose at that business again.

Jean took considerable steps at forty-five to stay in great shape. The Garbo incident had deflated him. Delacroix had her penciled note framed, and every waking morning it greeted him on the wall above the scale in his marble bathroom. He would stare in defiance at any slight weight gain. If he weighed above the 180 pounds that went with his six-foot-two frame, he immediately went to his personal gymnasium, one floor beneath his penthouse on Ile Saint-Louis. He then punished himself until he knew he had lost the added weight, plus one pound. It mattered not that he pumped iron for an hour or more. As his excess body weight normally hit him in his waist, he would do sit-ups, utilizing numerous forms, for at least another hour with no rest. His midsection would scream from the pain, yet he cared not at all. With every muscle crying out, he envisioned the Garbo note as if the incident had happened yesterday. No one would ever call him overweight again. Never.

℘

Marie was intrigued with Delacroix. She realized that with his interest and support, the only place she could go in her business was up. He was a ticket to people, places, and other things to which she, by herself, had no bridge. The thing that bothered her immensely was that she had no sexual interest in the man. It was not that he was bad looking. He was, in a manner, very attractive and masculine.

Of course, Marie accepted the dinner invitation. She would be a gracious guest, and should the occasion present itself where she might feel uncomfortable with Jean, she would think of a good excuse to alleviate the necessity of a sexual liaison.

℘

Jean's car would take Marie to Maxim's at 7:45. She wanted everything to be just right for that special evening. Entering her tiny apartment, she seated herself in front of the turn-of-the-century makeup table she had purchased at the flea market. It was a copy of a Marie Antoinette piece from Versailles. The aged, dark wood was covered with a lovely but faded nineteenth-century shawl depicting deer in a forest. In the center of the table was an art deco mirror with angels etched prettily in each corner of the glass, an expensive piece normally but bought for a few francs, as one corner was missing. Marie had draped that corner with part of the shawl to hide the defect. Small bottles containing her lotions and perfumes covered part of the little table, and a petite vase on one corner held a single lilac rose. The antiquated makeup table sat in front of an old wood-carved mirror from Mrs. Savoie's bedroom. It was in perfect condition and reflected pale light from a floor lamp next to the table.

Marie sat still for a long time, reflecting upon her image and her hopes and dreams. What would happen if she could fall in love with Jean and become mistress of the largest fortune in all of Europe? She could have her country chateau, all the things only the extremely wealthy own, and never have to think about work a day in her life. But, no, that was not what Marie wanted. A sudden thought came to her. She would not be tempted by wealth, nor dwell on anyone supporting her, owning her very soul. Never.

Marie had already decided to become a great actress and give to the world part of her talent. She looked long and hard at her reflection and decided she would succeed no matter what the price was. She would be the best or not succeed at all. With or without Jean Delacroix.

Although she took her time to make herself stunning for him, Marie had a single flaw, and that was the inability to apply makeup properly. When she was first allowed to wear makeup, she could not grasp the art of application. As time went by, no matter how hard she tried when she was alone, she could not master the technique. She had a tendency to apply too much makeup, and as a result, it actually made her appear older than her years. Only when she visited a fashion beauty shop was the makeup applied correctly. She had always recognized the problem and made the decision to hire a full-time makeup artist and hairdresser as soon as her films warranted it.

She did her best to prepare, but no matter. Her makeup might not be perfect, but she realized with great intuition that her indifference to Delacroix would win him over in such a manner that no woman on earth could.

∞

Leaving his apartment, Jean walked slowly around Ile Saint-Louis as he so frequently did. It was five in the afternoon, and the small shops located below the numerous apartments were thriving with shoppers. He enjoyed watching the action that encompassed the area, sitting at one of the small bistro tables outside and sipping an espresso or coffee. He mixed with strangers, trying to figure out what various persons did for a living. On more than one occasion, Jean had guessed the occupation of a surprised patron who chose to sit beside him. It was a harmless game, a practice he used in his business to outmaneuver or manipulate his adversaries in order to gain an advantage.

Returning to his nondescript apartment building, Jean took the old but smoothly running elevator to the third-floor apartment located within view of Notre Dame. On that level was a single doorway. The hallway inside was formal and immaculately clean yet gave no indication of the splendor beyond. Jean entered the apartment, a diminutive palace fit for a king, and passed through the spacious living room just off the entryway.

High ceilings ran throughout the apartment, and all the rooms were decorated in genuine Louis XVI furniture, each piece of museum quality. The living room had antique chairs and sofas in such pristine condition one hesitated before sitting, fearing a museum guard would rush over and say it was forbidden to use the furniture. The Persian carpets were of rare quality, each more valuable than the next. The walls were covered with Aubusson tapestries depicting great scenes of battle, hunting, or royal lodgings. Between the tapestries hung paintings, their equals only to be found in the Louvre. Degas, Renoir, and Lautrec were just a few of the magnificent oils that adorned the walls in places where tapestries were not hanging.

It was early evening as Jean entered his deep-green-marbled bathroom; even there hung the fine art of turn-of-the-century French masters. He walked into the adjoining dressing room where closet after mirrored closet contained the finest wardrobe in Europe. No famous designer was absent from the Delacroix collection. His own couturier was present, of course, but Jean greatly respected and appreciated the fashions of all the great designers — Brioni, Pierre Cardin, Yves Saint Laurent, and many more.

At one end of the dressing room was an elaborate makeup table designed exclusively for Jean. It was fashioned in an art deco motif, and the wood was entirely covered with burl. The oval mirror in the center was held in place by the wings of a pair of black sculpted swans. Ceiling spotlights could be adjusted from the table to enhance the reflection to such a degree that every pore of the skin could be viewed. On occasions when Jean was not in a mood to see the reality of life, the lights could be dimmed to show a gentler image in their soft reflection.

That night nothing would be left to chance, and Jean turned the lights up to their maximum intensity. Dark, gray-blue, piercing eyes looked out from an oval face that showed a strong man in the prime of his life. No softness there. Jean relaxed his body then to ponder his secret, innermost thoughts. He concentrated on what he had to accomplish that night. Rising, he walked back into the elaborate bathroom and looked up at the splendid Renoir hanging on the south wall. It was a scene depicting three young girls sitting in a park, having a picnic with an elegantly dressed older man. The man wore a monocle and was smiling at the pretty girls. Jean loved that painting above all of his Renoirs, as he fantasized each day what the man had on his mind and what he intended to do with his trio of nymphs so long ago. Jean showered, dressed, and prepared himself for his next great business venture, the conquest of Marie Savoie.

How very elegant it was to dine at Maxim's. Friday nights were special for the restaurant and its distinguished customers; the restaurant had live dance music. Near the celebrated bar, a small dance floor and a trio of musicians were present. A normal suit and tie could get a man into the dining room, but if he wanted to dance, he had to wear a tuxedo. Jean wore his famous company-designed tuxedo, the Valentino.

Rudolf Valentino had started his career as a dancer but was also famous in Manhattan for his menswear creations. One of those was his own tuxedo, and Jean had purchased one many years before from the estate, later having Delacroix designer René Beaumont redesign the suit to great acclaim in Europe.

ဢ

Marie had taken great pains to make herself as beautiful as possible, but also had been careful not to overdo it and stand out. Her floor-length dress was in shades of light pink, sequined at the waist and hem with a floral design depicting small roses. The sequins were also in a pale shade of pink, and the overall effect was very pretty indeed. Marie's luxurious dark-brown hair with a hint of auburn was braided in three parts and held back by a netting of pearls.

ဢ

The maître d' led Jean and Marie into the main dining room. Every eye turned to the fascinating couple. Of course, everyone knew Jean, and some made vulgar exclamations, having recognized the young French star. They made a fabulous-looking twosome.

Though their table was against a wall that permitted them to see everyone present, it was set away somewhat so they had total privacy and could speak without others listening. Jean — with what normally was a woman's insight — saw the one defect in Marie's appearance: her makeup was not right.

Dismissing the thought of Marie's cosmetic insufficiency, Jean saw only the beautifully elegant girl he wanted so desperately. As he studied Marie while she chatted about her film role, he noted she had a unique, tough attitude about her. If he commented on her makeup, she probably would just laugh and tell him to buzz off. It was as if she really did not care if he thought less of her or not. She had that kind of self-assurance. He decided the lady was not going to be an easy conquest at all.

"What are you thinking of now, Mr. Delacroix?" Marie asked with an amused expression.

"I'm looking at someone I'm in love with. Will you marry me?"

⍓

Marie laughed loudly, and those nearby looked at the couple. "Of course I won't. I'm not getting married ever. I don't believe in marriage." Marie coyly stared at Jean with sparkling eyes. "Why should anyone get married when it's so easy to divorce? Let the legal system figure out a way to make it difficult to get divorced, and I'll consider marriage. Anyway, I'm much too young to marry. I haven't discovered the man I want to spend my life with. He must be worldly, elegant, and above all, very rich." Marie was quite playful then, as she noticed that Jean seemed highly uncomfortable.

⍓

Jean had thought Marie much too young to keep up with his mentality, and was shocked at the level she was outmaneuvering him. How on earth did the little vixen manage to make him feel so inadequate? He stared at her intently, trying desperately to regroup his thoughts. A nineteen-year-old actress had him off guard.

"Garçon!" Jean snapped his fingers sharply to gain the attention of one of the waiters. "Good evening, Rafael. We need a bottle of 1958 Roederer estate-bottled champagne, at once please. Just one glass, and my usual, please." The waiter promptly returned with the champagne, one crystal flute, and a bottle of Perrier.

"Marie, a toast, my dear, to an elegant young lady who won't marry me because of my destitution, my lack of elegance and class. May you find the man in your life who will give you what you really need." *I'll play her game if it kills me.* His mind raced wildly as he envisioned getting that little bitch in his private amusement room and introducing her, by force if necessary, to his pleasures there.

⍓

As if she had read his mind, Marie smiled and followed with another great laugh that would become louder as the evening progressed. A bit of the bubbly had a tendency to make her laugh so loud that others around her, feeling a bit giddy from their own imbibing, would burst out laughing for no reason whatsoever. Marie's friends enjoyed being in her company to hear her contagious laugh.

⍓

The rather sophisticated Jean Delacroix did not know what to make of the happy creature. And that fact made him desire her even more.

Jean ordered a sumptuous meal starting with the restaurant's famous turtle soup. A small, delicious Beef Wellington followed, accompanied by Japanese pea pods and a rich mashed potato blended with Gorgonzola. Appropriate wines for his guest included a 1951 bottle of the famous Chateau Haut-Brion Gran Cru.

That wine had been blended for select customers, and when Jean had discovered the quality, he ordered half of the entire one-thousand-bottle production. The bottles were stored at various restaurants throughout Europe where he favored dining. Each world-class restaurant stored no fewer than six red and six white wines for him at all times. Among the wines were extraordinary years of champagne and the finest white Montrachet. Additionally, he owned half of the production of the best red wine ever blended in France, the 1945 Petrus. Jean Delacroix kept the exquisite wines for his company only; he never drank anything that contained alcohol.

The dinner was a splendid success as Marie had a taste of the wines, then a bit more, loosening up. Her natural energy, so full of life, flowed forth. She was quite the match for the worldly Delacroix. He, in turn, was more enamored by the minute and, by evening's end, would have given her anything to become a permanent fixture in her life.

At the end of the meal, Jean fairly pleaded with Marie. "Come home with me and allow me to show you my collection of the French masters in my humble apartment."

Marie squealed loudly with laughter. "Is that what you really have in mind for me, Mr. Delacroix? I'll humor you and see your paintings, but if you're thinking in terms of more, don't even think about it."

Laughing back, Jean was smug. *I'll make you an offer tonight you can't possibly refuse.*

∽

Jean's 1961 Rolls Royce Phantom V whisked them to the isle, and he led Marie into his spacious villa. A bit inebriated, she still recognized most of the artists and ran from one masterpiece to another, giddy with the beautiful paintings within such close proximity. Just to be in Coco Chanel's apartment was a trip for her, but seeing those spectacular paintings so closely that she could reach out and touch them was almost more than the French star could take in. Jean finally led her into the bedroom, and she wandered around like a child in a fairy tale come true. Inevitably, Marie found the great Renoir in the marble bathroom. Having run out of energy, she dropped down on one of the dressing room chairs and stared at the masterpiece.

ଛଠ

Jean had rarely allowed anyone into the sanctuary of his bathroom to view the greatest possession he had. An ironclad rule to have all his more-serious affairs conducted away from his apartments had been a lifelong policy. Rarely was anyone allowed beyond the living or dining areas or his prestigious office. The exception was the activity that took place in his Black Room, then again that room was designed for its special pleasures. At the moment, he could not resist the temptation to share with Marie the treasures of his life.

She finally spoke, still looking at the Renoir. "What a beautiful picture. Could I wish for anything in my life, it would be to own a painting like this. You must sit here for hours. I would if I could."

"It's yours, Marie." The words suddenly came out of his mouth with no thought of the consequences. Something had happened to Jean that night, and regardless of what would be, he had hopelessly, deeply fallen in love with the beautiful French actress. Taking a small settee, he sat next to her, gazing into her large brown eyes. Nothing mattered to him, only that he would win her over anyway he could, though it cost him everything he had.

ଛଠ

Marie stood up then and, facing Jean, saw the depth of love in his eyes. A great sorrow passed through her heart. Why did she feel nothing for such a generous man? Her life could be as no other in the world. Paradise was hers for the exchange of her body and soul. "No. I can't accept your gift. I know what you desire, and I can't give it to you now." Speaking tenderly, she said, "Perhaps another day, Jean, another time. Please take me home."

ଛଠ

The summer passed quickly for Marie. Of two splendid film roles offered to her, she accepted a part in a remake of *The Scarlet Pimpernel*. The original version—filmed in 1934, directed by Harold Young, and starring Leslie Howard, Merle Oberon, and Raymond Massey—was a classic. The new, French version would be directed by Jean Cocteau, and Marie would play the role that Merle Oberon made famous in the original. Young's film had been shot in black and white, but the France International production company was gambling on a color version focusing on elaborate sets and costumes of the late-eighteenth century.

A new Italian sensation, twenty-four-year-old Mario Galantin was to play the lead role. He was raised in France and spoke fluent French,

Italian, and English. Many of the international gossip magazines depicted him as a scandalous gigolo who propelled himself to the top by sleeping with anyone who could further his career.

Much of the filming would be in Versailles, on the vast estate where the kings of France had resided. Arrangements had been made for utilizing the royal palace and surrounding grounds, with the blessing of the French government, and the landmark would be closed to the public for nearly two months, except on Sundays.

Marie was in her trailer in the front parking lot, where tour buses were normally encamped. She was going over her lines for the first day's shoot when someone tapped on the trailer door. Opening the door, she saw an apparition that made her heart race. Mario Galantin was wearing only leather breaches and a well-worn black silk scarf around his neck. He looked well over six feet tall with a body that stirred Marie's interest at once. He bore a rather large grin and looked at her with mischievous brown eyes. His wavy ebony hair and small, neatly trimmed mustache, grown specifically for the film, made him quite striking.

Mario's eyes ran up and down Marie, lingering in the process. "Hello, I'm Mario." His voice sounded urgently sexual. "I just wanted to drop by and tell you how excited I am to be working with you. I've seen two of your films now and adore you." He gestured toward the palace. "They're serving lunch in front of the Latona pond. Will you join me?"

They walked the half mile along the north side of the palace and down the promenade that led to the fountains Louis XIV had installed at the beginning of the eighteenth century. The surrounding forest ringed the series of pools. Beside the Fountain of Latona, the "honey wagon" was serving lunch to the cast and crew. Marie and Mario sampled a small plate of the simple pasta and chacouette and drifted to the closest trees to seek shade, engaging in superficial conversation. Infatuated with each other, each spent the afternoon thinking about who might make the first move. Neither did, and eventually they walked back to their trailers to contemplate the next day's filming and daydream about each other.

❦

Another interested party observed their encounter—Roger Elonda, hired on as a grip. One of the film's financiers had insisted Roger work during the filming. Elonda had genuine credentials. He had worked ten years in London, mostly for Ajax Studios, and was a top grip with

France International. And he had been carefully interviewed in Paris a month and a half before shooting began for *Scarlet Pimpernel*. The meeting was on Ile Saint-Louis.

∾

Seated behind his Louis XVI writing desk, Jean had studied the man across from him. He had carefully selected that detective because of his background as a former British intelligence operator. The man had been a field operator during the war, and his reputation to maintain his cool was clearly stated in the confidential report Jean had acquired. "I expect a lot from you, Mr. Elonda. My distant niece, Marie Savoie, will start filming on *The Scarlet Pimpernel* in six weeks. My lovely niece is very talented but needs careful supervision on occasion. The family and I have decided to keep an eye on her through you. She is a bit of a romantic at heart, and our fears are she might have an affair or indulge in late hours that might affect her health. You will observe her at all times without bringing her attention to that fact. I am supplying you with this little gem to photograph her—a Sony 1412 mini-camera disguised as a pocket watch. Next week, my associate Mr. Price will demonstrate for you how it works. You will practice with this camera until you feel you're competent to use it comfortably."

Jean leaned forward. "Mr. Elonda, I will be paying you an annual salary equivalent to twice what you have ever earned in your life. Your employment with our family will be for an extended period of time. In addition, on any set where Marie is working, you will keep your production salary, as well. I expect only one thing from you: under no circumstances will you talk to anyone other than me about this arrangement. Should you do so, I will know about it. Should you break our agreement, you will never work anywhere in England or Europe again. This I promise."

∾

Roger had listened patiently as Jean spoke. Delacroix was staring at him, and he knew Jean was deadly earnest. As to the bullshit story about his "distant niece," Elonda had his doubts, but what difference did that make? He was going to make more money than he had ever dreamed of, and what other little goodies might be in his future during his alliance with one of France's strongest men? Roger would do his job well, very well.

ℰℴ

Filming went smoothly, and reviews of the daily shooting indicated the picture would be a huge success. Many agreed she would emerge as a major French star. She continued to see Jean once a week for a quick dinner in the little village of Versailles. A warm friendship developed between the two on the surface. Marie never suspected that Jean, who was a prince during the evening encounters, would leave the town in a silent rage. Roger Elonda had reported to him that, indeed, an affair between Marie and Galantin started almost immediately after filming began and that there were some evenings Marie did not emerge from his trailer until morning.

ℰℴ

The picture was in its final week of shooting. Although cast and crew had been whisked to nearby towns to utilize some of the farms and chateaus of the area, most of the film was shot in and around the main palace at Versailles. Mario was splendid as the Scarlet Pimpernel. His affair with Marie was stimulating, but as the picture neared its end, his mind was preoccupied with other things. Marie was proving to be a romantic creature, but his personal feelings on romance were quite different than hers. He liked her but tried to think of how he could continue the affair without her demanding it be exclusive.

Those thoughts were on his mind as he walked to the village nearby and toward the small inn located next to the main square. His mind was on the slim blonde waitress who had secreted a note to him the night before as he was dining with Marie. It was a simple statement: *I want to fuck your brains out. I'm off tomorrow at one, you'll find me at the inn in the upstairs studio marked 14.*

Mario opened the door to number 14, a small room with only enough space for a double bed and nightstand. As his eyes became accustomed to the darkness of the room, he saw the blonde waitress on the bed, stark naked with a huge smile on her pretty face. He walked over and gazed down at her — *God, what a body* — and looking directly at her pussy, noted she was not a blonde.

With no further ado, she said, "Take your clothes off and fuck me. I want you now." Wanting her just as much and not hesitating, Mario pulled his clothes off, tearing half the buttons from his shirt. He grabbed her roughly and placed himself on top of and into her at once. She was tight; with Mario's experience, he calculated she had not born children.

The woman started screaming the minute he was in her and continued so until they finished. The louder she screamed, the more excited Mario became. After ten minutes, she pulled herself loose and turned over. She rolled herself up, head down, and hissed, "Do it." He did, and the screaming intensified. She was very tight at that end, and his enlarged penis was chaffing. He lubricated himself with saliva and continued for another twenty minutes. The girl was having an extended orgasm and not releasing her enthusiasm at all.

They changed positions several times over the next half hour, and suddenly Mario, unable to hold back any longer, ejaculated every millimeter of semen in his glands. He lay spent on the bed and watched the young nymph look at him with what appeared to be a sarcastic smile. Her long white body still vibrated from the encounter. He marveled at the commotion she had made and hoped the room was soundproof.

Mario quickly dressed without washing and started to leave. The girl laughed deeply and said, "Is that all?"

Amused, Mario looked at her, recalling the sign-off for a famous cartoon, and said, "That's all folks," on his way out.

§

The woman got up from the bed and walked into the bathroom, turning on the shower. She removed the tight blonde wig and laid it on the floor. How delightful the hot water felt after good sex. She carefully washed herself and dressed in her Chanel suit that had been hanging in the closet. The black suit was a new design from the great fashion house, and at ₣10,000, not exactly worn by the average working-class waitress.

Lila Despardoux was good at what she did. A single lady of thirty-five but looking in her twenties, she loved her work with a passion. Sex was the focal point of her life, and her job was to enjoy that occupation to its fullest and be paid for it, to boot. She worked for Madame Alexandra's establishment, which was anything but the talk of Paris.

Few knew, or would ever know, just what Madame Alexandra supplied to the elite of Europe. Politicians, kings, the shah of Iran, the nobility of Europe were her customers. No whorehouse madam was she. If the top establishments in Paris charged ₣3–5,000 for services from one of their girls, that was cigarette money in Madame Alexandra's establishment.

There was a double knock, then three more. She opened the door.

Roger smiled at the beautiful brunette, wondering if the day would come that he could afford her. "How did it go, and how was Mr. Wonderful?"

"Good in bed, but a typical asshole as a person. The man didn't so much as say goodbye."

He removed the small makeup case lying on top of the dresser. Inside was an eight-millimeter motion-picture camera hidden behind a small hole covered with a dark glass lens. The case could be placed on any piece of furniture, the camera angled to frame in the desired filming area. In Mario's situation, the entire bed had been framed, with allowance for nearby activity.

Roger handed Lila an envelope and smiled again. He left the small room and walked back to the area set up for the stage crew, grips, and cameramen. He had served Jean well that day.

സ

August 1, 1961, was the last day of shooting for *Pimpernel* on location. A few interior scenes would be accomplished at the main production studio in Paris. Marie left her trailer and walked to the south wing of the palace. Her costume for the library scene was magnificent—a gown of blue and purple bands of silk threaded with small white pearls in a cascading style and larger white pearls about her neck. Hand-embroidered gloves and period jewelry placed her back to the court of Louis XVI just after the Revolution.

The scene was a meeting between Marie's character and the Scarlet Pimpernel when he would reveal his true identity. It was the last scene for the two principals in Versailles. Marie was seated at a large library table. At last, Mario arrived. It was a rather simple scenario. Mario entered the library and quietly embraced Marie. He then showed her his ring, which in reality was her own husband's, as the Scarlet Pimpernel *was* her husband, who had disguised his voice and manner so that no one had recognized him, including his own family.

Everything went almost perfectly on the first take, but director Jean Cocteau called for a backup shot, to be safe. The director called for action, and Mario entered the room, embraced Marie, and extended his hand to show her his wedding ring. As in the previous scene, Marie reached out to take his hand, but she grabbed the large glass inkwell on the table and lifted it high above her head, ready to bring it down on Mario's fingers.

Everyone froze, and sheer terror overcame the young actor. Marie must have gone completely mad. She brought the heavy crystal object down. He had no time to move, and just as he prepared himself for the impact, Marie dropped the inkwell on the table and burst into tears.

Marie lay her head down and literally drowned herself in her sorrow. She had fallen in love with Mario and had not been prepared for the envelope that was pushed under her door earlier in the morning. The photographs inside were so revealing that even Marie recognized the young waitress who had served them dinner the evening before. At first, she was crushed and cried endlessly. When her tears were exhausted, she became enraged thinking of Mario's conversations of love and future marriage. She had believed his lies and then some. When she calmed herself, she wanted revenge and the sooner, the better.

Having rehearsed that day's scene, Marie figured out how to get back at her lover. She would leave him something to remember her by the rest of his life. At least, that's what Marie had planned but then was unable to carry out. In reality, Marie Savoie was as capable of committing a criminal act as would Romeo betray Juliet. That lovely creature was quite capable of being in harm's way but would under no circumstances harm a living soul.

No one could coax Marie to leave the set. Head down, she continued to cry until there were no tears left and her emotions were spent. Jean Cocteau closed the set, telling everyone to leave Marie alone with her thoughts. She remained in the room for nearly two hours. The hurt was almost unbearable, but as she sat in the impressive edifice that at one time was the library room of King Louis XVI, inspiration came to her about the realities of life.

Marie matured in those hours, and though many other hurdles would impact her as the years went by, that experience was the first of several that heightened her awareness of man's follies. Her father, whom she worshiped, was not a warm person, and she had never received the bonding that was so necessary from him. Subconsciously, she looked for mature love from the men who entered her life. Marie did not know that in the wings of her life was one man who could more than give her that love. The clock was ticking.

଼ଠ

Leaves were falling from the trees; the weather was turning cold; and the sun disappeared behind the deep cloud cover over Paris. It was a time of sweaters and long coats, umbrellas and hats. The streets were a little dirtier, the buildings a bit darker, and the moods of the populace a little surlier.

Marie was exhausted from filming *The Scarlet Pimpernel*, having faced Mario Galantin on two more occasions for scenes at the production studio in Paris. She had shown no animosity toward her costar.

Mario was at a complete loss of why Marie had abandoned their affair. He tried unsuccessfully to see her alone and found to his dismay that her private phone number was disconnected with no referral to any other. His frantic letters went unanswered, and just after completion of filming, he discovered in his mail a large manila envelope containing all the mail he had sent to her — unopened.

$\wp$

The Scarlet Pimpernel was on its way to being nominated for Best Film in Cannes and Best Foreign Film in America. Marie would win Best Actress. Though calls came daily from the producer and director of her next film, Marie took a month off before beginning *Romeo and Juliet*. She did not think she was emotionally up for the part and had not committed to the film France International planned to start filming a week after the completion of *Pimpernel*. Sitting in her apartment, Marie talked to the one confidant she trusted.

$\wp$

Alexia listened attentively and gave Marie the compassion she desperately needed. Having experienced numerous rejections in her life until recently, Alexia was not only able to commiserate with Marie's complaints but to carefully impart from her own experiences the ways of men. "Men aren't like us. They're from another world. To me, men are mentally and chemically different. I, for one, think most men come from the moon and we from the very heavens. Man is an island to himself and can often go through life alone. He needs no one, not even another man. He might just as well live on a deserted island in many cases.

"But you and I are so close, as I am with some of my new friends. I love talking to you, and I know you always listen to me. You understand my problems. When I talk to a man, someone I'm seeing for the moment, he may occasionally do me a big favor and really listen. Then he'll proceed to tell me exactly what's wrong with me and how to repair the damage. They're imbeciles, for the most part, when it comes to communicating with us, and the best purpose they serve is how well they perform in bed."

Marie had a pained expression on her face. "I can't believe everyone is like that. The experience I had with Vincent Peret, though not sexually satisfying, was fantastic. He treated me like a queen. Had I liked him physically, I know it could have been—"

"There are men who have it all, but finding one is like searching for the needle in the haystack. Look at it this way instead. Trust no man ever. If you fall in love, prepare yourself for getting dumped at any moment. Get everything you can out of the relationship before the shit hits the fan, and always keep your eyes open for someone else to take the jerk's place."

The conversation went on for a long time before Alexia finally departed. It was a chilly night, and the sky was darkly overcast. As she walked along the Seine, distant lightning flashed, followed by a roll of thunder. Alexia hurried then as not to be caught in the coming storm. Her thoughts went back to Marie's last words: *I'll dream of the right man, and it won't be an impossible dream.* She laughed out loud, her voice carrying to a streetwalker huddled behind some trees, seeking shelter from the night.

Alexia remembered the words of the Gypsy Queen who had destroyed her dreams not so long ago. As she left, she had meekly said to Madam Tatiana, "I will not believe what you've told me today."

"Don't be upset, my dear. Should there be immortal gods in the heavens, they look down on all of us and smile their smiles. They have long planned for your destiny. Destiny cannot be changed for anyone. It can be altered for a brief time. In the end, the gods have their way."

∩

Alone with her thoughts, Marie was momentarily disillusioned. Two men had fallen desperately in love with her, and she'd had no romantic feelings for either. Then her first affair of the heart had ended in disaster. She wanted the rush she had felt when she and Mario first met. How did one distinguish who was genuine and who was not?

Marie sat in front of her oval mirror, preparing herself for a dinner out with Jean. He had proposed marriage a second time, promising Marie anything in life she wanted. She had been upset with him, and he promised not to bring the subject up again. But she knew somehow he would work around to it.

She was depressed over Alexia's convictions concerning men, but those thoughts were lifting. For a moment, Marie had considered Alexia's viewpoints, but she realized she would never look at men the way Alexia did. Life with that kind of attitude was not what she expected from her own convictions. Disappointment and a little bitterness, yes, but she was not ready to sacrifice herself or her life for a man like Jean Delacroix, even with his vast fortune.

Money was not what Marie wanted; she wanted the ecstasy that could only be found when a man and woman were bound to each other eternally, both hopelessly in love with each other and ready to share a life together. Marie wanted and dreamed what was almost the impossible.

℘

As Marie's depression continued, Adriene Truffaut asked her agents to plead with her to at least meet with him about *Romeo and Juliet*. He had been calling to convince her that she would be perfect for the role of Juliet in Shakespeare's classic of all classics.

Irving Thalberg had first produced the film in America in 1936. Adriene had always been interested in producing a French version of the love story for the ages. He was intent upon using Marie in the title role and did everything possible to convince her that the role would make her the number one star not only in Europe but internationally.

During his close contact with Marie filming *La Peau Douce*, Adriene had noted a classic example of an actress who needed something extra to push out the talented star that lay within. That film had not done well artistically or commercially because Adriene was hired to direct a script that could not be salvaged in any way. The sole salvation was his discovery of the talented Marie Savoie. Knowing he had no chance with her romantically, he concentrated his efforts on bringing her talent out in the role she was playing. The storyline was still so poor nothing could emerge from the finished product, and the film itself was a box office failure. He did not, however, forget that sensational young actress, and since he had finally succeeded in getting his precious Romeo financed, he wanted Marie as Juliet.

Marie never thought of herself as either beautiful or talented enough to play a film classic such as Adriene was offering. There were other reasons she did not want the role, but she kept those thoughts to herself. Additionally, she thought if she could not carry it off, she would be laughed out of France. Marie had avoided the French director until her agents explained it was in bad taste not to at least meet with him. Finally she agreed to go to his office.

Adriene greeted Marie cordially, and after both were comfortably seated, he said, "What is this about you not wanting to play my Juliet?

This can be a pivotal role in your career. Just tell me what's bothering you. I know we can work it out."

Marie hesitated before responding, not sure she wanted to confide the real reason. Deciding to trust the director, she finally responded. "Whoever plays Juliet must feel strongly about the role and, in reality, *become* Juliet. You worked with me on your last film, and though it wasn't successful, you know I gave everything I was capable of giving. Would you want less for your new film?"

A puzzled expression came on Adriene's face as he asked, "Why in the world would you give less for this kind of part?"

Marie felt wistful then, as she realized she must confess to him the real reasons for turning down the film. "I recently had a bad personal experience and don't feel I can give to the role what it needs. You're looking at me as if I've lost it. Perhaps I have." She looked away for a moment then faced him squarely. "I trust you, Adriene, and except for a few men in my life whom I consider mentors, I don't trust my feelings to anyone. I'm not right for this part, not at this time. A romantic role on my part wouldn't come across on the screen." Marie stood. Seeing the pained expression on the director's face, she went over to him and hugged him tightly. She walked toward the door and, without turning, whispered, "I'm sorry, Adriene. I hate all men for the moment."

Deep inside, Adriene knew Marie's feelings "for the moment" were just that, feelings for the moment only. He had not completed so many films in his life without seeing that scenario before. In desperation, he sought out Jean Delacroix, knowing he had made himself, if not her lover and benefactor, a close ally and confidant, which in truth was the case. Marie would not date any man, yet she was still seen in the company of Delacroix. Adriene made his case to Jean, and with enthusiastic entreaty from Delacroix, Marie accepted what was to be one of her early triumphs in film.

To the role of Romeo came Jacques Bunole. Born in Paris, Jacques had aspired to acting at an early age. While he was appearing in a French play at age fourteen, he was discovered by Laurence Olivier and brought to Stratford-upon-Avon to study at the renowned Royal Shakespeare Company for the next five years. The British adored him, and no seat went unsold in Stratford for any play in which he performed. When he played Romeo, no curtain came down without a sea of tears by men and women alike. Truffaut was more than aware of Bunole, and in his mind, the two attractive young actors would create on the celluloid screen a romantic tour de force. He had never been so accurate.

Against the passionate advice of Delacroix, Marie instantly recovered from the Galantin betrayal and fell in love with Jacques Bunole. He was at least six feet tall and after visiting the makeup room and costume department, resembled Adonis reborn. And Jacques worked with weights. To Marie, he appeared like a Greek god.

Jacque had been so engrossed in his acting career that he had never developed interest in a man or woman. On the day he met Marie for a talk-through with the script, he took one look at her and never completed six lines.

Their chemistry was so overwhelming Adriene canceled the rehearsal. The director decided the attraction between his two stars must be channeled into the film. Not wanting that kind of energy used off camera, he decided he would try to keep them apart outside the set and enlist other parties interested in the actors: Jean Delacroix and Laurence Olivier. Delacroix took residence in the village where filming was to commence. Olivier, keenly interested in Bunole's career, visited the set and joined the effort to keep Jacque and Marie from having a torrid affair until the film was complete.

Jean was in Marie's company around the clock, except when she went to bed. That alone would never have worked save the fact that Jean called in Alexia LaBrocque, knowing she was the one other person in Marie's life she might listen to. Though he had never met Alexia, Jean had his private helicopter whisk her in from Saint Tropez, where she had just completed a minor film.

Jean and Alexia temporarily prevented the affair, reminding Marie of the disaster with Mario Galantin, and the necessity of using all her energy for the film. However, Olivier, who appeared to be infatuated with Jacques, resorted to threats to keep his young stallion in line.

Mostly indoors, the filming went on for twelve weeks. A break from December 15 to January 10 allowed Marie to go home and be with her family. Delacroix was never out of sight. Jacques Bunole, hopelessly in love, was not allowed anywhere near her.

The relationship between Jean and Marie remained platonic. There were occasions when her sexual frustration almost won Jean what he had intended from the start. One of those occasions took place just before Christmas, in Jean's island apartment. Taking Marie to la Coupole for a late dinner, he enjoyed watching her imbibe too much wine with their meal. He convinced her to join him at home for an after-dinner drink, allowing Marie to wander the sumptuous apartment and eventually his bedroom suite. In the ornate bathroom, she again became mesmerized by the romantic Renoir painting. Jean decided the moment was right. He came up behind her and encircled her waist. "I love you, Marie. Marry me. We'll fly tomorrow to my chateau in Switzerland, and I'll announce to the world you will make me the happiest man on earth."

Though Marie leaned into him, some outside force prevented the union. Jean, raging under his outward demeanor of smiles, held himself in check. He would win. He would win.

℘

For New Year's Eve, Jean arranged for a private room at La Tour d'Argent, one of Paris's most celebrated restaurants. Only a select group of friends were to be at the formal affair. The designer of Jean's fashion house, René Beaumont, was in attendance with his exquisite male companion, Pierre Casadesus. Always in demand due to his outrageous sense of humor and classic looks, Casadesus could have stepped out of the time of Nero in Rome. He dressed in costume when attending private parties and that night wore the purple toga of a caesar. A complete opposite, René always dressed conservatively and usually wore a Pierre Cardin or Yves Saint Laurent suit if not dressed in one of his own designs. That evening he was immaculately dressed in a Brioni tuxedo.

The private party consisted of eleven elegant French men and women plus the Baroness von Tyrotsky, of Russian royalty and Jean's best customer. The baroness was sixty years young and sported a sequined dress made for her by Beaumont. Her diamond necklace and tiara would have ransomed a king, and a talented surgeon had taken away years from her face so she might pass for not even forty. Her seventeen-year-old escort was very handsome, and what he could not supply in table conversation he made up for in the baroness's oversize bed.

Jean had ordered a splendid meal for that evening. A large platter of seafood including shrimp, mussels, clams, and langoustines was served for the appetizer. Poached salmon in the restaurant's delicious tarragon sauce followed. Mashed potatoes whipped with cream and a hint of blue cheese accompanied the meal. Champagne and Jean's own house Montrachet accompanied the spectacle. Dessert consisted of platters of fruit, cheese, and, for those guests who had no concern for calories, tarts, cream puffs, brûlées, and a white-chocolate soufflé.

The evening progressed in a celebratory manner with much toasting to the coming New Year and to each other. Midway through the meal, Casadesus looked at Alexia LaBrocque, who was seated to one side of Jean, and asked, "Alexia, what's the funniest event that happened to you this year?"

Quite tipsy from the wines, Alexia laughed. "Well, it didn't happen to me, but let me tell you what happened to my good friend Muriel." The table conversation ceased, and all turned their eyes to Alexia. Sitting on the other side of Jean, Marie began to lightly snicker. It was a private secret the two girls shared that whenever Alexia wanted to tell a story about herself but felt it inappropriate to let others know it was she, she used the name Muriel. The real-life Muriel was a friend who had moved to America recently to study at UCLA.

"My friend Muriel met a man from America by the name of Charles Sawyer. He said he was on vacation in Paris, a carpenter who worked mostly at Bond Studios in Hollywood. Anyway, poor Muriel teased the man relentlessly whenever he tried to get her in bed. She really wanted to have an affair with him, but according to her, his being American and not speaking our language just turned her off. The man spoke no French, or even tried to. He demanded service from everyone around him and was a boor.

"Even through all of that, Muriel was still attracted. One day, he invited her into the country. He actually packed a rather heavenly lunch. Telling her he wanted to surprise her with a special chacouette sandwich, he disappeared into some nearby trees to prepare the meal while she sat on the blanket he had spread out for her.

"After ten minutes, he came out bearing in front of him a large porcelain plate with a French baguette containing ham, salami, cheese, and lettuce. The roll was nestled between olives, pickles, and fresh carrots. He asked her to get up and take a part of the sandwich. When she tried to lift it off the plate, it remained attached, or so it seemed. Looking closer at the large roll, she noted an unusual object at the end. It was Charlie's cock, specifically the tip of his cock. Muriel told me it was at least a foot long."

Marie had been tittering the whole time Alexia was talking. The baroness stared at Alexia and leaned forward. Pierre and René were also laughing by then and peering intently at her to get on with the conclusion. She smiled at everyone and asked the waiter for a fresh glass of Cristal champagne. The baroness's eyes were large enough to fall out as she said, "Do tell, dear, what happened. They did get it on, no?"

Alexia looked up from her champagne and with a warm smile said, "No, dear. I never asked." And with that the table came apart. Perhaps under normal circumstances, the story would not evoke such laughter;

but taking into consideration the evening, the good feelings, and the warmth of the wine, it was no wonder that everyone present lost their decorum. Marie, who had been laughing quietly with a snicker, started to howl so loudly that even those outside the private dining area stopped their celebrations to listen. Her laughter was infectious, and for five minutes no one stopped. Suddenly, Pierre looked at his watch and announced midnight had long since come and gone. Regardless, it was considered a fabulous evening by one and all.

₭

During the final filming for *Romeo and Juliet*, the fire between the stars vanished for reasons only the gods knew. Two young people who had so much attraction for each other one day found it had disappeared the next. *C'est la vi.*

Then the talent of Adriene Truffaut was put to the test to create the illusion the two were still passionately in love with each other. The production team and director were greatly relieved that the death scene between the two lovers, the most important part of the film, had already been shot, and the picture was finished in spite of the wane of passion between the stars. Another personal triumph for the director.

₭

Marie received rave reviews and, for the second year in a row, won for Best Actress in Cannes. That marked a serious turn in her life for several reasons. Artists International of France, the world's largest and most powerful talent agency, took Marie on as their premier actress. They not only furnished her with a French publicist but retained Patrice Clouzot in America to promote her films and act as a manager for possible roles in the United States. Marie's salary requirements tripled overnight, and she drew as much attention as Brigitte Bardot and Genevieve Dubois, France's number-one draws at the box office.

People other than theater enthusiasts became aware of Marie. Mohammed Reza Pahlavi, the shah of Iran, invited Marie to his palace as a "special guest." His ambassador in France, Houshang Davaloo, met with Marie for lunch and handed her a small gift from the shah, a token of affection. She opened the gift later that evening in her apartment—a diamond necklace with scores of blue-white stones, the center diamond over a half inch in diameter. Marie could not resist doing what so many women have done for time eternal. She went the next day to Cartier, the largest jewelry store in Paris, and asked for an appraisal. The necklace contained 140 carats of perfect blue diamonds, the smallest being one carat and the centerpiece twelve carats. When she heard the cash value, she had to sit down.

Marie never hesitated an instant. She had a courier return the magnificent gift to Houshang Davaloo with a note thanking the shah and stating that the gift and visit were not a possibility under the circumstances.

ℰ෮

Many were the playboys and the aristocrats of older French families who noticed Marie, as well. Every day she received invitations to the "in parties" throughout France, Germany, and Switzerland. Through it all, Jean Delacroix saw the love of his life being drawn into a world he could not control. He raged inside, but on the surface showed only kindness and companionship. After all, he was Marie's most important confidant and therefore privy to all that went on in her personal life. Except romantic interludes. If Marie was overexposed to the crème de la crème of men, she was probably seeking to satisfy the sexual desires he saw in her eyes. Then a certain person chanced into their company. Marie had developed numerous women companions, including aspiring actresses. It was time to take action.

ℰ෮

Jean's apartment was bathed in subtle light. Every bulb was in a soft shade of pink. Controlled by the master dimming switches in each room, the floodlights and lightbulbs did not produce an obvious pink cast. They illuminated the room in such a soft shade of light that one was only aware there was no yellow or white glare. Jean would meet with the young woman in the formal office next to the enormous living room. To Jean's annoyance, she was five minutes late. He paced the room, staring at the warm fire behind the marble-facade fireplace. Reported to have been in the castle of James I, at the moment it served a new master and was so large you could enter it standing up when it was not lit. The ancient mantel from Scotland was over five hundred years old.

The door chimes tinkled in the foyer and Cyril, his valet, brought Jean's special guest to the entrance of the study, where she stood silhouetted in the doorway. Such a marvelous-looking young woman. Why could he not be attracted to her instead of the obsession he had for Marie? Jean welcomed the woman into the converted study. He closed the double doors and invited her to sit on the small chair in front of his massive King Louis XVI desk. Taking a seat in his elaborate, comfortable leather chair, he examined his prospective employee for several moments. That she would take the job was never in question. He had investigated her thoroughly and knew she would be the best one for his secret employ.

"You're very beautiful, my dear," Jean said warmly, putting on all the charm he was capable of. "You received my note about not telling a soul you were going to see me. Have you said anything to anyone about this meeting?" He examined her carefully; if he made a mistake in reading her response, it could be all over between him and Marie.

The woman smiled, and in her response, he read clearly that nothing had escaped her lips about the meeting.

"Good. You've been trying for two years to achieve some headway in your career, but it hasn't happened. How would you like to become as big a star as Marie Savoie? What if I made it possible for you to become financially independent?"

The young woman looked at Jean, and her eyes asked him to continue.

"I will finance your films, and they actually will make money. I will use the best scripts, the best directors, and as you can't act worth a shit, I will get you the best acting coaches available." The girl paled, and Jean detected anger in her face briefly. "You can't pay the rent on your apartment with the roles you've been in. You are in arrears on all your bills, yet you continue trying to stay up with those around you who have made it. Your wonderful companion who was supporting you has fallen on hard times. You would be wise to dump him. I will immediately advance you half a million francs against your salary for a film I am currently backing. You will only costar in the picture with Brigitte Bardot, the principal star, but your director will be the best in France. I want the film to be a success for you, and that will only be guaranteed if the film can carry you, as you cannot carry the film.

"No one must ever know that I am financing your pictures. If you ever betray me, you will be out of the business, even if you have gone to the very top and feel you no longer need me. No one crosses me, ever, and if I have to, I will even go further than blackballing you. If you turn me down tonight and betray me to Marie, your life might easily be in jeopardy. Are you interested? If not, we will end this conversation and the evening now." Jean walked to the nearby side bar and poured a large brandy. He handed the woman the Baccarat glass.

ॐ

The young woman examined the fine crystal glass and smelled the expensive brandy. She stared at Jean in silence. Then her eyes wandered around the spectacular office. A Monet depicting water lilies hung on the wall behind Jean. Other walls held the works of nineteenth-century French masters. Her mind drifted as she took in the opulence. How in the world did someone have such vast resources? She reflected on her short life in that moment of decision. A window had opened for her that night. In life, some people never saw the window open; others didn't recognize the window when it was presented. Perhaps a window of opportunity would never again present itself to her. She looked directly at Jean with no expression whatsoever and said, "What do I have to do?"

New York City, 1962: Patrice Clouzot

Holding a dark, fragrant Havana cigar in one hand, Patrice Clouzot picked up the phone. Who the hell was calling at nine already? Her secretary wasn't even in yet.

"Patrice, it's Marcel Bijot, in Paris. I'm calling about Marie Savoie. John Taylor at Paramount Pictures wants her to appear in a cameo role in *The Carpetbaggers*. George Peppard, one of the principals, is insisting she take one of the guest roles. He's infatuated with her, according to Taylor. The part they've submitted to us stinks, but if we can get some changes, I've convinced Marie it's not a bad idea. We want exposure in the American market, and this is a start."

Patrice puffed on the stubby cigar as they finished the conversation. She strode to her worn Formica desk and reflected on the new French sensation, Marie Savoie.

A stout woman, Patrice was not born with what the world considered femininity. She had a round, jovial face with reddish complexion and had to resort to a hair remover for the noticeable mustache that appeared on her upper lip. Her brown hair was short and curly, illuminated by tuffs of red. To a stranger, her appearance was that of a woman who just went to the hair salon, wasn't sure what color to use, and just had the stylist sprinkle a little red here and there for effect.

Behind the facade was a truly fabulous woman. She had a sparkle in her green eyes and the energy of ten people. When promoting a client for a job, she was a great locomotive making others feel the project they had in mind would not work without the input of Patrice Clouzot. Because her primary job was to seek publicity for stars, she would wine and dine anyone who could further her clients' reputations. News, radio, and television commentators were the nucleus of her contacts.

Patrice's inner office was a disaster area, as her secretary, Judy Smoltz, was not an organized woman. Ms. Smoltz's filing system consisted of stacks of files piled high on her desk, mostly unmarked but tagged in various colors denoting what each star was doing. No one was allowed into the inner office. The outer office and reception area were immaculate.

Patrice had retained the best decorator available. Alphonse Lamada III utilized what he considered a respectable European flair. Although he had never been to Europe or attended design school, Alphonse relied on business from his networking ability. He had a personable attitude that his customers liked, and most of them had never been abroad either. In reality, Alphonse was a Jewish man born in Brooklyn, New York, who dropped out of school at fifteen and ended up in Hollywood looking for Mr. Right. He drifted into interior design and built a reputation in Tinseltown as a connoisseur of fine furnishings. Most of his clientele knew no better anyway.

The occasional Europeans who visited Patrice's offices would return to Europe with descriptions of Ms. Clouzot and her taste in decorating, confirming what most Europeans believed about Americans to begin with. In the large reception room, two matching Victorian sofas faced each other. Framed in mahogany, their fabrics depicted scenes from the Walt Disney picture *Bambi*. A series of oil paintings by Andy Warhol, depicting red-and-white soup cans, adorned each wall. Miniature plaster busts of Hollywood's greatest stars, most presenting comic expressions, sat in every nook and cranny of the room.

In spite of her decor, Patrice Clouzot represented the biggest names in show business, and for the European market, she also acted as manager and agent. Puffing on what was left of the rich Havana, Patrice greedily viewed the photo file on her new client, Marie Savoie. As she gazed at the photos, her mind toyed with hidden fantasies: What a beautiful face and figure. If only the girl had an open mind to sex. It would be incredible to get Marie into bed with her.

Patrice was still in the closet, as were many lesbians in the early 1960s. It wasn't socially acceptable to be in her position and announce her sexual preference. She was conscious of those thoughts as she marveled at the sensational photos. Patrice wanted very much to announce to the world that she was gay, but those in the motion picture business would probably be the last to come out. The theater world adored anyone connected to pictures and had a very narrow mindset for actors' sexuality, much less their publicists.

Setting the pictures aside, Patrice started making calls. Marie Savoie was coming to America, first to New York then on to Hollywood to appear in Harold Robbins's best seller, *The Carpetbaggers*. All of America had fallen in love with the book. Her new client was to have a featured guest role, and it was Patrice's job to make the most of that rather uneventful event. She placed her next call to an old friend at NBC. "Gloria, it's you-know-who. Put me through to Jack Paar."

New York City: West Side Story

The trip from Paris to New York was hardly notable until the comfortable Air France jet made its final approach. Paris, with only the Eiffel Tower standing so tall, had given Marie no warning of the vastness of Manhattan or the startling appearance of its famous skyline. The approach to the airport furnished a spectacular view of the city and surrounding area, awash in lights as daylight faded at only 6:00 p.m.

Marie had traveled lightly and cleared customs with ease. Her American publicist had flown in the previous day to greet her and escort her to all the meetings and appointments scheduled. Marie hit it off splendidly with Patrice, and that started a relationship that would endure for life. Her publicist had chartered a spacious limousine, and they were whisked away to the Mayfair Regent, where a suite of rooms had been prepared for Marie's arrival.

Dario Polata, the manager, greeted his guest and gave her a brief tour. The turn-of-the-century salon on the first floor was the best feature of the hotel. The room held elegant European furnishings surrounded by enormous floral arrangements, which were tastefully displayed. The staff was exceptional, and all spoke French, German, and, of course, English. Adjoining the hotel was the city's premier restaurant, Le Cirque, known for its French cuisine and outrageous prices.

Marie's suite consisted of two rooms: a living area and a bedroom, oversize by European standards. Both were furnished in nineteenth-century pieces, mostly French or English. Fresh-cut flowers were always present.

The suite's per diem price level would make an aristocrat blush. Excited to be the first studio to obtain a guest star of Marie's stature, Paramount Pictures had selected the hotel, and no expense was too high for France's ingenue. They instructed her publicist to make sure Marie enjoyed her first visit to America in style. Patrice should show her the best New York had to offer.

Don Simpson, the president of Paramount, had season tickets to all the shows on Broadway. His front-row-center seats were invaluable. Don enjoyed watching the actors perform and would only attend a play if he could literally see the performers sweat. He had personally called Patrice in Los Angeles. "I want Marie Savoie to see the best we have to offer on Broadway." Tickets for *West Side Story* had sold out six months in advance and were unavailable from ticket brokers, but Don told Patrice to use his tickets. He insisted everything be right for Marie.

"Everyone wants to see that show. And invite her to Sardi's afterward for dinner. I'll call ahead to Leslie Cole and make sure she introduces some of the performers. I'm sure Miss Savoie will be thrilled with Tristan Taylor."

℘

Marie stopped in front of the hall mirror in her suite and examined her appearance. The hotel beauty salon had sent up a stylist to do her hair and a cosmetics specialist to assist with her makeup. Even though she did not have a vain thought in her mind, she did like the way she looked that night. Marie's friends who had seen the play had raved over *West Side Story*, and several of the girls had noted an attraction for the lead singer, Tristan . . . She tried to think of his last name, but, la, she had to get going. Patrice was waiting downstairs. Not even time for a glass of champagne; how the day had sped by.

℘

Tristan was going over a change in the second act to see if it affected his role. No, it didn't. Good. He checked his makeup. What a drag, putting on makeup so as not to appear pale to the audience. On the table in front of him, a red envelope caught his attention. Usually, that was a serious line change. He opened the envelope and recognized Leslie's handwriting:

> Dear Tristan,
> You have a special guest tonight in the audience. A new French
> actress is visiting. Be a nice boy and join her at Sardi's for dinner
> after the performance. I'll be there to protect my interest.
> (ha ha, just a joke)
>
> > > Love and more,
> > > Leslie

The bitch. Protect her interest. She had worked with Tristan for five years and counting. Yes, Leslie had made him a Broadway star, had worked his ass off onstage. His dance routine was good, his voice better than ever, and much of it was her doing. She had provided the best dance teachers available, the best dramatic coaches, including sessions with Lee Strasberg at the Actors Studio. Leslie had made Tristan a serious and talented performer.

What the world at large did not know was the added price he paid on each and every Sunday night the show was dark. Each time, Tristan entered Leslie's penthouse suite on Park Avenue at precisely eight o'clock. Using a passkey she had provided, he entered her twentieth-floor apartment. He passed into the guest bathroom and, again using a special key, opened the wardrobe door. Hanging neatly inside the closet were leather shorts; suspenders riveted with small, round metal studs in sterling silver; and a long, slender whip. He slowly dressed in the scant costume and removed the whip from the closet.

A spiral staircase led to the second floor of the apartment, which consisted of Leslie's sleeping quarters. Her bedroom suite was decorated entirely in black with gold accents. There was no style. Black satin covered the walls, the bed, and the huge down-filled pillows upon the bed. The plush, deep carpeting was also jet-black. Supporting the canopy bed were metal poles gilded in gold. The headboard was a black lacquered swan with entwining wings that swept around to the front of the king-size bed.

The apartment contained a wall of glass on the side overlooking Manhattan's Central Park. The glass was treated so that one could see out but no one could see in, even when the lights were turned on, which was seldom done when Tristan was there. The city's many lights illuminated the bedroom, so it was unnecessary to turn on inside lighting for the purposes Leslie used the room.

Tristan entered the black cavern. Leslie, who never showed herself to the sun's rays, lay in the middle of the bed stark naked, looking at him. He never tired of looking at her white Amazon figure. She was perfect; daily exercise and proper diet kept her looking youthful. Her eyes moved to his, and he stood in front of her as he had been instructed to do so many years before. Bells tinkled lightly in the background — some kind of oriental music she played during the ritual.

A black lacquered ladder stood at the foot of the bed. Tristan ascended it and stared down at Leslie as he had been instructed. She was beautiful to look at — full breasts, no sag, long legs — a perfect body that years later might be called a "ten," but in reality, just perfect. Her angelic face appeared to reflect the epitome of innocence, but innocent she was not. He knew Leslie had been involved with every scene known to mankind dealing with sexuality. Men had used her; women had used her; and the result was dissatisfaction with anything considered normal.

Tristan reached down and undid the buttons of his leather shorts. He unclasped the leather suspenders, and the shorts fell to his feet. He dropped the suspenders to the floor and stood naked before the goddess. Leslie watched him as always, with a look on her face almost of amusement. Her eyes contacted his and told him what move came next, almost hypnotically, finally telling him to move.

Kneeling at the foot of the bed, Tristan unfurled the unusual whip. Its entire length was made with strands of soft hair, Leslie's hair, naturally blonde with a hint of honey. Moving forward, he reached over slowly and caressed her lips with the tip of his finger, lovingly and ever so softly. He touched her face in that manner, and she smiled serenely. Tristan's hands slid unhurriedly down the marvelous body, touching and caressing her so that each passing moment her body relaxed.

Tristan took the whip and carefully laid the strands of hair from the tip of her head to her toes. Slowly, he pulled the whip across Leslie, undulating the motion across her beautiful body. She moaned a little as the tickling continued. Moving her over carefully so she faced down into the soft mattress, he stroked her with the whip and caressed her with his free hand at the same time. If Leslie's back arched, he backed off. It was too soon. He tightly held her undulating body until she stopped moving. Again Tristan turned her, that time on her back, and started over again, more slowly. Tristan made love to her in that manner for nearly an hour.

She looked at Tristan with her doll-like eyes, bidding him to give her the climax she loved so much. With a practiced mouth, he orally made love to her until she was awash in her own substance.

℘

Leslie reached tenderly for Tristan then, knowing that he was completely unsatisfied with the act. She would hold him until she slipped into a deep, deep sleep, all her cares gone and fully satisfied within herself.

In the five years Leslie controlled Tristan's personal life, not once was he allowed to have intercourse with her. She would never share with anyone, not even Tristan, her secret that she hated all men except him. Some strange innermost feeling told her that if she allowed Tristan to penetrate her, the special feeling he brought her would leave. She loved her little game; it gave her the peace she wanted in life. Beginning with Tristan, she had decided no man would ever enter her again.

℘

At precisely seven o'clock in the Hellinger Theatre, the orchestra started the sequence of melodies that would be played during the show. Tristan heard the on-time knock of Jerry Eisenberg, his valet, at his door and rose to descend from the second-floor dressing room area to the stage below. Jerry was talking about the full house while complaining of the ongoing allergies that affected his breathing each night. Used to his devoted valet's complaints, Tristan feigned his usual yes to Jerry's chatter while descending the steeply curved, old cast-iron stairs. As he reached the last step, he caught his sleeve on the banister and slipped forward, hitting his tailbone on the metal stairs. He could not stop his right foot from going through the rails, causing him to twist the foot badly to one side. Tristan tried to rise but could not.

Jerry ran into the wings and brought back a terrified Leslie Cole. "Tristan, are you all right? You're white as a sheet."

Tristan smiled at her. He tried again but could not get up. His right foot would not respond.

Leslie took over at once. "Don't move. It may be broken. Jerry, tell Bob to signal the orchestra to repeat the opening overture." And with that, Leslie grabbed John Sparks, Tristan's backup. Engaged in half-hysterical conversations at the prospect facing them, many of the performers milled about Tristan. John was Tristan's understudy but had never stepped onstage in Tristan's role. Not only was Tristan incapacitated, but the second male lead, who played Riff, had the night off and his regular stand-in was out sick, leaving an inexperienced understudy to perform that role.

℅

Marie had no reason to suspect anything was wrong even though some of the audience were loudly voicing their discomfort when the orchestra started up a third time with the overture. *Odd, the Americans. They don't have any patience.* With that, the curtain parted and the musical began.

Having never seen *West Side Story* or Tristan Taylor, but having heard the music, Marie watched John Sparks in disbelief. As the performance progressed and the audience mumbled among themselves, the rest of the cast was affected, and it truly was a terrible evening for *West Side Story*. When the curtain came down on the first half, nearly half the audience left. Of those who returned for the second half, many booed at the closing curtain. The performance had turned into a complete disaster.

Marie knew almost nothing of Broadway shows except through their music. And she had loved the music of *West Side Story* until that evening's fiasco. She was not optimistic about a late dinner but, having eaten nothing for lunch, agreed to accompany Patrice to Sardi's with Leslie Cole.

Leslie was apologetic for the performance and hopeful that Marie would return to New York soon so she could see a first-class performance by the principals. Marie tried half-heartedly to convince Leslie that she thought the music outstanding and, of course, those things did happen. "I'll come back. I'd like to see the show again."

Marie looked over the menu the waiter had half-thrown at her when she was seated. "What can you recommend for dinner? I'm famished." She could not understand half the things on the menu and was not accustomed to descriptions like porterhouse steak, pot roast, southern-style fried chicken, and all the different pastas and casserole dishes.

She was examining the menu again just as a man at the next table took a bite of a monstrous sandwich half a foot thick and dripping with sauce. She was fascinated as the man managed to bite into the concoction while the sauce poured down one side of his face. Without blinking an eye, he wiped away the greasy residue with a napkin. Glancing around carelessly to see if anyone was watching, he used the sleeve of his shirt to wipe off a blotch that he had missed with the napkin. Then he lifted a green bottle from the table and chugged down most of the contents in a single swallow. The boy next to him was busy trying to stuff into his mouth a longish object that dripped a yellow sauce.

Leslie laughed politely. "Hamburgers and hot dogs are an American tradition, and even served in restaurants like Sardi's." The bottle, of course, was beer, and Marie acknowledged that too was consumed in France, but out of a glass, never from the bottle.

"I suggest the veal medallions," Leslie said. "You probably want something tasty and not too overbearing. I'll order a bottle of French red wine. The selection may not be as good as you're accustomed to, but it'll be passable."

The meal turned out exactly as Leslie described — very tasty and not too heavy. The wine was good, and the table settled down. At length, Marie said to Leslie, "Patrice arranged an appearance for me on *The Tonight Show* later, but I'd like to meet Tristan Taylor before I leave. Did you say he would be joining us for dessert?"

Leslie reflected for an instant, realizing it was Tristan who might end up as dessert for the breathtaking French beauty. "Yes, my dear, I'm sure he'll join us soon."

ဢ

The Kettering Emergency Hospital at Sixty-Ninth Street and Third Avenue was filled to capacity with a never-ending flow of emergencies that evening. With Jerry's assistance, Tristan had finally seen a doctor, who diagnosed him with a bad sprain, gave him a painkiller, and bandaged the ankle. He told Tristan he could walk with the assistance of a cane but make no strenuous efforts for at least a week. Tristan was not pleased, especially having to meet Leslie next and tell her the news. He glanced at his watch and noted it was after nine thirty. Shit, and he was looking forward to meeting the French actress, Marie Savoie. Well, if he was lucky enough to catch a cab, he'd just make dessert.

ဢ

Sipping her coffee, Marie noted it was nine forty-five. Patrice tapped her leg under the table and eyed the door. "La, it's getting late," Marie said. "Thanks for the evening, Leslie, but I don't want to be late . . ."

"No, no, just a few minutes more. Stay and meet Tristan, dear. You'll love him, and he might need some cheer."

"Well, maybe a few more minutes, but I really must be leaving soon."

ဢ

"Son of a bitch, what do you mean you only want to work the East Side!" Tristan yelled after the large yellow taxi as it fled up Third Avenue. Fabulous Manhattan and its cabs. No one in their right mind would drive in New York, so a sea of yellow cabs took people wherever they had to go. However, God forbid they were late for a meeting and needed to get to the West Side of Manhattan from the East Side. Tristan looked again at his watch. "Damn. Ten fifteen."

ဢ

Patrice looked restless enough to jump from her seat. It was quarter past ten. In front of Marie was the *West Side Story* cast program showing Tristan Taylor on the cover. He looked quite charming, and she had been looking forward to their meeting. Well, maybe just a few more minutes.

ဢ

When Tristan hobbled into Sardi's at ten twenty-five, Leslie ran over and hugged him tightly. "You're walking, thank God for that. Will you be able to perform tomorrow?" As she led him to their table, Tristan repeated what the doctor had said. Cast members were bubbling over with some merriment by then about the evening's disaster.

Tristan greeted everyone then looked at Leslie. "Where's Miss Savoie? I thought she was joining us for dinner."

"She did, Tristan, but she's gone. I can't believe you missed each other. She left as you came in."

ℰↄ

"What do you think of America so far, Marie?" Jack Paar asked, fully expecting a canned response. Her description of Americans eating hamburgers and guzzling beer, and the *West Side Story* evening had the audience in tears laughing.

"So, you think New York is interesting, wait until you see Los Angeles. In LA, the people ride horses to work, and the closest thing to a good restaurant is five hundred miles away in San Francisco." Jack was joking, but his deadpan expression, which did not fool the audience, left Marie saying only, "Oh my."

Los Angeles: The Beverly Hills Hotel

Marie and Patrice left New York early the next day. Having spent a whirlwind week in Manhattan doing two television and several magazine and newspaper interviews, Marie was tired and slept during the entire six-hour flight.

Patrice had arranged separate transportation for each of them in LA, as they were heading in opposite directions. When the limousine picked Marie up, she looked for the horses at once. Seeing none, she asked the elderly driver where they were.

He glanced up to his rearview mirror. "Horses, you say? Yes, ma'am, you can rent a horse in the park anytime you want. I'll take you there later if you want me to."

With that positive response, Marie continued to look for people riding horses, until they reached her hotel.

The Beverly Hills Hotel was the equivalent of the George V Hotel in Paris, except that gentlemen were required to wear a tie to enter the George V's bar for a drink. The Beverly Hills Hotel first opened its doors in 1912. Located on Sunset Boulevard in the heart of Los Angeles's most wealthy community, it was the meeting place of the rich and famous, Americans and foreigners alike. The hotel was known for its private bungalows, spacious suites, and world-famous cocktail bar, the Polo Lounge. Buster Keaton, Charlie Chaplin, Errol Flynn, John Barrymore, Douglas Fairbanks, Clara Bow, Marion Davies, Loretta Young, and Gloria Swanson were a handful of the motion picture stars who stayed at the hotel or consummated a contract in the renowned lounge.

The famous lounge area was divided into two sections. One first entered the cocktail bar with its plush green-velvet booths. Recognized stars and celebrities were led to one of a dozen such booths, all marked reserved. Country boys from Arkansas arriving for a meeting of the Rotary International Men's Club were pleasantly greeted by the maître d', Carlo Spimante, and led to the standing bar. It was not unusual for a celebrity to arrive early for a meeting and find most booths vacant yet the bar area three deep with looky-loos waiting for a glimpse of Mr. or Ms. Famous.

Having slept soundly on her flight, Marie was wide awake and anxious to see the famous studios she had heard about in Paris. Patrice met her in the Polo Lounge for a light lunch. It was just past two, and most of the lunch crowd had left. As the two followed the maître d' through the bar area, Marie quietly asked Patrice, "Who are those beautiful women seated at the bar? I don't recognize any of them. Are they actresses?"

Patrice smiled and laughed lightly, pulling Marie through to the garden area of the lounge. "No, my lovely. Most of them are hookers."

"Hookers. You mean prostitutes?"

"Yes, they're all girls who Carlo, the maître d', permits to sit and visit with the regulars who come by for their services."

"They're very pretty. In Paris, this is a no-no. The girls must be in special bars just for that purpose. Most of the high-class call girls in France are part of a service run by an elegant woman in Paris who provides the girls to only the wealthy. I don't know her name. However, the most beautiful young Parisians who want to earn a great deal of money are in her service. It is even said some do it for sheer pleasure and care little about the monetary rewards."

The conversation went on as the two were seated under a huge walnut tree that grew in the middle of the courtyard. Patrice ordered champagne, and lunch consisted of large goblets of fresh shrimp in a tasty red sauce.

Marie had been in America just over a week and was elated to be totally alone. She had managed to convince Jean Delacroix that she wanted complete freedom the next few weeks. She enjoyed her liberty immensely and loved her new companion and publicist who did everything to make her happy. La, that was a splendid journey, and possibly somewhere in that vast, noisy city she might even meet someone in a romantic way. For a fleeting instant, she reflected vaguely on the missed connection with Tristan Taylor in New York. She tried to bring his face into focus but couldn't.

⃝

On the other side of the patio was a man dressed conservatively in a Brooks Brothers English-style suit. He could have been a businessman staying at the hotel. His appearance might lead one to suspect he was even a studio executive. He was certainly neither. John Barber was an American private detective hired to watch every move Marie Savoie made. He had been given carte blanche expenses and utilized two of his best detectives in addition to himself to carry out the surveillance. She was to be watched twenty-four hours a day. The observation had started in New York and would be finished in Los Angeles.

Hollywood: The Carpetbaggers

The Carpetbaggers film was eagerly anticipated worldwide. The book was described by many as "you just can't put it down." It was a well-crafted roman à clef, leaving many to wonder if such notables as Jean Harlow, Howard Hughes, and a young John Wayne were the principals of the story. It was Hollywood in its heyday, set sometime in the 1930s. For such a huge best seller, casting was a bit unusual. George Peppard, Carroll Baker, and Alan Ladd were the leading stars.

That was Hollywood's first serious attempt at showing the inside workings of a major studio. The story, of course, was much broader than that, but in the attempt to portray the "Hollywood story," the picture fell far short.

Marie's small role as a guest star was that of a short love interest of one of Hollywood's fictional moguls purported to be Howard Hughes in real life. Her part was finished in two days of shooting on the sound stage at Paramount. Though she thought the scenes went well, they were eventually left on the floor of the editing room. In the end, Marie would not appear in *The Carpetbaggers*, and when she saw the film in France the following year, neither would she be disappointed that she had been left out.

Working opposite George Peppard was interesting, but nothing developed between him and Marie on screen or off. Alan Ladd, on the other hand, was very handsome, and Marie found herself instantly attracted to him. Like so many men who entered Marie's life only to be intimidated by her long, raven-colored hair and beautiful face, Alan placed himself in the role of mentor and protector. She sensed he was enamored with her, but at the same time, he clearly indicated he was to be her friend and nothing more.

It was George Peppard who persisted in attempting a conquest, and to Marie's dismay, she could not dissuade him from trying. Not wanting to be rude, she joined George for a drink one afternoon at the Polo Lounge. He immediately went on the attack. "Why not, Marie? Look at me—I'm charming, youthful, and will promote your working here in serious roles. I've great connections in this town. In a way, I own part of Hollywood. Have an affair with me."

George and Marie sat in one of the plush green-velvet booths. As he worked on a third double-gin martini, Marie sipped her third glass of champagne. A large platter of the lounge's famous liver pâté with garlic lay on the table between them.

Marie tried to be polite and direct at the same time. "I really don't want to get involved with a married man," she said, a little high from the effects of the champagne. "You have children. You love your wife. Why me?"

"You're driving me crazy. Do you know it was my idea to have you come here for the film? I saw you in *Romeo and Juliet* and fell in love with you like half the world did. I must have you." George reached under the table and caressed Marie's hand. He said huskily, "Let me get a room, no a bungalow. Let's spend the night together. Please."

After the frustration of so many nights alone and only the company of Jean Delacroix, Marie was greatly enjoying the attention of one of America's famous celebrities. How tempting that situation might be if she were attracted to him in the slightest way. La, what to do? "George, let's have coffee. I'm going to bed in my own bungalow tonight, and, so sorry to say, without you. I admire you, respect you, and I want us to be good friends always. Look, here comes Louella Parsons to say hello. She's interviewing me tomorrow for her newspaper. Hello, Louella. Sit down and have a cup of coffee with us."

Marie had met Miss Parsons on the set previously and was looking forward to giving Louella her views on her French films, along with her first reflections of America. With a dismayed look, George stood, greeted Louella warmly, and said good night to both ladies. Marie and Louella watched him leave, smiling at each other.

"He's quite the ladies' man, you know," Louella said. "He thinks every woman should be interested in him. I hear he went for Italy's Sofia Vaskeli without luck. Has he asked you to bed yet?"

"Not at all," Marie lied. "I find him very charming, very direct, and very sexy, but he is married with children, and my head is somewhere else right now."

"You're more than generous. I'll enjoy our interview tomorrow, to be sure." Louella glanced around. "Ah, no time for coffee after all. I'll see you at lunch tomorrow, the Ambassador Hotel. Have a good evening, Marie, and make sure your door is locked tonight. American actors are charming, but when they have a drink or two, they don't like taking no for an answer." Both women laughed. Louella moved a few tables away to begin a conversation with Charlton Heston, and Marie went to dress for dinner.

☙

Marie was to spend her last evening in Hollywood at Chasen's with Vanessa Daniells and her aristocratic husband, Baron Rolf von Snipes of Holstein, for dinner. Marie had heard rumors that the marriage was really one of convenience for Miss Daniells and that she kept an ongoing affair with some singer in New York.

Having adored Vanessa in her films, Marie was excited to meet her, and took great pains to prepare for the evening. Opening her wardrobe closet in the small bungalow, she carefully went through the six formal dresses she had brought. Most were long, sequined, one-of-a-kind designs made exclusively for her by Jean Delacroix's design studio. She tried on the crimson-red, full-length sequined dress. It was her favorite and set off her dark auburn hair perfectly. Matching shoes by René Mancini and a full-length Russian sable coat would complete the evening's outfit. Marie walked to the full-length mirror in the dressing room and studied her appearance. She would call in the hotel cosmetologist, Pamela Brown, to apply the essentials, and Gene Shacove himself would style her hair. She wanted everything to be perfect.

ॐ

Vanessa paced the lengthy bedroom and dressing area in her spacious Bel Air home. The baron was in his room, preparing for the evening. She had just terminated a ferocious fight with Rolf over Tristan Taylor. Rolf had accused her of having an affair with the singer, and she had vehemently denied it. So what if occasionally she had sex with Tristan? She was aware of the hold Leslie Cole had on him. When Vanessa occasionally got away to New York, she loved being with Tristan, mostly as just a friend.

Able to talk together about any subject in the world, Vanessa and Tristan supported each other completely. It mattered not if the subject were political, practical, or deeply personal. They were on the same wavelength and would be for a lifetime. Once in a great while, a little too much sadness in one of their lives coupled with a little too much wine and led to a comforting evening in bed.

Those occasions were never planned, and only Tristan yearned for a more permanent relationship. "Vanessa," he would murmur, "I love you. I understand you. Leave Rolf and come live with me."

Vanessa would inevitably laugh lightly and say, "Yes, yes, love, and who would take care of me in the style I'm accustomed to? Tristan, I'll always love you, but I must have extreme wealth and live in the clouds. You know me. I can't just be with one man or I'll die. I'm a big, bad romantic and will die one. The most exciting thing for me is to know I might walk down any street and meet someone new who I'll fall into instant and heavenly love with. Isn't that how we met, my bad boy? If I moved in with you, we would ruin the one thing I love most about you. You're the only male friend in my whole life. I can always come to you when I'm in trouble." Then Vanessa would disappear from Tristan's life.

As she paced the room, she fumed over Rolf's threats against her and Tristan. She loved the lifestyle Rolf had brought her into, but it was becoming a pain. It was perfectly okay for *him* to screw whomever he wanted, and there were many according to the press and her friends. The Europeans had a strange philosophy when it came to marriage. Somehow they accepted the man's having a mistress, but never the woman. What crap.

Vanessa snapped. She had thought always of Rolf's castles, yachts, planes, and endless costly gifts as something she could not live without. That was over. Not that she would divorce the baron right away. The relationship was finished, but she would gradually ease her way out. In a year, she would free herself regardless of the monetary loss. In the meantime . . .

Standing in front of the gilt mirror doors of her dressing room, Vanessa pondered what to wear that evening at Chasen's. She opened the custom closet that held her long, formal gowns. Her newest was in crimson red, a copy of a dress featured in Jean Delacroix's newest couturier line and not available for sale. She had attended the fashion show in Paris; and when the model wearing the splendid full-length, sequined dress had paraded the gown, Vanessa tried to buy it at once, only to be informed it had been designed exclusively for another. As there were photographs available of the entire show, she obtained a set and had Bond Studios make her a copy of the red gown. That night she would meet French sensation Marie Savoie and wear the new dress.

℘

The maître d' escorted Marie to the large booth. Baron Rolf von Snipes rose and took her hand, bowing slightly to kiss her extended fingers. "Welcome to Hollywood, Miss Savoie." He turned and introduced Marie to several elegantly dressed persons, including the consul general from Germany and his beautiful blonde wife, Sonja. The men all stood to say hello, and the women smiled. "You must forgive Vanessa. She's always late for her dinner parties. Let me order you a drink."

Marie was seated, and polite table conversation began. The baron was in the middle of describing one of his hunting lodges when he suddenly stood. "Here's our Vanessa." Marie stood to greet her.

Vanessa nearly froze in place. Though she recognized Marie Savoie at once from the film *Romeo and Juliet*, there in person an enormous wave of emotion swept through her—a recognition of kindred spirits. Everything appeared in slow motion as she neared Marie, but as the sounds ceased and the light faded, a dark wall came between her and the anticipated vision. It was not to be, as the light came back and the sounds of the restaurant woke her from the momentary trance. For an instant afterward, she saw herself in Marie but suddenly was overcome with laughter. It was Marie's red dress . . . the dress Vanessa had copied from the Delacroix collection. Immediately, she realized it was the original designer gown.

Marie reached out to embrace her. By then, Vanessa felt the blood rushing to her face. "My God, Miss Daniells. What have I done?" Marie asked.

Vanessa finally remembered she had made a last-minute change of her wardrobe—deciding against the red dress—and let out a cry of relief. As she put her arms around the red-faced Marie, she leaned close and whispered what had *almost* occurred. The conversation, and the laughter from both women, intermingled with the relief Vanessa felt, cementing an instant bond between them.

Rolf, who had tried to seat Marie next to him, and Vanessa against the opposite wall, found the two inseparable. No amount of joking could gain Marie's attention, and he finally gave up any attempt.

The evening was a smashing success for Vanessa and Marie, who chattered away almost as if no others were present. Both hardly ate anything but did imbibe a bit too much wine. They parted company that night, Marie having to catch a plane back to Paris and Vanessa ready to start a new film. They vowed to see each other soon. Not letting go of Vanessa's hand, Marie whispered, "It's as if we've known each other forever. Please visit me if you're in France."

§

Late that night, Vanessa stood in front of her dressing room mirrors again, lost in her thoughts. From the bedroom she heard Rolf talking about the evening and something about not getting any attention. His words faded. A sadness came to her, as the new friend she had made was leaving the country tomorrow. How strange was the special bond she felt toward Marie. The red dress? No, it was something else, and for the first time in her life, Vanessa closed her eyes and wished for a vision to tell her of the strong affinity she felt for the French actress. No vision came, no matter how much she concentrated.

Vanessa finished undressing with a warmth she had not felt in a long time. Her decision to leave Rolf was a great relief. They would remain friends, of that she was sure. She reflected again on Marie, whose energy level was like her own, as if she had a fire burning inside her. Marie's enthusiasm for everything was like her own, and Vanessa sensed Marie was genuine in all things.

Seated in front of her art deco dressing room table, Vanessa removed her makeup. She completed the process without thought, as always. In the large antique mirror, she glanced at the incredible Matisse painting that hung behind her — a forest and primitive animals. Next to the painting was the antique clock she had brought from her home in Beverly Hills. It had hung in her living room, and something about it drew Vanessa toward a memory. When she tried to recall what it was about the clock, the vision came, but it was not of Marie. It had been such a long time since she had a vision that the occurrence was more like a dream. The lights in the room faded, and the night sounds outside her window vanished.

Tristan sat near the edge of a narrow river with ancient buildings on each side. A strange boat with bright lights was passing through. The boat had a bank of windows — some kind of tour boat. It was evening, and large floodlights lit both sides of the shoreline. Tristan's face was illuminated then and showed a great sadness. Tears streamed down his cheeks. Vanessa could feel his desire to end his life.

Her heart contracted, and she let out a cry, finding herself back in the present. She reached for the phone and dialed Tristan's number in New York, where it was the middle of the night. The phone rang and rang. In complete panic, she called everyone, including Leslie Cole. The two had met several times and were not exactly great friends, each knowing exactly where the other stood with Tristan.

"No, Tristan is not with me. He has never slept over. We don't have that kind of relationship, Vanessa dear. It's three in the morning. Is there anything else I can help you with?"

Vanessa hung up. *Bitch.*

New York City: Mark Hellinger Theatre

It was 3:00 a.m., and Tristan sat on the empty stage, lost in thought. He had been there for three hours, reflecting on the past several years of his life. They had been exciting. He recalled the initial rush of being propelled into the Broadway spotlight and to the acclaim of his peers. Tristan had thought he wanted the life and energy of the popular musicals he loved. In the early years, he had loved going onstage every time he performed. The adrenaline rush had been indescribable, but he wanted more out of life than spending it on Broadway.

Tristan's agent had contacted him earlier in the year, asking him to take the lead in the movie version of *West Side*, but much to his own surprise, Tristan had turned it down. Finally, the reason came to him clearly: it was time to move on. To where, he did not know. In the morning, he would give the required six-month notice. That part of his life was over. What was next was anything but clear. He would find what was right for him.

Elated then, Tristan felt as if a heavy weight had been lifted from his spirit. He returned to his West Side apartment, where the phone ringing. It was 4:00 a.m.

Paris: Marie's Apartment

The Air France jet lifted off the runway for its ten-hour flight to Paris. Marie looked out of her cabin window and over the Los Angeles Basin. Even at the end of winter the weather was spectacular. Warm and warmer, unlike the cold conditions in Paris.

Alexia LaBrocque had called the day before to confirm Marie's departure. "Come home, Marie. We love you. We all miss you, and I can't bear your being away another day. You're asking me about the weather? Silly girl, you better wear a fur. It's as cold as the North Pole. See you at the airport. We're coming to pick you up personally."

"Who's we?"

"Delacroix and I, my love. Hugs and kisses. See you in the morning."

Marie looked out over the ocean before closing her eyes. Her mind drifted off slowly. Her last thought was of Delacroix — *I'll just deal with the inevitable. I've put him off now and won't think about it till he pushes me* — and Marie slid into a deep, wondrous sleep.

$$\wp$$

It had been raining for five days. A wind accompanied the April showers, and a chill was in the air. The landscape was coming alive with the approaching summer, and with the rains, the city looked crisp and fresh. Marie sat in her new apartment in Luxembourg Gardens. The large, luxurious apartment looked out over the park, which gave Marie a feeling of being somewhere in the country just outside Paris. The apartment was not her idea. Jean had wanted her to be more comfortable, and she had let him take over with locating and furnishing it. That had kept him busy while she was in America.

$$\wp$$

By using dozens of laborers working twenty-four hours a day, Jean had converted the apartment into a little jewel in less than two weeks. The furnishings were from his warehouse located just outside Paris. The end result was spectacular, with fine furnishings and all the necessary decorations to set them off. Knowing Marie was not phlegmatic in her taste, he mixed fine antiques from Asia, England, and France in such a manner that the result was truly superb.

The apartment consisted of two large bedrooms, two maids' rooms, a formal dining room, and a spacious living area. Utilizing antique furnishings of the different countries, he set each room up in its own style. The living room was decorated in French furniture upholstered in new fabrics and covered with soft down cushions.

The dining room was in Queen Ann style with one wall covered entirely by a sixteen-foot Chippendale mirror. That was actually a mischievous touch by Jean. A Victorian dining table ran the length of the room, and placing himself at the end, he could use the mirror to view every person at the table.

The master bedroom was the crème de la crème. Jean had outdone himself with Marie's bedroom and bath. In actuality, he had converted two large bedrooms to one and refurbished the elegant art deco bathroom that was last done in the 1920s. Utilizing his endless warehouse, he furnished the bedroom entirely in sixteenth-century Mandarin-Chinese style. Elegant tapestries adorned every wall, depicting scenes of hunting and horses; carp ponds and landscapes; beautiful geishas; and architectural masterpieces of castles. Adjustable lighting illuminated the walls in any tone Marie might desire.

In the middle of the vast bedroom was Jean's favorite piece of furniture, a bed he would not utilize in his apartment, as it was appropriate only for whom he had always intended: his mistress. The extraordinary Chinese wedding bed dated to a sixteenth-century Mandarin emperor. The elaborate carved headboard panels depicted the stages of a long life for the person who slept there. The bed was equivalent to two king-size American beds and could comfortably sleep six. The throw pillows were covered in Chinese fabric and filled with soft down. An original fireplace in one corner was covered in blue Mandarin tile. Fu dogs decorated each end of the fireplace and held in their paws a silver screen to keep back any spark from hitting the antique rugs that lay on the floor.

Marie's bathroom was a masterpiece containing an enormous shower and tub area behind a wall of glass. By closing the single door, one could turn the area into a steam room. The hand-painted tile walls depicted flowers of all kinds, but especially lilies, Marie's favorite. One wall bore a treasure Jean knew she would love. He had taken his beloved Renoir from his own bathroom and installed it in hers.

8⟩

When Marie had arrived to see the apartment for the first time, she said, "Jean, how in the world can I pay for this, even with my new success?"

Jean looked offended. "It's my gift, Marie." But the look that time in Jean's eyes was different.

"I can't accept this. You're going to want something I can't give you."

"I know, Marie," he said, his voice strained.

ℰℴ

They stood in the marvelous bedroom, and Jean seated himself on an oriental chaise at the foot of the bed. He bent forward and lowered his head. Jean Delacroix was incapable of gentle emotion. There was a lack in his chemistry, a biological malfunction that occurred only in certain people, both men and women. Jean actually stifled a cry then, but the cry was not of hurt, or that of a broken heart; it was the anguished cry of failure. Jean never lost at anything, and he did not lose face with anybody. He was hopelessly in love with Marie, desperately in love with her, and in that moment of despair, obsessed beyond reason with her.

ℰℴ

Having no boundary for her compassion, Marie put her arms around the man she so highly respected but had no sensual feelings for. "Jean, please. If I accept this, it means I must give up something dear to me. I want this lifestyle but need to earn it for myself. I know you love me, and I know you want me to be part of your life in a way I can't be right now. I can't even tell you that someday it will be different, which is why I can't take anything like this from you."

Jean had not achieved his success in life without being quite clever. In that moment, his mind formulated a new plan. He stood and hugged Marie. Putting on his biggest smile, he said, "Of course. I understand, but you do have the income to pay the rent, and even a small amount for the loan of my furniture. I'm going to my home in Saint Moritz this weekend. Please be my guest, and I'll explain how you can afford your new lifestyle."

Saint Moritz, Switzerland: Chateau Delacroix

Built in the 1920s by Jean's father, Bernard, Chateau Delacroix was situated at the highest point of Saint Moritz that was accessible by car. The view was, to say the least, spectacular. The valley in front and the surrounding mountains exposed the village and countryside in its entire splendor. The tiny village of Saint Moritz featured one of the best hotels in Europe: the Palace Hotel, where people stayed if they did not own one of the nearby chalets. Notables throughout the world lodged there, and one of Europe's most famous playboys, Gunter Sachs, owned the entire top floor.

A guest of Mr. Sachs once described a party given by Gunter when he was a young man. "A special elevator that was only used to take you to the penthouse deposited you at the hall entrance to the Sachs apartments. You waited at the door till it was opened by Mr. Sachs himself, who stood before two bulletproof plate-glass doors, one several feet behind the other. In the first glass door was a small opening. Next to you was a table with a small-caliber handgun. Mr. Sachs would stand behind the second glass door and invite each of the women to take the handgun, insert it through the opening in the first door, and take a shot at him anywhere they chose. He kept a record of who shot at what part of his body. As they arrived, the rest of his guests applauded the shooters' aims."

Saint Moritz was the playground of the famous and the wealthy. Marie had never been there. Most people journeyed up the narrow-gauge railway from the base of the mountain near Zurich, which took nearly half a day. Jean Delacroix would have none of that. His small Lear jet whisked Marie and him from Orly Airport in Paris directly to Zurich, where his Bell helicopter awaited them. The four-seat Bell traveled the fifty miles to Jean's mountain chateau. He escorted Marie to her suite of rooms.

The chateau had its own electric generators, and all the utilities were self-contained. Jean could reside there a year and not be dependent upon anything from the outside world. The staff for the twenty-bedroom chateau were fifteen full-time workers in the winter when guests were infrequent, thirty beginning in April when he welcomed his first guests of the year, and forty when Jean opened the chateau for the summer.

"The rooms are beautiful." Marie crossed to the large French windows. "My God, the view is breathtaking. I don't think I could leave here if it were mine."

"Marry me, Marie, and I'll give it to you as a wedding gift." Jean put on a false smile as if he might be joking. Marie didn't bite and kept running from window to window to see the different views. Above the main floors, her suite of rooms was housed in a corner turret and allowed a panoramic view.

Jean followed Marie onto the large balcony that stood on one side of the apartment. It was decorated with carved-marble furniture. "Now that you're here, I want you to know that I've contacted your agent and manager, as well as your attorney, regarding a business proposal for you. No, don't look alarmed. It's not marriage and it is absolutely genuine. I'll explain everything to you tomorrow at lunch, when your representatives are here. I've invited them to stay for the weekend, and I have some entertainment planned for all of you. Why don't I leave you to rest. Do come down for cocktails at seven. Dinner's at eight."

Jean embraced Marie, and she felt his firm body against hers. La, why did she feel no attraction? Why did she almost feel revulsion when he touched her? "Yes, Jean." She politely pecked him on the cheek. "By the way, please be a sweetheart and bring Alexia here. I really want her to be with us this week."

For an instant, Jean hesitated. With another smile, he said, "Of course, love. Anything you want," and he was gone.

Marie went back to the windows facing the village and tried to discern the antlike people moving to and fro. What was it Jean had in mind? She was certain it meant her freedom, and prepared herself to refuse even before she heard the proposition.

That evening was subdued, like the quiet before the storm. Normally animated and talkative, Jean was quiet. Marie tried a little small talk but to no avail. Jean did not even try to persuade her to stay for a Frangelico after dinner. She finally let it go and took her departure after dessert.

$\wp$

Jean sat by himself in the chateau's main room, in front of an enormous fireplace fully engulfed in flame from a pile of pine logs. Over the mantle hung a large portrait of Bernard Delacroix, dead for over twenty years. Jean gazed into his eyes. How much his father would have disapproved of his life. He had been so ethical, so very practical with his own life. His ethics would never have allowed him to be so dishonest in a relationship.

How Jean had both hated and admired the old man. He reflected for the hundredth time how his father was in the process of changing the will so that none of the future Delacroixs would have great personal wealth, only a generous yearly allowance. His father had been concerned that sooner or later an heir would come along and squander the vast fortune. How the Fates had interceded to end that life. Jean would never have wished his father to depart the earth in the manner he did. Ah, well, that was life. He smiled to himself; yes, life was a bitch for some people, but not for him. *I will never lose. I know I'm possessed with Marie, but I'll win her no matter how long or costly. Tomorrow will begin my new strategy. She won't refuse me.*

Those thoughts rambled in his mind as he ascended the stairs to his quarters. Taking out his passkey, Jean entered his bedroom suite. The sitting room was elegantly comfortable, decorated in a ballet theme. Six oils by Edgar Degas hung on one wall. A French chaise longue was beneath the paintings, and seated in the middle was the beautiful young woman he had retained to watch Marie and report back to him anything and everything his beloved obsession confided to her.

The girl wore only panties, and Jean studied her graceful body. A smile parted her lips, and she extended her hands to him. "How is the bitch?"

Jean slapped her across the face with no warning, but controlled the strike so it did no damage. The girl sat up, anger showing in her face, but instantly smiled again. "You're mad, Jean, and I love you anyway. Come. Take me now." She removed the panties and lay back on the chaise.

"Not here. Come with me." Jean led her to his inner sanctum, a strange room off limits to everyone but the cleaning staff. The walls were painted stark white and nearly covered in photographs of Jean from his childhood through his teens, plus several pictures of his mother, Grace. From a large oil portrait, she looked down at the twin bed Jean had slept in as a child.

There was nothing special about the bed—cast iron, white paint that had faded here and there. A normal twin mattress covered the bed frame, and a nondescript quilt covered a few warm blankets on top. Jean pulled the girl down on the bed and embraced her tightly with his strong arms.

She looked into his eyes. "What did Marie say today?"

Jean's smile was almost grotesque. He put his hand over her mouth to quiet her. Taking his rigid manhood, he entered her at once. Jean was well endowed, and she screamed with unmistakable delight, obviously loving the feeling of his fullness. Placing his forearm against her neck in sadomasochistic snuffing, he pushed tightly against her so she could not budge as he pounded her relentlessly. As she started to lose consciousness, he lessened the pressure. He worked on her in that manner for thirty minutes, allowing her to come to a complete climax on several occasions. At the very end, as she was again about to pass out, he released himself into her, yelling the name of his beloved Marie.

The girl looked up at Jean. "Amazing, love," she breathed. "But you haven't answered my question. What did Marie tell you today?"

He looked at her indifferently and responded, "She wants Alexia LaBrocque."

℘

Covered with a heavy wool shawl, Marie stood on her balcony in the cool April evening. The lights of the Palace Hotel and surrounding countryside homes were sparkling like small jewels. She walked to the retaining wall and let her mind drift to what Jean had in mind for her on the morrow. At the far end of the flat entry to the grounds, the helipad lights came on, nearly blinding her with their high-voltage beams. Directly beneath, two persons walked toward the Bell helicopter, which had just started its engine.

Marie instantly recognized Jean's tall figure, but the person walking beside him was covered by a long trench coat that also hid her face. That it was a woman Marie easily recognized by her walk. She studied the two until they reached the aircraft. Helping the woman enter, Jean waved off the pilot, and in a few seconds, the craft was gone.

Marie retired for the night. Strange. Who could the woman be? And there was something about the way she walked that reminded Marie of someone. *La, it just won't come. Maybe tomorrow.* The memory faded away as Marie drifted into a deep and dreamless sleep.

℘

It was a hectic morning at the chateau. Jean busied himself with his chef in the kitchen, making sure everything would be letter perfect for the late lunch that day. He also was meticulous with his choice of dress for the meal, as well as instructions to his staff for Marie's well-being. In fact, Jean had orchestrated the entire week's luncheons and dinners at the chateau, as well as at the chalets of a few nearby friends.

As a surprise for Marie, Jean had his pilots bring Solange Vinges, her hairstylist, and Lucy Saint James, her make up girl, for the week's stay. Alexia LaBrocque arrived with Emile DuBols, the director of a film she was to star in. After completing a film in Rome, Emile had flown to Paris to join Alexia, who had arrived home the previous evening. They came in on the Bell aircraft together, marveling at the view as the helicopter flew up the canyon between the two huge mountains surrounding Saint Moritz. At precisely noon, the aircraft delivered Marie's attorney, Henri Deroches; her agent, Guy Thoreaux; and her French publicist, Sylvie Carne.

The lunch was as exceptional as Jean had planned. Everyone seemed in an excellent mood for the meeting that was to follow. Jean led his guests into a room organized for exactly that purpose—a meeting room that could accommodate up to twenty-five persons comfortably around a solid-black teak conference table. Jean seated himself at one end and asked Marie to sit at the opposite end.

"I hope you have all enjoyed your brief stay so far. I know everyone is aware I want to make a business proposal to my good friend Marie regarding an idea I've had for some time now." Looking at Deroches, he continued. "Henri, I am having this meeting tape-recorded and will give you a copy so you can transcribe it later should you wish.

"Marie's film *Romeo and Juliet* has set new attendance records in France, as well as in every county it has shown. I conducted a poll of select theaters and determined that Marie's image as a new star has surpassed Brigitte Bardot. Many theatergoers feel she is a serious actress and want to see her in serious films.

"As to the potential of my good friend, let me share this. One of the questions we included was, who does Marie remind you of that you might consider your favorite actress of the past twenty years. Can anyone here guess the response?"

Guy Thoreaux responded at once. "I've known it for some time, and all of Marie's directors have told me that she resembles and has the same acting style as Greta Garbo." The table conversation buzzed momentarily in agreement—all, of course, except Marie, whose face paled at the statement.

"I conducted another survey in every country where Marie's films have been shown, to analyze advertising benefits for my clothing line as well as my cosmetics company, if Marie were my role model, my representative of sorts. I examined the advertising programs of Chanel, Yves Saint Laurent, and Givenchy. I studied the models they have used over the decade and note they do not utilize one face in any consistent manner."

Taking a moment to catch his breath, Jean signaled to his wine steward to serve champagne or drinks to his guests. The wine steward worked his way around the elegant table, memorized what every person wanted, and took leave to bring the drinks.

By then Jean had everyone's attention. "And so, my plan is to take the world's newest film ingenue, my beautiful Marie Savoie, and make her my companies' personal star. She will appear in all of our ads — clothing and cosmetics — and I want her to appear personally in Paris's annual haute couture show, representing our designer, René Beaumont."

Jean waited as the refreshments were served. "Marie will be given a lifetime contract to represent Delacroix Industries. I, in turn, will pay her an annual flat salary of ten million francs a year." For an instant there was silence, followed by a collective gasp. No one had ever made that type of offer to any celebrity, anywhere in the world. Not even Elizabeth Taylor or Marilyn Monroe in America had been approached with a contract of that magnitude.

"The 'lifetime' contract, in reality, means as long as Marie is active in film. I see the day when women will not just want the youths of the world to be their role models. Our studies indicate that it is women over forty who buy our designer line, women over thirty-five who buy the more expensive cosmetics and perfumes. I want to take a limited gamble that Marie will become one of the legends of film this next decade."

Jean paused to let what he had said sink in. There was not a sound in the room as he sipped his Perrier and lemon. Marie's representatives were speechless, as was the object of his obsession. She looked at him then, and he could feel in his bones that she believed everything he had said, every word. And why not? Nothing he had uttered was exaggerated in any way, except a fact only he knew and would never disclose: Had he wanted to, it mattered not if he were to choose any of the leading women of that time — Elizabeth Taylor, Sophia Loren, Marilyn Monroe, or Audrey Hepburn. He could have made any one of them the Delacroix Industries fashion model and representative. But that afternoon, with just the right amount of food and wine, the magnificent setting of his home, and above all, Jean's genuine enthusiasm, he had everyone in the palm of his hand, including Marie.

Concluding his presentation, Jean pointed out that each year, Marie would automatically receive no less than a five-percent raise and would, of course, be free to continue her career in film.

For an actress who was just being recognized as an international star, and yet to star in her first American film, F10 million was serious money. The contracts were signed in Paris on May 1, 1962. The world's leading fashion photographer, Peter Byrd, was called in from Australia for the first cosmetics ads, as well as shots of Jean's couturier line for release in twenty international fashion magazines.

Two weeks after the photo sessions began, Peter and Marie became lovers. Neither knew what hit them. He had ended a lengthy affair with Australian pop singer Noelle Calla and fallen madly in love with Marie upon sight. Marie, having finally found a man she was both physically and romantically attracted to, gave in to her heart. She desperately wanted his affection and was greatly attracted to him physically. And so Peter moved in with Marie, into the elegant apartment Jean had so elaborately furnished, and they soon married.

℘

Caught completely off guard by the disruption to his elaborate plan, Jean seethed in his apartment in Ile Saint-Louis. His father—in a strange way Jean's mentor—had once said to him, "Son, don't ever make a plan you know won't fail, especially when it's a plan of the heart. The heart of man is never as smart as the heart of woman. A woman's heart never responds to a plan."

Jean reflected on that conversation, but it did no good. A silent rage coursed through him, so he closed his eyes and entered a state of meditation. Only that concentration would keep him rational. He must go on; he must go on and in the end win, for there was nothing else in life but the game. He had lost that engagement, but in the end, he would win. He would win. Somehow, someday, he would win.

PART IV: JEAN DELACROIX

Paris, 1793: The Delacroix Empire

July 12, 1793, was a blazing summer day in Paris. Charlotte Corday, a self-appointed leader in spirit of the French Revolution had assigned herself that day to carry out a mission of utmost importance for the people of France. She wandered the streets of Paris before taking a carriage to the section called Rue des Cordeliers. Standing outside a prominent home, Charlotte rang the bell. A young woman answered the door.

Charlotte put on a big smile. "My name is Charlotte Corday, and I am here as a concerned citizen of France to see our dedicated leader Jean-Paul Marat. I have a list of conspirators to give him."

The woman looked askance at Charlotte. "Monsieur Marat is too ill now to see anyone."

Charlotte hesitated, then asked if she could leave a message. She hastily scribbled a note stating she could inform Jean-Paul of a plot being planned in the city of Caen by the Girondins, who were known to be conspiring against him.

She again paced the streets before eating a simple lunch and emboldening herself with a glass of strong wine before returning to the house of Marat. That time when she arrived, fresh bread was just being delivered. She passed in unnoticed and got all the way up to the bedrooms. The stench of illness was thick in the air, stronger as she approached the farthest room. He must be there. Just as she thought she could enter the room, the woman grabbed her arm. An argument broke out, and Charlotte raised her voice loudly to attract Marat's attention. "I have names of traitors that must be given to Jean-Paul at once."

A man's weak voice called from one of the rooms. "Let her in, Catherine."

The woman led her into the bathroom where Marat was bathing. He was slouched in the hot water, with a cloth tied about his brow, his arm slung over the side of the tub. Charlotte talked for fifteen minutes, describing the persons she thought were plotting to kill him. Proudly displaying her Jacobinic beliefs, she finished naming the plotters. Marat's response was quick and to the point. "Good. In a few days, I'll have them all guillotined."

Charlotte was seated by then in a chair next to the bath. Without warning, she rose and pulled a long dagger from the top of her dress.

She struck once, savagely, beneath Marat's right clavicle, severing his carotid artery. Within minutes, he was dead. When the police arrived, she defiantly screamed. "Vive la France! Vive la France! Vive la France! . . ."

℘

Marat had succeeded in all his ambitions, and only the ultimate fate stopped him from enjoying what he had won. He had instinctively known the power that would result from controlling the weapons factories during the Revolution. Long before, he had cunningly calculated taking over munitions and arms manufacturing. With a secret plan, he had carefully influenced those on the Revolutionary Tribunal with bribes or gifts of feminine services favored at the time.

One of those services was called the sharing of "assets" — captured aristocrats, women who would later face the Revolutionary Tribunal, after being "shared." Partaking of the little treasures was supposed to be a secret. Those who participated agreed that anyone talking publicly about the sharing of assets would be guillotined within twenty-four hours.

One documented account survived that period and translates as follows:

The revolutionary guards picked up the Duke and Duchess Le Guay in their chateau just outside Versailles. The duke's guards put up a small resistance but were massacred to the last man. The duke was taken at once to the Bastille and incarcerated. His notoriously beautiful wife, Nicole, was brought to my apartments near the Tuileries.

She was in a state of shock, and when I locked my bedroom door behind her, she burst into tears. She was wearing countless valuable items of jewelry, which could pay the expenses of a Parisian family for an entire lifetime. I found myself aroused by her antics and, approaching her where she was lying prone on the floor, reached down and tore her dress off. She struggled with a show of great strength, which aroused me even more so. I struck her once across the face to cut her resistance.

Momentarily, she stopped struggling, giving me time to remove the rest of her clothing with not too much difficulty. I removed my own clothing and again reached for her. She started to struggle again, so I pinned her down to the floor. She had the most beautiful body I have ever seen, and I will never forget the passion I felt as I took her on the floor that night. She started again to struggle violently, so I grasped one of her arms and pinned it against her back so she could not struggle without great pain.

I was so engorged by then, I found it very difficult to penetrate her. She was very tight, and it occurred to me she was probably sixteen or seventeen at the most. I finally managed to open her up, and she was now screaming very loudly. The louder she carried on, the more excited I became. I must have fucked her an hour or more before relieving myself.

I lay there listening to her weep for a while. Getting up, I walked over to my cabinet and poured a glass of cognac. The duchess was blubbering, just looking up at the ceiling. I watched her in complete silence for about thirty minutes. I could not take my eyes off her and, with no warning, became stiff once more.

I went over again and looked down on her. She was motionless, and I reached down and turned her over. Her behind was even tighter than her vagina, and it took me a few minutes to work myself into her. She was screaming again, and it aroused me to a feverish state. I went on with her the entire evening and was amazed at the way I found myself enflamed almost without end. After four hours, nothing came out of me, but I continued with her until dawn.

Calling my servant, I had her locked into a spare bedroom. I slept until late in the day and, upon waking, immediately rushed into the room to have at her again. This went on for three days and nights. On the fourth day, I turned her over to the Tribunal.

And so Marat had built his influence and wealth utilizing every means possible.

෨

Joseph Delacroix received the news of his uncle's death with immense shock. The relationship between them had been very close from the time he was a little boy. Brought up by Marat, at twenty-three Joseph had been placed in charge of the munitions and arms factories. The only heir to the vast fortune Marat had amassed, Joseph had the natural talent to continue in the role of his mentor.

Mastering the diplomatic mazes of France, Joseph made sure he was in the camp of the Girondins, the Jacobins, the sectionnaires, and other splinter groups that were fighting for control of the nation. He wove his way among the groups in such a manner that, in the end, he alone would survive the purges that destroyed others trying to create their own financial empires within France.

Joseph was a brilliant and naturally talented capitalist. The factories he inherited were the oldest in France, some dating back centuries. He kept the old family names on those firms, setting up a simple plan to distance himself so he could not be recognized as having the controlling interest. He had the words *For the People of France* added to most of the facilities. Joseph was wise, and almost 75 percent of his profits were earmarked for bribes, payoffs, and charities that actually housed and fed those in need.

Political unrest continued until the end of the eighteenth century, when a new power took the reins of France. On November 8–9, 1799, a coup d'ètat occurred, ending the residing government, the Directory. A new constitution was formed, and the popular general, Napoleon Bonaparte, was vested the power of First Consul. The end of the French Revolution brought about major changes throughout France. That influence reached all of Europe. Absolute monarchy was ended forever in France, as were the large feudal estates of the nobility.

In that climate Joseph Delacroix found himself. Working in a minefield, knowing that if he stepped on the wrong person, his life was over. One morning, he was having an early breakfast with his family when a knock at the door interrupted their conversation. The consul's own guard summoned him to his office, ordering him to come with them at once. He was not even given time to properly dress.

The First Consul's spectacular offices were in the residence of former French aristocrat Pierre Robier, who had been killed with his entire family during the Reign of Terror. The enormous apartment had been converted to elegant staff rooms where the business of state could be conducted under Napoleon's watchful eye. Each room had its own purpose, and that day, Joseph Delacroix was escorted directly to the office of the First Consul himself. Napoleon sat behind the very desk Louis XVI had used in Versailles. Tapestries from the king's palace had been draped throughout the room, as well. Bronze torches were everywhere, as Bonaparte often worked through the night.

Joseph had never seen Napoleon and expected to see a large person. To his surprise, a stocky man stood to greet him. "Ah, Citizen Delacroix. I'm very happy you have spared time for me on such short notice. Please, take a seat here next to me, and we will discuss your role with the new constitution in France. Your uncle and I did not agree on many matters, but his ideals were good and he served France well. An untimely and terrible way to end one's life, but it was his destiny.

"Do you know that every person's destiny is written in the stars? Do you follow astrology? It's absolutely amazing how accurate things can be. I have a man that forecasts my life chart on a daily basis. I won't start the day without meeting him first. Let me give you a perfect example. Just today I wanted to know the outcome of our meeting. I called in Robert . . . yes, it's Robert who does my charts. We sat together for twenty minutes, discussing how you would work into what I have in mind. He said your reaction to my proposal would be very sympathetic toward me and, of course, to the cause of France."

Joseph was astonished at the high energy Bonaparte transmitted. Although he was a bit skeptical about Napoleon before, he realized the man was actually exceptional. As the meeting progressed, Joseph was impressed with Napoleon's convictions and his serious love for France. He was fully aware that his future was on the line.

"Joseph—may I call you Joseph? I have asked you to see me today because as First Consul, I have decided to establish a new banking system called the Bank of France. I have received the names of many candidates for the presidency of the bank. Your name was frequently mentioned. Having read a lengthy report on your activities, I feel you would be appropriate as president.

"You will be directly responsible for all the bank's dealings and send me monthly reports on its progress. I will expect you to take adequate but minimal compensation. However, the position will provide you with privileged information. I suspect you might use that information for your own gain, and that is fine with me. I myself will allocate to you certain sums of money that I expect to enhance my own income. Of course, we will disguise those funds as you have disguised your own assets."

Joseph's breath caught at the consul's words. As clever as Joseph had been, apparently investigators had traced the factories to him. Sweat broke out on his brow, and the great general stared at him intently.

Napoleon laughed loudly and continued. "Don't be alarmed, my fine friend. Your future and my future are interwoven. I'm not going to interfere with the empire you are building. It is to my benefit to have you in my camp. France is still in an upheaval and will be for decades. I have expansive plans for our country, and access to its military production facilities is of the utmost importance."

After Joseph was appointed the first minister of the Bank of France, he immediately reviewed the simple plan he had originally put into effect regarding the ownership of the various plants. He enhanced the concept so that, as the political tides changed in France, it would not be easily discovered that, in truth, the factories belonged to him.

The new constitution decreed that all businesses were to be of public record and the names of the owners registered with the Republic. Joseph did exactly that. The title of each business was placed in the name of a manager, who became the legal owner. However, as the constitution allowed, Delacroix Industries held the mortgage of the land and improvements. Through carefully arranged contracts, the equity of each asset would never exceed the debt of the mortgage.

In addition, as Joseph advanced the initial capital for each company, Delacroix Industries was entitled to a percentage of the profits, carefully structured and closely detailed so that, in effect, 90 percent of all profits went to him. Delacroix Industries was careful to reinvest large percentages of profits to public benefit. Delacroix Charities ran the University of France as well as the Institute of France.

Joseph made sure that no member of the newly formed government could, or would, point a finger in his direction. As the political climate changed over the years, he changed or remade those policies, ensuring that nothing interrupted the empire he was building within France.

France entered the great Napoleonic Wars, which fed the enormous factories and created new industries as industrialization began. Fifteen years of tremendous progress went by for Joseph. He built his empire, and he secretly made an immense fortune for Napoleon Bonaparte. His monthly reports never faltered, and even the temporary abdication of Napoleon on April 10, 1814, did not deter the ongoing arrangements. In 1815, recurring turmoil among Bonapartists, the moderate Royalists, and the Republicans resulted in a victory by the Royalists. A surge in domestic recovery pushed the Delacroix Empire to new heights.

Joseph walked a political tightrope for the next thirty years as France tried to settle down from the Revolution. As each party vied for power, Joseph, with the assistance of an army of advisers, made sure each and every base was covered. Every person who aspired to great political office was in the financial hold of Joseph.

Toward the middle of the century, Louis Philippe, Duke of Orleans, took power in France and was instrumental for the expansion of the Delacroix Empire. In 1842, Joseph, then seventy-two years old, obtained the contract for construction of a railroad system to cover all of France. Through Louis Philippe's assistance, he received one of the most lucrative contracts in French history.

Joseph Delacroix died quietly on June 27, 1845, with his wife, Sabine, by his side. His son, Luis, was just twenty and took over the vast holdings of Delacroix Industries, aided by his father's countless advisers. He would prove as competent a manager as his father.

℘

The year 1850 arrived and along with it, Napoleon III. Under the guise of savior of society from radical revolution, the son of Napoleon

Bonaparte took power. Luis Delacroix secretly supported his rise, and his financial assistance enabled Napoleon III to make his mark. Under his administration, French industrial growth blossomed. The railway track tripled, banking institutions flourished, and the Delacroix Empire grew.

For years, Delacroix Industries had supplied the army with uniforms, and Luis decided to set up plants in Ireland and Scotland. Reaching for a secondary market, he experimented with clothing for the general public. He soon discovered that by producing high-quality fabric, he could overtake his competition. The first of his family to take a personal interest in his own wardrobe, Luis hired the best designers of that period. In a short while, Delacroix Industries was producing some of the finest fashions in Europe.

In 1895, as Luis approached his seventieth birthday, he looked to his eldest son, Bernard, to carry on the family dynasty.

ʕʘ

Having inherited the skillful genes of his forefathers, Bernard took to the management of the family empire with great enthusiasm. More than anything else, Bernard's tremendous accounting abilities improved the family's holdings. He soon discovered that fraud was rampant within the companies. Most of the managers were accumulating their own wealth through a series of false accountings, which in the past were not carefully audited. It was time for a major reform in the original plan of individual ownership.

All of the manager-owners, as well as the heirs of their company holdings, were required to sign a proxy giving Delacroix the right to vote on their behalf during company meetings. In a daring move, Bernard held a private board meeting for Delacroix Industries and used his proxies to acquire their holdings. He bought out each manager-owner at the specified sum described in the original contracts dating back to the early nineteenth century.

Joseph Delacroix had realized that a day would come when total capitalism would take place not only in France but worldwide. He had made provision for a day of reckoning. That day had arrived. The original contracts were structured so that if a manager made any contention to the buyout, he stood to lose everything. Within Delacroix Industries' 1206 major companies throughout the world, only two persons disputed the contract. After years of litigation, the empire prevailed, and the two manager-owners received nothing. Within a few years, speculators estimated the net worth of the centrally controlled organization to be $500 billion.

As the twentieth century began, Bernard continued building a vast financial empire that would survive through the century and beyond. That network of wealth was so well organized that no matter what political or financial catastrophe occurred, nothing could deter the growth of Delacroix's massive personal fortune.

With the coming of World War I, the great war machine poured billions of dollars into Delacroix factories. France suffered enormous losses both in men and resources. By the end of the war, Bernard himself had lost two sons and a daughter, who had served their beloved country in its crisis; but he, his wife, and one young son survived. And most certainly the fortune that monumental organization was building continued into the 1920s and '30s. Then the winds of war began to blow again.

Berlin, January 12, 1940: The Reichstag

The Reichstag was an imposing building during World War II. It was exceptionally cold that early January evening. The Führer had called Goering and his close advisers to a six o'clock meeting about the details to be effected upon the occupation of France. As usual, the meeting room was in strict order. Each chair behind the long conference table was perfectly placed, the floor immaculately clean. No smoking was allowed, and those staff members who could not give up the dirty habit had huddled outside the Reichstag, pulling a last drag into their lungs before the meeting started.

At precisely 6:01, with all staff present and seated, Adolf Hitler walked in and took his customary seat at the head of the table. Everyone rose and saluted the commander in chief. He waved for them to be seated and looked around the table casually. His eyes greeted each person individually — a twinkle of sorts here, a stiff look there, an indifferent look for those who had on occasion questioned the master's will.

৪১

Hitler took a sip of medicinal tea that contained an antigas remedy to relieve his constant indigestion. Few outside his closest comrades knew that Adolf Hitler suffered from a severe form of colitis, as well as Parkinson's disease. The smell that emanated from his body during the lengthy meetings was ignored.

Ordering an officer to pull down a detailed map of France, Hitler began. "You see these red swastikas placed on the French map? They indicate key factories for our war needs. There are three thousand and forty-two locations that must, and will, be utilized for the continuing production of arms and munitions used in our master plan of conquest. Without these factories, we will have tremendous hardship supplying our troops with clothes, food, transportation, and most importantly, weapons and munitions. In a moment, SS Commander Alois Brunner will describe specifically the plans for converting these factories to our standards and needs.

"However, before he speaks to you, I want one thing to be perfectly clear: these French bastards won't cooperate without resistance. They resisted in the first war, and they will certainly resist now. I have devised a plan to get their cooperation."

Having just had an injection of his "vitamins" from his personal physician after dinner, Hitler was smiling. But the smile was no smile of happiness. It was malicious and vindictive.

The twinkle in the Führer's eyes signaled individual messages to every person in the room: Obey the letter of my will, or die. You will listen carefully, and my orders will be carried out, with no exceptions.

Paris, 1940: Gestapo Headquarters

Bernard Delacroix, his wife, Grace, and their son, Jean, stood in a large conference room in gestapo headquarters. Paris had surrendered twenty-four hours earlier, but the actuality and enormity of the circumstances had not registered fully in Bernard's mind. Yes, of course, he'd had ample opportunity to whisk his family away, but they had refused to leave, thinking it best to face the occupying force and save the historical legacy that had been passed down to them. The three huddled at one end of the steel conference table.

Bernard was comforting his family when two uniformed storm troopers entered the room, carrying submachine guns. Their Nazi insignia identified them as special officers. A man dressed in the black uniform of the Schutzstaffel—commonly known as the SS—followed them. The man was good looking, about thirty years of age with light-blond hair, dark-blue eyes, and fair skin. He strode to the Delacroixs.

"My name is General Felix von Damm. Field Marshall Theodor Dannecker has appointed me to take charge of all interrogations and interviews in Paris. Please, sit down and join me for a coffee. I hope we have not inconvenienced one of our first families of France. I know your history and had a chat with the Führer about you just before our invasion. Please excuse our temporary occupation of your great country."

A large breakfast cart bearing fresh rolls and coffee was brought in and von Damm assisted Grace with her coffee. "Ah, sugar and cream? Just cream. Please sit down, and we will continue our little chat."

He sat next to Bernard. "As I started to say, we are here as your guests. I want our visit to be beneficial to everyone, French and German alike. No reason to unnecessarily disrupt or jeopardize the life of a single German or French citizen, wouldn't you agree?" Giving Bernard no time to respond, von Damm rose and started pacing behind them. He walked a short distance away with his back toward the family, then returned each time he spoke. His ever-present warm smile and courtesy were relaxing. The Delacroix family had their little breakfast and sat back, listening to the friendly officer.

సౌ

Felix von Damm was one of Adolf Hitler's favorite SS officers. Schooled in America, he graduated from Stanford University. He not only finished first in his 1930 class but outdistanced the rest of the class so far that he was given a two-year scholarship to complete his master's degree in political science at Harvard University. Felix was a skilled orator who could mesmerize an audience, if the subject matter interested him enough. He returned to Germany in 1934 and was personally introduced to the Führer by Herman Wilhelm Goering.

Hitler saw an immediate use for von Damm as a member of his SS and in particular chose him to head up political interrogations. He was a master of political manipulation. Over the next six years, von Damm proved himself completely reliable and efficient in interrogations dealing with uncooperative foreign agents. Then he was assigned as gestapo chief for the occupation of France and worked out of the Paris office.

℅

Von Damm continued pacing behind the family. His French was impeccable. General von Damm spoke six languages fluently. "It is critical that the factories under your family's control continue to operate for our mutual benefit. The German government will reimburse you, of course, with continued revenues from the factories as we deem appropriate. Your lifestyle will not be interrupted, and you and your entire family will enjoy the protection of the Third Reich. We will even allow you to travel in and out of the country without notifying us, except that one of you three will remain here while the others are away. In return for your cooperation, we will treat your factory workers with special consideration, as we will with you. Your plant managers will also enjoy the Führer's protection and be treated with due respect."

℅

Bernard was feeling quite well at that point, pleasantly surprised by the SS officer's promises. Von Damm's charm and boyish personality gave the heir of the Delacroix fortune a feeling that everything was going to be fine. As relief flooded through Bernard, von Damm patted him on the back and opened a briefcase he had brought in with him, removing a five-page typed agreement. "Please sign and date this letter. It is just a confirmation of what I have stated."

Word by word, Bernard read the draft. It stated all that the officer had said, but went on to elaborate the penalties for noncompliance. Bernard reddened as he finished. "But, general, this document provides for the execution of any worker not basically performing his job at the discretion of the SS. It states their families may be executed. How can I enter into an agreement like this?"

Sitting again beside Bernard, von Damm patted his cheek gently, much like a father might do to a child he is instructing. "But of course you understand this contract contains the dictated policies of the Third Reich. You must not look at all the small dots and dashes. Why question anything when you know the policies will be carried out without your assistance?"

Bernard lowered his head, realizing the trap he was in. For two hundred fifty years, countless families had labored to build the Delacroix Empire. With the enormous responsibility of that history, how could he betray the families working under his direction. He looked at the young officer, seeing only a kind expression on his face, and said, "I cannot and will not allow you to take over the factories in this manner and with my written consent."

Von Damm looked painfully hurt. He rose and started pacing again, as if pondering his next move. He walked to Bernard, motioned for him to follow, and led him to the other end of the room. With no warning, he pulled his Luger pistol from his holster and fired a single round into Bernard's head. The bullet exited the back of his skull, and a stream of blood spurted onto the gray wall. Bernard dropped to the floor, mercifully and instantly dead. Grace collapsed to the floor, unconscious.

ℂ

Twenty-four-year-old Jean Delacroix stood and stared at von Damm. Jean did not flinch a muscle, and his eyes never left the SS officer's face. Before the shot was fired, he had guessed the outcome of their meeting. He had followed the trap von Damm laid for his father. Obviously, a careful study had been made of both his father and him prior to that sham of a meeting. If he could have, he would have silenced his father and taken control, but nothing would have changed the outcome. Bernard's loyalty to the workers and to France would have prevented him from allowing Jean to take over.

Jean also realized that his father's murder was probably planned in advance. The officer's information file would have told him that Bernard was no longer acting manager of Delacroix Industries. Two years before, he had passed on the reins to Jean. The murder was an elaborate intimidation designed to put Jean in a panic. Though the young man destined to continue the Delacroix Empire exhibited a youthful appearance and composure, in reality, Jean's posturing was a sham.

The Delacroix Empire had lasted one and a half centuries with the head of the family dedicated to one purpose only: the extension of their empire for the mutual benefit of Delacroixs to come and their beloved France. Jean Delacroix would exceed even that. While attending Menlo Park's School of Business in San Francisco, Jean had taken an IQ test, registering a record-breaking 184. His mental ability for anticipating people and things around him was three times faster than a person categorized as a genius. His father could have continued as director of the Delacroix Empire for another decade but had realized there was a giftedness in his son that would carry the family's fortune to new heights.

୫୦

Fritz von Damm needed Jean Delacroix. Without the family head, chaos would prevail within the Delacroix factories. He was prepared to make minor concessions to achieve his goal. The Führer had been quite specific in January relative to the Delacroix management. "You will use your influence in any manner you see fit to get cooperation from them. I will count on your superior mind and cunning to do it any way you want, but either the father or the son must appear to take charge of the plants and run the daily business as if nothing had happened. You will not fail me." It was not Fritz's intention to fail.

He smiled and walked over to Jean, whose mother was still unconscious at his feet. Still holding the Luger in his right hand, he brushed Jean's cheek with his left. He spoke softly and in a normal tone. "I don't want to have to shoot your mother now, young man. Have I your attention?"

Jean responded, also in a normal voice. "Yes. I have just one small favor to ask you."

Paris, 1944: Ile Saint-Louis

The war that had ravaged most of the world was reaching an end. On August 25, 1944, the Allies liberated Paris from German occupation, and France again was free. For many in France, and throughout the world, it was bittersweet. Some had lost all or part of their family. Some had lost that and every material possession they had. For a select few, the war had brought prosperity, as they had benefited from it in some manner. Those few, most of whom had worked or cooperated with the Vichy government of France, would keep those gains. For one man, peace meant he had survived the war and owned even greater material wealth than before. His name was Jean Delacroix.

Two weeks prior to the surrender of the city, a meeting had taken place in a luxurious apartment on Ile Saint-Louis, located near Notre Dame Cathedral. The apartment complex was once the home of Coco Chanel. The meeting was between two men: Jean Delacroix, who owned the landmark apartment, and SS General Felix von Damm.

The two men were alone, seated in the living room under a massive painting of lilies by Monet. They sat opposite each other at a small chess table. The chess set was like no other — two sets of playing pieces cast in solid gold and solid silver. Tiny but exquisite precious stones adorned each piece. A decanter of 1834 Napoleon brandy sat on the table. The snifters were by Saint-Louis Crystal works and bore the Delacroix crest.

As the intense chess match ended, Felix sighed heavily. "It's over, you know. Paris will be occupied in two weeks. I'm to report back to Berlin at once." He glanced around the room. "We have played each other here these past four years at least once a week, and you haven't let me win once. I had never lost at chess until I met you.

"You fooled me in our first meeting. I never guessed how smart you were. You had total control of everything after that. I thought I was manipulating you, but all the while, you had the upper hand. I would not have believed in a thousand years that we would lose this war. Yet you knew from the start the Allies would kick our butts.

"You planned that whole scenario about announcing your arrest and then us releasing you to take management of your factories. It was your idea to sabotage useless equipment and give the Resistance information that led them to blow up empty rail cars. It was a good plan. It utilized their forces to work on stupid projects instead of using the same forces to destroy important military objectives. It made you a hero to the Resistance. It will make you a hero of France. It worked well for you, and now it will work for me. I only regret having to kill your father that first day. It was really Theodor Dannecker who gave those orders before I left Berlin. We never planned on letting him live."

℘

Jean looked intently at von Damm then. Of course, a madman like Hitler could never have won the war. Jean had figured out how to win in the end. He would have been dumb and dumber not to. He merely had fed von Damm's ego, along with giving him what he wanted anyway. He never had a choice in that matter. It was either cooperate with the Germans or die. Jean had chosen not to follow his father's path. What good would it have done him? What good would it have served the factories or the workers? And Delacroix Industries got special concessions as a result. The workers and their families survived as well as any might have under the conditions.

Jean reflected on that as he responded. "Yes, Felix, I do understand, and after all, four years have passed. I have accepted what happened." Jean paused then, filling up von Damm's glass with the aromatic brandy. "I have the suitcases packed for you with the diamonds. They're the two large cases you passed at the front door when you came in tonight. Your men can take them out for you when we finish the last game. You will play me one more time? Perhaps you will win. I feel it is your lucky night tonight."

The two men exchanged smiles, and the board was reset for a final match. Jean again looked at Felix. "You know, I really have come to like you. I would like to share with you my little secret. No one knows this secret—it is very egotistical, not something one boasts about. I think life is nothing other than a game of chess. One does not win or lose the game because of luck. One plays this game for all it is worth, and winning is all that life is worth. Only the winners survive. The losers lose and will always lose.

"I have no respect for the losers. In reality, I have little respect for anyone other than myself. Of course I respect you, Felix. Never doubt my respect for you. I wanted to share this last memory with you before you leave. You are going where? Oh, yes. You are not to tell me. Let us say Shangri-la, and I will continue with my heritage."

The two played awhile longer. Jean won quickly and said goodnight. He retired to his room, closed the drapes to the massive, luxurious suite, lay down in the great bed, and slept for eighteen hours. It was finally over.

છ

With its three engines humming loudly, the German Junkers Ju 52 entered Swiss airspace, leaving France behind. The plane had to climb to an altitude of twenty-four thousand feet in order to clear the mountains before descending into Geneva. Fritz von Damm looked down over the snow-covered mountains and let his thoughts drift to the life in front of him. A group of his family's friends would meet him in Geneva and supply him with a false passport and documents enabling him to continue on to Rio de Janeiro. A plastic surgeon would change his face in Brazil, and Felix would live out his life in luxury. As the aircraft continued its ascent over the mountains, he pondered what he might do in Rio.

Felix's thoughts turned to Jean Delacroix. How odd it had been to murder Jean's father in the manner he had and still go on to have such a close relationship with the son. What a cold and ruthless man Jean Delacroix was. In spite of his own father's murder, he had been warm toward Fritz those four years, as if they had been close friends forever. Nothing was too difficult for Jean to get for the SS officer, whether it be a girl for the evening or some unavailable delicacy. In a strange way, he would miss Jean.

Felix glanced out the window again at the snow-covered summit of the mountain in front of him. It was the last image implanted in the SS officer's mind. When the plane reached twenty-four thousand feet, two pressure bombs, hidden in the false bottoms of the diamond cases, ignited. Nothing was ever found of the plane, or the diamonds.

Jean never lost a single chess match in his lifetime. Jean Delacroix never lost at anything.

Paris, 1948: Annette Bjorg

After the end of the war, France began economic recovery under the leadership of Charles de Gaulle. To say France was becoming a country to reckon with internationally would not be true; then again, all of Europe was recovering from the devastation of Hitler's insanity. With one exception. The Delacroix Empire was flourishing.

Jean Delacroix threw all of his energy into the revitalization of company assets, principally the factories the Germans had converted for their own war machine. Having hidden cash assets safely in Swiss banks and vaults before the invasion, Jean utilized a fraction of those funds to modernize the factories and replace old equipment with new. Delacroix textile factories in Scotland and Ireland were converted to the most modern facilities anywhere in the world, and sales of the high-quality goods were monumental. The French government placed massive orders for arms and equipment with Delacroix contracts, as did other European countries that had not been attached by the communist arm of Russia. Overall, as France struggled, Delacroix flourished in the sunshine of good fortune.

At thirty-one Jean had changed from a rather gangly young man to one who radiated tremendous strength, both outwardly and inwardly. He was vigorous in his daily exercise workouts, spending at least an hour daily in his private residential gyms. A trainer was always present for his workouts to make sure he utilized proper form. The results held for him many good things. Men and women alike admired his appearance. He radiated a strong, mature look, and if he was conducting a business transaction, he had everyone's attention. If he was in a social situation, he also got attention.

Jean had always admired men and women who dressed well. He had just opened the largest women's couturier fashion house in Paris: Delacroix Designs. Jean had hired Chanel's leading designer, René Beaumont, away from them. Beaumont created a theme he had envisioned for years but was not allowed to produce for Chanel. As a result, in 1948, Delacroix Designs captured the market's interest and received worldwide recognition in their first year at the spring fashion show in Paris.

Stunning beauties from around the globe modeled clothing from the world's best fashion houses. As Jean watched the show, he noticed Danish model Annette Bjorg. Not one of Jean's girls, she had attached herself to Dior. They too made a fabulous showing that year. However, Jean was not interested in the clothes but the Scandinavian model.

Annette stood tall even for a model. Her hair was very blonde and very short. Her cleavage matched her body, a proportion which was not favored in the modeling circles of the 1940s. In effect, she was an Amazon, and Jean was immensely interested. Not only did her spectacular looks catch his attention, but the way she carried herself, like a queen. As he sat in the audience, he decided he wanted her, and he wanted her at once.

The show ended late in the evening, and Jean pulled René aside to ask about the Amazon from Dior. René boasted he had turned the girl away from their own fashion house because of her unusual modeling presence. However, he was sure she would still be interested in meeting Jean without hesitation.

The models were backstage, changing into street clothes. Annette Bjorg was putting on her shoes when Jean entered the crowded room with René, who introduced him to her. "Daaling Annette, you looked ravishing tonight. I'm so sorry we didn't grab you when you came to us last year. I want to introduce you to Jean Delacroix. He thinks if you should change your mind about modeling for Mr. Dior, you might give us a second chance."

In response, her tone was just right, and a clever, though young, Annette smiled mischievously at both men. "Why wouldn't I consider. After all, isn't everything negotiable?"

Jean laughed and took her hand firmly, coaxing her to leave as he invited her to dinner at la Coupole. Many of the crowd that night would head for the landmark restaurant, and he knew she would love to be seen with one of the heroes of France. After all, everyone in France had read at least one article about Jean's heroic acts of sabotage against the Nazis while supposedly working under their authority.

℘

Jean and Annette walked into la Coupole hand in hand. It was a marvelous vision as Jean, at six feet two, matched Annette's height in her heels. The maître d' seated them at once. The dozens of onlookers, who had been waiting forever for *any* table, watched in envy as Jean and Annette were seated in a booth with a white-linen tablecloth. Only special, regular customers were seated at those tables. Others got a paper-covered table. The eatery's wine list and menu were equally diverse. Bottles of house wine were a few francs, estate bottles were many thousands of francs.

Manuel Denard had been a fixture for years at la Coupole. His father had been maître d' since the 1920s, then Manuel managed the famous restaurant. There were a few customers on whom Manuel waited personally. Jean Delacroix was at the top of the list. Charles de Gaulle was on that list, but, in reality, the size of de Gaulle's check did not come near the size of Jean's tip. "Good evening, Monsieur Delacroix, and I see you have very pretty company tonight."

"Thank you, Manuel. Let me introduce you to Denmark's most beautiful model, Annette Bjorg. She will be enjoying whatever you plan for us tonight. I'm not in the mood to order. Just have Jacob prepare something light and tasty for the two of us."

"Yes, certainly. And should I bring you my suggestion for wines?"

"Yes, on the white wine, Manuel, but for the main course, I must have a bottle of 1945 Petrus. Please bring us a bottle of your best champagne to start. As a matter of fact, skip the white wine, we'll just have champagne with whatever appetizers you choose for us."

℥

As always, the meal was a delight, and again hand in hand, Jean led Annette to his waiting limousine and on to Ile Saint-Louis. He knew the apartment was the likes of which Annette had never imagined existed. As they entered the living spaces, she seemed to recognize the Monets, Renoirs, and exquisite Degases that filled Jean's apartment. Perhaps she had studied art? It was a paradise of wealth, and the delectable setting would have its intended effect.

Jean continued a mesmerizing conversation, all the while flattering the girl in the ways and manners a young woman wanted to be flattered. Jean was entering the prime of his life and knew the art and magic of sexual conquest. They were seated in a large love seat in his bedroom suite, and Annette was drinking anisette. The massive fireplace radiated a summer's warmth.

"How old are you, Annette?"

"I don't want you to know." Her eyes were glowing, and Jean was not considering whether he should have sex with her. He was considering how far he could go that first night. What he wanted that evening might just end the affair instantly. If he had read her eyes correctly, he could have almost anything he wanted that night. He toyed with bringing her to the Black Room, his room—the ultimate chamber of sexual gratification. A sixth sense told him she would not resist, but also told him to wait a bit. That one was special. Of course, they were all special, those he brought to the Black Room.

The girl sipped the anisette, and Jean looked deeply into her bright-blue eyes. How wonderful, he thought as he read her mind. She was behaving as if she knew everything. She must have some experience. If he judged her right, she was about sixteen and surely had sexual encounters with the persons who had brought her to where she was — probably a few photographers, agents, playboys, and the naïve youths in Denmark. She might even have been a "guest" of Sorte Che, Denmark's famous house of prostitution where only the best in the world were allowed in to ply their trade. Jean took the girl's hand and kissed her fingers. No, he would save that one; she was very special.

Jean ushered Annette to the front door, where his valet would escort her to his waiting limousine. He told her he would be in touch and gracefully brushed her cheek with a kiss. Aware of the disappointment in her eyes, he smiled inwardly. The young ones were alike no matter where they were born. She had been prepared to make love that night, but without warning, he had cooled himself and her from culminating the date with a sexual encounter.

The night was still early, and Jean was very aroused. He sat down in the living room and dialed a number he had long since memorized.

A woman answered in a husky voice. "Yes, may I help you tonight?"

"Yes, Madame Alexandra, you certainly may."

∞

Born in Paris, Alexandra Leclercq was a stunning young woman when World War II erupted. If fate and the warped mind of Adolf Hitler had not been a reality, she would have grown into womanhood, married well, and probably raised a family. But the course of her life came not out of being in the wrong place at the wrong time. That certainly was a factor, but one simple fact changed her life forever, along with those whom she touched later in life.

Alexandra was a Jew. Namely, an exquisitely beautiful Jewess, a fact which also changed her fate. She was arrested in Paris by the gestapo and taken to Dachau, where only her beauty saved her life. She was used in the worst way a woman could be, not to accomplish some kind of work but to be the sexual object of the officers in charge of the camp. She survived her tormentors, but the result was devastating. When she was liberated at the end of the war, Alexandra sought revenge against what she had gone through. In the end, she not only blamed the Germans, she blamed mankind, specifically any man who walked the face of the planet seeking sexual gratification.

As peace and a form of prosperity washed over France, Alexandra entered into the oldest business on earth. She not only opened a house of prostitution, she opened *the* house of prostitution. Not that it was a famous landmark; to the contrary, it was a highly secret establishment. Her house indulged only the wealthy of the world. Her customers were princes, kings, politicians, and men like Jean Delacroix, the wealthiest of the wealthy. She catered to those men's needs, providing them with any kind of service if the price was right.

"And how are you this evening, Alexandra?"

"I'm very fine, Jean. What service can I provide for you? It's a bit late, but for my favorite customer, I'll see that your needs are fully met."

"Thank you, my dear. Yes, I'll need the full treatment tonight. Don't forget, she must be blonde and, naturally, not shy. I'm feeling very aggressive. I'll need her for twenty-four hours. She will naturally have a little rest in between. As usual, she must be new and very young. No virgin, as you fully understand she must have the experience to stay on the level of my high energies. So nice chatting with you. Cyril will let her in this evening."

Saint Moritz, Switzerland, 1951: Robert Bolvin

Winter came early in 1951, and snow blanketed the mountain ranges around Saint Moritz. Jean had the private ski lifts closed that weekend so that he could ferry his guests back and forth without the traffic of the skiers. At Chateau Delacoix, his thirty-fifth birthday party would be the event of the year in Europe. He invited 310 guests from every walk of life. That is, every *important* walk of life, by Delacroix standards — dignitaries of Western Europe, titled nobility, and enough young actresses to cast a dozen films.

A few actors were invited, but only those who had headlined a film. From America came Rock Hudson with Doris Day, and Charlton Heston arrived with the legendary Cecil B. DeMille. Kirk Douglas, Bing Crosby, and Tony Curtis with Janet Leigh were a few more. From Europe came Sophia Loren, Anna Magnani, and Silvana Mangano. From France, Jeanne Moreau, Albert Rémy, Roger Vadim, and Brigitte Bardot.

As the guests arrived, Jean and Annette graciously greeted each person, leaving all the impression they were honored above the rest. A young woman with long, auburn hair accompanied Roger Vadim. Francoise Dorleac had just started her film career. As Jean watched her, he could not help but think she resembled Greta Garbo.

Jean's attention was then brought to Mohammad Reza Pahlavi, one of his most distinguished guests that day. The shah had confided to him that his guest would be a regular escort provided by Madame Alexandra. Jean glanced at her with envy. How wistfully beautiful she was. She had long, dark-blonde hair worn in cascading curls, full lips forming a delicious mouth, large brown eyes with flecks of gold in the irises, and the longest lashes he had ever seen. Her upturned nose and long neck made her utterly ravishing.

The party lasted from Friday evening until Sunday morning. As they tired, most of the guests were shuttled to the luxurious Palace Hotel in the village below. A few stayed on at the castle, mostly those interested in the late-evening festivities. Those included the single set, who could not be described as shy. Jean encouraged all and any activities that might be interesting for him to watch; however, he never partook of those activities publicly.

One man sat alone in the main reception room of the vast chateau, a respected senator from the newly formed French parliament. A new constitution was to give Charles de Gaulle broader powers, and as a result of that and the close relationship Jean had with him, added prosperity for the Delacroix fortune. While Jean had hoped for de Gaulle's presence at his birthday party, Senator Robert Bolvin had been sent in his stead.

Jean knew very little about Senator Bolvin. The Delacroix staff had been unable to determine just where the senator might be helpful to Delacroix Industries. The man was fiercely loyal to France and Charles de Gaulle. A member of the Resistance, he had been captured at the end of the war and brutally interrogated by the gestapo days before the liberation of France. He survived the questioning and was recently backed by de Gaulle in his bid for a senatorial seat in the new congress.

Jean walked over to the somber-faced man. "Senator Bolvin, yes, so nice to have you join us. I had invited President de Gaulle, but as he could not make it, I'm glad he sent you in his place."

Bolvin's composure bothered Jean. There was something strange about him, as if he were hiding something. He was a stocky man, but beneath the weight, Jean sensed a physical and mental toughness. He was almost bald, and had a round face. Jean judged him to be around fifty.

Looking directly into Jean's eyes, Bolvin responded. "It's a great pleasure to meet a hero of France. I've read so much about you and was certainly looking forward to our meeting. Is there a chance we can speak in private? I have something to discuss with you that is of the utmost importance."

Jean did not miss the hint of sarcasm. His intuition screamed at him that there was an immediate danger. "Of course we can talk. Follow me. I have a private office at the top of my chateau. I use it for confidential meetings."

He led Bolvin to the elevator that ran from the reception area to the top of the chateau. The elevator was operated only with a special key, and the office they stepped into was accessible only to Jean. The spectacular office occupied one of four corner towers of the chateau. About a thousand square feet, the room had panoramic views of the Saint Moritz mountains. As impressively decorated as all of Jean's homes, the office held classic furniture of the Napoleonic period. Great French master paintings adorned every wall—works by Jean Clouet, Georges de La Tour, and Nicolas Poussin.

The stocky man walked around the room with a critical eye. He viewed the artwork but made no comment. The somber expression remained as he was directed to a side chair in front of Jean's massive

Napoleon II desk. "What I am about to say is not complimentary to you, Monsieur Delacroix, and the only reason I am giving you this opportunity to hear me is that I feel myself to be a loyal citizen of France and a gentleman, as well. I have my reasons for confronting a man I believe to be a traitor and villain of my beloved country. I wrestled many nights with my conscience regarding whether I was going to speak to you first or to the proper authorities. I decided on speaking with you first, as it is my opinion that we can salvage much bad publicity for France, and for you, if you step down as director of Delacroix Industries."

Jean did not so much as blink an eye. He was the master of the game. A challenge was coming in the form of Robert Bolvin, newly elected senator. Inwardly, Jean relished the contest. Another man might be faint of heart if faced with some ugly skeleton that was going to come out of the proverbial closet. What did Bolvin have for him? Had he discovered Jean's unusual sexual appetites? Or perhaps the young woman who had taken her life not too long ago because her expectations for her services did not culminate in marriage. Perhaps a bribe to one of the officials had been unearthed. He smiled at Roger, waiting for him to continue.

"I have in my possession a diary, Monsieur Delacroix." He stared at Jean, and for the first time, his round face bore a slight smile. "I have the diary of Fritz von Damm."

Jean maintained his composure though he felt a slight tic in his neck.

"The diary covers the German officer's life from the time he joined the gestapo until he left France near the end of the war. Daily entries provide detailed descriptions of what took place. Von Damm names you, and I need not disclose to you the farce of your so-called cooperation with the French underground movement. He lists the phony leads you gave us, the empty railroad cars we blew up, the equipment we destroyed that no longer had any valid use for the occupying forces." Bolvin's voice had grown louder, and he paused a moment before continuing. "Von Damm goes on to describe the gifts you gave him and the luxury of your life in exchange. I am personally disgusted with these revelations and would enjoy seeing you publicly ruined."

Another man would certainly have blanched under those circumstances. But Jean's father had trained him well: "Never lose your composure under any circumstances. The man who loses his composure loses the game. It matters not what the situation is, whether it is for life or death. Whether it is for financial gain or loss. Play the game the way you see fit, but never let your opponent know what lies behind your outward composure.

"Be surprised by nothing in life. Life is the biggest game of all, and only that cannot be won in the end. Your death lies at the end of life, so enjoy everything in between. Always play the game with complete control of your composure. It is your inner strength that will always conquer in the end."

Jean reflected on that conversation as he responded to Bolvin. Feigning a sincere smile, he said, "Yes, I won't try to argue with you. Though I thought it was in the interest of France that I maintain control of the factories and lead at the same time a normal lifestyle for myself, I can see the majority of the citizens of my country would not understand this. I will step down as you suggest, and do so at once. I just ask one consideration. I would like to view the diary once briefly to see for myself that I am not being charged unfairly in this matter."

Bolvin displayed a rather large grin as he responded. "What do you take me for, sir, a fool? Yes, you may review the diary, but only in the presence of me and an officer at the Bank of France. It is in a locked safety deposit box in my name. I would be a fool to have it anywhere else. You certainly might take steps to have me killed and recover the diary, but I have left explicit instructions with Paul Pomares, the bank's president, to deliver it personally to de Gaulle if something happens to me." He glared at Jean, crossing his arms solidly across his chest.

"Naturally, Monsieur Bolvin. Can we meet in Paris tomorrow in the early afternoon? I will bring my letter of resignation with me and hand it over to you after viewing part of the diary." Jean led Bolvin out of his office and back to the reception area. He told him the car that brought him from the Palace Hotel would take him back shortly then on to the Zurich airport to catch a plane back to Paris.

Jean returned to his party, which was in full swing, and greeted more of his guests. What a special day it was, he thought as he wandered back and forth reveling in his birthday party. He glanced at his watch, realizing it was time to have Robert Bolvin picked up for his ride to the hotel.

℘

In the village of Saint Moritz and the surrounding countryside were a number of quaint villas owned by Jean Delacroix. Many of those homes were used as vacation favors to political factions within the Delacroix "family." Plant managers and their families also used the villas as a reward for work well done.

One small but handsome villa on Place de la Park was the exclusive residence of an extremely talented and faithful employee in the Delacroix network, George Saint-James, whose services were used infrequently. The forty-five-year-old man spent much his time in a highly specialized weight room in the basement. Bodybuilding was not a hobby for George; it was a livelihood. Six feet tall, he weighed 220 pounds, and his biceps were twenty-two inches of solid muscle. He was built like an ox and, in fact, could kill an ox with a single blow of his hands if he had to.

On the few occasions when George ventured out of the villa, he rarely engaged in conversation, whether shopping or having an occasional glass of wine in one of the local cafés. Four times a year, he flew to the Seychelles Islands for several weeks, spending time in a residence that Delacroix maintained. There George returned to a normal semblance of life, mixing with other visitors. He even allowed himself to speak his native tongue if he encountered a fellow countryman. Only Delacroix knew that George Saint-James was the name he had given to former gestapo officer Wolfgang Schmidt.

Perfectly trained in the French language, "Wolf" had administered beatings and killings while interrogating prisoners during the occupation of France. It was Wolf who personally assisted Delacroix during the war, keeping him informed of what was going on in gestapo headquarters. It was Wolf who let him know specifically what plans von Damm had in mind during the war. And it was Wolf who made sure the two suitcases containing diamonds and explosives were aboard the plane with the Nazi general.

After the war, it was Jean who called in a plastic surgeon to alter Wolf's face. It was Jean who provided him with papers showing him to be a Frenchman who had resided in Brazil during the war and returned to work for Delacroix Industries shortly after. And at the moment, it was Jean who placed a call to Wolf's villa in Saint Moritz.

Wolf was in the weight room when the phone rang. His blond hair was matted with sweat; his body and handsome face gleamed from a lengthy workout. Seated in a chair, he was doing bicep curls, fifty-pound weights in each hand. He dropped the weights on the wood floor and picked up the wall phone. "Yes, George here. May I help you?" His accent and response were French, as his training had engrained in him. Even so, he knew it was Jean; the phone only rang when his employer needed him.

"Ah, my good man Wolf. I must ask for the 'special favor' today. I know we have not utilized the favor for many years now, but I'm afraid I have an insect biting me on my backside. The insect is quite small, but his bite could be fatal, I'm afraid. Don't play with him, Wolf. It is important we eradicate him at once. I know you like to taunt our victims a bit, but please don't in this case. The man appears to be very strong, very wiry. As a matter of fact, if you did not recognize him when you picked him up yesterday in the van with the others, his name is Roger Bolvin. You interrogated him that last week in Paris. You removed one of his testicles, if I recall the story."

Wolf contemplated a moment before responding. "Oh, yes, the tough little Resistance fighter who wouldn't cooperate. Of course I remember. What do you wish me to do with him?"

"You will pick him up here at the chateau. He is waiting for you. Bring the special limousine. Start down the mountain road, then take the Lorre Pass road back up to the summit. The side road is clear to the Mannheim lift. I have checked at the lower gates. No one has entered today or will, except you. Take the lift key with you and use the lift to the top. You know where the out-of-bound markers are for the Mannheim Chasm. Drop the body into the chasm, I don't want it to surface in this century."

§

Robert Bolvin climbed into the Mercedes limousine and eased into the soft, black interior. The quiet ride down the mountain relaxed the huge adrenaline rush the meeting had evoked. It had been much easier than he expected. No begging or pleading for mercy. Then again, he never expected that. What he anticipated was a straight attempt at bribery. That it did not come was the only surprise of the day.

He glanced out the window and was puzzled at first by the view. They seemed to be heading back up the mountain instead of down. He had not noticed any abrupt road change. One minute they were going down, and the next the summit of the mountain was approaching. Robert leaned forward and rapped on the glass partition that divided the driver's seat from the passenger. The chauffeur did not turn around. Robert banged very hard the next time with his fist, but again not a move by the driver.

A sudden, loud clicking noise caught Robert's attention, and instinctively, he reached for the door handles. To his horror, the door would not open. The car accelerated as they reached a part of the mountain that had a long, clear run to the entrance to the ski lifts. What in the world was happening?

Robert started to scream, more in anger than in fear. The driver did not flinch, did not turn around. It was as if he were not there. Robert's body tensed, and he strove to calculate what fate might be waiting at the end of the trip. He had not long to wait.

The car came to a stop at the gated entry to the private ski lifts. Through the glass divider, Robert saw the chauffer lower the driver's window and wave to the guard to let him through. Robert waved frantically and called to the guard, but to no avail. Did the blackness of the tinted windows prevent the guard from seeing in? Was the vehicle soundproofed, as well? The driver glanced at him in the rearview mirror, the hint of a smile on his face as he drove the last few minutes to the base of the mountain.

Through the intercom, the chauffer spoke soothingly in French. "Please, Monsieur Bolvin. No harm will come to you if you do as I say. Monsieur Delacroix wants to meet with you to have another private conversation. He will be joining us at a small cabin not far from here. Do you understand me?"

"Yes, and I will be glad to continue the conversation." Robert's thoughts were running in different directions: Was he to be killed? Was Delacroix going to see him? He must buy time. He must cooperate until he had a moment of clarity to see otherwise.

The chauffer exited the car and unlocked the rear door. Bolvin came out and immediately sized up the larger man. He stood no chance against the driver. Even through the man's windbreaker and sweater, Robert saw the massive arms. He followed alongside the chauffer into the thick forest that led to the ski lifts. He realized then that there was no meeting, only his death sentence, and the man he was following was to be his executioner. That was the reason Delacroix put up no resistance.

Robert concentrated with all his means to comprehend where he had failed in his plan of personally disgracing Delacroix. He should never have sought personal revenge. But again, how could Delacroix get his hands on the diary when it was entrusted to the one entity in France that was above reproach, the Bank of France? Then, like all things in life that come crashing down after one has designed the perfect plan, with a gut-wrenching feeling, he suddenly remembered that Jean Delacroix *was* the Bank of France.

The ski lifts came into view. Realizing his life was about to end, Robert spotted a large, thick branch in the pathway ahead. He slowed slightly, noting his captor was not paying much attention. Reaching down quickly, he grabbed the heavy piece of wood and swung it down as hard as he could onto the skull of the big man. Reminiscent of David and Goliath, he hit him perfectly, and the chauffer dropped to the ground, obviously unconscious.

Robert turned and ran like never before. They had been walking in the woods for at least fifteen minutes. On several occasions, they had turned from one path to another. As he ran back down the mountain path, he was sure he was going in the right direction, but it seemed like an eternity trying to find the clearing where the limousine was. He hoped the keys were still in the car.

His mind raced on to the vengeance he would bring down on Delacroix. He would call de Gaulle at once; he would call the news media. He would personally see to it that the diary was published, so the world would know what a piece of shit the man really was.

Finally, a clearing was in front of him. Robert could see the long black Mercedes. Exhausted from the run, he would have to continue his race for life down to the gate if there were no keys. He frantically opened the front door and half-fell inside. There were keys in the dashboard ignition. What great luck! Pulling himself fully into the car, he reached to start the ignition.

A hand locked Robert's neck in a vise-like hold from behind. He looked up to the rearview mirror and saw the driver's face, covered in blood. He glared at Robert with wild eyes. His massive hand was choking Robert, who struggled with all the strength remaining in his body. He saw the man reach up with his other hand and bring down a small, rounded object. With blinding-sharp pain, Robert's world disintegrated into a flash of light, and he lost consciousness.

∾

Robert awoke and, after the first wave of pain ebbed, saw stars. The sky was black, and the stars appeared to be moving. He shifted his head slightly and was instantly nauseous. The stars were not moving; he was moving, in a ski lift. He felt the chill through his coat as the lift moved up the mountain. Tied to the lift, he was seated next to the monster who had accosted him.

The man was still bloody, and the moon lit his face. He had a strange look, a wild look, about him, and Robert felt a new fear in his gut. Why wasn't he dead? Why was the man taking him up the mountain? He asked his captor what was happening, but the man looked at him and did not respond.

Near the top, his captor jumped onto the receiving platform, ran to the lift control, and switched it off. He untied Robert from the lift, but his feet were still tied and his wrists cuffed. The big man dragged him by his coat along the platform and into the snow, then pushed him onto a small sled standing nearby. He pulled the sled along a path that ran beside tall red markers that indicated where the out-of-bounds area was. A sign appeared in the moonlight:

BEWARE
MANHEIM CHASM

Robert's captor pulled the sled into the trees alongside the ski slope. Smiling wickedly, he hoisted him up against a giant pine tree and, using Robert's own belt, secured him there. He leered at Robert, removing a long switchblade knife from a sheath near his ankle. Robert squirmed against his restraints as the man drew nearer. Deftly, he cut Robert's trousers so they fell at his feet. Reaching out, he pulled down Robert's long boxer shorts.

ᔒ

Looking his victim straight in the face, the chauffer spoke in perfect German. "Mein Freund, ich sehe das seit unserer letzten Begegnung, du hast noch einen Hoden übrig." (My friend, I see that since our last meeting, you still have one testicle left.)

Bolvin's eyes bulged. He tried to scream, but Wolfgang Schmidt pushed a handkerchief deep inside his open mouth. The mountains might echo the screams that Bolvin would certainly utter as Wolf played with his foe, and the last thing he wanted was for any report to reach Delacroix. He lit a cigarette and walked toward the high fence that surrounded the chasm. The top of the ten-foot fence was almost level with that year's deep snow. He peered over the side.

The Mannheim Chasm was a marvel of nature. In reality, it was a volcanic funnel, millions of years old, that at one time brought a flow of molten lava from the bowels of the earth to form the highest point in Saint Moritz. No one had ever descended to the bottom; it was considered bottomless. The sheer drop went straight down.

Wolf walked back to the little Frenchman and, opening the blade of his stiletto, spoke to Bolvin in a soft tone. "Monsieur Bolvin, we have some work to do now. And when I'm finished, you'll be going on a little trip. Do you like riding on a roller coaster? I've arranged for you tonight the fastest roller coaster on the planet."

℘

Jean awoke at five Monday morning and pushed the control button on his nightstand to open the mammoth drapes that covered the bedroom windows. The day was beautiful, with the sun's rays just coming up. He showered, dressed, and had a leisurely breakfast. At six forty-five, George Saint-James called. Jean took the call in warm anticipation of good news.

"Yes, George, how nice. You say the evening went well?" Knowing his servant, Jean went on to say, "Of course, I understand you had no time to play any games last night . . . no, no, I would never question your loyalty to my orders. I believe you. By the way, that cut on your hand, was it very painful last night? . . . No? Very good. I'll call you later."

At precisely ten, Jean placed a call to the Bank of France. He was connected to Paul Pomares, acting president. "Hello, Paul. How are you, and how are the wife and two little girls? . . . Yes, that's splendid. Please, let me remind you that you and your family will be vacationing next week at my villa in Gstaad. You may stay as long as you like, and all airline reservations have been made. By the way, our new senator, Robert Bolvin, has asked a favor of me. He wants me to place a little gift in his safety deposit box. As a matter of fact, it's a surprise for him. You're laughing, Paul. You know my little surprises, don't you? I'll be in on Wednesday. Will you have your assistant meet me at ten? See you then. Perhaps lunch later in the day."

Paris, 1952: The Black Room

Jean Delacroix's valet, Cyril, escorted Annette Bjorg to a three-room apartment on Rue Furstemberg in Saint Germain des Pres. Annette thought of the rooms as her own, but in reality, she was not allowed to occupy them unless Jean invited her for the occasion. She had known him four years and was his mistress almost from the beginning. He had arranged for her to use the luxury apartment.

Still modeling for Delacroix Fashions at twenty, Annette was considered the most famous model in the world. Her photographs appeared in every fashion magazine, and every newsstand displayed her famous figure and smiling face. Yet within herself, she was not happy.

As she settled into her suite, Annette contemplated her life. When she first met Jean, the whole world had opened for her. Though she had been well compensated at Dior, he made her his premier model at Delacroix Fashions. Within a year, she was the top model in the world. Photographers fought over her; magazines lined up to utilize her famous face. Her arrangement for fashion shoots was not exclusive; only for fashion shows did she work exclusively for Jean.

He wined and dined her and took her everywhere. From the beginning, she had given herself to him alone. She knew she was not the only woman in his life, that she was, in fact, his mistress. But Annette realized that unsurpassed success was only possible with his help. He had taken care of her in many ways that enabled her to reach the top. His surgeon in Switzerland had improved her facial blemishes and surgically improved her body so that the end result was a woman of perfect proportions.

She owed Jean a lot, and he took from her a heavy payment. He had initiated her in the rituals that were expected of her, and she performed them perfectly. She had to. One of the rituals was Jean Delacroix's Black Room.

ॐ

Jean's elegant bedroom had a unique feature. Near the entry, one wall bore a massive Henry Rousseau painting of ancient forests and animals. Next to the painting was what appeared to be a temperature-control system. The twin set of dials that indicated hot or cold settings were actually registration settings. Jean could turn the numbers to a set of pointers at the top, the correct sequence releasing a mechanism that slid the oil painting sideways to reveal a hidden room. Once the calibrations were set to open the door, a safety system automatically locked the bedroom doors so that no one could enter. Jean had designed the Black Room and hired contractors exclusively from South America to accomplish its construction. He had the workers flown in for that contract only and sent back afterward.

Jean Delacroix had two personal pleasures in life. One consisted of taking Delacroix Industries to unimaginable heights on the financial front. His second pleasure was sexual. He was a physically powerful man, and his libido was in constant overdrive. To fulfill that drive, he hesitated at nothing that would satisfy his sexual craving.

He had been introduced to the initiations of love at the age of twelve. A young French nanny, appropriately called Nanette, would tuck him into bed and tuck herself in at the same time. She fondled the boy and, with great glee, taught young Jean the art of sex, as she knew it. He learned everything about basic lovemaking, including numerous positions, extended lovemaking, and that there was more than one entrance into a woman's body. Nanette enjoyed being bound lightly, and with youthful zeal, he obliged her frequently. The nightly encounters went on for nearly a year before one of the butlers found out.

By the time Jean was sixteen, normal sex was passé to him. Taking a new young maid into his confidence, he started to experiment by utilizing a German publication on masochistic lovemaking. He would wait until his parents were gone from the residence before his experimentations. He took the paraphernalia from its hiding place and set it up in his father's workout studio. Utilizing the magazines along with his own unique devices, Jean became proficient in the art of masochistic sex at a very young age, engaging varying partners over time.

Jean awaited Annette that night. He enjoyed her and the pleasure both experienced in his special room. He would try a new experiment, a new way to explore the sensations of his body and hers. Per Jean's instructions, his valet was to call him on the intercom when Miss Bjorg arrived. Annette was to come to his bedroom suite alone, and Jean would buzz her through the main door. He had long ago instructed Annette on how to enter his special room. He would be sitting there, waiting for her.

Entering the Black Room, Jean had two hours to prepare. He held the remote selector in his hand and used one of the illuminated controls to bring the lights up to low dim. The black-velvet walls illuminated the wondrous paintings of Henry Rousseau that covered the entire fifteen- by twenty-foot room. Small, adjustable lights in various hues changed the reflection of the paintings at a touch. Jean played with the controls until the illumination suited his mood.

At the far end of the room was a door to a small but elegant dressing room. Jean entered with the leather bag he had brought in with him. The dressing room had one wall devoted to a full-length makeup mirror and high-intensity lighting. The mirror could accommodate six persons, if needed. Specially designed chairs allowed one to adjust them up and down or swivel them to see any angle of the face or upper body.

Jean opened the large makeup case lying on the counter in front of the mirror. It contained layer after layer of face and body paints in every color on the spectrum. He removed a small jar containing pure lampblack and applied it to his entire body, utilizing a long-handled brush to do his back. The process took thirty minutes. Jean stood and examined himself in the mirror, pleased with the result.

Next he painted his face in rainbow colors, much like an African warrior might before going into battle. He added colors to his chest and legs. Standing, he examined himself, again gratified by his appearance. Taking a spray canister, Jean applied a light coat of the contents to his entire body. That would hold the makeup in place until he washed it off with soap and hot water, and he could engage in almost any action without rubbing off the colors.

Reaching into the leather bag, Jean removed a magnificent costume. The headdress was an African mask covered completely in soft feathers of splendid colors. A short kilt was also covered in feathers, some projecting outward at a forty-five-degree angle. Those puffed up his appearance but were also designed for a specific purpose. Upon contact with another person, the feathers depressed enough to produce an exotic caress. Donning the costume, Jean examined his appearance a third time. He was satisfied, very satisfied. The process had taken nearly two hours. He was ready for Annette.

Jean switched on the video camera that projected a view of the interior of his bedroom suite. Only Annette was visible. He activated the door to the Black Room. She removed her full-length leopard coat, revealing only her naked body.

Annette was perfection itself. Not a blemish marked her light skin. She wore her hair up—as he always requested for that performance. Smiling as she walked into the room, she lay on the bed of ostrich feathers Jean had placed there. He approached and knelt beside her. On his hands were wristbands tied with short soft feathers, designed to produce a wondrous and sexual feeling. He lightly slid his hands over her entire body.

Straddling Annette, Jean lowered his body to within a millimeter of hers, caressing her with his body, lightly and gently. She responded with a long, gentle sigh and pulled him down onto her. He removed the headdress and, following the age-old ritual of lovemaking, reached inside her thighs with his mouth and tongue, kissing her gently and softly just outside her mound. She was completely shaven, as he required of all his lovers.

Annette shuddered and started to scream in obvious delight, reaching the beginning of a climax, which she frequently did in that position. Jean reached over to an open bowl lying next to him, plucked out a small, rounded ice cube, and inserted it into her vagina. Annette backed off the orgasm, and again he started the same pattern. That time he was able to prolong the foreplay a few minutes until she started to vibrate, indicating an orgasm was coming. He plunged his erect penis into her, and she cried out with her orgasm. He lay inside her, not ejaculating, and waited for her to finish the intense body spasms that followed. He lay that way several minutes before releasing her.

Sitting up, Jean caressed Annette in the same manner as before until she was ready again. That repeated for almost an hour until Jean had worked himself up to such an extreme point of heat that when he finally came into her, it was as if the world exploded. Afterward, they lay holding on to each other.

Jean was a vicious businessman, with few scruples for almost anything dealing with mankind, but he was able on occasions to give to women something most men could never dream of. And he loved giving it to Annette. She was a sweet, if not bright, young woman and did not realize yet the realities of her life. She did realize that the day would come when the marvelous body and face she was born with would be anything other than that. She was at the pinnacle of her life as Europe's leading model. But one could not remain at that pinnacle for long, and Jean would ask her to retire from modeling for Delacroix Fashions at age twenty-one. And perhaps he hire an American model next time, or an actress? Modeling was a cruel business. It always would be.

ৈ০

Annette's thoughts were more surreal. She loved Jean intensely and wished their relationship could be exclusive. She stroked his cheek and, seeing him becoming sexually animated once more, could not resist jesting. "Tell me, my master, how is it you can be so aroused after just making love? My past lovers, who were younger than you, always faded away for hours before becoming aroused again."

With a large and crooked grin, Jean spoke to Annette as a father would do. "Annette, my young puppy, most men and women make love with their bodies. Most look to what lies between their legs to make love. What mankind does not know is that love is not made with that extension of the body. Love is made with what man possesses in his head. It is the mind that makes love, not the body." They both smiled then, and Annette reached out for her lover with new admiration.

The lovemaking ended at nearly midnight. As always, Annette begged Jean to allow her to stay. As always, he politely refused, showering her with compliments and a small diamond bracelet to add to her rather handsome collection of baubles. "Sleep well, my love, and remember what I told you tonight. Only you will ever be allowed in my room of love."

She knew, of course, that was not the truth, that Jean would never tell her the realities of his secret life.

"You are and will always be very special to me. I love you as much as I can any woman. Maybe a day will come when you may spend the night. Please respect me until then."

With that, Annette left with the heaviness she always felt in her heart when he dismissed her. Reflecting on it, she realized that was how she always felt with Jean — dismissed.

ຂໍ

Jean took the elevator to the roof. Roses in every available hue grew 365 days a year. But the pride of Jean's gardens was his lilies, found nowhere else in the world. Red, yellow, white, pink, and one variety Jean had developed exclusively: the Nile Lily, which had been extinct for two thousand years. His staff had worked ten years resurrecting the unbelievable flower. The petals were almost twelve inches long and consisted of variegated red, orange, and yellow blooms all on one long green stem.

Jean walked through his gardens and finally sat on a bench facing an unfinished limestone bust of Queen Nefertiti, the wife of the Egyptian Sun King, Akhenaten. Jean smiled at the partly colored face. His mind wandered to the stories his mother used to tell him of reincarnation. Once she had shown him that figure, which was in her bedroom, and said, "Perhaps she was your wife in a former time." He smiled to himself. What utter nonsense; nevertheless, he fantasized for a moment what it might have been like living so many centuries before.

Glancing down at his watch, Jean noted it was nearly one. How exciting, the evening was about to commence. How nice to have Annette prepare him. He took the private elevator back to his penthouse and entered his bedroom. Everything was as before. He still had on his costume and makeup and only needed to put the mask back on.

Jean again looked at his watch. It was almost time, and he relaxed in an armchair in front of his splendid carved fireplace. As the flames illuminated the room in a pleasant, warming way, his thoughts drifted to the girl who was coming to provide him an exclusive performance. One of Madame Alexandra's girls, that one would be extraordinary.

A month prior, Jean had called the madam to set up the fantasy. "Yes, it is your illustrious, hardworking entrepreneur, Madame Alexandra. I want a very special favor from you. I'm aware you have a friend in Hollywood who is in the same business as you . . . How do I know? I know everything, my dear. Is it possible to approach a certain young lady I have admired in film? Last night I watched her in *War and Peace*. She is married to an actor named Mel Ferrer, but according to my informer, the relationship is on the rocks . . . Yes, obviously it is Audrey Hepburn. Will you see what you can do?"

There was a long pause. "Jean, I personally know Miss Hepburn, and let me tell you why this can never happen. You have selected the one woman who not only will not accept money for these services, she is a true romantic and has been very selective with her partners. I knew her family when they lived in Holland. In 1944, she was chased by German soldiers in a field near her home and raped by all the men. I'm not even going to approach her on this. If you want, I'll give you Madame Suzette's phone number in Los Angeles. You can talk to her directly.

"I won't lend my name to that useless pursuit. However, if you're interested in an exquisite actress who is challenged by men like you, I have an American who fits the bill perfectly. She has a great sense of humor and enjoys pleasing the men. Let me tell you about her." The madam went on a bit, and Jean became interested indeed. "You must not call her by her real name. She will use the name Eva when she sees you and will travel incognito while in Paris. The fee you will have to pay is ten times the normal rate, but please don't acknowledge her real status or name at any time you are with her."

Jean had made arrangements for the American to see him that evening. She flew in the week before, and Jean furnished her with a female companion to show her the sights and smells of Paris. It was the young woman's first trip to France. Jean wanted her to enjoy everything but also to become accustomed to the time change before meeting him for a performance.

ℰꝺ

As Eva waited, Cyril called Jean on the intercom, announcing her arrival. She followed him to Jean's bedroom suite, where he opened the door for her. Upon entering the room, she noted the luxurious decor and paintings. She was standing next to a stunning Degas when Jean activated the secret panel revealing the Black Room. Eva had been warned about that evening. It was not so much a warning as it was to prepare her for an experience even she had not engaged in prior to that night. She was told a special room would be used and that Delacroix's sexual appetite was bizarre, frenzied, and, to some, quite stimulating. It was that description that interested her.

Eva cared nothing for the sum she was being paid — $1 million for the night, and more if both agreed to a further indulgence. That doubled the amount she had received for her last picture. Her curiosity had been piqued, and then some. No sexual encounter was too much for Eva. She had agreed to the tryst with Delacroix, among other curiosities, to see if he could make her climax. Despite her motion picture success, she, like her predecessor Jean Harlow, had never experienced an orgasm. Perhaps he could do what no one else could.

The Black Room's lights were dim, and Jean turned them up a bit. Beatrice Garnier, Eva's escort in Paris, had dressed her in a 1920s Coco Chanel beaded, full-length white sheath that came out of Delacroix's personal wardrobe collection of vintage clothes. Eva was fitted into the dress, and the effect was alluring. She could see it in the way he looked at her.

"Hello, Eva. Walk to the opium bed and lie down face first."

Seeing Jean's costume, Eva was amused and at the same time warmed with the situation. That certainly was different. She lay face down on the large, antique Chinese bed and waited. Jean walked over, took her hands gently, and tied each one to the top of the bed with elegant silk scarves. Removing her white shoes, he bound her feet likewise to the bottom posts.

"I am going to tell you what I'm going to do to you now. For the moment, you are the slave and I am the master. Do you understand?"

Eva nodded.

"If there is anything you don't like, tell me before I start. If what I do to you bothers you as I'm doing it, say stop. I really want to please you very much, and myself also. First, I will take off your dress. I'll take off your undergarments next. I want to caress and kiss each part of your body very slowly and very deliberately. I will start at your feet and finish at the nape of your neck.

"I am going to use body oil on you and work it into your skin, slowly and gently. I will massage you like you have never been massaged. When I finish working on your back, I will turn you over and do the same. I will give you cunnilingus until you orgasm. If you don't orgasm, it is not important. You will orgasm at some point. Eva, you will orgasm as you never have in your life. This I promise you."

With great surprise, Eva was becoming wet with each word that came out of Jean's mouth. Something was happening that had never happened before. She had been tied up on occasions, going along with it when she knew her companion well. Never had it done anything for her. She marked that form of sadomasochism as stupid, a man's ego trip. With Jean, she felt none of that. There was something very different going on.

∞

What the American actress did not know was that Jean Delacroix was a magician. He was not a magician in the way of tricks, card stunts, or traditional magic. Jean possessed a tremendous gift of illusion. A talented and forceful hypnotist, he needed no props to put a woman under his spell. He simply hypnotized her with his voice, talked to her. He convinced her, and without knowing it, she just fell under his influence. If he wanted Eva to believe she was a queen, he could accomplish even that.

"Eva, when I'm done working with you, I'm going to untie you. I will shower while you rest, and when I return, you will do the same to me. I will be the slave, and you will be the master. Do you understand me?"

Again Eva nodded.

"When we finish, we will take a slight refreshment before continuing. I have some champagne on the table next to the bed. Also, there is any kind of artificial stimulant you might want to use. I myself do not drink or take any form of drug, but I understand that is unusual today. Feel free to do what you want at any time. I will stop you if you exceed a safe level."

Jean removed Eva's stunning gown and undergarments. Starting at the girl's feet, he massaged her slowly but strongly. He worked his way up her legs to her back and, with his strong fingers, rubbed the joints in her back until she relaxed completely. His cosmetics company had formulated an oil exclusively for Jean, and he used it only for that purpose. The oil was in a clay brazier heated by a small candle next to the bed.

He worked on each vertebra in Eva's back, and by the time he reached the nape of her neck, Eva was almost asleep. He untied the scarves and turned the girl over. She was someplace else then, and Jean smiled knowingly. He again started at her feet, but that time he massaged her small toes one at a time. At the conclusion of each pretty toe, he leaned over and, with his mouth, caressed the toe gently, then with no warning reached down and gave the toe a quick pull with his fingers.

℘

When Jean massaged the first toe and concluded with the pull, Eva let out a small cry. She felt nothing in the toe; she felt a release in the center of her body. She had experienced a small but pleasurable climax. It was her first, and she was startled at how easily he had accomplished that. Jean repeated the process, and with each quick pull, the orgasm was increased.

Eva had ascended to another plane, and as Jean began massaging her legs and thighs, every touch produced a shiver of sexual gratification. When his strong fingers came close to her inner thighs, Eva reached an orgasm again, and he had not so much as penetrated her. She had an enormous urge to reach out and pull him to her but could not, as he had retied her. At the same time, she felt completely possessed, and the feeling in itself was a high. He did not touch her center but moved up to her voluptuous breasts and gently massaged her, starting on the outside and working in to her nipples. He used both the warm oil and his tongue and very, very gently nipped her. Eva experienced a strong orgasm and let out a sudden, loud scream — not of pain but of ultimate pleasure.

℘

Jean observed Eva's state and decided not to cool her down with the ice standing nearby. He assessed from the great release she was going through that the young woman had never experienced any kind of orgasm and, more importantly, was capable of having multiple orgasms. He was delighted at that prospect, as it meant he could indulge greater fantasies with her. His penis was significantly engorged, but with practiced control, Jean ignored the compulsion to have his first orgasm.

Kissing Eva all over her body, Jean slowly worked himself to her center. She was moaning sensuously. He worked her body to a rhythm then, and she would continue to build to a climax as long as he orchestrated her to do so. He reached down with his mouth and entered her with his tongue, and Eva let out a loud scream as she released herself.

Sitting up next to Eva, Jean watched her vibrate with the orgasm. He untied her and took her in his arms, holding her tightly as the enormous orgasm subsided. It took five minutes before she relaxed in his arms. She looked deeply into his eyes and said, "I love you. Where have you been all my life?"

Leading Eva into the elegant bathroom, Jean turned on the water in the small spa. He poured her a glass of champagne and embraced her with a strong hug. "Relax and enjoy yourself. I'm going to take off part of my costume, and we will continue the performance. Are you having fun?"

ℰↄ

Eva was still in that faraway place where people go when they discover that life is not so predictable and new pleasurable experiences are yet out there. Jean had disappeared long before she responded yes.

ℰↄ

Jean entered the green-and-black-marble shower. Turning on the six water jets, he allowed the hot water to cascade over his body. His penis, still engorged, began to return to its normal size as he applied specially formulated soap to remove the paint. He spent a full ten minutes under the water until every particle of makeup was gone.

After drying himself off, Jean lay on the chaise longue and entered a state of meditation. His mind wandered to the life he led. As usual at that point, the small conscience that existed in Delacroix emerged and began arguing with him. It told him over and over that what he was doing with his life was wrong. Jean allowed his mind to listen for a minute or so before he dismissed the demon. *I'll live whatever life I desire. There is no hereafter. The rest after death is eternal. I'll taste life to the fullest now.*

Jean returned to Eva, and as he had expected, she was in a high state of excitement to continue the performance. She looked at him so innocently in her youth. He returned her look, giving her the strength of his will to enter into sexual fantasies she had surely never dreamed existed. He led her back to the bed and had her tie him as he had her. As he instructed her in what to do, she did so.

Eva was a magnificent student of love, and Jean could see in her face a look of triumph indicating she would take those lessons with her to another. Little did she know, that art of lovemaking would only work if the man or the woman knew the magic required. Eva would search the rest of her life for another man like Delacroix and discover that only returning to Jean gave her the pleasure he had taught her. When they finished their extraordinary lovemaking, both slept deeply only to awake and enter again into sexual fantasies.

That went on for two days and nights. Eva repeatedly turned to Jean to tell him how much she loved him. Jean knew the relationship was strictly sexual, and that the declarations were Eva's way of complimenting him. On parting, she smiled and said, "For you, my amazing lover, you can always address me with my real name." In the future, he would always do so.

ॐ

Jean paid Eva in emeralds of the highest quality, but never again would she accept anything of great value from him. He had changed her life forever.

Paris, 1959: Ile Saint-Louis

Annette arrived at Jean's apartment in a new winter coat he had given her, a full-length Russian sable. Made from the finest skins available, the coat had a lustrous sheen and was delightful to the touch. The valet let her in and brought her to Jean, who was seated at the desk in his library.

Like every room in the apartment-mansion, the library was spectacular. In the center of the room was a ten-foot wooden sculpture of a Roman warship in full sail. According to Jean, every detail of the ship was perfect. Sculptor Pierre van Dorn had taken five years to complete it for him. Each of the four walls bore a splendid Van Gogh painting.

A large canvas behind the desk depicted a vast field of wildflowers in brilliant colors. In the middle of the painting, a young girl sat among the flowers, her hair blowing in the wind. Annette lost herself for a moment, studying the masterpiece. It was the most beautiful thing she had ever seen.

"So you like the little work," Jean said, looking up from the papers on his desk. "May I send it over to your apartment for the winter? I can live without it for a while."

Annette broke into a rare laugh. "Oh, Jean, you can be so generous when you want to. No, keep the painting. Can I sit down and talk to you seriously?"

"Absolutely, my love. What's troubling you, or should I say has made you look so radiant?"

Annette sat silently for a few seconds, not really knowing how to reveal the purpose of her visit, the desires of her heart. She had not modeled since 1953, as Jean had requested. For a while she had wanted to enter the theatrical world, but he discouraged her. He would have done anything for her if she had chosen another field to become involved with. But no other occupation could replace the love she had for modeling. She tried; however, modeling—being part of a fantasy world, having people watch and admire her—was what she liked best.

In time, Annette became Jean's principal companion, kept in a style most women would envy. She was aware he had others, but he took Annette to the most important social functions. She made sure she looked stunning and behaved in a quiet and respectful manner. She never made a gaff at a party, never insulted someone important, and never became intoxicated. Indeed, she strived to be the perfect companion. Annette knew Jean loved her in his own way and still enjoyed the physical relationship they shared. She was special to him.

"Jean, I'm pregnant." It was a simple statement. Annette did not elaborate. She merely waited for him to respond as she knew he would, with great happiness and even perhaps offering her what she eternally hoped for, a more permanent relationship.

Jean looked down at his hands and did not speak for what seemed like an eternity. Annette was not sure what to make of his silence. He had told her he was unable to provide a woman any children. He had always figured he was infertile, as no woman had ever become pregnant, going back to when he was a teen. Jean's doctors had actually informed him that his sperm count was very low and that, should he ever want to have children, he would have to have injections to get his count up.

Finally, he looked at her and said quietly but firmly, "I don't want you to have my child."

Annette's world came crashing down. She knew she could be naïve at times and that men—including Jean—were attracted by her beauty, some like hounds in heat. No man she had allowed into her life had ever discussed deep things with her. But she was certainly not stupid, just not worldly. Yet how could she have been prepared for his response?

℘

Jean did not want to be with an intellectual. He wanted a beautiful companion to accompany him, look stunning, and be quiet. Annette was perfect. What made the whole thing work, of course, was that the chemistry between them was magnificent.

She looked at him now with such hurt in her eyes that he could not utter a word. "Jean, please let me keep the baby."

He looked down again and lost himself in thought. A great compulsion in his heart screamed, Take her in your arms. Tell her you love her, tell her you want this child. But another, stronger compulsion that really made up the character of Jean Delacroix said, "No."

℘

Leaving Jean in solitude, Annette exited the apartment and wandered across the bridge, past Notre Dame, and along the left bank of the Seine. She sat awhile at a table in one of their favorite bistros, where she and Jean so often sat holding hands and teasing one another about various things. They had laughed, never cried, and would always end the evening in each other's arms. She finished a glass of white wine and continued her walk along the great and ancient river. At the old, wooden pedestrian bridge, Pont des Arts, she crossed the river and walked through the Louvre grounds and on into the park next to the famous old palace. The air was cold, and snow was falling that winter day, turning to slush as it hit the ground. Sitting down on one of the park benches, Annette tried to think about what had just taken place. She tried to understand why Jean did not want their child. She wanted to understand his long lecture on why she could not keep the baby. But no matter how much she tried, only the tears would come. She picked herself up and walked slowly home.

⃝

Jean felt very uncomfortable with the day's events. A demon inside him had dictated the day. He sat at his desk, not having moved the past four hours. Why had he responded like that? If Annette wanted his child, what difference did it make? He would have to acknowledge to the world that the child was his. Was that the reason his reaction was so negative? Jean became angry with himself. If she wanted a child, he would let her have the baby. A realization came to him like a bolt of lightning: he was as close to loving and caring for a woman as he would ever get.

Having overcome his Mr. Hyde, Jean felt much better. He reached for the phone to call Annette and give her the news. They would celebrate that night at Maxim's with a special dinner. He would call ahead and have the chef make their favorite meal. There was no answer at Annette's apartment. It was past six, and she was always home at that hour.

A tremendous depression swept over Jean. The instincts passed on to him from his great ancestry cried out inside of him. He knew something was terribly wrong. An ache in the pit of his stomach put him into a panic. Not waiting to call for his car, he raced out of the building and hailed a cab that took him to Annette's apartment close by.

Jean's entire body was in a sweat. He ran up the stairs to the top floor and opened the door, frantically calling Annette's name. For one of the few times in his life, Jean was not in control of his mind or his body. He opened the bedroom door in a complete state of shock, not wanting to see what he feared the most.

Annette was dressed in the gown in which he had first seen her. He approached her and noticed she had taken great pains to make herself look beautiful, right down to her makeup and nail polish. Jean sank to his knees and, from the depth of his soul, cried out the grief that had resulted from his folly. He loved Annette deeply and never realized it until that very moment.

He was too late. Annette was suspended from the ceiling. She had tied a rope to the chandelier and hanged herself. An envelope was on the table below her. As from another world, Jean read the letter inside.

My dearest Jean,

Thank you for everything you've ever given me. Please don't be angry with me for taking my life. I love you so very much.

I saw today that you must've stopped loving me. I tried so hard to understand why you didn't want our child. I have nothing left to live for.

I hope you find a person someday who you will love as much as I have loved you.

I love you eternally,
Annette

PART V

Paris, 1962: Marie and Tristan

The storm had passed as dawn came to Paris. Tristan lay next to Marie, watching her. He had never felt so good in his life. Gone for the first time was the overwhelming obsession for Vanessa Daniells. Marie had come into his life like some magical, unexpected miracle. He raised himself to look into her face. She was sleeping deeply, as if she too had experienced something overwhelming and needed to rest and regain strength for another day. He caressed her face with his finger, tracing her lips, her cheek, and her closed eyes. She stirred then, and not wanting to wake her, he gently held her to him. Tristan had found his great love. No man could feel that strongly about anybody or anything. In his mind, he knew she felt the same. They would spend eternity together.

∞

When Marie awoke at noon, Tristan was gone. Two enormous vases containing yellow and pink roses were on each side of the bed. A note lay on one of the tables.

> Marie,
> Do you still love me?
> I'll be back soon, don't leave.
> Tristan

She rose and stretched. She felt like she was still on a cloud. The small, elegant hotel room had a sensational bathroom, and Marie soaked herself in the turn-of-the-century tub. She allowed her thoughts to wander. *Tristan Taylor, what a charming name. Will he finally be the person I've been hoping for? Will he love me, and will he love just me?*

∞

Born with a romantic soul, twenty-one-year-old Marie wanted more than anything else to find and love one man exclusively. She wanted that man to return the same love, free of wandering, and wanted her romantic soul to match his.

Such is the love of the young, and occasionally the gods allow this to happen. But in the lives of Marie and Tristan, as much as they might love each other exclusively and forever, fate of another kind was at work—fate by the name of Jean Delacroix.

October in Paris was a beautiful time of the year. When the sun shone in the cool, crisp air, it could be spectacular, especially for two people in love. Marie and Tristan were certainly lost in each other. The first week flew by with neither having a care in the world. With Marie in attendance every night, Tristan finished his engagement at La Poste.

He moved into her spacious apartment in Saint Germain des Pres at once. He was overwhelmed by the luxury at first, which exceeded even his quarters at Maestro Paulo's palatial home, but nothing fazed him about Marie. To him, she was made of magic, and to her, he was Prince Charming.

That anything would interfere with the special love Tristan and Marie had for each other was inconceivable. At the end of each performance, Tristan took Marie to la Coupole, and the two repeated the initiation of love they experienced that first night. They walked to Notre Dame, held hands and looked at each other, caressed each other. A few who noticed the two so engaged felt a pang of jealously, watching them indulge each other so intimately. The two behaved sometimes as if no others were around them. To them, the love affair took place in the clouds. The high was a natural high, and no love affair on earth could match theirs.

It is not unusual for two people to fall so much in love with each other that the other can do no wrong. Men and women are so different, in reality, that sooner or later, one will become disappointed in the action of the other. It is inevitable, but between Tristan and Marie, it never happened in those early weeks of bliss. Little habits that might annoy each other were lacking. Both were compatible in almost everything—careful not to upset each other, courteous in all ways, respectful of each other, admiring of each other.

A marriage of two souls must be accompanied by a serious mixing of the two in mutual admiration and respect. The highly combustible sexual attraction that they have for each other, which might and probably would ebb somewhat, must be replaced with a great friendship. The instant friendship between Tristan and Marie was apparent from the start. That love match was certainly made in heaven.

But like heaven, the other side called hell involved itself in that relationship. The most prevailing reason that two people break up is outside influence, usually from close friends, or even more so by family. Marie's family had met Tristan at La Poste on the third evening and fallen in love with him. However, unbeknownst to her, a man who considered himself more than a family member was standing in the wings, prepared to destroy their relationship at all costs.

Saint Moritz, Switzerland: Chateau Delacroix

Jean was seated on the veranda outside his bedroom suite, having coffee and looking out over the valley between the two mountains. It was the middle of October, and a sea of red, orange, and gold covered the terrain. The air was crisp, the temperature perfect as the sun's rays illuminated the surrounding area. He was in a splendid mood that day. Marie's divorce from Peter Byrd was final, and Jean had not needed to interfere to end their relationship. Marie would definitely be on the rebound, and conditions were ideal for him to take charge.

In Jean's secret employ, Marie's close girlfriend had called late the previous night and left a message that she was catching an early-morning flight to Zurich. She left flight information and requested that the Bell helicopter rush her to the estate. Smiling to himself, Jean anticipated a lengthy description of the divorce proceedings between Marie and Peter. He was relishing those thoughts when the phone rang next to him. It was Marie.

"Jean, good morning, my sweet. I can't make it up this weekend as you requested. Something's come up. Have you seen the proof sheets on the new photo spreads I did for you last week? They're great."

Jean's heart froze. What was that all about? He had specifically told her how important that weekend was. She had promised him. He held back the silent rage. "Certainly, my dear. Whatever you say. But what has happened? I need you this weekend. Can't you make changes and join me?"

"La, no, Jean. I'll explain later what's happening. It's really not anything serious. Bye now."

Jean held the dead phone in his hand. The bitch had hung up. The rage surged inside him, and a deep instinct signaled him to get indoors quickly. He headed for the basement.

℘

When Jean's father built the basement area of the castle, he installed cold storage areas for the large amounts of food and wine brought to the estate. Utilizing a contractor from a German firm, Jean had taken one room and specially designed it for meditation and exercise. Occasionally, he used it for more intimate purposes. Jean used the many pieces of exercise equipment daily in the long, narrow area. In the center of the gym were two thick ropes suspended from the twenty-foot ceiling. Jean often used those to climb to the ceiling with his legs extended in a ninety-degree angle, Olympian style. He was in magnificent shape.

He was an excellent marksman, as well. Against one wall was a gun collection consisting of both rifles and hand guns, the latter used for practice almost daily. Jean could bring down a jackrabbit nearly a hundred yards away with a small-caliber pistol. Though tempted to blast away his rage, Jean continued walking until he reached the exercise equipment.

Jean spent thirty minutes on the treadmill before moving on to weight lifting. Within an hour's time, he had worked up a sweat. He paused, waiting for the rage to dissipate. The girl would be arriving shortly. She must know why Marie had canceled her trip. Looking up, Jean focused on the two ropes hanging down. He stood very still and let his body relax from the strenuous program he had just completed. A vein in his neck throbbed incessantly. The rage was still there, and it was much worse—a dangerous rage—and Jean fought against it with all his will. He moved to the opposite wall and seated himself into the first position of yoga. He would meditate until the rage was gone.

℀

Jean had meditated for two hours before returning upstairs, uncalmed and unstable. He sat rigidly in the formal meeting room used previously for the successful meeting with Marie and her agents. It was past two in the afternoon when Cyril finally brought the girl in, closing the door as he left. With a firm grip on her arm, Jean ushered her to a chair next to his.

A black veil covered her face, as was the custom when she came to the chateau. She removed her veil and looked up at Jean with fear in her eyes. Stuttering, she informed him of the new man in Marie's life. "He's a noted singer from America: Tristan Taylor. He starred on Broadway, and he's performing at La Poste now. *Paris Match* has an article on him. I brought it with me." She rambled on. "I've never seen Marie like this. I met with her the day after she heard Tristan sing, and she was in the clouds. Marie's other affairs excited her. But this time she's fallen completely in love, and from what I understand, so has he."

Jean listened intently, his anger building. He responded almost in a hiss. "Good. Keep close. I want every detail of what's going on between them. I have some calls to make. Join me for dinner at eight. Cyril will take you to your room." And with that, she was dismissed.

Jean sat at the large black conference table, and his mind drifted. Would the nightmare ever end? Why couldn't he rid himself of his obsession for Marie? He had access to any woman in the world, and he could only think of her. He loved her and he hated her at the same time. Jean reached for the phone and dialed a number he had memorized long ago. Roger Elonda had served him before; he would be required to work around the clock, watching the two lovers. There would be a way; there was always a way. Jean's second call was brief. "I want her at the airport in one hour. My plane will meet her and bring her to my chateau."

℘

It was eerie having just two people dine in the chateau's cavernous dining room. Additionally, Jean did not speak at all. It was as if there were no one present. He had never frightened the girl before, but that day there was something sinister in his eyes. She tried speaking, but her conversation was met with distant coldness. She finally gave up and finished the meal in silence.

As they got up to leave the table, Jean said sarcastically, "I won't need your services tonight. Cyril will wake you for breakfast early. I'll talk to you in Paris."

The girl followed Jean's valet along the elegant corridors with the old master paintings looking down at her. In her room, she sat down to remove her makeup and examined herself in the mirror. A pang of guilt swept over her. A beautiful woman looked back at her, but she was a Judas, if ever he really existed. Well, what else could she have done? She had money that she could never have earned otherwise, and a career where none would have been. She finished her bedtime ritual and retired for the night.

℘

Jean entered the dark gymnasium in the basement and switched on the overhead lights. He went to a large Manchurian cabinet set against one wall and opened the cabinet doors. Inside was the best stereo system available, a Blaupunkt from Germany. He selected an album with a concerto in D minor by Beethoven.

He walked to the center of the gym and inspected the two nooses he had made earlier. Taking a stepladder that was lying next to the wall, he tightened the nooses and set them for what he considered to be ample openings. The rage had returned, and the migraine was coming in alarming force. Marie's friend, his Judas, was safely tucked away in her room, and he could focus on what he must do.

A knock came at the door, and Jean opened it. Cyril was standing there with a young blonde. As always, she resembled Marie somewhat but the hair had to be blonde, even if the girl had to have it dyed for the occasion. That one was exquisite. The robe she arrived in dropped to the floor, revealing a nude figure that immediately lessened the rage inside Jean's mind. Her body was perfect. As was the custom, she wore a blindfold.

Jean dismissed his trusted valet and led the girl to the middle of the room next to the stool. He quickly undressed himself then walked to the music system and started the heavy German concerto, amplifying the volume so that nothing else could be heard. Taking the girl's hand, Jean assisted her until she was standing on the stool. He carefully climbed up beside her. The stool was specially designed so that it accommodated two persons, and the metal struts were loosened so that it felt unsteady once they stood up. Jean reached up and slipped one noose over the girl's head, the other over his own.

Leaning close to her then, Jean whispered. "Do not move. Do not struggle. I am not going to hurt you." He lifted her straight up against his body and entered her. Jean had the strength of three men his age. The control he exercised over his body was absolute. He held the girl rigidly against him and began the even rhythm necessary to complete the act. His headache subsided with each thrust of his body. The rage subsided along with it. The explosion that came after a brief time removed all the rage and all the pain, and he was again at peace.

Holding the girl firmly with one hand, he removed the two ropes from their throats. He lowered himself and the girl to the floor with ease then placed the robe over her and led her to the door. Cyril was outside to take her to a dressing room and give her the customary envelope for Madame Alexandra. He could count on anyone she sent to remain quiet. He bought their silence. Each session cost Jean ₣350,000. Those were his therapy sessions and worth every franc.

The girls would never know the jeopardy they were put in. If they knew, it would not be a matter of yes or no, but a matter of price. Madame Alexandra would just pump up the charge. Those thoughts were going through Jean's mind as he returned to his rooms for a well-deserved shower and a long and deep sleep.

ॐ

Jean sat behind his priceless Louis XVI desk and listened to Roger Elonda make his daily report. Roger had hired sufficient men to work in tandem with him to follow both Marie and Tristan as they moved about the large city. That was not a difficult assignment in a city like Paris, as hardly anyone used private cars. The antiquated underground subway system was convenient to all and, during the day, quite safe to use. Cabs were the other means of transportation for most. Roger handed Jean a printed list of what Marie and Tristan had been doing. They had been together for two weeks, and neither was out of sight of the other for more than a few hours.

All of Marie's phones had been tapped, and information was easy to obtain. According to Roger, Marie was going over scripts from her agents, and Tristan had been calling Rome to postpone his engagement there. Marie's bedroom had been wired for sound, as well, and Roger was a bit fidgety as he handed over the tape. "This is the master bedroom tape you requested. I haven't heard the contents, per your instructions. Telephone conversation just this morning indicates Taylor is leaving for Rome in two days to perform at the Regent. My informant in Rome told me it's a dinner theater much like La Poste. Taylor has reserved rooms at the Excelsior."

Jean interrupted the conversation with unmasked disdain. "And Marie. Is she also planning to leave with Taylor?"

"Yes. They've booked two first-class seats on Alitalia. She put off her agents here indefinitely, telling them she needs a rest before starting another film. Additionally, Taylor booked rooms at the Royal Danieli in Venice following his appearance in Rome."

Jean was fully disturbed then, and Roger avoided his glance. "Anything else, Roger?"

"No sir. Am I to set up surveillance in Rome? Getting into their rooms is going to be hell, and expensive."

"Expensive?" Delacroix nearly yelled the word. "What in hell do I care about expensive? Do whatever you must. I have to know what's going on. Leave tonight. I want teams set up at once—one in Rome, one in Venice."

ॐ

Marie was excited as she packed for her trip with Tristan. It would be her first real vacation in . . . she could not remember ever having taken off just to enjoy herself. Alexia was out of the country, doing her first serious film role. Marie talked to her every few days but wanted to share her newfound joy with a close friend or two and had called in Gabriel Dubols and Veronique Ophuls, actresses she had met during the past two years.

"I've never taken a vacation of any kind. Imagine. I've fallen in love, hopelessly in love, and I'll be spending nearly a month with Tristan while he performs in Rome then Venice.

"He's scheduled for three nights at the Metropole Theatre in Venice. It's his first concert outside of a dinner club, and it's been sold out for months. Eight hundred people will be there, even though he changed the date.

"Venice. Can you believe it? I've never been to Italy, and we'll be in the two most romantic cities outside of Paris."

Marie threw her wardrobe together, paying no attention to the large stack of suitcases piling up next to the bed. Gabriel, or Gabby as she was referred to by her friends, started laughing. "Marie, what are you doing with that huge closet of clothes? You can't take it all with you. The plane won't be able to take off."

An open bottle of Dom Perignon stood on the nearby table. The women had been sipping the bubbly and were a little tipsy. Marie came forth with her famous laugh, threw open her shoe closet, and with no organization whatsoever, piled suitcases full of shoes, laughing louder and louder with each handful. Her laughter was always contagious, and that day was no exception.

℘

Tristan arrived at that moment. Walking into the room, he was greeted with even louder laughter. He smiled heartily and said, "Am I that funny looking, or has everyone gone off the deep end today?" He strode to the bed and examined the ten suitcases Marie had managed to throw together. "You're not really taking all this, are you?"

"No, Tristan, this is just my coats and shoes. I haven't started packing my clothes yet," Marie said with a straight face.

Tristan shook his head, speechless.

Having just taken a gulp of champagne, Marie held a serious look on her face for several seconds before exploding into laughter. The champagne exploded from her at the same time, spraying Tristan thoroughly. He was both pained and surprised until it all sank in. He ended up on the floor with all three women, laughing at length until he cried out that his sides hurt.

ഔ

Marie would finish her packing in a more proper way the following day and, to her credit, only have six suitcases to accommodate her on the journey. Tristan would have one.

ഔ

When Gabby left Marie that afternoon, she slowly walked the short distance to the Seine, where she rented her small apartment. The light high from the champagne was still refreshing as she walked, but another feeling was there too. Why was Marie so lucky? She owned the world at twenty-one, and every opportunity that came along led to something special. Sure, a few men had disappointed her, what else was new in the universe?

A whole new career was opening for Gabby, with two films lined up in which she would first costar then star. That fact did nothing to stop her from being envious of Marie. Self-pity overcame her, and by the time she reached her apartment overlooking the river, the pleasant high was gone. She hesitated a long time before reaching for the phone.

Rome: Excelsior Hotel

Located at the top of the Spanish Steps, the Excelsior was Rome's finest hotel. Every major city in the world had at least one luxury accommodation, and the Excelsior was that and more. With expansive views from all sides, its famous penthouse restaurant looked out over the great city. The hotel employed Rome's finest chefs. The rooms and suites were elegant, and the service unmatched in Italy.

Arriving late in the day from Paris, Marie and Tristan took the one-hour taxi ride to the hotel. They were on an incredible high. Love knows no boundaries when two young lovers have found an ecstatic, loving relationship they believe will last forever. During the ride, they talked incessantly about their first evening in Rome. Marie's agents and friends had given her lists of restaurants, clubs, and dear friends to call when they arrived in the ancient city.

The lovers made elaborate plans for their first evening but procrastinated about making decisions. Should they call anyone the first night or be by themselves? Should they go to a traditional Italian restaurant or a trendy new place? In the end, as in all things, their best-laid plans went asunder.

After checking into the Excelsior, Marie and Tristan had a drink in the bar at the top of the hotel. They held each other tightly, oblivious to everyone around them as they viewed the Vatican from the restaurant's large picture windows. They looked deeply into each other's eyes, silently saying how much they loved each other so very much and so very dearly. Then they went back to their room and made love. They left open the shades of the large, panoramic windows of their suite and, locked in an eternal embrace, awoke early to the sun's rays. Looking at each other, they never moved, never twitched, just loved one another from the depths of their very souls.

The two were not lovers for the first time in that plane. The passion was too immense, the intensity sincere. Somewhere, in some other time, they had been together as lovers, and as friends. But the gods had other plans for them. Jean Delacroix had other plans for them. Yet that night, and for a few precious weeks, the gods would let them have their happiness.

℘

Tristan's appearance at the old Regent Theatre was a smashing success. Paulo Nolanza, attended his concerts on three occasions. Each night, Tristan's performance was clearly enhanced by the new love in his life.

Paulo fell instantly in love with Marie, and the threesome made the rounds of early luncheons at homes and restaurants at the direction of his former teacher. He introduced the two to the so-called nobility in Rome. Those experiences were delightful and, on occasion, surprising. The White Elephant was a favorite dining place of the rich and famous. From the brocaded booths to the clear crystal set on each table, elegance was tradition at the restaurant. They served bottled water before S.Pelligrino or Perrier was ever heard of in America. Of course, the water was Italian not French. Fine Italian dining was similar to dining in the finest restaurants of France. Light meals were the mainstay of Italian gourmets. Sauces were a bit heavier, but even that was arguable.

℘

Maestro Paulo introduced Marie and Tristan to the Duke and Duchess of Verona and their elegant guests, all Italian nobility except for one. Tristan had never met persons of that station and was interested in their conversation, most of which was politely done in French for Marie's benefit. She and Tristan were seated together at a corner of the twelve-person booth.

The member of the Verona's group who was not Italian was Claire Hawthorne, a wealthy American who had recently married an Italian count. (Much later, Paulo said the count was really a fraud who married Miss Hawthorne for her money.) The luncheon would not have been terribly noteworthy except for the incredulous conversation between Claire and the nobility. Tristan came to comprehend the absolute absurdity of moderately new money trying to upstage the more-real old money.

Miss Hawthorne rambled on about her wealth. "You see, my dears, my father left me all this dreadful money to spend, and frankly I can't spend it fast enough. Look at my new necklace I purchased in Paris last summer. It's from Cartier and made especially for me. The centerpiece is a perfect six-carat diamond, and the smaller stones total one hundred and twelve carats. And do look at the emerald bracelet I bought myself for my birthday last week." Claire lifted a thin wrist into the air and waved the beautiful green bracelet for all to see.

Tristan took Marie's hand under the table and gave it a squeeze. She smiled back, obviously sharing the same thoughts. How strange that anyone could be so unhappy with their life that only physical possessions represented the highs of life but, in reality, were unimportant. What really left an indelible memory with Tristan that night was that, even with the pretty, expensive items Miss Hawthorne carried on about, she was unaware of the treasures the other guests were wearing. The Duchess of Verona had a diamond-and-ruby tiara that was easily worth ten times the rings, bracelets, and necklace Claire bandied about.

Tristan knew nothing about the cost of such baubles, but his strong instinct told him what was of real value and what was not. He knew Marie liked, on occasion, the fluff of life that made women feel special, but she wasn't obsessed with that. Later that night after Tristan's performance, he and Marie laughed until their sides hurt, reliving and trying to mimic Miss Hawthorne's descriptions of her jewelry.

ॐ

Tristan and Marie's last evening in Rome was spent with Maestro Paulo in his magnificent villa atop the hillside next to the ruins of the Forum. Only the teacher, his pupil, and the lovely Marie were present.

"Paulo, you must tell us about Venice," Tristan said. "Where shall we dine? What should we see?" The two lovers were seated in the maestro's comfortable library, sipping Franjelico.

"Ah, my beloved Venice. What is there not to see? Where is there not to go? I'll prepare a list before you leave tonight. I understand you're staying at the Royal Danieli. I'll call ahead for you and make sure you're well taken care of. I know the manager well and will request a suite for you.

"I can only tell you this. Venice is for lovers. You need do nothing but walk the narrow streets, lie together in a gondola, or sit at a small table in Saint Mark's Square watching the people go by. You're very much in love and have chosen the perfect place to be. It's not important where you go, or even what you do. Venice will do it for you."

After embracing the beloved teacher responsible for the start of Tristan's career, Tristan and Marie left his splendid home and walked down the little mountain road toward Rome. Tristan looked back and waved one last time to Paulo. It was the last time Tristan ever saw him.

ॐ

The gods had given the maestro a long and happy life. It was time to move on, and when autumn turned to winter, Paulo would die quietly in his sleep, dreaming of his young students and the richness he had given to the world with his teaching.

Venice: The Royal Danieli

One of the most luxurious hotels in the world, the Royal Danieli was once a palace, and when it became a hotel, it remained a palace. The rooms would suit a monarch, and frequently did. The amenities were splendid in every manner — antique furniture, carpets, and drapes; old master paintings; enormous rooms covered in beautiful fabrics and bordered with crown molding. From the twenty-foot-wide balcony, visitors could look down at the Grand Canal or see the Island of Murano in the distance.

Making a reservation in that hotel compared to deciding whether to rent a Mercedes Benz or a Rolls Royce Corniche. For most persons, renting either was an impossible dream. For the wealthy, a line of distinction was drawn between even the Mercedes and the Rolls. If you drove a Rolls, you had truly made it. And if you could spend a week at the Royal Danieli, you had made it.

Tristan had yet to earn the money he would when his destiny in the music business put him at the top financially. Over the past several years, he had saved his *Westside* money, and adding to that the great generosity he wanted to lavish on Marie, he did not hesitate when he signed the registration card listing his luxury suite at £4.1 million per night. However, the price did include a continental breakfast. To the rich of the world, the hotel was a bargain. For two people newly in love, it was paradise.

∞

Paradise was not on the mind of the man who registered just an hour after Tristan, carrying a small overnight bag and an attaché case. Roger Elonda was tired. His flight from Paris was over rough weather, and the pilot of the Alitalia flight had bounced the plane off the runway upon landing, jolting Roger so badly that an old injury was inflamed in the lower part of his back. He was limping to one side, and the fact that he was staying at one of the finest hotels in the world was not an inspiration.

Roger was not in a suite, but no room in the famous hotel was less than splendid. Splendor did not help Roger's pain. He ordered a double Scotch on the rocks, which somehow lessened the discomfort. His work for the week was almost around the clock, starting with that night. Inside the attaché case was F1 million, mostly for bribes. Rooms must be bugged, workers hired for a myriad of jobs. The bribe to the hotel manager was enormous.

છ

Fabritzio Vascassio was a lifetime employee and above reproach. In the entire world, the hotel manager would bend to only a handful of individuals making requests against hotel policy. Of the six or so persons in that category, most were breaking rules like bringing in a prostitute or setting up one of the rooms for a serious card game between the great gamblers of the world.

The day before Tristan arrived, a caller contacted Fabritzio at the hotel. "Yes, I'm fine, Fabritzio . . . No, I'm not coming to Venice but look forward to seeing you soon, my old friend. I have a modest request for you. My niece will be arriving tomorrow with Tristan Taylor, who has booked rooms with you, I understand. You have his reservation, yes? . . . Well, my dear friend, I think Mr. Taylor might be hooking my niece on heroin . . . No, no. We won't involve the police. I have to prove it first, and then as long as she's not involved in the scandal, I'll consider the police. In the meantime, please work carefully with Roger Elonda, who will protect her in this matter. Please, do whatever he requests of you. For your assistance, he'll take care of you in my little family way, which you know so well."

છ

Harry's Bar was one of the happiest dining experiences in Venice. It was not glamorous in a traditional sense; nevertheless, the ambiance made it a must for anyone who liked to look at other people, have a fine meal, and try a first Bellini, a mixture of champagne with a little peach puree.

Working on their third Bellini, Tristan and Marie sat in a small booth at the rear of the first-floor restaurant looking out at the Grand Canal. Neither could keep their hands off the other, and for those who recognized one or the other, it was difficult not to feel a tinge of jealousy. The two obviously were very much in love and oblivious to those around them that first evening in Venice.

After dinner, Tristan and Marie strolled along the winding, narrow streets back to their hotel, lost in a world of innocence and love that was winding down. A clock was ticking without their having any idea that their time together was very short.

Paris: Madame Alexandra

Jean sat behind his desk and dialed the number. It rang several times before the husky voice responded. "Madame Alexandra, and how are you today, dear?" Jean had known her forever and knew he was by far her biggest customer. His business activities caused him to use her glamorous services quite frequently, for himself and others, and he never once questioned her fees.

"I have an unusual request for you. I have never made this kind of request, and I don't want you to refuse me. I want the services of one of your girls, and she only has to act out a few lines for me. There should be no problem with that request, as she is an actress anyway. I want Genevieve Dubois to do a job for me."

Madame Alexandra was silent for a long moment. "You . . . can't have Genevieve Dubois . . . how did you know she works for me?"

Holding back his laughter, Jean said in a controlled voice, "The king of Morocco is my personal friend, my dear. So is the shah of Iran. I know she only sees them and that the arrangement is known by only the four of you. I want her for this assignment. It is urgent. And there will be no sex involved, only an acting job. I'll provide you with a full background for the scenario so she can accomplish the task accordingly." Jean was enjoying every second of the game. He knew she could not refuse him, and he knew that Genevieve Dubois, the young sensation of Europe, would not refuse the madam. He was in his element, controlling the situation and winning.

"I'll see what I can do, Mr. Delacroix."

Jean laughed loudly then. "It's Jean, my dear. Remember, you haven't addressed me by Delacroix in years. I'll await your call. Don't make it long." He hung up the phone and sat back in the deep chair. His headache gone, he could enjoy the rest of the evening.

Venice: Aphrodite

The sun's rays woke Tristan as he lay in the soft canopy bed in the bedroom overlooking the Grand Canal. He looked into Marie's peaceful sleeping face. For the first time since he had left New York, he thought of Vanessa. And for the first time, his thoughts were memories of a close, loving friend. He suddenly understood where their relationship really was, had really always been. Naïve for so many years, Tristan realized in that moment that Vanessa had long ago accepted him as a friend, a loving friend but nothing more.

In her own way, Vanessa had maintained the relationship, allowing herself and Tristan the indulgence of an occasional romantic evening. He realized with a great shock that this amazing person, who had originally been attracted to him physically, was long since indulging him sexually only out of a great desire to remain friends. That insight was a powerful awakening, and never again would he want Vanessa in any other role than friendship. Vanessa was his touchstone, and he wanted more than anything to share with her the person he would spend the rest of his life with.

The sun slowly brightened the pretty bedroom at the Danieli, and Tristan pulled Marie close. She stirred in his arms as he gazed at her. His thoughts wandered, and he tried to imagine why he was so much in love with the beautiful young French woman. Her physical presence was vital to him. Life without Marie was incomprehensible. He kissed her cheek, her lips, lingering softly on her mouth. He gently caressed her long, dark-auburn hair and pulled a lock against his cheek, feeling its smooth texture.

Marie's eyes opened slowly, and she gazed into his face. The warmth of their chemistry began slowly, and they caressed each other gently, lovingly. Then the fire, as if a volcano had erupted. They could not quench the immense rush they felt for each other. Time went by, how long neither knew. It could have been minutes; it could have been hours. The sun was higher, the room ablaze with light. Tristan and Marie were covered in sweat, covered in all the wondrous juices of great passion. The distinct perfume of love permeated the room.

When they could love no longer, Tristan and Marie lay in an intimate embrace, holding each other as if they might never see one another again. They looked into each other's eyes deeply, lovingly, and fell back into a very deep sleep.

When Tristan awoke again, it was late afternoon. Marie lay sleeping with a contented smile on her beautiful face. He got up carefully so as not to awaken her, then showered and dressed quickly. Somewhere in Venice he would find a little surprise for her before dinner. Setting out, he allowed himself to become lost in the maze of streets and alleys that made up the unique city. Tristan went in and out of dozens of stores, clothing boutiques, candle shops, and jewelry stores, looking for some special gift he could surprise his love with. He lost track of time but knew he had wandered far from their hotel.

Tristan came out of a narrow passage and into a large square. In one corner of the square was a quaint church with stained-glass windows ablaze in the late afternoon sun. Across from the church was a cluster of small shops. He walked by the stores, looking into the windows at the merchandise. The last shop displayed a single item: a small, elegant, brown-leather bag trimmed in gold thread and tied with a gold, braided strand of rope. Tristan read the inscription at the top of the windowpane: OIL FRAGRANCE, THE ULTIMATE GIFT.

His curiosity piqued, Tristan entered the small shop. He was instantly aware of the pleasant scents that filled the air. His first thought was that of walking into a perfume store, except no evidence of actual perfume was in sight, only identical amber-colored bottles marked with the names of different fragrances.

A woman appeared from behind the curtains that closed off the rear of the store. She was blonde and unusually pretty. Her face revealed an ageless quality, but Tristan knew she was perhaps thirty, maybe a bit older. She smiled at Tristan and said, "Hello, Tristan Taylor. I hoped you might come in. Don't look so surprised. I have tickets to see you perform tomorrow night. I'm Aphrodite, and you're here because you want something splendid for your lady friend, yes?"

"Yes. Please tell me what's in these little bottles. Are they fragrances used to make perfume?" Tristan watched Aphrodite move about the store, retrieving some of the amber bottles. She was very slim and walked with an elegant grace.

Standing behind a small counter, she placed the bottles of fragrance on top and opened their lids. She held one out to Tristan so he could smell the fragrance. "This has a lavender scent," she said as she took Tristan's hand palm down and poured a small amount on his wrist. Gently, she rubbed the oil into his skin. The content was not perfume but clear oil. After a few seconds, the oil became very warm, and Tristan rubbed his wrist rapidly in surprise. She laughed gently at his reaction. "Yes, the oil becomes warm as soon as it's exposed to the air. No one else has this formula. It has stayed in our family for hundreds of years. The formula is special, as is the purpose of the oil."

"And what is the purpose?"

"It is, in reality, a love potion. I blend the fragrance of your choice with our formulation, and it's used to massage the woman you love. The oil penetrates the skin, revitalizing the surface and, at the same time, giving pleasure to the one you love as you apply it. I'll give you a little book to study and use in the application of the oil. You must use care, as some parts of the body are not good for the application. You mustn't apply it near the eyes or inside any intimate part of the body. You also need not wash off the residue, as this will, in a short time, penetrate the skin and help to keep the skin forever youthful."

Tristan listened to the elegant woman for nearly half an hour. He studied her closely as she spoke, and became curious about her age.

Eventually, she said with a lovely smile, "You're wondering about my age. How old do you think I am?"

"I'm sorry. I didn't think I was so obvious. You're young. I would say early- to mid-thirties, no?"

"No, Tristan. I'm fifty-five. I can't sell you water from the fountain of Ponce de Leon, but I can provide you with our oils that will keep you and those you love youthful. Tell me now, what fragrance does your lover like best? No, let me tell you. It is lilies."

"And how did you know that?"

She laughed then, a rich laugh giving Tristan a happy feeling. "Because, young man, it's still all over you from your lovemaking."

Tristan left the little shop, content with the gift resting inside the attractive leather case. He was anxious to try it out on Marie after dinner that evening.

Venice: Roger Elonda

Jean took the call on a Saturday morning. In Venice, his beloved Marie would be leaving with Tristan to return to Paris on Monday. He had two days to put his plan into its final act, having made an ultimate decision to spare the singer's life. How much easier it would have been for Jean, in such a powerful position, to just have Tristan killed. He had toyed with that idea in the beginning, but some strong inner instinct kept him from following that line. It was not because of any conscience that he would spare the man. Jean was a dysfunctional human being but, with a clever veil, hid that part of his character from the world in general. He was well aware of his sociopathic malfunction. He didn't give a damn about Tristan's life, just the effect his death might have on Marie. In the end, he opted for a more complex solution.

Roger Elonda spoke in a tired but concentrated voice. "I have everything ready to go for Sunday. As per your orders, the man who will meet Tristan Taylor cannot be traced back to me. I used two middlemen to set up that operation. The window for Sunday will be narrow. I must have your girl here no later than one p.m. I've retained the Italian actor, who will be on hand for the entire day."

"Roger, I cannot tell you how important it is that the singer not be hurt. If Tristan or Marie becomes suspicious, you must call off the operation."

ຂາ

That Sunday, Tristan and Marie's last day in Venice, was to be a special day. The hotel's launch would take them to the Island of Murano, where representatives of the principal glass factory would be waiting to escort them through the modern showroom as well as the famous museum. A private lunch would then complete the afternoon.

Tristan's agent, Greg Manning, had called the previous day to give him some exciting news. Alphonse Luccessi, who owned the largest theater in Florence, had called and wanted to meet Tristan after lunch to discuss an engagement at his theater later in the year. Greg stated he was prepared to offer Tristan a figure exceeding twice what he was currently receiving. Having expended a rather substantial amount of his savings, Tristan decided it was important to listen to the proposal. He did not want to miss a moment with Marie, but Greg told him Luccessi would not hold him up more than a half hour.

Everything went well on Murano, including the tour and the lunch. Feeling just a bit of the wine and their natural high, Tristan and Marie held each other tightly at the rear of the small hotel launch for the return to the main island. All of Venice could be seen that sunny day as they neared the shoreline—Saint Mark's Square, the Gritti Palace, and, of course, their beautiful hotel.

When Tristan and Marie exited the small craft, a middle-aged man was standing at the hotel's dock. He was dressed immaculately in white, with long blond hair tied in the back much like Tristan. He had warm blue eyes, and his greeting was cordial. "Mr. Taylor and Miss Savoie, I am Alphonse Luccessi. Such a pleasure to be meeting both of you. I hope your visit to the Glass Island was pleasant. Miss Savoie, I must congratulate you on your performance in *Romeo and Juliet.* My entire family was captivated by your interpretation of Juliet."

The three walked from the dock adjoining the Danieli to the front of the hotel. Tristan embraced Marie warmly in farewell and followed Luccessi toward Saint Mark's Square. The two men selected a small table in the middle of the square, where the view of the church and the promenade was the most spectacular. Both ordered double espressos, and Luccessi described his small opera house in Florence.

Tristan listened with one ear, but his mind drifted to thoughts of Marie. He heard Luccessi's voice but couldn't concentrate. A strange melancholy overcame him. The day, the week, the past few weeks were the best of his life. An urge overcame Tristan, and without offering a reason, he excused himself from Luccessi. "I'm so sorry. I have to leave. I feel a bit dizzy—must've been the espresso. Please call my agent. I look forward to coming to Florence." Tristan stood up. He was sweating. The urge to join Marie was overwhelming, and he walked in the direction of the Danieli.

§

Alphonse immediately flashed Roger Elonda the agreed-upon emergency signal. Having hoped the meeting would continue for the full thirty minutes planned, Roger felt the color drain from his face, but only for an instant. Without a moment's hesitation, he rushed over to Tristan. "Excuse me, sir, you must be Tristan Taylor. Your friend Marie Savoie gave me a description of you and told me I could find you here somewhere on the square. There's been an accident."

Tristan tensed and stopped walking. "I knew something was wrong," he muttered. "How bad, and what's happened? Is she all right?"

"Yes, yes. It's not life threatening. She fell down the hotel stairs and broke her wrist. She's in a lot of pain. A launch has taken her to Cipriati

Hospital. She's asked me to bring you there. Follow me. It won't take long."

&

Tristan followed the man through the crowd to the front of the Grand Canal, where fifteen minutes later they were able to hail a passing launch. After the ten-minute ride, they took a short walk through the strange alley-like streets to the hospital. The old Cipriati Hospital was constructed in white marble both outside and in. A huge reception area bustled with people—doctors, nurses, and patients.

The man took Tristan to the reception counter. A young girl behind the counter smiled and in proper American English asked how she could be of assistance. With much concern, Tristan described Marie and what had happened. The girl disappeared for nearly five minutes. When she returned, she looked at him and said, "I'm sorry, sir. There's no Marie Savoie here."

Tristan felt light-headed for a moment. "There must be."

"No, I'm really sorry. I've checked all our records for the past two hours. She's not here."

Tristan was becoming disoriented. He looked around to find the man who had brought him. He was nowhere in sight.

&

Marie was exhilarated as she returned to the hotel. She had no commitments in Paris that couldn't be put off. Tristan was finished with his short tour, and they just had not seen enough of Venice. Her heart full of joy and excitement, she rushed to the reservation counter and ascertained that they could extend their stay.

"Yes," Fabritzio said. "Your rooms were reserved for a week, but what luck for you"—lowering his voice, he leaned over the counter and whispered—"Vanessa Daniells had made reservations but got into a fight with her husband and just canceled. Shall I keep the room open?"

"Please, Mr. Fabritzio, hold it until Tristan returns. I'll ask him and have him call you right away."

Bursting with happiness over her idea, Marie ascended in the old bronze elevator to their third-floor suite. She opened the door to their rooms, humming happily as she entered the bedroom. Her smiling face froze instantly. Lying in the middle of their bed was a woman entirely naked. It was not just that the woman was naked; it was the woman herself—Genevieve Dubois.

Genevieve sat bolt upright, a look of complete surprise on her face. "Hello, Marie. I'm . . . so sorry. I was supposed to see Tristan in Paris but couldn't because I was completing my film with Robert Bresson. Tristan's agent told me I could find him here. I asked at the front desk, and having recognized me at once, they just had someone let me in. They never told me you were with Tristan now. He told me all about you from Paris but said he wanted me to come back. He was supposed to tell you in Rome."

Marie seated herself on the rug and cried silently, tears streaming down her pretty face. She wanted to talk, but nothing would come out. Genevieve Dubois was one of France's most famous and beautiful actresses. She was virtually on a par with Brigitte Bardot for beauty and popularity. Through her role as Juliet, Marie was just being discussed as a new French sensation, but she certainly did not have the film credits the slightly older actress had. If it had been anyone other than Genevieve Dubois, Marie might have hesitated. The idea that the situation was a staged theatrical hoax was not conceivable. Tristan had fallen in love with Genevieve first and, for some reason, had not told Marie. Those thoughts went through her mind as she sat heartbroken on the floor of the bedroom.

Genevieve came over and embraced her as a close friend might have. "Men. Marie, you must learn all about them. They tell you they love you the whole time while thinking of someone else. Have you not had any of these experiences?" Marie's shoulders fell as she remembered the men who had betrayed her. "Marie, my love, I'm so sorry. I'm going to leave. I won't ever see this man again, you can be assured. He should have told you. By the way, you know he's still seeing Vanessa Daniells. He promised me he'd break off that affair, but I can see now I want nothing to do with him." All the while she was talking, Genevieve was dressing herself. She gave Marie another tight hug and, pulling her to her feet, kissed her cheek and was gone.

For a fleeting second, Marie's subconscious noticed Genevieve did not have anything with her aside from her shoulder purse. But in Marie's state, the thought disappeared quickly. She sobbed and felt like her heart was certainly broken, if such a thing were really possible. The ache in her chest was unbearable. What to do, who to call? She instinctively reached for the phone and dialed the one number where she knew there was someone she could count on to help her anytime and anyplace.

"Yes, Marie, I understand," Jean said. "I'm here for you, my dearest, and always will be."

"I can't believe this is happening. If I could just . . . I'm going to pack up and—"

"No. Don't pack, just leave. I'll call Fabritzio and have his staff pack all your things right down to your toothbrush. It will all be delivered to your apartment in twenty-four hours. He will personally escort you to the airport outside Venice. My plane will be there for you."

"Not until I have a little talk with Tristan Taylor. How could he do this to me?"

"No, no, don't confront him now. Come home and we'll talk about it. He could get violent. You need a rest, Marie, a long rest. There's a small island in the Seychelles. I'll take you there. It's called Denis Island."

"Yes, Jean, I'll come home. I'm so unhappy." And Marie ended the call.

Had all of her time with Tristan been a lie? *I loved him so much,* her thoughts cried out. *I know he loved me. Tristan, Tristan, why did you destroy us?*

℘

Exasperated from his bizarre ordeal, Tristan finally returned to the Danieli. It was early evening, and his concern for Marie was overwhelming. He ran into the hotel and up the three flights of stairs to their suite. The room was totally empty, and all of Marie's clothes were gone. He frantically called reception and spoke to the assistant manager. "Mr. Taylor, I'm so sorry. Miss Savoie checked out an hour ago. No, I have no idea where she went. No, there was no accident. She was fine. She was smiling when she left."

Tristan sat down on the bed, completely bewildered. Then he saw the small envelope next to the pillow. The letter was short, and when he finished it, he felt as if his life was over.

> Dear Tristan,
>
> Thank you for such a wonderful time. I really like you and will remember you with fondness. When I met you, I was getting over a man I loved very much. I just called him in Paris, and I want to be with him again.
>
> I'm so sorry, please don't call me.
>
> Marie

Tristan felt completely numb. Marie had never once hinted of another romance. On one occasion, she had mentioned that she had only once fallen in love but in retrospect realized it was just a strong infatuation. She held Tristan close that night and told him he was her first love. He, in turn, told her of Vanessa and how he too realized he had been caught up in an infatuation. The lovemaking that night was intense, but tender at the same time. Both expressed that they could never love another as they did each other.

With a great sadness in his heart, Tristan felt as if he were dying. One of his favorite aunts had died some years back. His beautiful aunt was young, and the two were inseparable. When she died prematurely, his heart broke. With the loss of Marie, the feeling was the same.

Tristan lay on Marie's pillow, inhaling her fragrance. Finally, the tears came, silently at first then in wrenching torrents until he could cry no more. Rising slowly from the bed, he picked up the phone and called the concierge, who scheduled him on flight 412 to Paris the next day.

જી

Jean sat in his apartment on Ile Saint-Louis, staring out the window. Though the Notre Dame Cathedral glowed in the red-orange rays of the setting sun, he saw nothing. His fingers tapped absentmindedly on the top of his Louis XVI desk as he contemplated the call from Marie that afternoon. He was not gleeful; he was not ecstatic; he was satisfied for the moment. Past failures with his attempted conquest of Marie had taught him to be patient. That romantic creature could change her mind in a second and simply confront the singer. She was capable of anything, but a strong hunch whispered in his ear, yes, Jean, you've finally won. He had left nothing to chance. He was not the kind of person who ever forgot any detail. Jean never lost at anything he attempted. He never would.

Venice: Marco Polo Airport

The woman climbed the stairs to the DC-6B, glad to be leaving Venice behind. At least she had a first-class seat. She had not calculated the eight-mile trip from the Port of Venice and had almost missed the departure of flight 412 to Paris. The sky was overcast, and she hoped it would not be a bumpy flight. With any luck, the passenger in the window seat would miss the flight.

She walked up the aisle and located her assigned seat, but unfortunately, a young man sat by the window, staring outside. Good God, he looked so sad. She hated to ask, but, "I'm sorry. Do you mind if I sit next to the window? I get claustrophobic when I can't see the sky."

The man turned his vacant deep-blue eyes to hers. After a moment, he seemed to focus. "Oh, uh, yes, that's fine." He stood at once and let the young woman take the window seat. Most men did anything she asked.

"Thank you." She smiled at him and sat down. Luckily, he did not recognize her; that would have put an end to all hopes of a quiet flight. He was in his own world that day, anyway, it seemed. Her thoughts were elsewhere, also.

Genevieve wanted to be back in Paris as soon as possible and away from the ugly scene of the day before. She closed her eyes as the plane taxied down the runway and took off. Her mind drifted to the events leading up to the previous day.

Her arrangement with Madame Alexandra was unique. Genevieve was not interested in the money generated by her special services anymore. It was amusing to be paid in diamonds by the shah of Iran. It was equally fascinating to control the sexual appetite of King Moulay Ismail of Morocco. Those were her two exclusive clients. Bored and angered with the sexual appetites of the men she had met in the past, she used her sexuality to influence the two great monarchs.

Genevieve was mostly bitter over her first so-called love of the heart. Pierre Rousseau was a film director who misled her into an alliance resulting in an illegitimate son and a sexual betrayal. He wooed her when she was yet in her teens, moved her into his vast, exciting life, then proceeded to fuck every good-looking young girl he came across. With Rousseau's help, she had started her career in film, but she was coming into her own.

When Madame Alexandra first contacted her, Genevieve refused to talk to her. However, when she separated from Pierre and had a new son to take care of, she agreed to meet the famous madam, more out of curiosity than anything else. Madame Alexandra made her an overwhelming offer. The shah of Iran had seen one of Genevieve's early films and was prepared to pay any amount for her services.

The shah brought in his private plane to Orly and whisked Genevieve to his palace in Iran. The man was kind, very gentle, and exceptionally generous. Her first liaison gave her enough money to live out a year in comfort. He would see her not more than six times a year, sometimes for a single evening only.

Genevieve experienced an added bonus with the relationship. Knowing just how well she could please a man, she managed to control the shah, in a manner of speaking, and as a result, the enormous power she had over him was of great conciliation. He frequently whispered secrets of state that no one else in the world knew. He possessed international knowledge of events taking place that were enormous in scope and, in some cases, affected world politics and finances. He gave her financial tips that she could use to her advantage. Never once was the shah wrong in any suggestion he made, and she amassed a great deal of wealth.

Time passed, and Genevieve lost interest in the petty conflicts and sexual obsessions of the common man. When she occasionally indulged herself sexually outside the shah, it was always for power and never for love, which was a forgotten extravagance for her. Love was for moonstruck teenagers, like she had once been. Never again would she allow herself the luxury of that kind of love. No man would enter her life in any meaningful way unless there were some form of power or money to go along with his other attributes. She recently had agreed to visit the king of Morocco. But the high was fading. The past few years, she had put away enough money from her services to last her a lifetime.

As Genevieve sat in the soft luxury of her first-class seat, her thoughts went to Hotel Danieli. At first, the assignment had sounded intriguing. Madame Alexandra had told her she must take the assignment because it would cause a serious problem for both of them if she didn't. The madam carefully explained her relationship to Jean Delacroix and his, in turn, with the shah. Genevieve understood the jeopardy of the situation and reluctantly agreed.

Once she got herself into the right mental state to make her little performance in front of Marie, she became excited about the situation. After all, that was Marie Savoie, the little bitch who had won the role of Juliet over her. Genevieve had been informed by the director that he was leaning toward using her in the epic film, but at the last instant, they opted for Marie. A close friend of the director whispered to her that they thought Marie looked much younger and would be more suitable as Juliet. She still fumed at the thought, and when the opportunity presented itself, she was excited at the prospect of getting back at Marie. She had actually enjoyed her role, and the possible risk it offered if the singer showed up. Well, the singer did not show up, and she left a brokenhearted Marie crying herself into despair. *Good,* she thought at the time, *she can go through a bit of what I've had to deal with in life.*

But a day later, Genevieve was not happy with what she had done. She realized how bitter she had become with men in general, but a tiny spark flamed in her heart when she awoke that morning, and that spark became a fire. What right had she to tempt the fate of someone's life? Had it been worth the revenge she thought she wanted for Marie?

Besides, Genevieve's film career was ascending. Some said she had replaced Brigitte Bardot, and even America's Audrey Hepburn, in popularity. If any of her assignments from Madame Alexandra came to light, it would jeopardize her stardom. She no longer needed the money, but she would be categorized as a common whore. That business with Marie had served one purpose at least. Genevieve would break away from Madame Alexandra completely.

Those thoughts came to a conclusion in her mind as the plane entered French airspace. Feeling a bit relieved by her decision, she cast her attention toward the good-looking man next to her, who was obviously still lost in his own thoughts. Tears were running down his face, yet he uttered no sound. He looked like some wounded animal, and something inside Genevieve that had long ago vanished came back briefly, touching her heart. Impulsively, she reached out to take the stranger's hand just as the captain's announcement requested that everyone fasten their seatbelts. She quickly retracted her arm. *My God,* she thought, *what's happening to me?*

Paris: Saint Germain des Pres

When Tristan arrived at L'Hotel in Paris, Guy Louis Duboucheron, the owner, came out to greet him. "Welcome to your home away from home, Monsieur Taylor. But can this be the famous star of *Westside Story*? By all the gods, you look like the wreck of the Hesperus."

Exasperated, exhausted, and emotionally spent, Tristan did not want to even know what the expression meant. He just disappeared to his old room like a recluse and called down for a bottle of vodka. For two days and several more bottles of vodka, he made no appearances. Blissfully, on the third day, Tristan passed into a sleep that lasted forty-eight hours.

When he awoke, he did not know where he was. He reached for the phone and dialed Marie's number. A recording stated the phone had been disconnected. Another moment passed, and again Tristan's world unraveled in front of him. With a rush, memories of Venice came back in all their unreality.

Tristan had slept soundly and had no traces of a hangover. A single thought then entered his mind. He must get himself together. Somehow he would find Marie. Somehow she could explain to him what was happening. How could it be that two persons so much in love ended up like they had?

Tristan had not eaten for three days and was suddenly famished. He must feed his body. Then he could concentrate on what was in his mind. He ordered heavily from room service, then phoned Greg Manning in New York to ask about Alphonse Luccessi. It was no great surprise to learn that Mr. Luccessi did not exist. The owner of the small opera house in Florence certainly existed, but his name was not Luccessi and he had nothing to do with any Luccessi.

As Tristan's head began to clear, some inner sense told him there was something phony about the entire incident in Venice. He hired a young French secretary to make calls on his behalf in order to find Marie. Two days passed and still no word. Marie's agents would not talk to him or his secretary. Finding her friends was like finding spring flowers in winter. No one was willing to talk. His secretary could trace not even one friend. There had to be a way.

As dinnertime approached one evening, Tristan entered the small bar inside L'Hotel. He vaguely remembered having seen the duck pond in the center of the room during his previous visit. A bar that seated no more than six patrons was on the right side of the room. To the left, small tables for other patrons who just wanted a cocktail or glass of wine. He passed to the rear area, which seated no more than forty or so restaurant customers, and sat in a booth.

As he looked over the menu, a man approached his table. "So sorry, but very happy to make your acquaintance. My name is Akio Marakaya." The small Japanese man was barely more than five feet in height. His hair was short and jet black. He wore a small mustache and had large, pearly white teeth, all perfectly formed. His smile was genuine, and for the first time in almost a week, Tristan could not help but smile.

Mr. Marakaya bowed to him. Knowing nothing of Japanese customs, Tristan rose and extended his hand. Marakaya took it and once more bowed in front of him. A natural instinct made Tristan do the same.

Marakaya spoke again, that time looking directly at Tristan. "I so pleased to meet you. My wife and I see you in America, in New York, see you in *Westside Stories*. Very good voice. We like you very, very much. I hear you in Paris, too, four week ago at Poste place. Very good music, very different than *Westside Stories*."

The charming little man amused Tristan. "Please, Mr. Marakaya, would you care to join me in a drink?"

"Ah, noo, thank you soo much. Cannot drink when working. Perhaps later when I finish work."

"You're working, Mr. Marakaya. What kind of work?"

"Ah, so kind you ask. I president of small company in Tokyo. Name is Yamaha. We making electronic sound systems. We making some music instruments, too. Also, we developing new kind of lighting for concerts. I coming to meet you after listen to your songs. When you sing in Poste place, music loud 'cause you have big voice. When hearing you in America, voice very good but not too loud. My company, we give you our equipment, all new. The music for you be very loud in large opera house, like in New York. You will give me try, I make us very, very famous."

Seychelles: Denis Island

The beach stretched forever. The sea was a deep shade of aquamarine, and only the sound of an occasional gull could be heard. A carpet of tropical foliage, which began in the mountains, cascaded gently down the slopes and expanded to the white, sandy beaches. Thatched A-frame huts dotted the beach but not very close together. Visitors could sun alone in the comfort and knowledge that no prying eyes would disturb their rest, whether they wore a bathing suit or not.

A small, sandy trail led from the huts to a larger hut set back from the beach. That was the hotel's main building, where they served meals. The hotel's capacity was for no more than a few dozen guests at a time. The atmosphere was not conducive to mixing company. Almost everyone who came to Denis Island came to get away from everyone and everything in general. Couples were the predominant visitors, occasionally a single person wanting the solitude the small island offered.

Marie lay stretched out on the sandy beach, only a bikini bottom covering her. She was asleep in the noon sun, a solemn look on her face. Jean approached her silently, concentrating his thoughts on his beautiful new conquest. She was finally his alone.

He stood looking down on her. All the years, all the desire. His obsession was fulfilled. At last she understood how much she needed him to protect her against a world of Tristans. He had finally won.

Tokyo, 1963: 1 Yamaha Square

Wind swirled through the streets of central Tokyo. The skies were bright blue, the air crisp for the normally warm June weather. Tristan had never been to Asia. He had arrived three days before, and his host had provided him with a personal guide to show him the sights of Japan's most famous city. The destruction of World War II was nowhere visible. Eighteen years of Japanese rebuilding had replaced the war-torn city with a new, modern facade. Tall buildings stood where wooden shacks had existed before. Japan had become one of the world's big industrial powers, and that was evident in the busy capital — new skyscrapers, elegant restaurants, and just outside Tokyo, the sprawling industrial zone with its high-tech production factories. Many products once made in America still bore American labels but were manufactured in Japan.

Arriving at 1 Yamaha Square, Tristan looked up at the impressive building. The all-black glass exterior was highlighted with cast-aluminum panels. The Yamaha building certainly had an imposing entrance. Two young men dressed in military uniforms of an earlier history stood outside the automated entry and bowed in respect as persons entered or left the building. He wondered whether it had to do with Japanese customs or the watchful eyes of the Yamaha Corporation.

Within a few days, Tristan would understand the different type of bow each person received. The two well-trained guards recognized each individual and what he or she represented to the Yamaha Corporation. Depending upon the person's position, the bow was either low or high and the attendants' eyes would either meet or not meet with the individual's. Even when Tristan became familiar with Japanese customs, he would never know the real purpose of those security guards: looking out for any competitor who might enter the building without Yamaha staff knowing beforehand.

The lobby was quite formal and, aside from a security counter, bare. A small lobby with elegant leather chairs was to one side, but in order to enter the elevator area, you had to pass the security counter. Wearing a conservative suit and tie, a young man sat behind the counter, carrying a clipboard with a list of names. He found Tristan's name on the list and asked him to fill out a printed questionnaire stating the person and reason he was visiting at Yamaha's main headquarters. After filling out the form, he received a pass to attach to the outside of his jacket.

Tristan's personal guide was a stunning young Japanese woman dressed in traditional black-and-white ceremonial clothing. Umeko Hashimoto was a niece of Akio Marakaya. They took the special elevator to Mr. Marakaya's penthouse offices. When the doors opened, they entered a small reception room and, after being announced, were led into the man's office.

The ceiling of Mr. Marakaya's office was twenty feet high, and one wall made entirely of glass revealed a spectacular view of Tokyo. But it was the wall just to the left of Mr. Marakaya's desk that caught Tristan's eye. A set of worn-leather body armor was attached to the wall and, on either side, beautiful samurai swords with hilts fashioned in an ornate pattern, apparently cast in solid gold. The body armor was immense, and Tristan could not conceive a Japanese warrior had ever been large enough to actually wear it. In front of the wall was a full-size bronze casting of a warhorse in full battle attire. The saddle was also apparently cast in solid gold.

Mr. Marakaya came from behind his aged teak desk and bowed to his visitor. "Ah, welcome to Tokyo, Tristan-san. I trust you journey a pleasant one."

Tristan bowed in response, his gaze returning to the magnificent body armor and warhorse. Mr. Marakaya walked over to the display and stood erect beside the great bronze warhorse. "This be armor suit of my wonaful ancestor Shogun Tokugawa Ieyasu. He born over four hundred year ago in part of Japan call then Sekigahara. He be very strong warrior, kill thousand of his enemy before he die. Establish domination of Osaka castle in year 1616. He die in battle defending his home. Enemy take most family, make into slavery. He my ancestor. I velly proud."

Marakaya beckoned Tristan to follow him to the panoramic view of his ancient city of the Far East. He spoke quietly. "Great man of the time. He come into world to serve all those peoples a specific reason, a reason for his life. Is his karma. You and I, Tristan-san, we here on planet for reasons only the gods know." He looked up into Tristan's face. "Do you know why you here Tristan-san? Have gods placed you here to sing, maybe just bring new sound to music. Gods put you here for their purpose, Tristan-san. You not here for you pleasure."

Looking out the window then, Marakaya said, "You have same sadness I see in Paris. I have many years, possess some small wisdom. I see you sing in great city New York. I see you in La Poste. Sing wonaful. I see you two month ago New York again. You not sing good. You have in mind big problem. I not know your problem. It not for me my business. I know from heart it be a woman. Is in your eye. Only one remedy for sadness from woman. Man be very busy in job put here on earth for. I make you very busy man. I believe from you greatly." Marakaya bowed slightly. "Come, Tristan Taylor. We have lunch now and talk of 'show biz.' My people tell in Hollyland, music business call show biz, is right?"

Tristan came out of the place Marakaya had taken him and, resisting a large smile, responded kindly. "Yes, Mr. Marakaya, it's called show business, and it's Hollywood. They make films in Hollywood, but my business really has no specific home. I take my music all over the world. I'll be making my first album next month, in a studio in Hollywood called Capital Records."

Marakaya looked at Tristan with such an unhappy expression that Tristan stopped talking.

"Have I said something wrong, Mr. Marakaya?"

"Ah, no. Very sad story, Capital Record contract. We go America, to Hollyland, five year ago, to convince honorable Mr. Wahlich, the owner, use Yamaha equipment. He say want American equipment. We tell our system much better, make even very good demonstration. He say no. Very sad day for Yamaha. Please, you continue. I sorry interrupt."

"No, I've come on your invitation because I'm interested in what you told me in Paris. And thank you so kindly for your words just now. I've gone somewhere this past year. I was on a journey. You've comforted me with your words. I don't know why I was taken on that journey. Perhaps, as you say, it was my karma. But let me tell you, something did come from the pain you've seen in me. I've written some new music — fantastic new sounds and words, songs of love found and love lost. They were written for a large sound system.

"A few of my songs were written with a talented black singer from Chicago, Sam Cook — my father found him singing in the cotton fields of a southern state called Georgia. One song is called 'Cupid.' I'd like to perform that for you while I'm here. Also, please, Mr. Marakaya, tell me about karma. I don't really understand it."

It was time for Tristan to get on with his life and its purpose, though for the rest of his life, never a day would go by without a moment's thought of Marie. But the obsession was gone, replaced with a great drive to create new music for the world.

සහ

Umeko, her uncle, and Tristan went to a splendid lunch that day. Tristan had too much rice wine, and she accompanied him back to his hotel. Just turned eighteen, she had fallen completely in love with him on sight. As he lay on his bed in a deep sleep from the sake that afternoon, she took his clothes off and marveled at his body.

Smiling to herself, Umeko stroked Tristan's face, his neck and arms. Leaning down, she kissed him gently. His maleness awoke even through his sleep. So, he too had the experience of rejection. She let her long black hair fall on his body, deliberately moving it back and forth to caress him. *Careful,* she thought, *I don't want to wake him. I want him to want me as he must have the other.*

She carefully put his clothes away, then covered him under the sheet and blanket, placed a Do Not Disturb sign on the door, and left.

Outskirts of Tokyo: Yamaha Factory

The vast expanse of factories outside Tokyo was endless. It was there that companies like RCA, Frigidaire, Motorola, and countless other age-old American firms turned for cheap production beginning in the 1950s. Yamaha's facilities were among the largest, and a new building had just been completed to manufacture sound systems for theaters, new amplified musical instruments, and a complex lighting system that allowed performers to coordinate their music in rhythm with the lighting effects. The combination would revolutionize the entertainment business for all time.

Iwo Takahashi was the production supervisor for the Yamaha Sound and Light Systems division. Schooled in America, he was considered the top electronics engineer in his field. With Yamaha's vast resources, he had put a design-and-research team together that toiled three years, studying existing sound-and-light systems. They came up with two radically new systems: high-output speakers and computerized light-and-sound coordination.

Taking existing speaker components, the team was easily able to double the size of a speaker system's output capacity without enlarging the actual speakers. The sound coordination was another matter. A complex central computer was needed to coordinate light and sound. Using a primitive sensor keyboard, they could control the color and intensity of the lighting. That was a marvelous advancement, as computer-chip technology was not yet invented.

Two large vans housed the computer system outside the theater. One day, the entire system would fit in a desktop computer. The cost of the equipment was unaffordable except by renowned entertainers — Frank Sinatra, Dean Martin, Tony Bennett, and the new breed just coming into fashion, Elvis Presley, David Bowie, and the Beatles. Yamaha realized that improved science would greatly cut the cost of their products, but wanted to be first to market the new sight-and-sound equipment. Akio Marakaya wanted Tristan Taylor to be their experimental figurehead. He would be that and more.

୫୨

Tristan spent three days becoming familiar with the electronic systems before having his band join him for a demonstration at the Yamaha factory. A makeshift stage was set up in building number three, a warehouse containing a floor space of five thousand feet. Prominently located on the stage with the band, the sound system consisted of six three- by four-foot speaker clusters connected together on each side of the stage. The multi-colored lighting system was suspended from the ceiling, near the front of the stage. Tristan had called in Greg Giuffria, his pianist, to work the lights from the massive keyboard hidden by a curtain behind the stage.

There was no rehearsal. Tristan had practiced with the band in Los Angeles on two new songs he thought might work for the demonstration. They were both songs he and singer Sam Cook had composed in Chicago the previous year — "Cupid" and "Kansas City." Sam had recorded both songs, which reached the top of the black music charts. In America, black music still played on black radio stations but was rarely played on white stations, so most of the white population had not heard either song.

Tristan's composer, John Stiles, took over and, utilizing the small Japanese orchestra he had rehearsed for that demonstration, started into "Cupid." The first try was without the lighting system, and the effect was satisfactory. At the conclusion, Tristan's unique presentation of that popular rhythm-and-blues song was applauded enthusiastically by the small Japanese staff sitting in the audience, including Umeko.

The musicians experimented with several other songs, raising the volume of the new speaker system to its highest output and adding the lighting effects. After twenty minutes, Tristan called off the demonstration, hiding his disappointment with a radiant smile.

The musicians and Japanese technicians intermingled and had coffee, tea, and the small rice cookies that had been set out for everyone. Iwo Takahashi approached Tristan with a broad grin. He had been educated in London and spoke perfect English. "So, it was really great, no? Three years of sweat, and you would never believe the money expended for this project. We have a winner, don't we?"

Never wanting to offend anyone, Tristan looked at Iwo closely and decided to be direct and honest. "Yes, it was very good. Here, in this small warehouse, the acoustics are okay, but our little audience was right on top of the sound system. I could've used normal speakers, and the difference would not have mattered that much."

Iwo's face blanched. His smile evaporated, and he appeared hurt. "How is it possible? Our testing equipment shows the sound to be one hundred percent louder."

Tristan patiently responded. "Iwo, look around you. This building is five thousand square feet. I envision performing in open areas that have half a million square feet, or more. I want the sound to travel from the front to the back as if you were on the stage. There's a football coliseum in Los Angeles that holds over a hundred thousand people. I literally want to blow my fans right out of their seats."

Iwo's mouth was open by then, but he nodded his head. "What do you want us to do?"

"You will increase the speaker capacity to ten times what you have now. I also want each cluster to contain ten speakers, in double rows, five on top of another. I want the maximum sound capacity to reach a hundred thousand people. If that means ten or twenty clusters, that's what I need."

Iwo's eyes were protruding. "But what will Mr. Marakaya say? It will cost a fortune to give you that kind of amplification."

Tristan smiled happily. "Mr. Marakaya will do exactly what I ask of him. If he questions you, tell him Tristan says it's our karma. Just do it."

Paris, 1963: Saint Germain des Pres

Marie sat in her beautiful Luxembourg Gardens apartment, reading some of her fan mail. Alexia LaBrocque, Veronique Ophuls, and Gabby Dubols were on the Persian carpet in her living room, reading excerpts from the letters. All four ladies had been sipping champagne and eating caviar from an iced crystal bowl on the floor.

As usual, Marie was laughing so loudly that Alexia could not resist saying, "Marie, if you laugh any louder, you'll lose your voice completely. You're leaving this week to film *Kilimanjaro* in Japan. Should I call the director and tell him you lost your voice and the film will have to be a silent picture?" That resulted in even louder laughter, and Alexia stopped trying to silence Marie.

The girls carried on reading the outrageous letters to each other. Gabby held one up and demanded Marie listen to it. "Listen to this one, girls. It ends with, 'I am your real-life Romeo. I have studied Shakespeare in England under Sir Anthony Frisbee and starred in *Romeo and Juliet* this past summer when we finished our studies in Sir Frisbee's School of Drama. Though I have no financial support, perhaps you can assist me until I land a starring part in a film or go on stage. Please find enclosed my photograph.' " With that, Gabby passed around the photo.

When Marie took the picture, she went into an uncontrollable spasm of laughter, finally not being able to catch her breath. She immediately started hiccuping and could not speak. No matter what the girls did, for the next hour no one could get Marie to stop hiccuping. At one point, even she thought she might have to cancel the film because Alexia informed her some people went on hiccuping the rest of their lives. Fresh tears of silent laughter ran down Marie's face, and the day ended merrily with Marie finally able to catch her breath and speak again. The women went home feeling the inebriation of the laughter and the champagne.

§⊃

Marie made several films in 1963. *Kilimanjaro* would have been a fine film, but she lost her friend and mentor, director Pierre Remet, in the middle of filming. As everyone loved him so much, something just went out of the production. Marie herself became melancholy, and the film ended up quite flat with the new director. She returned to Paris, to Jean, and was soon offered a part she became enthusiastic about.

Rio de Janero: That Man from Rio

That Man from Rio was the first film Marie felt was really suited to her since *Romeo and Juliet*. It was a light comedy involving a museum theft in Paris and a chase for the thieves, ending in Rio de Janeiro, Brazil. Marie insisted that Gabby and Alexia accompany her to Brazil, with the production company footing the cost. For the record, they would assist with her makeup and hair, but in reality, both Solange and Lucy would be with her for that during filming.

Marie arrived at the Royal Brazilian Hotel on the beach in Rio and, after the long flight, prepared to take an early nap before dinner. She sat alone in her suite, her two companions nearby in another suite of rooms. It had not been a pleasant flight, as Marie could not forget her parting from Jean. He had argued with her for weeks to give up acting. He wanted her to become his wife and bear his children. Marie shuddered at the thought. She wanted children but, by God, not by Jean Delacroix.

She loved the lifestyle they led together, the wit Jean possessed, and the roller-coaster ride they experienced traveling together to meet some of the most interesting and important men and women of their time. He was generous with her without precedent. Nothing she desired was too costly or unobtainable.

Every major film producer on the planet tried to cast Marie for his or her films. Jean handled her contracts even though she still retained AIF in Paris as her principal agents. His tenacious negotiations doubled her monies, which then were at the top of the international scale.

Jean was many things to Marie except for one. She did not love Jean in a romantic way, and it was difficult to hide that aspect when they were intimate. She acted out the part, the whole time knowing he knew she was acting. Then the enormous fight over her career. He had wanted *Rio* to be her last film, and she had refused. She loved acting; it was part of her life. And without romantic love, acting *was* her life. They had parted with words for the first time, and Jean had revealed to her another side, a dark side she never suspected existed.

Marie picked up the house phone and asked for the concierge. A polite man answered the phone, and hearing some kind words, she relaxed a bit. "Yes, Joseph, thank you, I'm fine. Could you please do me a big favor? . . . Of course I'll give you my photograph before I leave. Is there a newsstand in Rio that carries American magazines about the recording business? Will you be a dear boy and see if they have any? I don't care what edition it is. The name of the magazine is *Billboard*. . . .

Yes, it lists the names of all the singers and the best records. Try and find one for me. I'll give you a favorite picture of mine when you bring it."

Tokyo, 1963: Yamaha Music Facility

Umeko was again Tristan's escort and hostess while he was in Japan. They had not become intimate, but she was very much in love. When she delivered him to the music building earlier, why could he not see in her eyes what he meant to her?

The first time Tristan tried out the sound system at Yamaha, Umeko had watched in front of the stage, smitten with his singing. He went to another place the minute he walked onstage and never once so much as looked in her direction. He seemed oblivious to everything except the music and the musicians he was performing with.

Her heart still ached, as she very much wanted Tristan to notice her. Her pace quickened as she approached the music building. She was anticipating the music that day more than anyone else. She nodded at Iwo as she entered and took a seat near the back.

ᔕᗩ

Tristan saw Iwo sitting anxiously on one of the metal chairs in front of the stage. Along with the Japanese staff seated around him, he wore large earmuffs to protect his eardrums from the explosion that was about to emanate from the new sound system. The musicians onstage were equally protected, as well as most of the stage crew. Only Greg Giuffria operating the volume controls of the immense keyboard behind the stage had his earmuffs propped up on his forehead. He would only use them if he had to.

Onstage, Tristan wore the traditional earphones used by musicians when they recorded albums. By utilizing such earphones, he could hear the music as played by the musicians onstage, without having his ears blasted away from the sound system. Not fully knowing what volume would be achieved, he had all the musicians wear them in anticipation of the enormous sound they expected. Thinking ahead to the open stadiums he envisioned playing in later, he realized it would not be necessary to use the headpieces in such a vast space, but he would take no chances.

Tristan had recorded his first album in Los Angeles some months earlier, an instant success that had earned him the status of having gone platinum. But he was not satisfied with either of the two songs they had attempted to do during his last visit to Japan, including "Kansas City," which had reached number one in *Billboard* just before he came over. Those rhythm-and-blues songs were fine but really did not improve greatly with amplification.

He had experimented in the recording rooms at Capital Records and come to the realization that not all music would create the effect he wanted just because the volume was increased. After considering the type of music suitable for heavy amplification, he came to the conclusion that all types of music, including classical, could be amplified for special effect. But it would take a certain type of music to create what he wanted to achieve with the new sound systems.

When he got to Japan, Tristan had rehearsed on regular speakers the two songs they would perform using the new sound system. He had worked with the small Japanese orchestra that would back up his small band.

He chose "Greensleeves" to start the equipment test. John Stiles, his accompanist, walked out and started the music. Tristan began singing. He had instructed Greg Giuffria to start slowly with the volume and work his way up. They had twelve enormous speakers at the front of the stage. Each stack of six was nearly twenty feet tall.

§⊃

Aside from "Ave Maria," "Greensleeves" was one of Tristan's oldest, most popular songs. Amplifying the sound made it interesting, to say the least. No one expected the physical sensation that occurred with the amplification. A vibration started within their ears and moved through their entire bodies, something never experienced before from that type of presentation or on that level. Many in the small audience tingled with the sound sensation. For Umeko, it became a sexual experience. For most, it was a kind of natural high. As Greg increased the sound, some removed their earmuffs. The experience was exhilarating. The sound was awesome. Tristan's voice penetrated everything and everywhere.

When he concluded "Greensleeves," he immediately went into "Ave Maria." To the end of Tristan's career, many would believe his version of that classic was his finest song. Greg turned up the volume. The audience was captivated. Some reached up without realizing it and placed their earmuffs over their ears. Some of the musicians, caught up with the new feeling, removed their earphones and tried to get the high the sound was producing. As Tristan reached the last crescendo to conclude the song, he hit a very high note just as Giuffria applied a last surge in the sound system.

ॐ

Hiro Yamaguchi, a Yamaha technician, was across the street from the new music facility when an explosion almost knocked him to the ground. Bits of glass littered the street. The music unit's doors burst open, and people ran out, some holding their ears. It was a bizarre sight. No smoke or fire, yet people were running out of the structure with musical instruments of all kinds. Amazingly, some were laughing, including Iwo Takahashi. "Iwo! What's happened?"

"We have just broken the sound barrier, Hiro-san, and our eardrums with it."

ॐ

Evidently, when Greg Giuffria had turned the volume up to maximum power in combination with Tristan hitting the highest note of "Ave Maria" in his tenor's voice, every window in the warehouse was blown out. All agreed afterward that the sound system was just fine, but never again would they experiment with it in that kind of setting. A few musicians not using their earphones wandered about Tokyo without hearing for days.

ॐ

Tristan was completely satisfied with the sound test. But one important thing was lacking. He had to find the right music to entertain a large audience. His repertoire of classics, pop music, and rhythm and blues was fine, but he really needed something new to attract the large audiences he envisioned. He would find it in rock and roll.

Paris, 1963: Montparnasse

"I'm finished with this business, Alexandra. It was never anything I wanted to do for just the money. I'm not interested in only money. It was curiosity that started me, and the fact that I would be around men of such great power." Genevieve Dubois sat in a pretty pink-and-blue chaise longue in Madame Alexandra's apartment suite, having a late afternoon tea. She was dressed in Yve Saint-Laurent slacks and a silk, cream-colored blouse of impeccable quality. Her shoes had been custom made for her by René Mancini.

Genevieve's blouse was revealing, and Madame Alexandra momentarily resisted the urge to caress her face. She was attracted to her and, though not a lesbian, felt Genevieve to be so beautiful that any woman, straight or gay, could love her physically. But so what? Sex was the madam's business. She could afford to feel any way she wanted. She hated most men for what they had done to her during the war. Should some day come that she took a woman as a lover, so what?

She looked into Genevieve's wondrous large brown eyes and spoke affectionately. "But what will you do about the shah? I know he adores you and will be unhappy about not seeing you again. What was it that changed your mind? I know you enjoyed these outings."

"It started with the assignment you gave me with Marie Savoie. I initially enjoyed the act. But when I came back to Paris, I realized I had destroyed a person's life. I destroyed two people, and I feel only remorse now. This man, this Delacroix, he knows about me. I intend to end it here and now. Never again will I be put in a position of blackmail." Madame Alexandra raised her eyes, and Genevieve continued. "Yes, my dear, blackmailed. What else would you call it? I'm tempted to call Marie and tell her the whole thing."

Alexandra gasped and raised her hand to her face. "No, I know this man. He is capable of killing you — and me. Promise me you will never utter a word of this matter to anyone."

Genevieve sat for a while with no expression. After a time, she looked directly into the madam's eyes and answered. "This part of my life is over. I won't talk now. As for never, I won't say that. Never is a long time. I've paid a price for this interlude in my life.

"My film career is really just beginning. I've been offered the best part of my life in a new picture, and I'm excited about it. I love working in film. I love acting, always will. I never thought I would, but it's become my destiny. To not act is like not breathing for me, but what I've done with you this past year must be as if it never occurred. If the world became aware of it, they would paint me as a common whore. No. I'll bury this part of my life.

"You know, Alexandra, there was a famous actress in America who for some reason cloaked herself in mystery from the public as I shall. Her name was Greta Garbo."

Beverly Hills, California

Tristan sat in the living room, staring into the fireplace. Vanessa had lit the pine logs an hour before then left to change into something elegant before taking him to meet friends at the Beverly Hills Hotel. He had returned from Japan the previous week to interview a lead guitarist and review some bold new music that someone had sent him. A heavier music was becoming popular, called rock and roll by its new fans. He would try out that new sound at Capital Records the following week then return to Tokyo to sign contracts for his first Japanese-backed tour of the United States.

Vanessa was currently working on a remake of Mika Waltari's *The Egyptian* and had fallen in love with her costar, Richard Denton. To complicate matters, she had married oil baron Swifty McCall only three months before. She walked in to join Tristan in a glass of champagne. "It's so good to have you with me, Tristan. Here's to the only soul I know who understands me." She raised her glass before taking a sip. "After all, how is it my fault I fell in love again? Help me. What is wrong with me? Just when I think I'm with the right person, another Mr. Right comes along and I just can't help following my heart."

Tristan, who seldom laughed at anything during the past year, broke into a rare spasm of laughter. "Vanessa, it's me you're talking to. Don't tell me about an affair of the heart. You're having an affair of something else, and though it's part of your body, it's not the heart. Look down a little farther, just past your belly button. That's where your urges are coming from."

She looked seriously at him, took a sip of bubbly, and promptly sprayed it across the room as she burst into laughter. Fortunately, Tristan was able to dodge the liquid, and both collapsed on the couch in tears.

There was a long silence, and they looked at each other with great affection. The two had been on the same wavelength for the past few years. Each would disappear from the other, usually into work or love, or both. A crisis would arise, and one would seek out the support they needed from each other.

Tristan took Vanessa's hands in his. He raised them to his lips and kissed them, put his arms around her, and drew her close. Leaning his head against her, he cried then. The tears ran down his face, and Vanessa held him tightly. He had long ago poured out his heart about Marie, but the pain was still there. It would never go away. He whispered in her ear, "Why, why does a woman love a man so much one day and is gone the next without telling him why?"

Vanessa, holding him close, replied quietly. "My dear love, won't you ever understand a woman? Men are so emotionally different. They think differently than we do. God put men here thousands of years ago to do the hunting and protect the family. And now the twentieth century is here, and we don't need your protection, and we don't need you to provide for us. Not all of us, anyway. Men have to rethink their roles in a relationship with a creative woman. I want my freedom. I love my freedom, and, yes, Tristan, I know what my problem is maintaining a lasting love. You're as close as I'll ever get to eternal love. You've come to understand me. I love you above all."

Tristan felt the familiar desire for Vanessa, the physical attraction that would remain between the two for their entire lives. They stood and held each other, crying silently in each other's arms, each feeling the pain of the other.

$$\wp$$

Tristan's version of "Kansas City" and "Cupid" went to the top of the charts nationally. Throughout the United States and Europe, many who had never heard of him through *West Side Story* thought the singer was black. It came as a complete surprise to some that he was not. He was one of the first white singers to transcend that barrier. Like Elvis Presley, who also was considered a white singer with a husky soul sound, Tristan had a new following of fans. The timing on his two hits could not have been better. Never before had anyone attempted the kind of concert tour he envisioned. The new sound systems, the new lighting effects, and the right music would revolutionize that part of the entertainment business forever.

Paris, 1964: New Year's Day

Jean called Marie with an invitation to join him for New Year's Eve. She was in Cap d'Antibes, working on her third film in six months, *La Chasse à l'homme.* "I just can't leave now, Jean." She sounded tired. "I'm very sorry about New Year's. This film is not going well for me. I'm exhausted and really don't need your coming after me, too. Perhaps we'll have a personal talk about our relationship when the film is done. I can't be to you what you want. You're better off with someone else. You keep talking about having children, and you know my feelings on that subject. Find another girl who will have your children. If you want your contract back, you can have it. I'll give you back the apartment, too."

Jean sat speechless. Catching her just before she hung up, he apologized profusely. He begged her to forget any thought of their ending the relationship. Calling inwardly for every cunning argument he could think of, Jean eased Marie into submission. She ended the conversation, telling him how tired she was. He was furious.

Sitting back in the deep, comfortable chair behind his massive desk, Jean tried to think clearly. What was the matter with him? Why could he not just end the farce once and for all? He could not control Marie and could barely hang on to the relationship. He constantly had to come up with new things to keep her interest, and that left him exhausted. Finally managing to calm himself, Jean meditated awhile and found new energy. He would outwit that bitch if it killed him. He just wasn't going to lose. He could not tolerate the thought that he was going to lose her. For the first time, he realized the true nature of his feelings for Marie. He was not in love; it was obsession alone.

Jean picked up the phone and called Cartier in Paris. He had been in the fabulous store the previous week and initially resisted the urge to buy the necklace he had seen. Nothing was too costly for him, but the necklace was, in reality, not only priceless but had a history of greatness. It had once been the property of Alexandra, the queen of Czar Nicholas of Russia. It was a combination of emeralds and diamonds. Ten centerpiece diamonds with a total weight of 280 carats were surrounded by smaller-size emeralds. The necklace had a staggering price tag of F60 million. The Russian government had made a claim against the consignor and present owner, and an out-of-court settlement would return half the money to Russia.

He gave detailed instructions to the manager of Cartier, Rudy Dastills, for delivery to Marie in Cap d'Antibes. "Yes, Monsieur

Delacroix, it is no surprise you have decided on the czarina's necklace. I expected none other than one of your exquisite taste and capabilities to accommodate such a purchase. I will see to the delivery arrangements personally."

ℰↃ

Jean's call had reached Marie on a Sunday. She was in her room at the famous Hotel Cap d'Antibes, located between Cannes and Nice. The film was tiring, and Marie, experienced enough in her profession to judge her own work, decided that film was not going to enhance her career. The filming had one more week before completion, and she had decided she wanted to get away from both acting and France to take a break.

She also wanted another break — away from Jean Delacroix. He was not emotionally in tune with her, and she yearned for someone or something to come along and take her back where she had gone with Tristan. Could there be another Tristan out there somewhere? Jean's monetary assistance was wonderful, but there was more to life than money.

Marie looked at the clock on the nearby desk, startled to see it was almost six. She had promised to join Veronique, who was also acting in the film, for a drink at the nearby home of Johnny Hallaway, a French rock singer. Johnny's home was just off the highway on the road to the Nice airport. Veronique was to pick her up at six thirty. Marie hurried into the bathroom to shower and dress, and was putting on her makeup when Veronique knocked on the door.

"You're not ready. I promised we'd be there by seven. I want you to meet Johnny. I think something could happen between the two of you. He really likes you. He confessed to me last week that he fell in love with you after your Juliet."

"You know my arrangement with Delacroix. I'm not in the mood for a new affair. As far as I'm concerned, all men are basically the same. They want your body, your soul. They want you to have their children while they look for others while you're pregnant. And if by chance you can support them financially, they like that as well. No, thank you. I'll stay with Jean. I've been in love once and didn't look for it. I was hurt and don't want that experience again. I'll go with you, but if this rock singer comes on to me, I'm leaving."

As the evening turned out, Johnny Hallaway was very polite and did not chase Marie around his villa. By the end of the evening, the two

Michael DuBasso

became friends. However, several hundred miles away, the news of Marie's new friendship did not fall on happy ears.

෨

Roger Elonda sat in Jean's apartment office, deep in conversation, reporting the activities of Marie the past few months. He told of her constant interest in Tristan Taylor's life, via the recording newsmagazines. He concluded with a description of her visit to Johnny Hallaway's home in Cannes. She and Veronique had left about one in the morning, quite inebriated, and both girls had been laughing loudly. "I don't think she had an affair. As to my best information, it was their first meeting. They did embrace at the door, and Mr. Hallaway did seem to hold onto her a bit longer than one who was just a friend."

Jean reflected on the news and told Roger to keep him posted of any new events. He led him to the door and said goodnight. He returned to his seat behind the great Louis XVI desk and meditated for nearly an hour before reaching for the phone. "Hello, Wolf, how's the weather in Saint Moritz? . . . Pleasant. That's good. The weather here is nasty. . . . No, not that kind of weather. I have a small job for you. Bring the special duffel bag that has all your little toys. The helicopter will pick you up in the morning. We'll have a private dinner together here in my apartment. It has been a while since you've been here in Paris, and I look forward to seeing you."

Los Angeles: Shrine Auditorium

The remarkable old building was built near the central business area in 1926, when Los Angeles was a sleepy, quiet community. Many splendid houses located within walking distance were home to the rich and famous in the 1920s. By 1964, LA and the world in general had changed. No longer was that area of the city prime real estate. The Shrine Auditorium still attracted performers, and it was there that Tristan's new agents, Marks & McKay, had booked his first concert on the tour. The word on the street was that he was going to surprise a few people with something revolutionary in the concert business. Three performances were booked, and every seat was sold out.

Leading up to the event, Tristan closed the auditorium to the news media and virtually anyone who was not performing or part of the elaborate sound or light system. Only his musicians and backup singers would be allowed in for the two-day rehearsal.

He still had one problem to deal with. He did not currently have a top record in the charts and wanted to introduce the new sound with something spectacular. After spending weeks considering the options with his composer, John Stiles, he decided to borrow two key songs of that year. Not only would the advanced equipment be used but both scores would be presented in a different format.

Tristan and his band rehearsed the songs for two days, but he intentionally did not heighten the volume. Excitement was building with his crew, and he did not want to peak too soon. He decided that only during the concert would they maximize their new electronics.

Saturday, April 4, 1964, was the debut of *A Night with Tristan Taylor*. A raucous audience greeted the warm-up band and lead singer, Bobby Crowe, who had just produced the hit song "Kissing Cousins," listed at number twenty in *Billboard*. A twin set of curtains shielded the elaborate set that Tristan would be using for his performance. Crowe finished his set to impatient but polite applause. Storming off the stage, he looked at Tristan and shrugged. "Good luck with that crowd, man."

There was chanting from five thousand rowdy fans. They yelled Tristan's last name, clapping their hands in unison. It was time. In one hour, Tristan's labor of love to produce something special would have been successful or not. As the audience became rowdier, he nodded to John Stiles, and with the curtain still closed, Tristan's drummer, Danny Rourke, broke into Gene Krupa's classic version of "Caravan." It would be hard to find a rock fan anywhere who did not appreciate the work of Mr. Krupa. The fans certainly did not come to a Taylor concert to hear jazz, but there was jazz and there was JAZZZ. Nowhere before had an amplified drum set been heard on that scale. Danny Rourke was the best drummer in the business, and that was the warm-up for Tristan's opening song. As the band joined in for the finish, Greg Giuffria turned the sound system on for effect.

The curtain parted to deafening yells and applause from the audience. A New Orleans street appeared as background, right down to several balconies filled with ladies of the night. The pretty girls, in reality Tristan's backup singers, wore short, revealing costumes in brilliant colors. From stage left came a great roar, and Tristan drove out on the Spider, a customized black-and-red Harley-Davidson made specifically for him. He stopped the bike at center stage as the audience rose in unison, screaming the singer's name.

On each side of the stage, two tiers of gigantic speakers reached to the ceiling. In the middle and rear of the auditorium, additional tiers of speakers stood. They had not been used during the warm-up, and Danny's drum solo had utilized only part of the stage speakers. The overhead lighting system, only subtly lit, awaited its debut.

Tristan waited for the audience to quiet down. It did not happen rapidly, and his thoughts turned to his opening song. From Liverpool, England, a small group had produced a song called "The House of the Rising Sun." He and John Stiles had reworked it into a moody, powerful ballad. The auditorium became almost silent, and he broke into the song with enormous emotion.

Never had an audience heard a powerful voice combined with a truly great song and amplified to such an extent. The vibrations of the huge Yamaha sound system drove much of the audience into a frenzy. The elaborate multi-colored lights, which came on periodically in time with the music, created a spectacular show. Not a soul stayed seated from the opening number to Tristan's closing version of "Ave Maria." He encored with "The House of the Rising Sun." Although it normally ran four minutes and twenty-five seconds, he carried the song twelve minutes to an audience that refused to leave.

∞

After Tristan exited, John Stiles came out and announced the famous words "Mr. Taylor has left the auditorium" to five thousand screaming fans. Tristan had left, fortunately for him. Several hundred out-of-control fans rushed the stage, seeking their idol, and could not be restrained by security. Some of the dressing rooms were destroyed. Greg Giuffria, who had done a magnificent job on keyboard, fled the auditorium but suffered a broken arm when confronted by fifty young women seeking special attention. As a result of the chaos, a whole new concept of security was born. From then on, local police would be retained to control those new rock concerts.

ℰↃ

Five thousand miles away in Paris, a tearful Marie read the headlines in *Billboard* magazine several weeks later. Her tears were of both happiness and pain. She was thrilled with the article describing the success of Tristan's concert. It left her so elated she wrote a beautiful note congratulating him for the success. Reflecting on the pain of his betrayal, she tore her note to pieces, all the while sobbing to herself that she was not with him in his moment of victory. Why, why had he not been truthful?

Marie picked up her discarded script of *La Ronde* and memorized the lines for the morning's take. Jean would be meeting her for dinner that night. She had to get away from him. He had become particularly obsessive lately. Putting down the script, she picked up a recent edition of *Paris Match*. Johnny Hallaway had been hospitalized after being badly beaten up by some stranger who stalked him while he was leaving a late-night party in Saint Tropez. One of his ears had been sliced off but was fortunately replaced by doctors.

Calling in her friend Gabby, who was visiting, Marie asked her to send flowers and a card to the hospital. It was the last week of filming for *La Ronde*, and Marie, caught up in the last days of work, did not notice there was no response regarding the flowers sent to Johnny Hallaway.

California Desert: Temple Bahari

Vanessa had just won her third Oscar and dumped her fifth husband, bandleader Art Torres. The marriage had lasted six months. Art had wooed her like no other, showered her with gifts and promised eternal love and fidelity. She had come to his Acapulco summer residence two weeks early as he was entertaining guests in the Jacuzzi. One was his sax player, the other a thirteen-year-old Mexican beauty he had hired to take care of Vanessa's children. When she walked in on them, he reacted with an enormous grin. "Surprise."

Having just completed his first concert tour, Tristan took over completely after learning of her latest fiasco. A private jet picked her and the children up in Mexico and flew them to Los Angeles. His limousine then whisked Vanessa to his Palm Springs home.

Tristan had already told her about his California desert home, which he had designed and built with the advance fees he received from Yamaha. As the limousine pulled up to the gates, Vanessa decided *home* was no description for Tristan's spectacular desert retreat set against the San Jacinto Mountains. A sign at the private entry announced: STOP. 24/7 Security. A guard waved the limousine through, and the chauffeur parked inside as the gates closed again.

"We'll take the van now, Miss Daniells. That's the only vehicle Mr. Taylor allows beyond this point." The driver helped Vanessa out and directed her to a white van waiting nearby. As he transferred her luggage, she seated herself in the second seat and put her head back on the headrest.

The driver took Vanessa to a one-story, adobe-brick building. There she changed into clothes provided by her host—a simple wardrobe consisting of a light toga and warm robe for the sometimes-cool evenings. Tristan had told her he had everyone dress that way there to enhance the feeling of retreat. Their personal things were allowed inside the main house, but he asked them not to bring in stimulants of any kind. However, the rule was never enforced. Tristan's home, which he called Temple Bahari, did not lend to any other indulgence than the enjoyment of what its host provided.

When Vanessa exited her changing room, a young man approached her. "Miss Daniells, please follow me. I'll guide you to the main house. Mr. Taylor is expecting you."

The path was a mile long, but as she walked she only noticed its peaceful beauty. The walk was lined with desert palms, enormous groves of bougainvillea, and endless jasmine. She heard no noise of any kind except the cicadas.

The house came into view, and Vanessa stepped back in time four thousand years. The young man acted then as a tour guide. "It is magnificent, isn't it? What you see is a miniature of the magnificent living area within the Temple of Deir el-Bahari in Egypt, which was built by the pharoah-queen Hatshepsut. She ruled Egypt in the eighteenth dynasty. Her temple was built in Abydos against an Egyptian mountain range."

Finally arriving, Vanessa climbed the limestone stairs to the expansive front porch. The front door opened, and out walked Tristan, a wide smile on his face. "Here at last. Come in, come in. Let me show you around." The residence was built in the shape of a mastaba. All the rooms had views of the desert and the inner courtyard.

Tristan gave Vanessa his personal rooms. "I had this main room decorated in an Egyptian theme, using a Thutmose I motif. He was the father of Hatshepsut, a beautiful princess who became the pharoah when he died." Vanessa looked at the lovely pastel colors that illuminated carved-limestone figures on the walls—scenes of hunting and fishing. "This wall depicts the capture of the Hittites two thousand years before Christ. Hatshepsut ruled Egypt for nineteen years and kept her army from expanding the empire." He sighed. "In her final year, the Hittites rose up and were about to capture Thebes itself when the queen's brother, Thutmose the Great, struck down his sister in a coup and not only defeated the Hittites but expanded the empire as never before. Hatshepsut only sought peace for her country.

"Peace. I've tried to duplicate her fine summer residence in a very small manner."

Well. He had succeeded beyond imagination, Vanessa realized. There was no modern convenience of any kind once she left the guesthouse. Tristan had not only stepped back into time, he lived as the ancient Egyptians did so long ago. And she would, too, for a time. No electricity, no news media, no city noises, only the desert peace and quiet one could only experience in a secluded setting such as that.

There Vanessa got very well enjoying the luxurious pleasures of riding bareback in the warm evenings, swimming in the small lake adjoining the house, and partaking of simple cooking provided by master chefs trained in meals eaten thousands of years ago. She missed nothing, feeling only a sadness when she left, that perhaps people were not meant to live in the modern world, where they never had time to reflect on inner thoughts, or to spend with their children in a meaningful way. Time to hold a man or woman they greatly loved in their arms, or truly reflect on the meaning of their lives.

Versailles, 1965: Marie Antoinette

Refreshed after her stay with Tristan, Vanessa flew to Paris to star in the film *Marie Antoinette*. John Huston would be directing, and her costar was a new actor from the Shakespearean Theatre, Richard Harlow. She heard he was a brooding young man from Wales who had spent years doing Shakespeare without any interest in films until then. She was not anxious to have any conflict after her last relationship.

When Vanessa had announced plans to come to Paris, the French consul had coerced her into visiting historical places. Versailles was one of the stops. On a day the palace was closed to the public, Vanessa followed a private guide through the palace and grounds. Walking through the large rooms of the palace, Vanessa could not help but think how terribly boring it must have been to live in such a barn. One could get lost in the cavernous rooms and halls. The tour guide explained that the original furnishings were lost or stolen during the Revolution and the existing rooms were really shells of a once-magnificent palace. Those rooms were filled in the eighteenth century with hundreds of busy court figures dressed magnificently in the gowns and costumes of that period.

In the gardens adjoining the palace, the consul general, Claude Donchet, had a tasty lunch prepared for his guest under an ancient tree in front of a large pool. In the middle of the pool was a bronze grouping of angelic figures among dolphins spouting water. Tables were laid out with a selection of cold chacoutte, delicious hams, salamis, and tasty salads. Dom Perignon white wine accompanied the meal, and Vanessa began to enjoy the day. When the meal was finished and she really felt like going back to her hotel and catching a little sleep, Claude announced he wanted her to see one last thing before leaving. The group got into the waiting limos, and a few minutes later arrived at two outbuildings called the Trianons.

The larger of the two homes was built for Louis XVI as a hideaway from the main palace, where he could entertain a small group of intimates. It was used, in reality, for romantic liaisons. The other, much smaller building was constructed for Marie Antoinette for her secret outings, and in both cases, the French government had gone out of its way to restore the beautiful *cachettes*.

Vanessa was impressed with the Grand Trianon, as the furnishings were beyond description. The guide explained that designers had acquired and put into place whatever was available from the original time period, decorating the home as it was in 1790. The building had two levels. The first floor contained a ballroom and dining area; the second floor contained the bedrooms.

She wondered about the events that went on in the Grand Trianon during that time period, but it was in the Petit Trianon that Vanessa felt a strange rush of excitement. That jewel of a home was a miniature of the other and could certainly hold no large group of people. She got the feeling that it was designed for no more than a handful of the queen's best friends. And, of course, that was what Marie Antoinette had wanted, according to the guide. In reality, it was used for only three of her intimates, and history did not say for sure what occurred.

As Vanessa walked through the second floor and its small bedrooms, she marveled. "How tiny the beds are."

"Oui, madame," the guide said. "People were petite in the eighteenth century compared to today." He went on to describe the main bedroom. "We have in this room some of the original furnishings of Marie Antoinette that were not destroyed in the Revolution. Please note the bed and quilting . . ."

The sun, shining brightly through the clear, leaded windows, dimmed, and the guide's voice faded as the vision came.

The colors before Vanessa were as no colors she had ever seen, or would on earth. It was as if she had enhanced her sight and viewed shades and depths of color she knew on that plane, but so intensified that her skin tingled. Sitting on the floor in front of the four-poster bed were two stunning women who looked enough alike to be sisters, dressed in long, beautiful gowns of rich fabrics. Beside them sat a magnificent man dressed in clothes of the same period. On the floor next to the young women lay two discarded silver wigs. The women had long, dark-brown hair, untidy but not disconcerting. Their faces were feminine perfection and classic in appearance — mouth and nose small but beautifully sculpted; tiny, perfect ears; and large, dark-brown eyes. Slender fingers held some kind of playing cards, and Vanessa could hear their laughter.

The man seemed to be a smaller version of Tristan. He reached out and caressed the cheek of the woman in a gown of different shades of yellow, all beaded with pearls. The other young woman had a gown of an intense blue that did not exist on earth, and diamonds, good lord, Vanessa had never seen the likes of that in any film she had made. The necklace at her throat consisted of pear-shaped diamonds in various colors of pink. The smallest must have been a carat, the centerpiece fifty carats or more. The center stone was identical to Vanessa's own, given to her by her husband.

As she watched in amazement, something occurred that never had before. The three astonishing persons stopped what they were doing, looked directly at her, and smiled. Vanessa wanted to leave her pitiful world and join them. Why was she stuck in the twentieth century when their inviting time period beckoned? She hesitated ever so briefly as they looked at her, and just as she felt a great urge to reach out to them, the vision ended and she was back in the reality of 1964. Tears rushed from her eyes, and she fainted.

Not knowing what she had seen, Vanessa had not recognized Marie Antoinette or had any idea that the other, Marie Antoinette's own cousin, was her lady-in-waiting, Marie-Louise de Savoie, Princess de Lamballe. The young man with them was Louis de Guilbert, the king's personal guard, provided for his wife. He was killed by the mob, lanced to the wall in the Petit Trianon as he tried to protect his beautiful wards on the first day of the French Revolution.

France and America, 1965–1967

Vanessa completed her film with Richard Harlow, and the two became lovers. The relationship would go on for years, built on strong emotions, both loving and hating. The two stars would clash but stay together until both were emotionally spent. Vanessa did not work for two years, mostly due to her obsession with Richard. When tempers became too heated, she ran to Tristan for support. He knew her so well by then that he was always able to calm the situation.

శ

As to Tristan, he recorded seven top-ten hits in three years. His contract with Yamaha Entertainment made him rich and richer. He received commissions on their sound systems, which were sold internationally. Working carefully with a team of established financial advisers, he grew his personal fortune to enormous proportions. During his first concert year, he appeared onstage five days a week with only two days between for rest and travel. The second year was no different, and when his band asked for a break, he allowed them to take off, then used backup players while he continued the road shows.

All the while, Tristan played in large but enclosed auditoriums, like the Shrine in Los Angeles and Madison Square Garden in New York. Not satisfied with those audience sizes, he continued to press Yamaha for more-sophisticated equipment. It was his vision to be the first performer to stimulate audiences of one hundred thousand or more at one time using the advanced sound systems Yamaha was working on in Tokyo.

Friends and family began to see the fatigue Tristan was going through, and when they approached him to take a break, he defiantly said no. Finishing an evening's work, he would avoid the young girls who clamored for romantic attention, go home, and just crash. He would fade into a deep sleep and, on many occasions, just as he was drifting off, take a few seconds to reflect on another time far away in France.

శ

Marie completed five feature films between 1965 and 1967. Two of those films were particularly noteworthy. Roman Polanski directed the first, *Cul-de-sac*, which costarred Donald Pleasence. In the film, critics noted her resemblance to Greta Garbo, and many predicted Marie's

career would take her to the United States to star in some of the epic
pictures made there in the late 1960s.

Les Demoiselles de Rochefort by Jacques Demy costarred George
Chakiris, who had starred in *West Side Story.* Marie was aware that he
was still close to Tristan, and time after time, she resisted the urge to
talk about him during filming. She would go to the set armed with
endless questions for George only to back off at the last moment.

$\wp$

George came to adore Marie, even letting her cut his long hair one
weekend. They would take her small rented car and drive into the
countryside looking for small inns where they could dine. On one of
those occasions, Marie stopped her roadster along a highway and
stepped to the middle of the street to remove a small cat that had been
run over. When he asked her why she had done so, she said, "What if
it were you run over in the middle of the road? Wouldn't you want
someone to carry you to the side?" George would remember that the
rest of his life. He would never forget Marie and told his friends how
incredible she was.

$\wp$

Jean continued his loose hold on Marie. Cajoling her, wooing her time
after time, being there when she was low enabled him to keep her tied
to him. He had long since given up on any thought of having a child
with her. She would become adamant and disappear for weeks.

Roger Elonda reported back that Marie would usually drive to her
small chateau outside Paris and sit in her garden, lost in melancholy,
occasionally crying, sometimes for days. She would busy herself with
the flowers or plants and eventually come to some kind of peace. The
information came from the woman Jean had long ago employed to
watch Marie.

Jean simmered all the while, realizing Marie, in all probability, was
still in love with the American singer. There were many occasions he
seriously considered ridding himself of Taylor, but some nagging
premonition stopped him. He would bide his time and figure a way to
win Marie permanently to himself.

Paris, 1968: Ile Saint-Louis

Marie sat in front of Jean with a defiant look on her face. "Don't tell me what to do, Jean. I've been your friend and lover now too many years, and you won't control my life anymore. I'm tired of your little words of wisdom. I know you mean well, but I must live my own life. I appreciate everything you've given me—the clothes, the jewels—but you can have everything back. I'm missing something important in my life, and I want to see Tristan again. You say he doesn't love me. Fine, but I want to hear it from him now. I'm not whole, and, yes, let him say he betrayed me. At least I'll hear the words, and maybe then I'll be free."

Tears streamed down her face, and Jean felt helpless, as he always did under those circumstances. Again he was on the brink of losing her. He had to release her or lose her forever. "Yes, Marie. I understand." He stood and, reaching over, lifted her up and hugged her tightly. "Go. It seems everyone on earth wants to see what Tristan Taylor is going to do with this new concert. Even I'm tempted to go with you. Just one thing: let me have one of my guards accompany you so you won't be hassled at the show. I'll feel so much better."

§Ω

Later, the elegant apartment on Ile Saint-Louis was quite still. Jean retired to his bedroom suite and, sitting on the edge of his bed, contemplated his next move. Reaching for the phone, he dialed the well-known number in Saint Moritz.

Wolf answered on the first ring. "Yes, George Saint-James here. May I help you?"

Jean hesitated then hung up the phone. Immediately he dialed another number, in Paris.

The young woman was not surprised at the call. It had been a while since Jean inquired about Marie, and she was full of news for him. "Oh, you already know she wants to see Tristan. What can I do for you?"

§Ω

Marie knew instinctively that Jean would send a spy as her escort, but she was happy the confrontation had ended as it did. *Yes,* she had thought, *anything to get away from you.* She walked all the way to her apartment as if she were in the clouds. The April night had turned quite cold, but she felt only warmth inside her.

Finally seeing Tristan again. How fabulous. Her mind drifted to whom she would have join her trip to America for the concert. *I'll have all my friends – Alexia, Veronique, and Gabby. I'll call them tonight. We'll have a party from the time we leave Paris right through the concert. And I'll take Solange with me and have Pamela Brown join us in Los Angeles.*

Marie entered her beautiful apartments and danced through the rooms, feeling like she had been reborn. As she looked out over Paris from her bedroom windows, the sun was setting and the entire city was a brilliant shade of red. She raised her hands to the red sunset and said quietly, "I'm going to see him again. I'm going to live again."

Cabo San Lucas, Mexico, 1968: The Luna Baba

It began in Cabo San Lucas, Mexico. In 1968, Cabo was a sleepy little seaside community hidden away from most of the world. Its pure-white beaches and geography were unbelievable. Located at the farthest tip of the Baja peninsula, Cabo San Lucas formed a boot much like the tip of Italy. On the ocean side of the boot was enormous surf that had brought endless ships to a watery grave. Within walking distance was the harbor side of Cabo that enabled people to swim easily, even though just a few hundred yards away the surf could easily drown them.

The harbor and its long beaches boasted of cozy villas where not-so-wealthy Americans retired to join in a life of relative comfort. Everything about Cabo was that of comfort, good dining on fresh fish, and mostly *no mucho trabaja* (not much work). People sat in the sun on the white beaches during the day, dined at one of the cafés in the evening, and got to bed early to awake to another sleepy day.

The single exception to that lifestyle was a large group of mostly young Latino men and women who frequented a certain nightclub in town called the Matador, at precisely ten each evening. The club and its unique show were not commonly known outside Cabo San Lucas. A young bolero dancer from Mexico City, Tony Alejandro, had perfected a new, exciting dance routine called the Luna Baba. He had tried to open a club in Mexico City with his routine but was banned by the Mexican authorities for his "indecent" performance.

Tristan had been looking for some kind of dance routine to introduce into his concert performances, but no matter what he worked out, nothing was exciting enough to interrupt what the audience had come to see: him singing. While he was on Broadway, Leslie had instilled in him the love of dancing. He had made up his mind that someday, somehow he would find an exciting dance routine to bring into his concerts.

While taking a short break from his concert tour, he saw Tony Alejandro's show at the Matador. Tristan too thought of the likelihood of the dance being banned in America, but he would perfect his own routine and, if need be, fight to get the act shown. He brought John Stiles and Jim Clancey, his choreographer, to Cabo San Lucas to watch Tony perform. After paying a small fortune for the rights to perform the dance, they spent two weeks working with Tony Alejandro during the day. Tristan learned the basics, and when he returned to Los Angeles, he worked out his own concept of the dance with an added routine that he felt would shake up the planet. It certainly would.

Pasadena, California, 1968: The Concert

Rose Bowl Stadium in Pasadena, California, would seat 125,000 fans for Tristan's concert, which sold out for all six performances. Throughout America, rampant rumors predicted that Tristan Taylor was going to stage something extremely controversial, which led to a nationwide stampede for tickets. Orchestra tickets were selling under the table for a staggering $1,000 each. Backstage passes reached $5,000, and no one except immediate family could get comps. Airline traffic was affected for all concert dates. Limousine service was pushed to its maximum, and security for the concert was maximized.

Alerted to something out of the ordinary, the press was not allowed into the stadium until the concert due to the special performance about to be attempted by the superstar. No one had any idea what Tristan had planned, as rehearsals were closed. The only crew present were the sound technicians, Tristan's personal choreographer, and John Stiles, naturally.

Speculation flourished. Did the star plan on appearing stark naked? Was he going to fly in on a helicopter, hanging from the struts — something Bob Morrison had tried in London the previous year? That had been a disaster, as poor Bob had fallen from the aircraft twenty feet above the stage, breaking both legs and half his ribs. Perhaps Tristan was going to make a surprise announcement like he had decided to turn gay or run for president.

Unbeknownst to Tristan, many of those rumors were started by the star's publicists. Popular performer though he was, he did not like any false publicity. However, Tristan attracted a staff so dedicated to making a legend out of the singer that on many occasions, they lost control of what they were doing and failed to listen to what he wanted. His female staff adored him; the men were loyal right down to the lowliest worker. The excitement of working with one of the biggest entertainers in the world was worth everything, and the longer they were involved, the more dedicated they became.

❧

The weather was splendid on April 15, and California's blue skies were ideal for the crowds of people coming from every state in the Union. Tristan opened the concert by singing his best hits. Thirty minutes into his performance, the audience began to wonder if the sensational rumors were just that, rumors. After one of his most popular hits, "House of the Rising Sun," he walked offstage. The band was doing an instrumental that usually preceded another song. They finished the solo, and the audience anticipated Tristan's return to the stage.

The Rose Bowl had a perimeter of high-intensity lights that could be intensified or dimmed by a team of technicians in the main control booth high above the stadium. In addition, they operated the new, experimental laser lights on the stage and the towers. Never did the lights totally go out during Tristan's performances. That night there would be an exception.

The stadium fell into complete darkness and silence. Set at one end of the coliseum, the stage was suddenly illuminated by a single bank of white lights. Tristan stood alone on the empty stage. On a small, wooden table next to him were a bottle of tequila and six shot glasses. Huge video screens above the stage projected a close-up of the setting, and the audience could see every detail of what was unfolding. Tristan stood next to the table, motionless. Dressed in tight black-leather pants, a white shirt, and black-leather suspenders, he held a long black whip in his right hand. In his left, he held an unidentifiable object. Breaking the silence, the band started a Spanish bolero.

ℰℴ

Tristan pounded the heels of his traditional black alligator-skin boots in rhythm to the music. He slowly danced to the front of the stage. Then the music stopped. He looked out into the sea of people and announced, "I want a dance partner. Who would like to volunteer?" Fifty thousand screaming women acquiesced at the same time. Looking directly at his security force at the foot of the stage, Tristan pointed to a stunning blonde and said, "You."

Several of his crew offstage had signaled him who might lend to what he had in mind. The blonde was television's Kitty Fletcher from the daytime soap opera *Daydreams*. Kitty came up on the stage, and as she came close, Tristan unfurled the whip and struck at her, hitting the stage next to her within an eyelash of the actress. He used the whip repeatedly, all the while concentrating on her eyes, letting her know she was perfectly safe. The audience, which at first was silent, screamed with every snap of the whip.

Tristan flicked the whip out again, neatly tying it around Kitty's waist without hurting her in any way. He had practiced that routine with professionals for months and could hit a fly with the whip from twenty feet away. He suddenly raised his left arm and snapped open a twelve-inch stiletto. He handed the sharp knife to the girl and said, "Do what you want."

Mexican music began, which was, of course, for the Luna Baba. Sweat poured down from Tristan's face, and he looked intently at the blonde woman, defying her to use the blade. "Do something creative," he said. She hesitated, but as the music continued and he stared at her, she inhaled sharply and sauntered slowly toward him. He read a fiery desire in her eyes. The whip was still coiled around her, and Tristan pulled at it, bringing her body directly into his own. He ran his arm up her body, plainly revealing his intentions.

Kitty took the stiletto and cut the whip, releasing herself. She had become part of the drama, just as Tristan had known she would. He moved into her and placed his hands around her waist. He kissed her passionately on the neck. "Use the blade." She reached out and cut his suspenders. They fell to his side. One hundred twenty thousand fans screamed their approval. She pointed the tip of the knife to his manhood and circled the knife around the front of his pants. The audience went crazy. She pulled out his shirt from his pants and began to cut off the buttons. She worked on his shirt until it was shreds and pulled it off his back.

Tristan had added the whip and the knife to the routine, knowing what might happen in that situation. Had she cut him, he cared not. The intense adrenaline rush was worth the gamble. He wanted and needed the mortality he could not achieve in real life. The woman he really desired was not available to him and never would be.

He stood there, gleaming with sweat. The audience reached a crescendo, and the music became louder. The laser lights came on, their shafts of colors playing over the entire stadium and stage. A single beam of white light illuminated the two onstage. Tristan took the knife out of Kitty's hand. He filled all six shot glasses with tequila and handed her one after the other until they were gone. Then he grabbed her by the waist with his left hand, turning her so he was behind her. He pulled her hair aside with his right hand and kissed her neck again. Everyone in the audience was standing by then. Tristan took the pretty blonde and, reaching up with both hands, placed them tightly on her breasts. The audience screamed, and a surge started at the front of the stage, but the sea of security guards pushed everyone back.

Tristan grabbed Kitty's head with his right hand and forced it back as far as he could without hurting her. Then he firmly guided her into the Luna Baba, keeping her head in a horizontal position facing the evening sky. It was a total act of bondage, a dance of bondage. As he led her through the dance, he pushed her through his legs, allowing her to do what she wanted as she eased through. He let her escape into her fantasies, oblivious to the multitude of screaming men and woman who encouraged her.

Kitty rested in Tristan's arms at the end of the dance, breathing rapidly. He escorted her to the side of the stage and returned to an ovation. Had he stopped there and continued his normal concert program, everything would have been fine. But Tristan, too caught up in the adrenaline rush, walked to the front of the stage, sweat pouring from every part of his body. And he then made the biggest mistake of his life.

On that warm evening in April, in front of the largest audience to attend a concert performance anywhere in the world, Tristan Taylor went into another time and place. Usually very aware of his surroundings, especially the audience, he did not heed the signals in front of him. He did not observe the surge of young ladies who had run down the aisles and were being held back with great difficulty by his security force. He did not hear the volume of screaming in front of him. It was as if he were the only person on earth. Tristan walked to the front of the stage and asked, "Who would like to be next?"

Pasadena, California, April 15, 1968, 10:22 p.m.

Another boring Saturday night at Pasadena Community Hospital. Phil Hilton, the emergency room doctor, was looking at the clock just outside the ER and munching on a Big Mac and fries. The usual cuts, contusions, and one bad traffic accident that resulted in a broken arm having to be set were the results of the evening's action. The phone rang sharply next to him, and his staff nurse picked it up, listening to the caller for several minutes before putting the phone down and turning to Dr. Hilton. "There's been a riot at the Rose Bowl. Their emergency ambulance says there are hundreds of injuries, many extremely serious. UCLA is dispatching helicopters but can't handle all the severe injuries."

Hilton dropped the remnants of his Big Mac into a waste can and grabbed the phone. Reaching the central switchboard operator, he instructed her to stop all incoming non-emergency calls and have every doctor come in at once, the same for nurses, assistants, and technicians. And she was to call the central blood bank. He then called USC County Emergency Hospital in Los Angeles and informed the emergency room staff to stand by for all the assistance they could give.

Ambulances arrived two and three at a time. In the organized chaos of the triage area, an unconscious young woman was brought in from one of the ambulances, along with a burly man who, though injured himself, refused to leave her side. "Never mind me. She needs immediate care, at any cost. My employer will see to that."

&

Positioned in the audience at the front of the concert stage, Marie, her friends, and two bodyguards had been encroached upon by the impending disaster unfolding behind them. George Saint-James had anticipated the riot that was going to occur momentarily. Without a second's hesitation, he grabbed Marie and, motioning to the others, bulled sideways to the far end of the stage. There he studied the tunnel leading out and pushed his group toward the exit. At that, the lowest level of the coliseum, the length of the underground tunnel was about a hundred yards. Marie, apparently not comprehending Wolf's actions, was still resisting his efforts to get them to safety. With no warning, he picked her up as if she were a feather and began the long sprint to safety. The others followed, pushed in turn by the other guard. A roar was coming from the stadium as they ran toward the exit.

Wolf's group had just left the tunnel and was running toward the parking area when the mob bore down on them. Marie's friends ran sideways away from the frenzied stampede. Wolf did not change course because he was carrying Marie. He was bowled over at once, and he and Marie were crushed by the people behind them. Marie's other guard waded in to pull her out of harm's way, but by the time he reached her, she was unconscious.

Paris: Ile Saint-Louis

Sweat poured out of Jean as he held the girl against his body. Rhythmically he pounded into her from behind. Her ass was tighter than any he had fucked before, and her screaming was of pleasure and not pain, something that always heightened the experience. He came into her with a great flood and waited for her passion to subside. Removing the loose cord from around her neck, he lowered her to the floor from the leather chair. He took her, still blindfolded, out of his special room to the bedroom and, picking her up, carefully laid her on the huge bed. Taking her hands and feet, he chained her to the four-poster.

Jean had made himself up as a leopard that night. His body was covered in large black spots over the fawn color he initially covered himself in. A mask made from a beautiful leopard covered his face. His feet were covered in the same leopard's paws. Jean's eyes glazed as he relived the animal's lusts in his own mind.

As the years had progressed and Jean's own fulfillment with Marie could not be achieved, his imagination had become more and more vivid and real. He had once tried to initiate her into the Black Room, only to have her laugh hilariously over his well-thought-out costume for the evening. Thinking he was just playing a practical joke on her, she teased him unmercifully for weeks over the episode. Jean never tried again to entice Marie but, in his mind, lived the fantasies he so much wanted out of life. He longed to become his creations—a great cat, a wild bear, a king of Egypt, a prince of the darkness. With his resources and inventiveness, he could be anything, and he fulfilled those fantasies with the young girls from Alexandra.

Jean looked down on the blonde Amazon lying on the bed and removed her blindfold. She looked up at Jean, seeing his magnificent attire for the first time, and let out a cry of real pleasure. He became engorged again and reached for her. Then the phone next to the bed rang.

Only a handful of Jean's employees and staff knew the bedroom number. When it rang, it seldom brought good news. That line was for serious emergencies only. With measured fury, he picked up the phone and listened to Wolf's description of what had just occurred in America and Marie's condition.

"I did everything possible, Mr. Delacroix." Wolf went on to describe every instant of the panic and its outcome. "She's at UCLA, recovering from a concussion and one broken rib. She hasn't regained consciousness, but the doctors don't think it's serious. I had them do a CAT scan, and there's no indication of serious injury to her head."

When Wolf concluded his description, Jean asked him about his own injuries and Marie's friends'. He asked in detail about one of the other women in particular.

"No, they're all fine. That one ran like a jackrabbit caught in hell. I'm fine. I have a concussion and three broken ribs. My arm was broken. It's in a cast. I wouldn't take any narcotics. The pain is meaningless to me. If I had been sedated, I couldn't report to you."

"The big TriStar Constellation is at the Rome airport. I'll make arrangements to convert it to a hospital plane and send it at once to Los Angeles. I want Marie back in Paris as soon as possible."

℘

Marie was flown to Paris three days after the concert, when the American doctors agreed it would be safe to fly her. On the way home, weak as she was from the ordeal, she had her friends gather every newspaper they could describing the riot. According to reports, after Marie's group had left the building, the stampede of fans to the stage was completely out of control. The *Los Angeles Times* described the scene:

> *It seemed like a world gone mad inside. The scene turned into a panic to get out of the stadium as fast as possible or be trampled as a consequence. There was no order at all. Security was the first to suffer injuries. Most of Tristan Taylor's musicians and crew escaped through the rear of the coliseum, led by a special team of security trained for just such a situation. Taylor stated later that as security dragged him backward, he realized his grave error of judgment and was in agony over the prospect of anyone getting hurt. Security had to carry him off by force.*
>
> *No one was killed, though many were injured . . .*

Talk of banning Tristan Taylor from ever performing again was in several papers. An outraged group of church organizations labeled him a reincarnation of the devil. Nightclub owners who discovered where the new dance originated flocked to Mexico to learn the routine. A bootlegged video of the dance sequence was shown on television news throughout the world. Publically apologizing for the riot though not for his performance, the singer became a cult figure overnight.

Only a few yards away from Tristan, at the front of a sea of fans, Marie had stood spellbound by the intense sexual act going on in front of her during the Luna Baba. She was too professional to think for a second it was anything other than an act of fantasy. She had known what Tristan was doing and enjoyed every second. His performance only heightened her sexual attraction, and feelings long dormant came alive again. She yearned even more to be with him again.

Sitting in her flower-filled hospital room in Paris, Marie listened to her girlfriends retell for the tenth time what each had experienced that evening. The girls had secretly brought in a bottle of Cristal and, locking the hospital room doors, were eventually beyond tipsy. They talked of Tristan and the inevitable meeting Marie would have when she recovered. When she laughed loudly, her friends declared she was well.

The afternoon was delightful, and when it ended and the young ladies got up to leave, Marie handed one of them the letter she had been working on for days. It was for Tristan. She had poured out her soul in the letter and would not rest until she had a response. Carried carefully by her loyal friend, the letter was delivered directly to Jean Delacroix.

Paris: Central Intelligence

Henri Piollet was the assistant officer for the central intelligence office in Paris. He had been in that post since World War II ended, and relished his work. He was a document expert and carefully examined any international intelligence that ended up on his desk, to see what political implications it might have for France. Many of those documents were obtained by loyal spies who had been placed into foreign offices by the French government.

Before the war, Henri had been involved in another business that very few knew about. He was one of the greatest French document forgers of all time. He was brought into the Resistance to make up documents allowing the Allied spies of Europe to move throughout France unencumbered. His work was so good that on the rare occasion a person was apprehended and his papers reviewed, even German intelligence marveled at the work, right down to the watermarked paper.

Henri was happily humming a tune at his desk when his secretary interrupted him with a call. "It's Mr. Delacroix, Mister Piollet, and he says it's very important." Jean was a very good, old acquaintance. He had used Henri's services after the war for a few illegal documents he needed to acquire French companies where the owners had not survived the war. Jean took over those companies cheaply with the forged documents, making a vast fortune in the bargain. When Henri was brought into the new French government, Jean remained supportive and provided him with vacation homes and "special favors." Henri was one of the boys.

Delacroix came on the line and, after asking about Henri's welfare, told him what he needed. "Just a little job for me, Henri. I'll have my plane available for you as soon as you can leave Paris. In America, there's a singer by the name of Tristan Taylor. You'll have a complete report on him waiting on the plane. He's residing in his apartment in New York. I need an original letter from Mr. Taylor to a friend of mine. I want it on his stationery, and it must be in longhand. I'll provide any assistance you need in America to obtain handwriting samples.

"Time is of the essence. My friend here in Paris has written him, and in normal circumstances, a response would take about three to four weeks in total. I know you'll do everything in your power to accommodate me and want you to have a little bonus for having to explain to the French authorities about your sister's fatal illness in America and how you must assist her now."

$\wp$

Four weeks to the day of Marie's recovery, a letter from America arrived to her apartment. Having been almost without sleep since sending Tristan her letter, she became light-headed when she found the envelope. It was stamped from New York and had been mailed to her two weeks earlier. She ran into her bedroom. Seated in the luxury of the chaise longue next to the windows, she tore the envelope open, anticipating the reunion she felt was paramount to her life.

> Dear Marie,
>
> I received your letter, and at first I was not going to reply. I remember our affair in Europe, and it was a great deal of fun. I guess you know I'm not a man who can love just one woman. It's in my blood to be very romantic, as I must have been with you, and then for some reason I don't know myself, I just find another and the cycle starts again.
> Good luck in your films. As they're in a foreign language, I don't have the patience to read subtitles and have not seen one yet. However, I will one day try to do so.
>
> Best wishes

Marie opened the large picture windows looking out over the Paris skyline. It was late morning, and the sun was shining. The flowers of May were blooming in the park across the street, and fragrance from her jasmine tree on the balcony floated into the bedroom suite. There was an unusual stillness in the air, and the park at that hour was uncommonly empty. The quiet amplified the moment as Marie sat in her chair, tears streaming down her lovely face. She released no sound, just the silent tears. She felt as though someone had died that day. Marie left the apartment, and as she walked the streets of Paris lost in her pain, she realized someone had died that day; it was she.

When she returned later in the day, Jean was waiting for her in the apartment. He asked her nothing of why she was so grief-stricken. Taking her hand, he said, "Jacques Demy has been trying to reach you all day. He has a new film for you. It sounds very interesting, and part of it will be done in America."

Marie looked at Jean, her old friend, always there, always to be counted on. She took his hand and smiled. "Yes, Jean. It's time to start a new film and get on with my life."

Saint Moritz, Switzerland, 1969: René and Pierre

Summer came, and with it the exodus of the more interesting personalities who made up the city of Paris. Many left for the South of France to enjoy Saint Tropez, Cannes, Nice, and neighboring Monte Carlo. Others traveled to countries outside France. Jean went to his chateau in Saint Moritz for the summer. His fully staffed office kept him in tune with all the business dealings of his empire and operated twenty-four hours a day, seven days a week, if need be.

At Chateau Delacroix, Jean planned a series of weekly dinner parties. A Bell helicopter was available around the clock to pick up his guests at nearby Zurich airport. René Beaumont and his very handsome companion, Pierre Casadesus, were the expected guests for the first weekend in June. In addition, Jean invited only Marie, as René and his lover were pleasurable and amusing companions when they had no outside distractions.

He had arranged for René and Pierre to arrive at the same time as Marie. And so, late Saturday morning, the two men were escorted to a top-floor suite overlooking the town of Saint Moritz. Marie was escorted to Jean's suite, where the two embraced. "Why don't you get settled and freshen up," Jean said. "Lunch will be on the main veranda in two hours." He kissed Marie firmly on the mouth. "I'm famished."

§O

On a perfect day of sunshine and fresh air, lunch was served under umbrellas on the chateau's first-floor veranda. Fresh smoked-salmon tartare on toast, accompanied by Beluga caviar and Roederer champagne, was the simple repast served to much laughter and antics by Jean's gay companions. The bubbly soon produced the predictable merriment that marked time immemorial. Everyone enjoyed stories of rival fashion houses.

When the sun faded behind the mountains, the group decided to retire for a siesta and meet again for dinner at eight. A French rock group had been hired to entertain the small party later; Johnny Hallaway would bring his version of rock and roll to the chateau that night. As Jean started to take leave of his merry company, René took his arm and asked if he could have a private word with him.

René often chatted with Jean privately about the fashion lines. He was a dedicated worker, and Jean was closely involved with the designs he created. Jean told Marie to make herself at home in his suite, and went with René to the conference room.

"What would you like to drink?" Jean asked, opening the liquor cabinet.

"Make it another glass of the bubbly if you don't mind."

Jean opened the small refrigerator door and removed a bottle of the house champagne. "What have you on your mind, my good man? Are you planning a last minute change to the fall designs?"

"No, Jean, and don't forget, any designs not revealed yet to the public belong exclusively to the designer. That's why I asked you to see me. I'll come right to the point. Christian Dior's top designer has moved on, and that has left Dior a bit in need. They've approached me with a deal I can't refuse. That is, unless you match it."

Jean watched René with an amused expression. Good God, the weekend was picking up. Perhaps something challenging was in the wind. "It never dawned on me that you would be tempted to leave me. What monumental deal have they made you?" Jean asked with a hint of mockery in his voice.

"Ah, as I've stated, an excellent proposal. Firstly, they matched your very generous salary. In addition, they've offered me twenty-five percent of the net profits. If you'd like to match this offer, I'll give that careful consideration."

Jean did not so much as flinch an eyebrow. He poured his guest another glass of champagne. In all of the Delacroix Empire, not one person was allowed the luxury of a commission. With the twentieth-century takeover of the financial industry, the family had decided that never again would ownership by an outsider be tolerated in any form. It was even against company policy to allocate serious commissions.

Walking to René, Jean gently placed his hand on the man's back. "Of course, René. I fully understand your position in the matter. For clarification, I don't understand what you meant regarding our fall designs. Those belong to the company, do they not? They were done these past three months and paid for by the company."

It is interesting what happens to many persons who have total control of their minds and their tongues when they are sober. What is even more interesting is what happens to some when they are under the influence. "You financial people are the scum of the earth." René was slurring, and his eyes began to stand out from his face. He reddened as he spoke. "You think you can dominate a business you know nothing about just because you have money. You couldn't design your way out of a woman's purse, sir, without us, the creative people.

"I know you for what you really are. Do you know the people that whisper about you behind your splendid back? They know who you see in your precious little special room. They know the kinky shit that goes on in your so-called private life. I have my spies, Mr. Delacroix. They keep me informed of your comings and goings. And there are other unmentionable rumors about you, sir, so don't fucking tell me who owns my designs. The fall designs are mine and go to Dior if I decide to leave you.

"I don't work nine to five. I work around the bloody, fucking clock getting these designs turned into acceptable working clothing. I've busted my ass for you this past year to get the recognition so a firm like Dior would look at me."

Jean noted the slip and smiled to himself. The afternoon was becoming a delight. He interrupted the inebriated man briefly for his amusement. "So you have your spies on me. How naughty of you. René, you're a bad little boy, and certainly, we are going to have to match Dior's terrible offer. Not only match it but better it. You sleep on it tonight. I will cut short my vacation here and meet you during the coming week in Paris to work out the details."

Leading René out the door, Jean walked him to his luxurious rooms on the top floor. Jean just listened and nodded his head in agreement as René kept babbling. "I want my name to be used if I decide to stay on with you. I want exclusive use of the chateau here in Saint Moritz for one week during the winter season and want anyone I desire to join me at your expense."

"Yes, yes, René, and you deserve everything you ask for and then even more." Again the sarcasm, much stronger, but Jean was well aware that the man was completely drunk. He opened the door to René's room and could see his companion passed out on the bed. "See you at dinner, my good fellow." But he knew that both men would sleep through the night, especially René. While pouring him the last drink, Jean had put a little something extra into his glass.

&

Jean had work to do before dinner and wanted to complete it quickly. Upon entering his office, he called for the chateau steward and informed him that the small staff and cleaning crew could leave for the evening. There would be no dinner, and Jean required that the chateau be cleared of servants that night. He ordered them to cancel the evening entertainment, as well. And no one was to come back until after midnight. Jean explained that his two male guests had imbibed too much bubbly and would sleep a while before returning to Zurich later in the evening.

The door closed after the steward, and Jean picked up the phone once more. After completing the call, he used the private elevator to his penthouse suite and joined his beloved Marie for a short nap. My, what a wonderful evening they would have at the Palace Hotel in Saint Moritz that night. He made a mental note to call his friend Gunter and invite him and his Swedish wife for dinner.

၈၁

The dawning sun came over the mountains and filtered its rays through the trees onto the roof of a log cabin. Wolfgang Schmidt had been up an hour and was finishing his breakfast of veal schnitzels, eggs, and various breakfast pastries. He drew open the shutters to let in the early sunshine and fresh air. Looking out the window, he noted the nearby ski lift, closed for the next few days. Additionally, he saw none of the visitors who occasionally hiked in those woods. Delacroix had instructed the gatekeeper below to allow no one into the private area for the next two days, and to phone Wolf at once if anyone tried coming up without authorization. Wolf took in a long breath of fresh air and went back to his breakfast, which was turning cold. He finished the meal with a large cup of freshly brewed coffee and rinsed the dishes.

Wolf left the cabin in his jogging pants and sweatshirt and ran down the path that led around the wooded area and back to the cabin. It took about thirty minutes to negotiate the surrounding woods and its labyrinth of paths that surrounded the cabin and ski lift. Satisfied that there were no trespassers, he returned to the cabin, exhilarated.

Without stopping to rest, he walked to a corner of the cabin, where various barbells were strewn on the floor. Sitting in a small leather chair, he lifted the various weights in a sequence he had followed for over twenty-five years. He did not even think about the routine any longer, just went through his disciplined program, always ending with a set of twenty-five bicep curls, utilizing a fifty-pound weight in each hand. The program took thirty-two minutes precisely, and at the end, he was in a full sweat.

To the naked eye, the rather-large, rectangular wooden cabin was used for nothing more than a visit in summer or winter to perhaps get away from the city. It was anything but that. Jean Delacroix had Wolfgang Schmidt design the interior for various purposes, including interrogation. Another function was even more forbidding. A set of stairs descended into the large basement, where one section was set up as a communications office containing closed-circuit television cameras that utilized their own communication dish. A cable on the peak of the mountain enabled visual transmissions to Paris as well as Chateau Delacroix, where Jean could see and speak to anyone being "interviewed."

Wolf showered in the small but adequate bathroom on the main floor. A much larger bathroom, with a Jacuzzi and walk-in shower, was located in the basement area, but that was used for another purpose. He dried himself in front of a fresh fire, dressed in shorts and tennis shoes, and descended to the basement area.

Two guests were sitting on the cots where he had placed them the night before, their wrists chained to the wall. The chains were long enough to let them lie down but nothing more. Smiling, Wolf greeted his visitors in perfect French. "I see by your eyes you did not sleep well. Perhaps the mattress was not soft enough? Monsieurs Beaumont and Casadesus, why don't you relax a bit while I chat with both of you."

René had been in a deep stupor when Wolf arrived at the chateau the night before, but young Pierre had to be slapped to get his cooperation and had a large bruise on the side of his head. Wolf had taken their unconscious forms quickly from the chateau and brought them to the mountain retreat. In the middle of the night, he had heard Pierre tugging frantically at his chains, but René had only just regained a groggy consciousness. Both stared wide-eyed at Wolf.

As the men looked him over from head to toe, Wolf lit into a huge smile and sneered. The simpletons did not know in the least what was happening. "My dearest children, let me explain what is happening so you will not continue looking at me with the hatred and fear I see in your eyes. I am not here to harm you really. I just need a tidbit of information for the man we all admire and love, our great benefactor, Jean Delacroix. Look into the television camera, please, just behind me."

Wolf moved slightly to one side, revealing a large, modern television camera. A red light came on just above the lens as Wolf activated it. "I'm so sorry this is just a one-way video today. Our host is busy entertaining a friend, so he can't personally converse with you, but do not fear. I'll deliver the video to him myself.

"Let me explain now what we will be doing so you will not have any surprises. René, I'm going to unchain you from the wall and have you join me around the corner for a little chat. Please don't do anything silly because then I'll have to hurt you, and I really don't want to do that. Do you understand me?"

René looked at Wolf and responded with a yes. His eyes betrayed him. He would do everything he was told. However, Wolf noted the look of defiance in the other man's eyes. He was going to be trouble, but delightful trouble.

Wolf released René from the wall, still cuffed about the wrists, and led him into a small, soundproof room where two chairs faced each other. A television camera was mounted in the corner of the ceiling, and Wolf activated it before seating and chaining René into the chair that was bolted to the floor. "René, I understand from your conversation with Mr. Delacroix that certain rumors have been speculated on concerning our employer. Can you elaborate?"

"Mr. Delacroix, rumors, well, I did hear a thing or two from others . . ."

Without warning, Wolf lashed out with his large, open hand and hit René across the mouth. The little man spun sideways off the chair and rolled as far as the chain permitted him. A large red welt mushroomed from his face. Tears coursed down his cheeks, and he shrieked uncontrollably.

Wolf took out a pack of Camel cigarettes and lit one, inhaling the smoke with pleasure as he waited for the wailing to subside. "Now, as I was saying, you told Mr. Delacroix you have spies watching him, that these spies are giving you confidential information about his personal activities. I want to know the names of all the informers who are talking to you. Do I make myself clear?" He leaned forward and ground the end of his cigarette into René's face. The man screamed again, and Wolf lit another cigarette.

He held the glowing end in René's face.

ᏚᎣ

René opened his eyes and said, "Well . . ." He had never experienced pure terror. He was raised in a pleasant middle-class environment. Discovering a love for women's fashions at a young age and at the same time a great attraction for men, René had led a protected life. Only recently, his relationship with Pierre had changed him. Pierre was not content with the income of René and had encouraged him to seek a better situation elsewhere. Pierre had come up with the idea of pitting the House of Dior against Delacroix in a bidding war to obtain the maximum amount of remuneration.

René's face was beginning to swell, and he found it difficult to speak. The words came out slowly. "I'll tell you whatever you want. Please don't hurt me anymore. I've been getting information from only

Michael DuBasso

one person. He's considered above reproach, as he's been with Mr. Delacroix for twenty years, working in his Paris home. It's his assistant valet, Marc Piollet."

&

Wolf took a deep drag on his cigarette. Exhaling the smoke directly into René's face, he asked, "What are the so-called secrets you have been given that might prove embarrassing to Mr. Delacroix?"

"I've been told there's a secret room where bizarre sexual activities are carried out, according to Marc. He says Mr. Delacroix sometimes spends twenty-four hours or more locked up in the room with different women who're brought in for the occasion. He told me he recognized one famous American actress, even though she had disguised herself."

"What other secrets do you profess to know, René?" Wolf spent another hour with the man, "assisting" him to try and remember anything of interest that Jean Delacroix might want to know about. A few minor incidents came to light regarding some of the assistants in the design firm, but for the most part, the added information was worthless. René had been ground down and pulverized, as were all the persons Wolf interrogated.

When he was finished, Wolf unchained the half-conscious René and carried him to another room. Wolf dropped him on the floor and closed the door. Removing his silver-plated Luger from a cabinet on the wall, he fired a single shot into René's temple. The body jerked spastically for a few seconds then lay still. René Beaumont had committed the ultimate betrayal. Wolf had committed the ultimate act of punishment. He had been René's judge, jury, and executioner.

As the room was slightly chilly, Wolf turned the heat up a few notches. He wanted the cabin to be quite warm. He had accomplished what Jean had asked of him. It was time to relax and have a little fun. Jean had given him permission to do whatever he wanted in the seclusion of the cabin basement. It was his reward for work well done.

First, Wolf would grab something to eat before his tasty dessert. He returned to the main floor and looked in the refrigerator. Jean was generous in all things, and the large pantries in all of his residences were stocked with the best foods and wines available. The cabin was no exception, as the events that occasionally went on there were vital to the ongoing interests of the Delacroix Empire.

Wolf arranged for himself a fine meal of chacouettes, fresh bread, and sausages, accompanied by a fine, cold German malt liquor. He leisurely ate, then took another jog in the woods to dissipate the meal while confirming there were no persons in the area. Returning to the cabin, he took a short nap before going back to the basement for dessert.

છ

Pierre was lying face down on his cot, asleep. The sheets were rumpled, the pillow bunched up under his head. Suspended from the wall, his arm was hanging at an odd angle. Wolf pulled up a chair and looked at the young man, not at all interested in what information he might have. Obviously Pierre knew whatever information René had acquired, but nothing more.

As he considered René's lover, Wolf's cock became erect. His large penis protruded above the waistband of his shorts. He reached down and unfastened Pierre's belt, removing his pants. As he removed Pierre's small shoes, the man's body jumped and he quickly rolled to his back, awake. Pierre's eyes grew wide as he looked first at Wolf then his own state of undress. He opened his mouth, but no words came out that could be construed as recognizable.

Unaffected by Pierre's state of shock, Wolf unshackled him from the wall. He picked up the small man and carried him like a sack of flour into another room. The room contained nothing but a king-size bed and a small refrigerator. Wolf locked Pierre's handcuffs to a heavy iron ring hanging from one of the walls.

He grabbed the back of the man's beautifully embroidered shirt and ripped it off like it was made of tissue. He pulled Pierre's tight bikini underwear down to his ankles and, grasping his own cock, ground it into the other man's anus. He plunged it deep inside the screaming Pierre and crushed his body against him, pinning him to the wall as he fucked him energetically. The tightness of the fit told Wolf that Pierre had never experienced a man of his size. Though Pierre squirmed in obvious pain, Wolf screwed him for a full thirty minutes before ejaculating an endless stream of warm sperm into the man's behind.

Having satisfied himself momentarily, Wolf opened a bottle of cold German beer and sat on the bed to examine the attractive Frenchman, who was sprawled on the floor and crying softly. Wolf belched loudly and said, "So you convinced your companion to turn on Mr. Delacroix. There is always a payment for betrayal, and you have been given to me as a gift for two days. What do you think of the arrangement?"

Pierre stopped crying and looked up at him. "What have you done with René?"

"He's in hell, where all bad boys go. If you are very good, my friend, you will not go there. I wish for your cooperation. Should I receive it, I will reward you with your life."

"What do you want from me?"

"You are very attractive. Let me unchain you and have you take a shower. We'll have a little dinner together, and then we will lie down and you will allow me the freedom to play with you a bit more. I won't be rough, I promise." Wolf was talking softly in French. The terrified, naïve sap would tolerate whatever he must in order to gain his freedom, as well as his life. He would please his German master no matter how much effort it took.

"Yes, we could have some good fun," Pierre said quietly, "and I am hungry. That would be very nice."

Wolf led Pierre from the basement into the main room. He prepared a great feast, opening a bottle of good French wine. The Frenchman chattered away during the meal as if nothing had happened. Afterward they returned to the basement, where Wolf entertained Pierre. He was not gentle, and after tying him face down on the large bed, he did things to him that would have received the approval of only the Marquees de Sade.

Los Angeles, 1969: David Benjamin

Tristan was in his Sunset Boulevard office when the call came through. His secretary, Karen, announced that Jean Claude Briac was on the line. Tristan smiled to himself, knowing that crazy French playboy would be announcing the cast for the weekend party. His parties were always interesting since Jean Claude was the biggest star-fucker in Hollywood. His "cast" would probably consist of every aspiring starlet available in Tinseltown. His male guests would be limited to a select few. The girls came in droves since Jean Claude would have the best champagne, appetizers, and to top it off, marijuana from Maui and that white powder that was coming back into popularity after decades of nonuse. He kept a special bag of large white pills marked "Lemon" for the special lady who might want to entertain him and his wife after the party ended—if and when the party ever ended. It was not uncommon for his parties to go on for days.

Tristan had met Jean Claude in Ibiza the year before aboard the yacht of a wealthy Saudi gentleman. Tristan had been standing in line at the ship's bar when he noticed that the bartender was pouring a bottle of Dom Perignon champagne into several glasses and that there were absolutely no bubbles. Not knowing many at the party and wanting to make an impression, Tristan announced quite loudly how rude it was to pour flat champagne. The bartender never hesitated pouring and in a heavy British accent announced, "Sir, the Dom Perignon that I'm pouring is the ship's house white wine. It is not champagne."

With that, a middle-aged, handsome Frenchman cracked up, thinking Tristan had made a joke. Jean Claude introduced himself and his wife, Madeline Mane, then proceeded to show Tristan around the ship. Jean Claude invited him to his home in the hills above the harbor after that, and by the weekend, he insisted Tristan join him at his villa as his houseguest.

Jean Claude was more than entertaining; he filled Tristan's life with constant amusement. Ibiza was a rebirth of Sodom and Gomorrah. Never had Tristan seen people act in such a crazy way. "Drugs, sex, rock and roll" was the name of the game. Tristan had never used drugs but was fascinated by those who did. Though seemingly happy, those people appeared to be a tragic group seeking happiness through drugs and sex because something extremely important was lacking in their lives.

The many experiences of watching people in their pain or joy had inspired Tristan to write the lyrics to some of his most memorable songs. Something was lacking in his life, too, and had been for many years. But he would not reflect on that. He would lose himself while observing others, and occasionally find solace with someone who resembled the one he loved so long ago.

Jean Claude had purchased Vanessa Daniells's old home off Benedict Canyon Road, behind the Beverly Hills Hotel. Tristan arrived at his party late. People were milling here and there, some apparently high from either alcohol or something stronger. He seated himself on the edge of the large marble fireplace, taking in the warmth from the fire and reflecting on the scene.

David Benjamin, from *Asian Combat* fame, approached Tristan and sat down. They had met through Jean Claude about six months prior. David was attempting to raise money to distribute a film he had made called *The Merry-Go-Round*. He was famous in America for his martial arts television series but had sold his television rights to finance his film project. Tristan knew Jean Claude would not finance the film and had a suspicion David was going to approach him for a loan.

"Where the hell did I go wrong, Tristan? Should I've sold my rights to do the film I wanted? No one'll talk to me about it."

Here we go, Tristan thought.

"The film is fantastic. And it's done now, but I don't have money to get it out there."

David was bombed. From what, Tristan did not know, nor did he want to know. He decided to leave. It was Saturday night, and he wanted to spend Sunday resting. On Monday, he would start pre-production on a new album. He wanted to review song scores for the LP.

David stared intensely at Tristan and persisted. "Hey, rich-and-famous, why don't you lend me the money? I'll give you a hunnerd percent profit."

Tristan gritted his teeth. Why the hell did he have to deal with that crap? He worked sometimes eighteen hours a day getting a record finished, did live concerts almost half of the year, and was not in the mood for any unpleasant confrontations. Then that asshole wanted Tristan to rescue him.

To avoid the torment he could not get rid of, Tristan filled his life with work. He could find no one in life to share his ecstasy, or his agonies; he had no real friends except for Vanessa, and when she was "in love for the moment," there was only the loneliness.

Memories of Paris returned. *Why did Marie run away, what did I do? Where is she now, who's holding her now?* Tristan read about her continually; but the news was only about her films, what she liked to eat, her favorite flowers, what she might like in a man, and absolutely nothing about her personal life. She might as well have been Greta Garbo.

"Okay, David. You want the facts? I'll give you the whole nine yards. You're a first-class jerk! Talented, yes. I've seen your TV series and enjoyed it since it does contain a good concept, and it plays everywhere in the world where they have television. You sold the television rights to produce your movie. Now, why in hell would anyone ever make a film without a distribution deal, at least enough to cover the cost of the movie? You basically took ten million dollars and flushed it down the toilet! You can't expect Jean Claude, or me, or anyone else to bail you out!" Tristan had lost it. His frustration with life, and with people, was overwhelming, and he unloaded all of his hostility toward that walking powder keg, David Benjamin. "And get off the fucking shit you're taking! You're joining all the other actors who aren't working because of their damn drug abuse!"

Tristan immediately regretted the outburst. His level of martial arts training could never prepare him for an angry David Benjamin. But it was too late. Every person in the room was silently staring at them. No one had ever spoken to David that way. He had an ugly reputation, drunk or sober. His mastery of the martial arts that he practiced on television was genuine, and his skill was unprecedented in all forms of karate.

Staring at Tristan, David backed away slightly, his shoulders slumping. He looked around at the staring crowd and dropped his gaze to his hands. "Well, uh . . ." He cleared his throat hoarsely.

80

Tristan had not perceived what his words would do to David. He had humiliated him in public, crushed him personally. Someone other than David would have broken down and cried; another might have fled. Had that been the case, Tristan's future would certainly have been different. But that night, the gods decided Tristan's fate. They chose to direct David's fury against him.

David had been previously arrested on several occasions for using his hands as weapons against people who had merely not responded to a question the way he wanted. Tristan ended a part of David's life that night. He also sealed his own fate in the bargain.

ℰᴈ

In a split second, David approached Tristan. Turning his back to Tristan's chest, he reached up with one hand behind Tristan's neck and the other around his waist. He hoisted Tristan into the air and threw him through a large plate-glass window. As the glass smashed into a thousand fragments, Tristan felt nothing; he was unconscious the moment his head struck the window.

ℰᴈ

Tristan landed in a bed of brightly colored summer flowers, a large piece of glass protruding from his neck. He lay in the flowers, slowly bleeding to death.

Newspapers around the world reported the tragedy. Doctors furiously labored to save his life, and succeeded. That was the good news. The bad news was that his voice box had been severely damaged. In time, Tristan Taylor would recover most of his voice but would never sing again.

ℰᴈ

Tristan lay in his private room, guarded around the clock from his fans, who stood outside the hospital vigilantly, awaiting word of his daily condition. He could not speak and was aware of the prognosis. His sanity remained because one man who had come to see him gave Tristan the comfort he needed in that crisis.

Akio Marakaya had caught the first plane available from Tokyo to Los Angeles when he was informed of the accident. When Tristan was well enough to receive visitors, Mr. Marakaya was one of a few allowed to see him. "Ah, so kind you let me visit Tristan-san. Please, I tell you story now about my great father who lived one hundred year before me. He have great enemy who capture him and hold for very big ransom money. Family pay money but captor take from great father his tongue, cut from him in front of family. Great father not cry out in pain. He possess special gift, not to feel pain with control of his mind. Now father not have tongue to speak, so write words of great wisdom for all generation to see.

"Great father go home and, in time, he raise army to kill captors. He leave legacy, and he leave for all family his writings. I have writings and memorize all. I use the teaching from him to all my children and for their children. I find in writings answers for things much difficult in life. Please to tell you something now for your own understanding.

"Great father say all things come to life have meaning and reason. Man not understand reason many time in life. Supreme Being give to you tragedy now. He have reason for this, Tristan-san. You not question his reason. You get well now, see me in Tokyo soon." Akio Marakaya had bowed to Tristan and started to leave the room. Standing in the doorway, he had turned and smiled sympathetically. "It is your karma."

∽

After the hospital, Tristan went to his desert retreat near Palm Springs, welcoming the solitude. Outside the stage, his new life was one of seclusion. He used the home that offered the past in every way possible. The meals became simple. He slept very well in the desert. It was autumn in California, and though most of the state was not affected by seasonal changes, the deserts had their seasons. The days were warm, and the evenings turned very cold.

Nestled against the mountain, Tristan's surroundings had a host of visitors at night. He saw mountain lions wandering the perimeter of his property, as well as other desert creatures, large and small. Coyotes roamed in search of mice and rabbits. The rattlesnakes had long since gone into hibernation in the rock crevices.

Tristan rambled through the hills, waiting for his voice to return, or some part, hopefully. He did nothing relative to his work. Inside, a song was trying to come forth as in all true musicians. He attempted to bury its silent tune and lyrics. The song was about love, and he wanted nothing to do with love.

Riding bareback during the day, he transferred himself back in time thousands of years and, in his fantasy, became the architect of his dreams: Senemut, who with his queen created a temple that still stood in Egypt. Tristan questioned his life as he awaited the healing. But each time he sank into depression, he brought to his mind Akio Marakaya's kind visit and his soothing words. There was a reason. It was his karma.

Vanessa would come and go on a regular basis and was one of the few people allowed inside the compound. But in November, a special guest arrived. Akio Marakaya sent Umeko to help Tristan in his need. When she arrived, he welcomed her warmly, remembering the compassion she had always shown him. They spent many a day together in solitude. She asked no questions; he spoke seldom and with great difficulty.

One unusually warm evening, Tristan barely heard Umeko enter his room as he sat on the floor, opening and closing a small leather pouch. He took out some small bottles and held them close to his face, caressing each one, all the while with his eyes tightly closed. His relationship with Umeko was very close, and he was willing that she should see what he was doing.

"Tristan-san, what are you doing? What are the little bottles you hold so closely?"

He gazed at her sheepishly. "Come here, and I'll tell you my little secret of the oils." With a rasping voice not nearly healed, he poured his heart out to the little Japanese girl who was so faithful to him. Tears ran down his face as he told the whole story. His heart felt as if it would burst from the years he had not shared with anyone the agony of losing Marie. Not even Vanessa had heard the full story, only pieces. Until that point in time, Tristan could not really express the way he felt about the love he had lost.

Umeko raised her eyes to Tristan's, tears sliding silently down her cheeks. As he described Marie's bewildering disappearance, she gathered him in her arms. Finally, his tears subsided, and Umeko whispered, "In my heart, I have always known you are in love. Your eyes speak of her. Even when you are surrounded by beauties, you are lost in her. I have sadness for you, Tristan-san, but maybe I can help you now."

She gently pushed him down on a soft blanket on the floor. Taking the fragrant oils from their pouch, she applied them as Tristan had told her he did to Marie. Gradually, he relaxed under her strong fingers. Slowly and wondrously, he fell into a deep sleep. He dreamed of lightning and thunder. He was back in Paris, with the storm. He was back in Paris, with his love.

New York City, 1969: Christmas

As December approached and Tristan's voice began to return, he went to New York. He would find what he was meant to do. His spacious apartment on Madison Avenue was two blocks from the Metropolitan Museum of Art. Bertoli Felini, one of the best decorators in Manhattan, had carefully designed the apartment for the comfort of the star. The living and dining rooms were combined with a large kitchen for easy dining. Adjoining the dining area, a bar opened to the kitchen, allowing those seated in the zebra-skin barstools a view of what tasty tidbits Tristan's chef was preparing in the kitchen.

The apartment was part of an 1880s brownstone that had originally been a single residence. Once popular in New York, brownstones required impossibly expensive upkeep, and most had been divided into apartments. The building consisted of six apartments, and his was on the third floor, overlooking Central Park East.

Tristan's two-bedroom suite was decorated in French-country-style furniture. A small Matisse adorned one wall, and directly over his large bed was an elegant white-period Louis Icart oil painting displaying a sleeping model reclining in bed. Another wall displayed a double-size poster of Toulouse-Lautrec's fabulous *Moulin Rouge*. The walls were covered in red brocade, the overall effect quite sexy. Hardly anyone other than Tristan used those rooms. But occasionally, Vanessa Daniells and recently Leslie Cole, whom Tristan still loved in his own way, came by to say hello and encourage his recovery.

Since the accident, Tristan had avoided the music studio in his apartment, where he had once spent most of his time. Along with a keyboard and recording equipment, the studio had every electronic device necessary to edit a master recording. None of Tristan's recordings had gone into production without his spending hundreds of hours amplifying and adjusting every song. He had fine tuned some of his biggest hits in that room.

Tristan had played the piano since childhood but not well enough to do so in public. In the beginning of his career as a recording artist, he used the piano to work out his music; but in time, when the electronic keyboard came into being, he was caught up in the myriad ways that device could be used. Yamaha provided him with experimental models years ahead of their time. Tristan could create the sound of any instrument known to man—from the basic piano to the lightest flute—and only a professional would know the difference.

As Christmas approached, Tristan had a final examination of his throat to see if he could sing again. Three of America's best doctors agreed the damage was permanent. His singing career was really over. Melancholy, he reminisced about his life. He must do something or slip into a depression he might not be able to recover from. But a force within was crying out in anquish. A part of his life was finished forever. The great highs he had experienced singing in front of an audience would never occur again. Deep inside, something compelled him to allow his mind and body to break down. No matter how hard he resisted, no matter whom he talked to about it, he really felt his life was over.

On December 24, after calling family and friends to wish them a merry Christmas, Tristan went into the music room and sat at the enormous keyboard. Smiling to himself, he let the melody that had been hidden inside come out. With no conscious thought, he sang the words in his feeble voice as he taped the music. He recorded and edited the song in just a few hours. Satisfied with the recording, he sealed it into an envelope with a note to John Stiles.

Tristan had written and recorded "Dedicated to the One I Love." It would be recorded that year by numerous artists; but, per his instructions, the first recording was by "Mama" Cass Elliot, whose stirring rendition would be considered a classic.

From his window, Tristan looked out over the vast park. Opening his wardrobe closet, he selected some warm but worn winter clothing including a heavy coat. He walked to the corner and put the stamped envelope to John Stiles in the postbox. Removing all his cards and identification from his wallet, he tossed them in a large metal trash can nearby. The wallet still contained nearly a thousand dollars in cash. He crossed the street to the park and went up to a grizzled old lady sitting on a bench, obviously destitute. Her eyes widened as she speechlessly accepted the cash and stuffed it in the pocket of her tattered coat. Tristan continued through the park, turning one more time to look at his apartment. Removing the elegant set of keys from his pocket, he threw them in a nearby snowbank. He then disappeared off the face of the earth.

Paris — Rome — Hollywood, 1970: And the First Runner-Up Is

Jacques Demy received a script from America, elated that he finally had an opportunity to show American film producers that a Frenchman could indeed make a decent film primarily designed for an American audience. Calling one of the principals at Cine France, he tied up the film rights at once. Susan Day, the American writer who sent the script at the urging of her mother, had tried unsuccessfully to even get an appointment with the Hollywood studios.

Miss Day had graduated from Southern California University, and the script was her first project coming out of school. Jacque knew of her mother, who was born in France and had spent years writing minor scripts for documentary series and low-budget films in Europe. Her claim to fame was her European contacts, and when her daughter was rebuffed with the script, Mrs. Day decided the project should go back home. She apparently had good taste, as the script was surprisingly decent.

With her script, Susan Day had included a synopsis of her fascination for all the women caught up with beauty pageants. She had watched the Miss America contests since childhood. She also watched the Miss Universe contests and was completely swept into the world of those young women. She had made the pageant process her graduation thesis — which she also included in with the package — and from that wrote the script, naming it *And the First Runner-Up Is*. The title said it all.

As portrayed in Miss Day's thesis, the Miss Universe contest was the prestige event of the year, culminating the hundreds of worldwide contests for the quest of finding the ultimate ten. Thousands of contestants worked, hoped, and prayed they made it to that pageant, supposedly the adoration of womanhood. It was far from that in real life. Many of those remarkable, young women sold their souls in the quest for number one. Her research into the realm of beauty contests exposed the inner workings of the system — the corruptness of some of the officiating that led to the Miss Universe contest and the intense pressure put on the lovely ladies who walked the final mile.

Jacques had known about the contests and, upon reading the script, realized Miss Day had a winner. The studio and director would create the film and portray the story in an exciting, true style that hopefully would result with a box office success. Casting was the key element.

The principals must be three beautiful women who could act and portray the contestants on whom the story was based. From among the three, the winner would ultimately emerge. The minute he finished reading the script, Jacques knew which actresses would be dynamite performers for these roles.

§∋

Sofia Vaskeli sat with her director husband, Sergio, at the White Elephant, having a quiet dinner. The elegant restaurant was not crowded, as it was only seven o'clock, Rome time. She was excited about the script that had been sent from Paris earlier in the day. Sergio was brooding and angry. He did not like the concept and argued vehemently that she not accept the role. She suspected he wanted her to do another mediocre, low-budget film for him in Italy. His films were not bad, but the six they had done together those past years had not done well internationally. The film she had done costarring Cary Grant gave her an Academy nomination. It also paid her a huge salary, and she wanted to work again with other stars. The meal ended with Sofia insisting she do the film, basta!

§∋

Marie was having a pleasant dinner at la Coupole with Jean and his new fashion designer, Marcel Bigot. Bigot had taken over when René Beaumont mysteriously disappeared. Marie thought Marcel's designs were superior to his predecessor, but greatly missed the first designer's entertaining sense of humor.

Jean finished a conversation with Marcel in which René's name came up, and Marie interjected. "Jean, what do you think ever happened to poor René?"

Smiling, he said nothing for a moment, then responded with a rather morbid grin. "Probably ran into a nasty German who didn't like his personal tastes. Perhaps he invited him home for dinner and ate him." And with that, Jean burst into an odd display of uncontrolled laughter. Marie exchanged glances with Marcel, not appreciating the humor at all.

Wanting to change the subject, Marie interrupted Jean's snickering. "I'm starting a new film next month and can't even tell you how excited I am. It will costar Vanessa Daniells and Sofia Vaskeli." Marie described the plot and locations, and the evening appeared to end on a happy note.

ℭ

Later that night, Jean was still fuming at the thought of being separated again from Marie. He had just started winning his way back into her trust after the Taylor incident; he did not want to lose her again. And something bothered him about the American actress, Daniells, but he could not recall at the moment what it was.

ℭ

Vanessa Daniells was in her Beverly Hills home with her new husband, agent, and manager, Jay Goldstein. The two had finished reading the script that had come from Paris and were elated. After she relayed her enthusiasm for the script, hesaid, "It sounds great, but have you given thought to who's getting which role? I note Mr. Demy has not cast specific parts for the three women. I don't want you to take any of these parts except for the lady who wins it all."

Vanessa's man-of-the-moment, Jay would be a brief part of her intimate life. However, he proved to be the best manager she ever had, and he would continue to represent her his entire life. As they continued discussing the ramifications of the script, the phone rang. Jay answered it and after a moment handed the phone to Vanessa with some concern. "It's John Stiles calling from New York."

"Hello, Vanessa. I don't have good news. The police can't find Tristan. Aside from the streetwalker who found all his personal charge cards in the trash, nothing's new. They don't suspect he's met with foul play because of the package I received from him.

"The envelope contained only a new song he recorded and a short note. He wants me to contact certain singers he thinks will be interested in recording the song. And he said to contact his attorney, Leon Fleishman, to make sure his properties are maintained from his royalty account. It ended with: I'm going away for a while. Tell my friends not to worry.

"Maybe he just decided to go somewhere and be alone. He hasn't gotten over the loss of his voice— it's understandable. But I'm very upset, Vanessa. My personal life is in limbo. I can't conceive working with anyone else."

Vanessa quietly told John it was okay, but deep inside, her intuition and special gift told her otherwise. Tristan was in trouble, real trouble, and her heart went out for the man in her life who meant more to her than anyone. *Thank God for this new film. I must take my mind off Tristan.*

ဏ

Filming on *And the First Runner-Up Is* started a month later in Florida at the famous Miami Beach Auditorium, where many pageants had been held. They would be shooting the closing sequence first. Filming would also be on actual pageant locations in France and Italy. Everyone was present for the first day's walk-through except Sofia Vaskeli, who was detained by her doctor for a checkup before she left Rome. She was due on the morning's flight into Miami International, and a limousine was already at the airport to meet her.

Gig Young would play the host of the pageant and had agreed to work sober. No one outside of Hollywood knew that Gig had a problem, but it had reached the attention of the producers from an independent investigator when they tried to obtain insurance for the film. Upon being confronted with his drinking, Gig told Mr. Demy that he need not drink on the set. Working with three of the most beautiful women on the planet would offset any urges he might have. Both had laughed heartily, and Gig got the part.

Jacques Demy was in a delightful mood as he breakfasted with his leading ladies and Gig Young. They were having coffee when a telegram arrived from Sergio Vaskeli. It contained a short sentence that on many occasions had caused directors near heart failure. *Sofia Vaskeli must cancel by doctor's advice, as she is pregnant with first child and there could be complications.*

He was speechless. He read the telegram to the actors and just sat there. In his mind, Jacques had already set the cast in stone. Any changes then would complicate things for him. Like so many good directors, he had become part of the film emotionally. In his mind's eye, he saw the parts played a certain way by each of the actors. He envisioned the sets, the sounds, and, most importantly, the presentations he wanted each actor to perform. The one thing that had not entered his mind was dealing with a major cast change. Sitting at the early-breakfast table, he looked off into space and said aloud, "Who the hell can I replace Sofia with?"

Seated next to him, Marie took his hand, looked him straight in the face, and without hesitating said, "With another French actress, obviously: Genevieve Dubois."

He looked at her for a moment, surprised. "How can I do that? France can't have two finalists competing."

Marie smiled. "Of course not, but you forget she's been living now almost three years in Venice with Mario Pavaroto, the great opera singer. They even have a daughter together. He left his wife of fifteen years for her. Genevieve speaks fluent Italian, and don't forget, even though Sofia is brunette, the Italians in the north are blonde."

Jacques looked at Marie with new admiration but was still pessimistic. "I love the idea, but with my luck, she's probably working."

Vanessa, who had been following the conversation, interjected. "No. She's available. It's in this week's *Hollywood Reporter*. According to the story, she's back in Paris, incommunicado. Mario left her high and dry in Venice and returned to his wife in Rome. Seems he's developed some kind of growth on his ass that's been diagnosed as cancer. The doctors think they can remove it and he'll live, but poor Mario has heard that the church condemned him for living with Genevieve, and he won't be able to enter heaven unless he goes back to his wife. He apparently went back to Rome, moved in with his wife, and made confession with his priest. The priest told him to say the 'Hail Mary' a hundred times, and he was forgiven." And with that, everyone burst into uncontrollable laughter.

℘

Genevieve jumped at the chance when she was contacted, and within a week, the filming began. No one mentioned the story in the *Reporter* to her. Jacques Demy had warned the entire cast and crew they would be terminated at once if they spoke even one word.

From the commencement of filming, the four principal actors worked together as if they had done so for years. Each was enamored of the others and Gig Young, being the sole male lead, had the wondrous position of playing opposite the three most beautiful women on the planet. He made the most of it on camera and off.

The filming went perfectly to schedule, allowing a respite on most Sundays, when Mr. Young escorted the three women to brunch and was the envy of every man no matter where they went. He would sip tea or coffee or a soft drink while the ladies got tipsy on champagne. Their table conversation fascinated him as the lunches progressed in conjunction with their drinking. Marie would start laughing outrageously at Gig's sense of humor. The volume of her laughter would increase with each drink until not a soul in the restaurant was doing anything other than straining to hear their conversation.

The three women certainly had one thing in common. They all enjoyed talking about men, especially Vanessa. By the end of each meal, and certainly by the end of the filming, Gig Young had learned enough about what women liked in a man to open a male call service.

To his chagrin, the one thing he was not able to achieve was having an affair with one of those beauties. He certainly tried and would sometimes lie awake at night, fantasizing what it might be like to sleep with all three at one time.

Susan Day's fabulous script came alive with the four principal actors, each character playing to the others in a stimulating manner. The artistically powerful story was about each of the women's own lives just before and during the pageant. The three actresses mastered their roles as contestants. Gig's extraordinary performance as the emcee would earn him an Oscar. His character's life away from the pageant was sad and meaningless. He would only come alive for the annual pageant then disappear into oblivion for the rest of the year, unemployable due to being typecast by his role in the pageant. Small vignettes of the principal actors ran through the film. The four were so caught up in their roles that they actually sat in on each others' performances.

₧

Genevieve decided from the first day of shooting that under no circumstances would she share her dreaded secret with Marie. She buried it in her mind so it would not distract from her acting. It would have stayed there except for the perennial situation in life that allows unplanned things to happen.

₧

Jacques observed the special bond that developed among his four actors. He had a reputation of being very clever and very observant. He let their bonding continue to a climax. They were near completion of the film, and only a few scenes were left. They had traveled to France and Italy and just returned to Miami for the last scenes.

At 7:00 a.m. in the Miami Beach Auditorium, the three ladies were seated onstage with Jacques and Gig. The camera crew and other technicians were ready to roll. Jacques explained that the day's shoot would involve the emcee asking a surprise question to each of the contestants. When the ladies asked for the script for the morning shoot, Jacques said there was none. He looked at his actors, and like a child who had kept a big secret from his family and was going to finally reveal it, he made his announcement.

"All of you have given me, and this film, some of the greatest performances I've ever elicited from any actor." He waited for that to sink in before continuing. No one said a word. "I didn't give you a script for today because I want each of you, from your heart, to make your own performance with nothing planned ahead. You all know that in the real Miss Universe pageant, the finalist must stand in front of the audience and answer a question that they haven't been told about previously. As to the audience, I'll film them later this afternoon with you. I didn't want any distraction at all for your responses. Mr. Young knows the questions. Let's get started, and I want this on one take only. You'll have to live with your responses. I won't shoot any of you a second time."

Jacques studied his leading ladies. He could see that they were excited about the little game, as he knew they would be. "Each of you will be asked a different question. Let's start. Roll the cameras."

To a silent room, Vanessa and Marie answered Gig's philosophical questions. Jacques knew he was getting great performances on both occasions. The two women had long ago become the contestants, and their answers and acting were very natural. It was Genevieve's turn next.

℟

Fate plays a considerable part in all our lives. The questions that the director had prepared were not designed for any one person. After considering doing precisely that, he opted to just let the questions come from Gig in any order he wanted. Gig himself gave no thought to the order. He just took the slips of paper in his hand and picked each at random.

℟

Ready to speak on any subject known to man, Genevieve enthusiastically stood before the cameras and Gig's solitary figure. "Now for contestant number three, Miss Italy, answer the following question for me. You three finalists have been together as a family for many weeks. Describe to me as best as you can *loyalty to one another*."

Time stood still. During filming, the past had not existed, only the present. But in real life, the past, present, and future are all tied together, and that forms people's lives. That philosophy is followed by many persons, but just as many others never think about it at all. Genevieve had never really thought much about anything other than the present. That day, her past caught up to her.

Genevieve froze, looking only at Marie. Jacques motioned her toward the camera, but still she looked at Marie. Without uttering a word, Genevieve walked to her, wrapped her arms around her, and began to cry. She stood a long time holding Marie, sobbing until she finally shuddered to a stop. In time, Genevieve stood back, looked at her, and whispered, "I love you, Marie. Come now. We must speak." Nothing else was said. The two young women walked off the set and did not return that day.

Los Angeles, 1971: The Academy Awards Ceremony

And the First Runner-Up Is was released in October of 1970 and was the biggest box office draw of the year. The film was popular in every country it was shown. In the US, it received ten Academy Award nominations: Best Costumes, Editing, Cinematography; Best Original Screenplay, Susan Day; Best Actress, both Vanessa Daniells and Marie Savoie; Best Supporting Actress, Genevieve Dubois; Best Supporting Actor, Gig Young; Best Director, Jacques Demy; and Best Motion Picture. The film was not a high-budget production, and for that reason, no one in the motion picture business conceived it would garner those nominations.

୫

The evening of April 15, 1971, was rather cool in Los Angeles. At the Dorothy Chandler Pavilion, where the Academy Awards were being held, the traditional red carpet led from the street to the auditorium, with grandstands lining the entire one hundred yards. Fifteen tiers of benches had been built to hold around three thousand enthusiastic movie fans. Lois Derson was the principal interviewer for television viewers that night. As each limousine pulled up, the screams of the fans indicated by volume which celebrity had arrived.

Vanessa Daniells received the loudest acclaim of all. She was dressed in a brilliant-red Christian Dior gown with sequins laced throughout. The dress showed off her cleavage in the most appealing manner, and a tiny crown of diamonds rested atop her jet-black hair. She looked like a princess as she was escorted to the auditorium.

୫

Vanessa was feeling radiant and elated. Up for her fifth Oscar, she cared not if she won as long as *Runner-Up* won its share of Oscars, and especially if Marie won her first. Vanessa was accompanied that evening, of course, by her husband, Jay Goldstein. Jay was shorter than she, and his hairline was receding. Offsetting his physical limitations, his ever-present humor had attracted her to him.

Moving forward, Vanessa tried not to catch the eyes of her fans, as she was concerned someone would start a conversation or ask for an autograph. She normally did not mind, but for some reason, that night she felt edgy, as if a strange presence were about. She wanted to get inside the auditorium as soon as possible. The line in front of them bogged down briefly, putting them at a standstill.

Jay turned his head toward the crowded benches. Nudging Vanessa gently, he whispered in her ear, "Christ, you should see some of these people. We come decked out as if we were meeting the queen of England, and some of our fans dress like they're going to a barbecue. Look at the nut at the top of the stands just alongside of us. He looks like a vagrant."

Vanessa glanced up and instantly looked away. She grabbed Jay's hand tightly and, putting her mouth to his ear, said, "Don't question a word I tell you, just do exactly what I want. I see two security guards in front of us. Walk over and tell them to help you grab the man you just described to me."

Jay looked at Vanessa with such a wide mouth that she could have put her small purse inside. "And shut your damn mouth. Do what I say, or I'll never speak to you again as long as I live. That man is my best friend, Tristan Taylor. Now get your ass moving."

No one who knew Tristan would ever be able to identify him with his full beard, his dirty hair and clothing. Except Vanessa. He certainly did look like a bum, but she had the special gift of vision and the ability to know one's eyes. She would never forget Tristan's eyes. The instant she saw him, she knew who he was.

Paris: Saint Germain des Pres

Marie had decorated her living room for the small Academy Awards party she was having for her best girlfriends. The ceremony would be telecast to Paris during the morning, but no matter. She had slept late and was buzzing around the apartment happily in anticipation of seeing her friend Vanessa Daniells win her fifth statuette. Marie would rather have attended the awards ceremony in person, but she had started rehearsals five days earlier for a new film to be done in Tahiti and could not leave Paris. She was disappointed at not being there but happy with the day and night off to watch the event.

She had invited six of her closest friends, including Alexia, Gabby, Veronique, and Sylvie Carne, her beloved publicist. Handing each of them a flute of champagne as they arrived, she directed them to the living room. That would surely be a day to remember. Marie's joy would have been more complete had she been able to speak to Tristan, but according to Vanessa, he had disappeared.

When Genevieve had told Marie in Miami that she was hired to betray her and Tristan, his supposed dishonesty had exploded in front of Marie. Too naïve to place suspicion on Jean at that time, Marie pushed Genevieve for the identity of the man responsible. Genevieve said she did not know, but the look of terror on her face told Marie there was a dark reason she could not reveal him. Later, Marie realized Jean had probably done it, but there was no proof. And until she worked up the courage to face him, she would accuse no one.

Marie tried to put Tristan out of her mind as the Academy program unfolded. The flood of awards for her film began almost at once, with Gig Young receiving the Best Supporting Actor award. As Bette Davis announced the Best Actress nominees, Marie and her friends fell silent. When she announced the winner was Marie Savoie, Marie's friends went crazy, shrieking and congratulating her. All but one; in the pandemonium of emotion, one of her friends embraced her tightly, said she had a bad headache, and left.

ॐ

Gabby headed through the lonely streets of Saint Germain to her small apartment overlooking the Seine. A slight breeze scattered papers along the empty streets. A street gypsy approached her with her hands out, asking for a few francs. Gabby reached into her jacket and gave what she had. Listless wisps of vapor drifted across the afternoon sky. A side street led her to the Seine, and she walked along the bank, thinking about her life. She reflected on that morning. Marie had everything; she had nothing.

Not far from Ile Saint-Louis and close to Notre Dame, Gabby's third-floor apartment was small but adequate. Turning on the lights, she walked directly to her small balcony overlooking the river and sat down in one of the worn cast-iron chairs that had been there when she first took the flat. That was seven years ago, and her hopes and dreams of becoming a star had not materialized. Yes, she had been given roles through Delacroix's power, but nothing had come from them. Deep inside she knew she was not the actress Marie was. She did not have Marie's magic.

The sun was setting, and shadows darkened the river in front of her. A distant bird sang pleasantly with the approaching cool of the evening. Soon the lights of Paris would adorn the great city, replacing the brightness of the sun.

Gabby left the terrace and closed the windows. She removed her clothes and washed herself in the small bathroom. Looking into the mirror, she saw a young, beautiful woman who could still dream, would still dream for years to come. She would somehow outlast Marie. She still had the support of Jean Delacroix. Putting on her best peignoir, she lay face down on her soft down bed. Closing her eyes, she dreamed of fairy tales; she dreamed she was Marie Savoie.

Beverly Hills, California: Tristan

Tristan had risen early the past few days. He awoke in the guest bedroom of Vanessa's elegant home, showered, dressed, and walked into the spectacular gardens outside his room. There were Vanessa's beloved flowers that bloomed nearly year-round in the warm Southern California weather. He nodded to her full-time gardener, Iwo Hashimoto, at work even at six in the morning. Iwo lavishly planted in Vanessa's two-acre backyard whatever flowers were in bloom. Set between deep-green palm trees of all kinds, the flower gardens had overwhelmed Tristan the first time he saw them — truly paradise found. If he were a little down, that setting always put him in better cheer.

He had been with Vanessa almost two weeks. Jay had been eyeing him warily, probably thought he was Vanessa's lover. And why not? They held each other closely when they thought him gone or out of sight. They caressed, even kissed, but never did it end up in bed. Jay had been a Hollywood manager for a decade, a man of the world. He knew enough to be suspicious. Tristan could tell he loved Vanessa passionately — his longing looks at her, the gentle way he held her hand. Poor guy was on borrowed time and probably knew it. Even afterward he would continue to idolize her. They all did.

The sun was just rising as Tristan settled on one of the deck chairs in front of the pool. An enormous blue jay lit near him on the lawn and pounced on a worm. He watched the tug of war, smiling to himself. Wasn't that perhaps what life was, a tug of war? The jay pulled the long worm from the ground and flew off. Then Tristan laughed aloud.

From behind him, Vanessa put her arms around him and nestled her head against his. "Tristan, are you coming back to us? We missed you. I've been waiting to tell you something very important. Are you ready, darling?"

That April day was going to be spectacular. The sun's rays lit the deep-blue California sky, and a gentle breeze came in from the Pacific Ocean. Softly holding his hands, Vanessa sat next to Tristan and gently told him what had occurred in Miami, what Genevieve had told Marie. How Marie had confided to Vanessa, knowing that if anyone would find Tristan, it would be she. Genevieve had warned Vanessa to talk to no one else about the matter, as it could be dangerous for Marie.

After a long silence, Tristan looked at her. "Seven years, Vanessa. Seven years I've been without her for no reason." Rage surged inside him, but the look in her eyes calmed him.

"There must've been a reason. We both believe in that philosophy. You yourself call it your karma."

He thought of the wisdom of Akio-san. Yes, there was a reason. Holding Vanessa closely he asked, "Where is she?"

"You can't reach her now. She's on some distant island away from phone contact. We'll call her agents in Paris and leave word to call us as soon as she can be reached by phone. Go home, Tristan. Go to the desert, or New York. It's over. You'll be back with her very soon."

New York: Dream a Little Dream

Tristan returned to New York. Before dropping from sight, he had lived on such a high level of energy regarding his work that he had been unable to cope with the loss of his voice, the loss of his work. He had drifted all over America for nearly a year, taking odd jobs here and there to support himself. In the beginning, when it had been cold, he had slept in various missions set up for the homeless, and during the summer, he had slept outdoors. He had tried to find himself. In a way, it was a blessing Vanessa had rescued him. In the past year, Tristan had not found any great revelation of where he was going with his life. He might have continued to wander for years seeking an answer, but clearly his karma had led him back to reality.

Vanessa's home had been enjoyable, but he'd had enough rest. Life took on a far different meaning, and he felt fabulous being in New York again. If he could get into his studio, he might busy himself with his music. The power of his voice was gone, but he could still get out a soft ballad on a personal level. While he awaited the call from Vanessa on Marie's return to civilization, he had an idea for a special song. The prospect of Marie coming back into his life was a driving force.

Sure that Marie knew "Dedicated to the One I Love" was for her, Tristan wanted desperately to write another song for her. But no matter how hard he tried, nothing came. Not a singer who felt he had to have original material, he called a few of his friends and mentors. Then it occurred to him. *Mama.* A Tristan Taylor fan since *West Side Story*, Cass Elliot had gone out of her way to meet him when she could to discuss her using some of his material. Mama had recorded "Dedicated to the One I Love" just as Tristan wanted. *Maybe she has something for me instead this time.*

On tour in San Francisco, Mama Cass returned Tristan's call from the Fremont Hotel several days later. "Finally a chance to help *you*? And where the hell have you been? Thanks for sending me that tape. We'll both earn a bit from that one, yes?"

"I love you, and your version was by far the best. I need a big favor, Mama. I want to tell someone very dear to me that I love her, I've dreamed of her, I've missed her so much. I want to tell her with a recording. Do you have something for me?"

"You must be clairvoyant. I've just written something, but your voice . . . How can you sing it?"

"I can't sing professionally, but even with my poor voice, I can let a loved one know how much I adore her. What's the name of your new song?"

" 'Dream a Little Dream of Me.' I'll send it to you by courier. God bless you, Tristan."

As promised, the recording reached Tristan the next day. In his music room, he listened to the lullaby and lyrics — perfect. Sitting at the new keyboard Yamaha had sent before he decided to drop out of the world, Tristan experimented with his voice. It sounded all right as long as he did not try to project the tune. He worked all day and most of the night on his own version. By dawn, he smiled as he played back the music. Satisfied, he had a messenger service pick up the package and deliver it to Air France. It would be in Paris at Marie's apartment when she returned.

A week later, he was having lunch with Leslie Cole in his apartment. His valet came onto the balcony where they were dining. "Tristan, it's Marie. She's calling from Tahiti."

Nearly tripping over himself, Tristan managed to get to the phone, worried he might be disconnected. Marie's voice was soft and magical, as he knew it would be. He was instantly in another space, alone with the one he loved most in the world. "I want to see you now. How can I get to you?"

"You can't get here. I'm on a small island near Tahiti, talking by radiophone. You have to wait till I'm back in Paris. I miss you so much. We have so much to catch up on. I'm leaving tomorrow for the main island, and I'll be in Paris in three days. Then I have to see someone before we can be together. It will take just one more day. Today is Monday. Come to Paris Friday, and we'll have each other forever." She was crying, and Tristan could detect in her voice the emotion she was feeling. He could not stand to wait for her.

"I'm going to catch the next flight to Paris. I'll meet your plane when you arrive from Tahiti. I can't wait any longer."

"No, Tristan. Trust me, I love you, but I must do something very important for both of us first. I love you. I have to go. I'll leave a note for you at L'Hotel."

And just like that, he was holding a dead phone and she was gone. His emotions came in waves. He had wanted to ask her what happened, who had happened. Marie had not really explained much to Vanessa. Only that they had been set up for years by an unknown person, to prevent their relationship. Vanessa had tried to question

Marie, but she was evasive, almost as if she suspected someone but did not want to name him.

Tristan returned to Leslie and decided to put out of his mind the delay in seeing Marie. His emotions betrayed him instantly, and Leslie laughed. "I see I'm not at the center of your interest. You look like a schoolboy fallen in love for the first time. It must be your Marie. Good luck, Tristan. You're one of my favorite people. You always will be. Go off wherever she is and live happily ever after."

After she left, Tristan tried to calm his feelings. He could not sit in New York waiting until the end of the week. Having considered a few thoughts, he picked up the phone and called Vanessa. "I want you to meet me in Paris tomorrow. I'll take rooms for us at L'Hotel . . . Separate? Of course separate rooms. You're not going to seduce me while I'm waiting for Marie." Both laughed heartily, which greatly eased the tension that had been building in Tristan.

"No, darling, not that soon," Vanessa said. "Why don't you go first. You sound like you're ready to jump out of your skin. I want to pack carefully for this meeting of the century. I'll join you Friday. Make a reservation for lunch. We'll celebrate for you and Marie."

Paris: L'Hotel

Deciding he could occupy himself better at home than in France, Tristan waited in New York and took a flight late Thursday evening. When he arrived in Paris, it would be Friday morning. Just one more day. He had not slept well all week and closed his eyes, trying to relax . . .

"Mr. Taylor?" The stewardess was leaning over him. "Sir, we've landed. Will you need help with your carry-on?"

Tristan rubbed his eyes. "Uh, no, thanks. I'm . . . I'm fine, thanks."

℘

Catching a cab from Charles de Gaulle Airport, Tristan returned to where it had all started: L'Hotel. Guy Louis, the gracious hotel owner, seated him at a private table in the pretty restaurant and handed him a sealed envelope. It was, of course, from Marie.

He held the envelope for a long time before opening it. Would there be something inside he did not expect? The letter felt very thick, very long. Finally, he tore open the envelope and examined the contents. The letter was ten pages long. Marie had written it while coming back from Tahiti. It was a beautiful letter expressing how she had felt the past seven years without him. How she thought he had betrayed her. It explained about Genevieve Dubois, her role and her confession just recently, all but who the person who hired her might be. She talked of Jean Delacroix, whom she had thought was her protector all those years. It went on to say she was seeing him then, ending their affair, and concluded with, *Tristan, that beautiful song you left for me, I love it. I'll think of the lyrics while I'm away. Can't wait to have your arms around me again.*

Marie had signed the letter with a big lipstick kiss in bright red. The pages smelled of her perfume. Tristan did not know what the perfume was, but it smelled of lilies. He finished the letter and read it again, that time slowly. There was no mention of who could have plotted to deceive them. When he read it a third time, he noticed Marie said she had thought Jean Delacroix was her protector. The words *had thought* stood out and made Tristan very uncomfortable. Who was that man, Delacroix? He had never heard of him. Perhaps Guy Louis could tell him.

Tristan took the small elevator leading to his rooms at the top of the hotel. Vanessa would be arriving in a few hours. He would catch a little sleep and worry about the letter later. He went into a deep sleep and was awakened by the phone. The hotel operator informed him Miss Daniells was waiting for him downstairs. He hurriedly showered, dressed, and went down to meet her.

Saint Moritz, Switzerland: Chateau Delacroix

Jean sat at the dressing room mirror. Not an attractive reflection, as at fifty-four he was not aging well—an ever-receding hairline showed above the deep lines etched into his granite face. He did not believe in reconstructive surgery as did so many of his acquaintances. What for? He had power, and he did not need to have a handsome face to go with it. He was in tremendous physical condition with proper diet and never a drug, prescribed or otherwise. No alcohol and plenty of exercise. He had lived an exceptional life, to its fullest. The family fortune had grown to astronomical levels; no business he had a hand in failed to make a substantial profit.

Only his personal life left a void inside him. Marie refused to marry him, refused him a child. An heir. How he had hoped to change her mind, but as the years passed, nothing developed. His obsession for her prevented his changing relationships to another who would bear him a child.

Jean thought of Annette. He had never forgiven himself for her death. Why did Marie not care for him the way Annette had? He had tried everything to force her to change her mind, to win that game. It had never happened.

The rage started to build again. For ten years, he had supported Marie—financing her films, influencing directors and producers to cast her in leading roles. For ten years, he had helped her through her frequent bouts of depression. When Marie was working or about to begin a film, she was fine; but, lo, if nothing was going on, she became morose and impossible to be around, occasionally quite nasty, as if she possessed a scorpion within her. And the privacy she insisted on during periods of time that she did not want his company. He knew that early on she had lovers, but since Tristan Taylor, that was not the case.

In 1962, Marie had fallen in love with that idiotic young singer. With a simple plan, Jean had ended their affair quickly, with neither person knowing the better. After that, she should have wanted someone she could fully trust. He had made sure it was he to whom she attached herself. It had almost worked, it still could.

But after ten years, Marie was going to tell Jean she was reuniting with that has-been singer! He looked at his watch; it was almost eleven. Soon she would be in the dining room for lunch, waiting for him with that lovely piece of news. Every day Jean's men watched Marie—twenty-four hours a day, 365 days a year. He would not allow any person in his life to come even close to betraying him. And that romantic creature, who was always searching for what she once had with Taylor, needed to be watched.

When Jean was sixteen, he had fallen hopelessly in love with a distant cousin, whom he had told his father he could not live without. Bernard asked him how the girl felt about him, and Jean lamented that she did not even know he was alive. "Jean, no one falls in love forever, especially when the love is not returned. We can love passionately for a while, even for a great period of time, but man is, for the most part, not monogamous in his relationships with women.

"I, too, met someone I thought I couldn't live without. When I was married to your mother and had just turned twenty-five, I was in Basel attending a watch-and-clock show we were exhibiting in—and keep in mind I was deeply in love with your mother. It was noon, and I decided to have lunch on my own. I was walking down a quiet street when suddenly coming toward me was a young girl, startlingly beautiful. Our eyes met . . . and we both stopped. Neither of us said a word. I just took her hand and led her to my hotel. We made love for two days. Neither of us left the room. And then while I was sleeping, she left. I never saw her again. I searched everywhere, but she was gone. And that is life.

"You cannot control destiny, especially romantic destiny. In time, you will forget this girl and fall deeply in love with one who will love you in return. Forget her."

Jean reflected on those words from long ago, but his mind and temper were not like his father's. The hatred grew as he left his bedroom suite.

໘

Marie had arrived in Zurich by Jean's private Lear jet, and his helicopter had swiftly carried her over the mountain range to the chateau. She sat at the large oak table, sipping strong coffee. Reflecting on what she would say, she stared out the window and watched the nineteenth-century narrow-gauge rail locomotive move slowly up the mountain.

Spring flowers were everywhere, a wondrous sight normally. But that morning she could not enjoy the spectacular view. She was nervous about ending her lengthy relationship with Jean. The good times and affection she had for him were not enough to keep her from true love. Reuniting with Tristan was all that mattered. She just wanted to end her affair with Jean and remain as friends.

Tristan was in Paris; she would be back that night and join him and Vanessa for the best dinner of her life. How in the world could she feel any better than having those she loved the most around her? She glanced at the clock. In only minutes, she would be free.

℘

Steeling himself, Jean entered the dining room and warmly embraced Marie. "How was the flight, love? Are you feeling well today? And what have we ordered for lunch?"

After a moment, Marie chattered on with small talk. Everything was fine; a new film was to start in three weeks about the life of Renoir. She talked for a while then paused. "Jean, I want to go back with Tristan Taylor. I love him, and we'll be married this summer in Normandy. I love you as my friend. Please understand and remain my friend." She was shaking.

Jean maintained rule of his emotions. Their final chess match. For years he had managed to win every time with this emotional girl, but the situation suddenly was backing him into a corner. "Marie, how wonderful, but have you really thought this through? He betrayed you once. He might do it again."

"No. I was set up." Taking a deep and shaky breath, Marie met Jean's gaze and said, "Someone played a cruel game with me, tricked me into believing Tristan didn't care for me. But now I know better."

For an instant, Jean almost lost control of himself. He was not prepared for that at all. His entire strategy was based on love betrayed. He had planned to work that angle endlessly, until she gave in. She had always given in before. He had thought time was on his side. It was not. Who would have ever thought his game would be discovered? Jean's mind worked feverishly. If Marie had been told of the plot, certainly she would guess who the schemer was—if not already, then later. In a moment, the chess game had finished. Checkmate.

Jean played at every game in the world, and usually knew long before the finish if he were going to win or lose. When he won, he relished every second leading to victory—at business, cards, sports, anything—but when he knew he was going to lose, he immediately did what he could to avoid losing face. In a game of cards, he would say, "I wanted you to win today." If it were a business deal going sour, he would say, "You should have this deal. It's better for you actually than I." Jean never allowed the other to gain face over him.

After a long look at Marie, he said, "Yes, of course, love. I can see in your eyes you are his now. You always loved him very much. Let me walk with you one last time to the point so we can see all of Saint Moritz. You know, the village is holding a festival. We can watch them a bit." He smiled warmly, extending his hand. Marie had stopped shaking. She took his hand, smiling in return. "Marie, I need to get my walking cane and jacket. Meet me on the terrace."

An odd feeling descended upon Jean as he and Marie exited the chateau. He glanced behind him then searched upward. From one of the windows high in the chateau, a silhouette studied the two. "Oh," Marie said as she came beside him. She was looking at the window then, too. The woman backed into the shadows, a lock of blonde hair falling into her face.

"I see my servant was enjoying the view, as well," Jean said.

"Hmm."

He took Marie's hand again, and they walked in the lush, green blanket of dewy grass, under the pine trees, and along the path toward the front of the mountain. The air was refreshing. When they reached the point, all of Saint Moritz lay below. The bright-green slopes were blanketed here and there with patches of wildflowers, and the little town flew bright, multi-colored banners on every corner. The sound of festive music wove its way up to them.

"Spectacular," Marie said.

Jean stood behind her, lost in thought.

With her back still to him, Marie said quietly, "Jean, it wasn't you, was it?" She turned slowly to face him.

His face set, he reached into his pocket and touched the beautiful nineteenth-century Henry Derringer pistol. It was identical to the one used by John Wilkes Booth to assassinate President Lincoln. Jean glanced briefly at the fabulous winter setting. "Marie, I love you dearly and would never betray you, not ever."

Marie smiled at Jean and hugged him. "I knew you would never do that to me."

They walked back hand in hand, Jean smiling to himself, fully aware of the event about to happen in Paris.

Paris: L'Hotel

Vanessa gazed at Tristan. It seemed Marie was all he could talk about. His deep-blue eyes shone as he spoke. "I can't wait to see her again after all these years. Imagine we're the three musketeers, even better than the original since you two are the most beautiful women in the world. There you go, let's write a Broadway show and create women in the role of the musketeers . . ." And Tristan just kept going, as one in love would. She looked at him with only that doting kind of affection one can for a very old friend, a sentimental one at that.

They were seated in a corner booth at L'Hotel. Tristan had Guy Louis order a delicious luncheon accompanied by a cold bottle of Cristal champagne. The meal started with a small iced platter of shellfish.

Vanessa was rejoicing in Tristan's excitement when the lights dimmed and nearby table conversation ceased. His voice faded. Never would a vision be as devastating as that one. Worst of all, she did not see a conclusion. It ended abruptly, but she felt intense sadness, knowing something terrible was about to happen. She put her arms around him and held him ever so tightly. She wanted to speak, but nothing would come out.

&

Within hearing range, Wolf sat at the bar, inconspicuously dressed in a formal suit and tie, a large coat concealing his powerful body. His fake mustache was itchy, and he squirmed a bit resisting the temptation to rip it off. He studied the pair, awaiting the moment Jean Delacroix had rehearsed with him.

The Daniells woman turned to Taylor and whispered, "Have to go to the loo, love. Back soon."

As soon as she disappeared, Wolf approached Taylor and in English with a hint of German told him, "Marie is arriving at the airport and wishes you to meet her."

&

Immediately Tristan stood. He briefly hesitated, then motioned for the waiter to come over and emphatically told him to relay to his guest that he had to leave.

The big, black Mercedes stretch limousine outside the tiny hotel stood out. It looked almost too large to navigate the narrow street. A large black bird perched on the roof of the car flew off as the chauffeur opened the rear door, an odd grin on his face. Moments later, the engine started, and the door locks clicked as the car pulled away from the curb.

When they approached Orly Airport, Tristan knocked on the glass divider to get the attention of the driver. There was no response. As the limousine passed the main entrance without slowing, he knocked harder without acknowledgment from the driver. The limousine continued to an area far from the main hub of the airport and paused in front of a security gate. Tristan reached for the door handle, but it wouldn't work. For a moment he panicked but instinctively knew he must gain complete control of his emotions if he was in danger, and he was in extreme danger. The gate opened, and they approached a small private jet far from the other planes.

The little window inside the car slid open, and the driver said, "My name is George. I'm here to escort you to a private meeting." He held up an old but polished German Luger. "Should you try to escape, I am instructed to put a bullet in your head." Tristan calmly nodded his head.

George opened the door for him, holding the gun to the side of his body where the pilot could not see it. For the first time, Tristan examined him—a massive man with huge arms and torso, surely capable of taking care of any man who might think of an escape, even without the gun. Tristan walked slowly to the small plane, where the pilot was standing next to the retractable steps. "Everything is in order for our flight to Zurich, sir."

"Very good," George said as he nudged Tristan toward the stairs.

Zurich? What the— Tristan entered the plane and was directed to sit in a very comfortable seat facing his captor. The pilot disappeared into his cabin, locking the door. George fastened Tristan's seat belt firmly then handed him a small glass of "orange juice" and instructed him to drink. All the while, the Luger was placed against his forehead. If Tristan was to be killed, it would already have been done, so he drank the liquid. He passed out at once.

∽

The plane landed an hour and a half later. Wolf removed the unconscious Taylor and put him into a new British Land Rover, again secured in the rear seat. The drive would take four hours.

Delacroix would join them in Saint Moritz. He had instructed Wolf not to disclose anything and not to harm Taylor unless he tried escaping. Wolf fantasized the delights that awaited him.

৪০

Tristan awoke with a slight headache from whatever he had been given, but came instantly aware of his dilemma. There was no security barrier in the RV, and he addressed the driver. "George, where are you taking me? Who am I seeing?"

He did not as much as glance at Tristan. "You will find out soon." Tristan realized no information was coming and prepared for the worst, concentrating on his training to meditate himself into a state of calmness. With each mile of the long drive, Tristan put himself more and more into a state of utter awareness and calm. He put his hand on the heavy money belt he always carried in Europe and the large buckle that carried a weapon that might save his life.

It was nighttime when the RV stopped deep in a wooded area. The lonely chirping of crickets filled the air, an owl calling mournfully in the distance as Tristan was removed from the car and led into a cabin. He was seated in a chair next to the fireplace that George lighted while still aiming the gun at him.

The interior of the cabin was spotlessly clean, and over the fireplace hung a black-and-white photo of Adolf Hitler. On the picture was scrawled, Für meinen Freund, Wolfgang. Friend of the Führer? Silently and with little motion, Tristan released the weapon from his belt and enclosed it in his left hand.

Wolfgang eyed him and finally spoke. "A token of better days" — he gestured at the photograph—"but you are not in Saint Moritz to reminisce with me. You have guessed by now who will be visiting you. Yes, Mr. Delacroix will see you briefly and will decide your fate. I also note you are wearing a money belt, how much is inside?"

"About fifty thousand French francs, all in gold coins."

Wolfgang pointed the gun at Tristan's head. "Give it to me now."

"As you wish." With a smirk, Tristan stood up, clutching the small stiletto switchblade hidden in his left hand. The blade was much like an ice pick, four inches long when sprung, and lethal in the hands of one practiced in using it. He had long ago learned from his martial arts instructor, hands were never enough when life was at stake. He had taught Tristan how to use the stiletto, along with the heavy belt it was hidden in.

Paris, France: L'Hotel

Vanessa had not believed what Tristan told the waiter for an instant, yet there she sat next to Marie in the pretty little suite of L'Hotel, trying to convince her otherwise. "Tristan is fine, Marie. If he has unsettled business, he'll call shortly."

"Maybe you're right, but it just seems like . . . Vanessa?" Marie's voice was faint. "Are you all ri . . ."

Tristan was standing up in a room somewhere, facing a giant of a man pointing a gun at his head.

Saint Moritz, Switzerland

"Take off the fucking belt. Now." Wolfgang came to just a few feet away. Tristan slowly removed the heavy belt with his right hand then doubled it at his side. With lightning speed, he swung the belt full force into the center of Wolfgang's face. The belt hit precisely on the bridge of his nose. *Bullseye.* Bone and cartilage into the brain. *kuPOWW!* A bullet whizzed past Tristan and hit the wall behind him with a *thunk*. He tossed the open stiletto to his right hand, buried the blade between Wolfgang's eyes. He'd be dead before he hit the floor.

Tristan had never used the weapon and never come close to killing a human being. The adrenaline rush left him on a strange high. That man was just one of two who wanted him dead. To relax for even an instant would be fatal. Jean Delacroix would arrive at any minute, and Tristan must be even more prepared. He closed his eyes and allowed a strange presence to direct him to the next step.

Dragging the dead man to the fireplace chair, Tristan managed to sit him up. Wolfgang's eyes were wide open, showing the horror that had been inflicted on him. Picking up the Luger, Tristan made sure there were more rounds left.

၈၁

Jean was all smiles as he drove his Mercedes 300 Gullwing through the dark forest. This was to be a crowning day of his life. He would tell Tristan Taylor what his fate was, and especially enjoy the moment he told him Marie would be Jean's forever. He was unusually relaxed, with no thoughts of anything but revenge. He parked his favorite car in front of the cabin. A night wind ruffled the leaves of the trees as he walked slowly to the cabin door and opened it. The interior was nearly pitch black. He had instructed Wolf to have Taylor in the main room when he arrived. In the dim light of the fireplace sat Wolf, not moving. Suddenly the room was lit, and the horror of the scene hit him like a thunderbolt. Taylor sat across the room, and in his hand was a Luger. He motioned with the gun toward a chair next to Wolf.

This couldn't be! How this worthless singer could kill one of the best-trained assassins on planet earth! Had to be pure luck, Wolf must have been completely off guard. Jean carefully felt his own weapon, a Beretta Pico designed for him and not yet sold commercially. It was the smallest and most powerful handgun available. However, that was not good news, as the Pico was holstered beneath his jacket. To reach it and get off a round would be nearly impossible. He must stall. For the first time in his life, he might not survive.

℘

Tristan was exhausted from the past twenty-four hours, and the original adrenaline rush was subsiding. He was facing a man who was possibly unarmed but capable of killing him nevertheless. But as he studied Jean Delacroix carefully, he saw the slight bulge in the left breast area of his jacket—a handgun. Tristan's instinct called out for an immediate kill, but he hesitated, desperately wanting to hear what bullshit Delacroix would say to save his life. He had not long to wait. The absurdity of the words enraged Tristan:

"I regret the things I have done to keep you and Marie apart. I can make it up. You will be the wealthiest couple in the world when I give you a substantial part of my assets. Just give me a chance. You will never regret it." As Delacroix spoke, he slowly unbuttoned his jacket, fidgeting with his right hand as if he were nervous, but slowly reaching into his jacket.

A familiar woman's voice sounded in Tristan's mind. "Kill him now." Tristan fired a round at Delacroix's heart. The bullet hit him so hard he fell backward, carrying the chair against the wall. He fell sideways and lay still.

A second adrenaline rush passed through Tristan. All the pain and suffering that man had caused him and Marie! He stood and looked down at the man who had tried to destroy their lives. The urge to empty the gun into his body was overwhelming. But the noise could attract attention if someone happened to be nearby, and Tristan resisted. Both the monsters were dead, they could never harm him. They could never harm Marie.

He let the adrenaline subside a little; he needed to carefully think out his next move. He looked around the cabin. On a shelf was a pair of work gloves. He put them on and with a cloth cleaned every area he might have touched in the cabin. He especially was careful with the stiletto buried in Wolfgang's head. He would leave no fingerprints at this scene, not one. With a sudden thought, he carefully took the Luger, pressed Wolfgang's hand around it, and dropped it near his limp body. Not that the police would suspect they killed each other, just a chance.

He dismissed any thoughts of setting the cabin on fire because that would draw attention. Aside from that, the charred remains of two homicide victims would attract even more scrutiny from the authorities.

The keys to the Land Rover were inside the car, a map in the glove compartment. Tristan hoped there was enough gas to drive back to Zurich. If not, a twenty-gallon gas can was strapped to the car. During the long drive, he concentrated on just driving and pushed away the thoughts of what he had just done. The time flew by, and exhilaration swept through him. He would see Marie very soon. However, he must not be careless with the trip back to Paris.

The faint glow of a new day was touching the horizon when he arrived in Zurich. He drove to the train station and parked far away in the lot. Still wearing the gloves, he opened the rear door and cleaned every square inch so no fingerprints would be found. He threw the map back in the glove compartment and headed into the station.

A train would depart for Paris in one hour. Tristan put on a pair of sunglasses he had found in the glove compartment and waited. At the Swiss border, he showed his passport. The conductor, half asleep, never even opened it. Tristan was in Paris a few hours later. He had made it.

℘

Tristan took a cab to L'Hotel as distant thunder rolled and a light rain started to fall. Marie opened the door and fell into his arms. "My God! What happened to you? I was so worried. I'm so happy to see you." Tears poured down her face as they held each other.

Through the tight embrace, Tristan could see Vanessa in the room, a big smile on her face. Holding Marie's hand, he walked over and kissed Vanessa gently, whispering in her ear, "Was it you?"

Vanessa just smiled. "Tristan, what a naughty boy you've been. I think I'll leave you two lovebirds alone. See you both soon."

After she left, the storm intensified—lightning flashed, followed by a huge clap of thunder. Marie and Tristan smiled at each other remembering their first meeting. They disappeared into the elegant bedroom. It was over, all over.

EXANDU

Most Beautiful Butterfly

In the village below La Malanese
Sits Miguel, the old storyteller of his people.
The sun has been shining all day now
And is setting behind the ancient mountain.

Miguel has lived to a wisened age,
Teaching the children about the wonders of life
And appreciating all the incredible
Joys we can share loving each other.

His apprentice, Rosa, sits by his side, adoring
Her benefactor, who has given her all the
Knowledge he has learned.

Miguel talks now again about the mystical butterfly
That touched his life so very long ago,
The kind lesson of life that no one
Can possess another, not ever.

The sun has now set, and all the children
And even adults have left, and Miguel is
Alone. He looks to the mountain and sees
A very bright light.
The light twinkles in the dark sky.

Without a second's thought, Miguel knows
The light is for him. It is his time now.
With great effort, he begins the climb to the light.
The climb is laborious, but as he comes closer
To the light, he feels great energy.

And suddenly he is there and the light
Is not white, it is colors he has never
Seen on this plane, colors of such intensity
He is nearly blinded. Then the colors
Transform to a beautiful angel.

The angel reaches out to Miguel,
And he embraces the spirit he realizes has
Come for him.

Made in the USA
Monee, IL
06 November 2020